Praise for *The Accomplice*

"Masterfully plotted, *The Accomplice* is both a keep-you-guessing mystery—like, seriously, I didn't see any of it coming—and a keenly and tenderly observed character study and portrait of a beautiful friendship complicated by a strange body count that keeps growing around them. I was rooting for Owen and Luna, but murder has a way of testing the bonds of even the tightest of best friends."

—ATTICA LOCKE, author of *Bluebird, Bluebird* and *Heaven, My Home*

"There's no one in crime fiction more inventive than Lisa Lutz, and *The Accomplice* is her greatest sleight of hand yet. Wry and menacing, with the gravity-defying grace of a skipped stone, *The Accomplice* is a suspenseful thrill ride, a deep and disquieting meditation on friendship, and a Wes Anderson comedy rolled into one. After this, I'd read her grocery list."

—AMY GENTRY, bestselling author of *Good as Gone* and *Bad Habits*

"Lisa Lutz just gets better and better. . . . *The Accomplice* may just be her best so far." —*CrimeReads*

"[An] atmospheric, well-plotted, and brilliantly narrated story, which is at once mysterious, suspenseful, and witty."

—*Booklist* (starred review)

"Quirky characters, humor in unexpected places, and a twisty but plausible plot keep the pages turning. Readers will be torn between eagerness to get to the bottom of the novel's mysteries—and reluctance for the adventure to end." —*Publishers Weekly*

"The fiendishly well-plotted action unfolds over a twenty-year span, but the focus of Lisa Lutz's attention in this wry, playful, off-centre saga is the unconventional enchantment that binds its two lead characters together. . . . Lutz writes brilliantly about young people, and the sequences in Markham University ('a safe haven for lazy stoners who wanted a break from life') are superbly cast, set and staged. I enjoyed the scenes in the Berkshires with Owen's charming, tony, roilingly alcoholic parents, who 'act out *Who's Afraid of Virginia Woolf?* every night.' . . . There is always a sense with a Lisa Lutz novel that artful misdirection is not just confined to the plot: something is happening, and we don't entirely know what it is, but the pleasure in trying to pin it down is considerable. With a flavour of Wes Anderson and a spritz of Alan Rudolph, this whimsical psychological thriller grips and teases in equal measure." —*The Irish Times*

Praise for *The Swallows*

"Riveting, caustic, and refreshingly funny, *The Swallows* is so full of imagination and power that my hands were shaking as I turned the pages."

—CAROLINE KEPNES, *New York Times* bestselling author of the You series

"Wes Anderson meets Muriel Spark in this delicious and vicious battle of the sexes set within a private school. Wickedly fun and wildly subversive but packing an emotional punch, *The Swallows* is as powerful as it is timely."

—MEGAN ABBOTT, *New York Times* bestselling author of *The Turnout*

"Extraordinarily fun and blood pressure–raising . . . *The Swallows* goes surprising places (axes are employed) and isn't afraid to let everyone roll around in the muck—though some characters come out smelling sweeter than others."   —*Vulture*

"In her witty and charming style, Lutz offers a genre-busting work of fiction that will satisfy readers looking for a seriously engaging read. The story itself is disturbingly plausible, and the humanly flawed characters make choices, good and bad, based on their backgrounds, all blending smoothly into a darkly comedic mystery. . . . This novel keeps readers on the edge of their seats while opening a conversation about public shaming, economic privilege, gender inequity, and revenge versus justice."

—*Booklist* (starred review)

"Lutz draws on the droll humor and idiosyncratic characterizations that make her Spellman novels so appealing. . . . An offbeat, darkly witty pre-#MeToo revenge tale. The patriarchy doesn't stand a chance."
—*Kirkus Reviews*

"Liza Lutz is a treasure. Her Spellman Files series manages to be both charming and shrewd, and *The Swallows* promises to follow suit—it looks witty and caustic, winsome and clever. It's also, and this is a classic Lutz move, a fresh, unique spin on a genre that already has been reworked a million times. . . . Lutz, searing as ever . . . illuminate[s] how various institutions excuse the oppression or silencing of women and girls."
—*CrimeReads*

"Sharpen your axes, ladies, and get ready for this fierce, fun, unsparing novel of female rage, power, and friendship."
—CAMILLE PERRI, author of *The Assistants* and *When Katie Met Cassidy*

"I devoured *The Swallows*. You'll laugh out loud even as you anxiously flip the pages."
—*New York Times* bestselling author TESS GERRITSEN

BY LISA LUTZ

The Accomplice
The Swallows
The Passenger
How to Start a Fire
How to Negotiate Everything (illustrated by Jaime Temairik)
Heads You Lose (with David Hayward)

THE SPELLMAN FILES SERIES

The Spellman Files
Curse of the Spellmans
Revenge of the Spellmans
The Spellmans Strike Again
Trail of the Spellmans
Spellman Six: The Next Generation

The
Accomplice

The
Accomplice

A NOVEL

LISA LUTZ

BALLANTINE BOOKS
NEW YORK

2023 Ballantine Books Trade Paperback Edition

Copyright © 2022 by Lisa Lutz
Book club guide copyright © 2023 by Penguin Random House LLC

Published in the United States by Ballantine Books, an imprint of Random House, a division of Penguin Random House LLC, New York.

BALLANTINE is a registered trademark and the colophon is a trademark of Penguin Random House LLC.
RANDOM HOUSE BOOK CLUB and colophon are trademarks of Penguin Random House LLC.

Originally published in hardcover in the United States by Ballantine Books, an imprint of Random House, a division of Penguin Random House LLC, in 2022.

LIBRARY OF CONGRESS CATALOGING-IN-PUBLICATION DATA
Names: Lutz, Lisa, author.
Title: The accomplice : a novel / Lisa Lutz.
Description: New York : Ballantine Books, [2022] |
Identifiers: LCCN 2020046879 (print) | LCCN 2020046880 (ebook) |
ISBN 9781984818287 (paperback) | ISBN 9781984818270 (ebook)
Subjects: GSAFD: Mystery fiction. | Suspense fiction.
Classification: LCC PS3612.U897 A63 2021 (print) | LCC PS3612.U897 (ebook) |
DDC 813/.6—dc23
LC record available at https://lccn.loc.gov/2020046879
LC ebook record available at https://lccn.loc.gov/2020046880

Printed in the United States of America on acid-free paper

randomhousebooks.com
randomhousebookclub.com

2 4 6 8 9 7 5 3 1

Title-page image: copyright © iStock.com/shayes17

Book design by Victoria Wong

For Mark & Beverly Fienberg

The
Accomplice

September 2002

O wen Mann first noticed Luna Grey in an Intro to Ethics seminar. He would watch her, fascinated by the way she hunched over her notebook, scribbling, glancing up occasionally to see if anyone was watching her. Owen thought she was pretty, pretty in a way that might last or grow on you. She definitely wasn't one of those beauties who made you do crazy things. By all objective standards, Luna appeared normal, reliable, and even a bit square. Owen, however, saw past Luna's ordinary armor. He recognized a feral quality in her. He saw a girl roiling with secrets. And he would have paid good money to know a few of them.

Luna always knew when someone was watching her. Sometimes she'd wait it out. Other times she'd stare back and force the prying eyes to withdraw. When Luna glanced back at Owen, he smiled brightly, even though they'd never met. What the hell was he smiling about, she thought. Luna had seen Owen before. It occurred to her that he might know who she was. But the smile was wrong for someone who had her number. The girl sitting next to Owen was trying to get his attention. When the girl saw where Owen's eyes had landed, she fixed her gaze on Luna, shifting it from curious to withering within seconds. Luna quickly turned away. She'd seen that expression too many times to count.

In her head, Luna repeated, *They don't know, they don't know.*

. . .

A FEW DAYS later, Owen ditched the glaring girl and sat in Luna's row, a few seats away. Luna felt her whole body tense up, until Owen fell fast asleep and didn't stir, even after the lecture was over. Luna tapped him on the shoulder to wake him as she climbed over his legs, clearing out of class. Owen rubbed his eyes, shook himself awake, and chased after her.

"Hello . . ." Owen said, as he caught up with Luna and began to walk in stride. "I don't know your name."

"I don't know *your* name," Luna said.

Owen had a stupid grin on his face. If she didn't have a secret, he thought, it would be deeply disappointing. Luna couldn't decide if the smile was taunting or goofy. Owen stepped in front of Luna and extended his hand.

"Owen Mann. A pleasure to meet you," he said.

Luna kept her hand by her side, debating whether to respond in kind.

"What can I do for you, Owen Mann?" Luna said.

"Has anyone ever told you that you have the social graces of a mobster?"

Luna fought hard not to laugh. "That might be the nicest thing anyone has ever said to me," she said.

Luna offered her name; Owen explained why he'd followed her. He'd slept through the Kant lecture and wanted to borrow her notes.

"Why my notes?" Luna asked.

Owen shrugged. "Don't know. But they have to be your notes."

Luna weighed the request. Then she leafed through the notebook to confirm there was no personal information in there and handed it to this Owen guy. They agreed to meet an hour later at the library.

Markham University was a small liberal-arts college in the Hudson Valley. It sat on twenty acres of dense woods and prided itself on self-directed independent study. It was also a safe haven for lazy stoners who wanted a break from life. Think summer camp with cushier accommodations. Markham U was Luna's first choice and Owen's third-backup school.

Owen chose a seat on the third floor of Bancroft Library, at a desk nestled by a wall of windows. He opened Luna's notebook and poised his pen over a blank pad. Once he examined her text, he dropped the pen and visibly slumped in his chair. He couldn't decipher a single sentence of her handwriting.

As he stared at the mysterious script, it occurred to him that she was writing in code. Either way, it was aesthetically pleasing. He took out his sketch pad and rendered an abstract interpretation of Luna's notes. Then he removed his headphones from his backpack, blasted Mogwai on his MP3 player, and looked out the library window, watching the human traffic on the quad.

Luna arrived at the library five minutes before the one-hour mark.

"Done?" she said.

"Can anyone read your writing?" Owen asked.

"No. Never," Luna said, relieved.

"Then why did you give your notes to me?"

"I thought you might be the first."

Owen liked her voice. It was deep, deadpan. Her pitch rarely wavered, even when she asked a question. Most people were cautious and slow to warm around Luna. Owen just barreled forward, unafraid.

"I'm going to need you to translate," Owen said.

He pulled out a chair and slid the notebook across the desk. He waited for Luna to sit, not even considering that she wouldn't. Luna accepted the chair and reviewed her notes. Sometimes, even she had trouble reading them. Above her head, a fluorescent light was flickering its way to death. Luna clocked it with annoyance.

"They should fix that," Luna said.

The flickering light unsettled her more than a light should, Owen thought. Luna spent thirty minutes summarizing the lecture for Owen, who took notes in his own hand, which was so clean and concise that it almost looked like a font designed to resemble human script. Luna felt the heat of the flickering light. Her head gave her that familiar warning signal, the one she often ignored. It was like the police standing outside her head, knocking on her temple.

"There are two duties that are part of the categorical imperative," she said. "Um, there are negative duties, like don't kill or be an asshole. And positive duties to help others. But then, okay, say you're helping another person—you're just supposed to promote their happiness. Kant didn't believe in paternalism, which is pushing your morals and ethics on someone else. He was super into autonomy. And, um—"

Luna made a choking sound. Her eyes rolled back, her body went stiff, and she began to vibrate and tilt to the side. She fell off her chair onto the hard linoleum floor. Owen winced as he watched her head hit the ground and bounce up again.

Owen called for help, but the entire floor was empty. He crouched next to Luna, balled up his jacket, and put it under the base of her neck. She made a gurgling sound, which Owen misinterpreted as choking. He stuck his fingers in her mouth, trying to press down on her tongue, remembering something he'd read or heard or seen on TV about people swallowing their tongue in the midst of a seizure.

He called for help again, but Luna's convulsions had begun to fade. He removed his fingers from her mouth and wiped them on his sweatshirt. He pulled out his cellphone and dialed 911. He told the operator what had happened. The operator asked if Luna was breathing. Owen turned his head and let his ear hover above her mouth. He could hear her soft, wispy breath.

He told the operator that she was breathing but unconscious and provided their location. Then he sat on the floor next to Luna for several minutes, watching her inhale and exhale. It seemed to Owen as if she were in a deep, luxurious slumber.

Luna opened her eyes. She first saw that flickering light again, and then she saw the boy staring down at her. He looked familiar, but that concerned gaze was even more familiar. A trail of drool slid down her cheek.

Owen covered his hand with his sleeve and wiped it off.

"What are you doing?" Luna asked.

"Wiping drool off your face," Owen said.

"Do I know you?" Luna said.

"Not well."

"What happened?"

"I think you had a seizure," Owen said.

"I know that," Luna snapped.

"I called 911."

"Where am I?" Luna said. Then she noticed books. From the angle on the floor, it looked like she was trapped in a library maze. "Oh yeah, right."

When she sat up, her brain felt like an eight ball in a glass of water. She reached up and touched a small lump on the side of her head.

"The ambulance should be here any second."

Luna stumbled to her feet. "I need to get out of here before they come."

"You should see a doctor," said Owen.

"Why? I'm fine."

"Has this happened before?"

"I'm epileptic. Of course it's happened before." Luna picked up her notebook and shoved it in her bag. She turned to Owen. "Thanks for . . . whatever you did."

"I just put my jacket under your head."

"That's it?" Luna said, with a note of skepticism.

She slung her backpack over her shoulder and checked her close perimeter for any lost or forgotten items.

"I made sure you didn't swallow your tongue," Owen said, as casually as one can say that.

Luna froze and then slowly looked up at Owen. Her eyes narrowed. "Tell me you didn't stick your fingers in my mouth," she said.

She could tell from his expression that he had. Her profound disappointment was hard to miss.

"I—" Owen started.

"It's a myth," said Luna. "You can't swallow your own tongue. *Think* about it, dude."

Owen curled his tongue back and thought how obvious that seemed right then. But he figured all tongues were different.

"I'll remember that for next time," Owen said.

"If you want to help, you turn someone on their side."

"Good to know."

The ambulance pulled up in front of the library, sirens blaring and lights reminding Luna of the one that had set off her fit.

"I'll see you around," Luna said as she took the back stairs, like a robber making a getaway.

Owen promptly gathered his belongings and followed her.

"Wait up," he said.

Luna didn't. She knew he could catch her if he wanted to.

Outside, Luna was revived by the fresh air and a rush of adrenaline as she breezed past the incoming paramedics.

Owen caught up with Luna and walked in stride with her through the quad. "You hit your head pretty hard. You might have a concussion."

"I don't."

"How do you know?"

"I've hit my head before."

"Maybe I'll just stay with you to make sure you don't develop any symptoms."

Luna wanted him to stay. She'd wanted him to follow her out of the library. But she was good at not saying what she wanted.

"It's a free country," she said.

As they walked in stride, Owen was greeted by a gauntlet of students, cheerily acknowledging his presence. Owen would raise his hand in a half wave or nod as a response.

"You running for class president?" Luna asked.

"Never. Why?"

"You have a lot of friends," she said.

"Acquaintances," he clarified. "People like me. Don't know why."

Luna thought he probably did know and didn't want to say. He was handsome but not manly or rugged. Attractive without being threatening. And, judging by his egalitarian greetings, he was friendly. Luna didn't mention any of that. She did, however, ask a question no one had ever asked him before.

"Do *you* like people?"

"Not as much as they like me," Owen said. "Hmm, I think that came out wrong."

"I get it, in a way," Luna said.

Her experience was the exact opposite, which allowed for a certain inverse understanding.

Luna seemed wise beyond her years, Owen thought. She was subtly enigmatic. It would take some time to figure her out, but he was willing to put in the effort.

"Tell me something about yourself," Owen said.

"Like what?" Luna said.

Vague questions never seemed vague to Luna.

"I don't know," Owen said. "What do you do when you're not convulsing?"

It was a dangerous joke. When a moment of silence passed, Owen thought he'd gone too far. Then Luna laughed, a big, deep laugh, the kind of laugh you can't fake. He loved the sound of her laugh. It was like the first time you take a drug.

"I think we're going to be friends," Owen said.

"Let's not get ahead of ourselves," Luna replied, even though she secretly hoped that would be the case.

That was the day it all began. Luna and Owen. Owen and Luna. Their names would be inextricably linked for years to come. The one steady thing in their unsteady lives. Before long, neither would be able to imagine a life without the other. It would be hard not to admire the strength of their bond. However, if you were in their orbit, you might come to realize that it was a dangerous place to be. Not everyone there made it out alive.

Luna was watching coffee brew. It was seven-thirty A.M., caffeine withdrawal ramping up, brain still fogged and incapable of any heavy lifting. *Still,* Luna thought, *this is not a good use of my time.* Not that she could think of a better thing to be doing at the moment. Her husband, Sam, had a thing about waiting for the coffee to finish brewing before you poured a cup. He once suggested it was like the grown-up marshmallow test. Luna didn't think that was the best analogy, but the mere suggestion that she'd fail that test had changed her entire morning habit.

Luna heard two quiet knocks on the back door. Only one person used that door. You had to unlatch a side gate and circle around the house. It was just easier to use the front door. Irene Boucher, however, didn't care about easy. The doorbell took a picture of you, which was stored on some random company's hard drive. They were not going to take her picture.

Luna opened the door, got a look at Irene, and laughed. That morning, Irene was wearing a red Fila shell suit. It wasn't one of her better ones, Luna thought. She also had on a thick gold-plated chain that Luna had given her for her last birthday. A joke of sorts. It was the kind of thing that a movie mobster might wear. Irene really liked the chain, in an unironic sort of way.

"Is Tony Soprano your fashion icon?" Luna had once quipped.

Irene's earnest response: "Paulie and Christopher wore the best tracksuits."

Irene had a closet full of them. Some velour, some polyester, in a strange rainbow of colors. She was most loyal to Fila and Adidas. She wore them for comfort and because she could exercise at a moment's notice when she had them on. Irene was compulsive about physical activity. She ran, hiked, lifted weights. She was the sort of person who would suddenly drop to the ground and do a set of push-ups or lunge her way across the room.

Irene exercised so she could maintain the diet of a teenage boy under no supervision. She was the only middle-aged woman Luna had ever met who ate doughnuts and pizza on a regular basis.

While on occasion Luna might join Irene for a run, most of the times Irene dropped by, she'd end up in Luna's kitchen drinking coffee for an hour. She'd hit the pavement after that.

"Am I interrupting something?" Irene asked.

"No. Come in," Luna said. "Coffee is almost done."

Irene followed Luna into the kitchen. Luna's phone rang. She showed Irene the caller ID. Leo Whitman.

"Ignore him," said Irene.

"He'll just keep calling," Luna said. "One minute."

Luna answered the call. "Hi, Leo. I told you ten. Yes, it's still ten. Okay. I'll see you then."

Luna silenced her phone and placed it screen down on the counter.

"You're still helping him?" Irene asked.

"I'm vetting résumés and arranging interviews. He swore he'd hire someone this week."

"Remember," said Irene, "he's really good at asking for things and he doesn't know when to stop. You have to have boundaries with Leo."

"I know," Luna said.

"Thank you," Irene said.

Irene knew the only reason Luna was helping him out was so that she didn't have to.

"What's new?" Luna said as she removed two mugs from the cupboard.

"I've been listening to this podcast about Bigfoot," Irene said as she opened the refrigerator, checked the inventory, and closed it.

"You've mentioned it," Luna said. "You want toast?"

"Nah. If you want to survive a Bigfoot attack, offer it food and don't cry."

"What happens if I cry?" Luna asked.

"It'll punch you in the face," Irene said, smiling. "I think that's my favorite Bigfoot fact."

"Sure you want to call that a fact, when the existence of Bigfoot is already in question?" Luna said.

"The punching thing may be bullshit. But there is a Bigfoot or Sasquatch, whatever you want to call it."

"Okay," Luna said. "You're the expert."

The coffee maker beeped. Luna removed the full carafe and aimed at Irene's mug.

"Owen's got a side piece," Irene blurted out.

Luna poured half a cup of coffee onto the counter before sharpening her aim and filling the mug.

"What?" Luna said.

Irene grabbed a sponge and cleaned up the spill. Luna wiped down the mug and slid it over to Irene.

"I shouldn't have said it that way. I sound like a misogynist. Owen has a paramour. I think. No. I know. He has one."

"'Paramour,'" Luna repeated, thinking what a polite word for a wife to use. "Why do you think that?"

"Because now he tells me where he's going and when he's returning."

While this was indeed out of character for Owen, Luna felt confident that her best friend wasn't hiding a mistress from her. Maybe from Irene. Not from Luna.

"I promise you, he isn't," Luna said.

"How do you know? Would he tell you?"

"I think so," Luna said.

For almost two decades, Owen had been the one person to whom she'd confessed all her sins. It never occurred to her that he didn't do the same. So she stalled—sipping her coffee and wiping a smudge of jam on the counter with her sleeve—and bluffed her way through the rest of the conversation.

"I don't know what to say here, Irene. Are you okay?"

"Yeah. Yeah."

The first *yeah* had no conviction; the second one was solid. In fact, Irene seemed a little too okay to Luna. Okay in the way someone who is making big changes is okay. They're okay because they have a plan.

"What are you going to do about it?" Luna asked.

Luna tried to picture life without Irene. What would it look like?

"I'm not ready to say," Irene said.

Both women understood why Irene wasn't answering the question. Luna and Irene were good friends, maybe great friends, but Luna's primary allegiance was to Owen.

"I understand," Luna said.

"I better go," Irene said as she left her mug in the sink. "Is there any chance you can keep this conversation between us?"

"Of course," Luna said.

They both knew she was lying.

LATER THAT AFTERNOON, Owen texted Luna.

Owen: Halfway at 5?

He was suggesting a drink at their local bar. After her morning conversation with Irene, Luna wondered whether that was a good idea.

Luna: Maybe you should go home.
Owen: Why?

Luna wasn't ready to answer that question.

Luna: One drink.

Owen: Be there in 20.

Luna arrived at the Halfway House first. She ordered a bourbon and checked her phone to get Owen's ETA. She'd convinced him to install the app years ago after he'd left her waiting over an hour at the train station. At least she'd know if he was stuck in traffic, almost there, or truly off-grid. She could see the Owen dot moving on Route 9. He was less than ten minutes out. She then texted her husband to tell him she wouldn't be home for dinner. Book club, she lied.

After five minutes, her husband replied: K.

The Halfway House was a dive so divey that Owen and Luna could safely assume they'd never run into anyone they knew. Finding a place in a small town where you could remain entirely anonymous made up for a sticky bar-top and filthy restrooms. After a few drinks you didn't notice the grime or the sour stench anyway.

When Owen arrived, he ordered a dirty martini with three olives. He would switch to an entirely different drink after that, never able to stick with just one. He was obsessed with variety, which Luna had only recently correlated with his inability to stay faithful.

"What's Irene up to?" Luna asked.

"I don't know," Owen said. "She left this morning and I haven't heard from her all day."

Owen and Irene weren't the kind of couple who routinely checked in. In fact, it was fair to say they were the opposite. Early in the relationship, Owen established a pattern of going AWOL, which Irene soon learned to mimic so she could feel a sense of parity. That said, if Owen repeatedly texted his wife, she'd usually respond.

"I saw her this morning," Luna said.

"What did you talk about?" Owen asked.

"Bigfoot," Luna said, after a pause. "Apparently the secret to surviving—"

"I've heard it already. She's been listening to that podcast non-stop. It's getting weird," Owen said. "Do me a favor and send her a text. See if she gets back to you?"

Luna typed: Run tmrw? 8:30? and immediately felt virtuous, as if she'd already taken the run.

"Maybe she's ignoring you," Luna said.

"Why would she do that?"

"Maybe you did something bad," Luna said.

The bartender served Owen his martini. Owen lifted the toothpick of three olives from his glass and offered them to Luna, who bit the first one off. Owen took the second one and dropped the third back in the martini glass. He was debating how to answer. His silence gave Luna the impetus to keep pushing.

"What did you do?" she asked.

"Nothing," Owen said without any conviction.

"Who is she?" Luna said.

"No one."

"Why didn't you tell me you had a no one?"

"Because I can't stand that judgy way you look at me."

Owen finished his martini and slid the empty glass with the lone olive in front of Luna. She ate the olive and finished her bourbon. They ordered another round—bourbon for Luna, a gimlet for Owen.

"She's a student, I assume," Luna said.

"Why do you assume that?"

"Where else are you going to meet women?"

"Women are everywhere, if you haven't noticed," Owen said.

"So, a student?"

Owen nodded.

"You're so boring," Luna said, disappointed by his lack of originality.

"That's it," Owen said, pointing at Luna's face. "That look. That's why I didn't tell you."

Owen picked up Luna's phone as if it were his own and looked for a response from Irene. "Now I'm worried," he said.

"Don't be. She links me with you. When she's angry at you, she's also a little angry at me."

"So, she knows?" Owen asked, trying to read Luna's expression.

"I don't know," Luna said.

"Spill it. What did she say?"

"She said you had a side piece," Luna said.

Owen took a sip of his sour drink. He liked the idea of gimlets more than gimlets themselves. "She actually said *side piece*?"

"Yes, but then she switched to *paramour*."

"Huh," Owen said. "It's enough that she dresses like a mobster."

"You have any other response to what I just said?"

"How'd she find out?" Owen asked.

He felt mildly queasy and took another sip of his drink, which didn't help.

"Don't know," Luna said. "Tell me about her, your . . . paramour."

"She's just a sculptor with spectacular tits."

"You need to listen to yourself sometimes," Luna said, rolling her eyes. "Does she have a name?"

"Amy. It didn't mean anything," Owen said.

"Did it mean something to *Amy*?"

"No," Owen said. Although he couldn't say for sure.

"Was she the first?" Luna asked.

Owen tried to ignore the question.

"How many?" Luna asked.

Owen knew that she was asking not as a concerned friend but as an advocate for Irene.

"Not many," Owen said.

"Oh god. Jesus, Owen." Luna made a face like she'd swallowed a bug.

"Only two. I really tried for Irene," Owen said.

Luna finished her drink and threw a few bills on the bar.

"Don't tell her I told you, okay?" Luna said. "Whether you stay together or not, she's my friend too. I'm not taking sides."

"Bullshit, Luna. You can't be Switzerland."

"Watch me."

That night, Owen returned to an empty home. He left a few more messages on Irene's cell and wondered how she had learned of the sculptor. Another man might have called the police. Owen went to bed.

IRENE WAS STILL gone the next morning when Owen woke up. He texted Luna to see if she'd heard back. Luna said she had not.

She remembered her invitation for an eight-thirty run and thought she might find Irene doing laps around Dover Cemetery, where they often met. Luna threw on her sweats and sneakers and headed out.

She walked through the greenbelt behind her yard. Her elderly neighbor, Mr. Kane, had bushwhacked a clearing years ago. He maintained the passage year-round, in winter driving his snow-blower through the woods. It gave him a shortcut from his house to his wife's grave. Other neighbors began using the same shortcut, and soon it was a well-worn path that led not just to Dover Church and Cemetery but to town.

Luna began running under the tunnel of foliage, the dirt soft and tacky underfoot. Her body felt stiff and creaky. Within just a few minutes, her breath became hard as an asthmatic's. She hoped Irene wouldn't show up and race around her like a gazelle. Luna slowed down, caught her breath, and walked along the edge of the grave-yard, noting the names and dates of the dead as she had so many times before.

Then she heard the squawk of carrion birds looping overhead. She spotted a swath of red fabric against the stone and greenery. She stumbled up the hill, past the graves of those who'd died last century and before. There hadn't been a new burial in more than sixty years.

Luna's knees buckled; her body understood before her brain. Irene was lying on her side in a fetal position. For the briefest moment, Luna thought Irene might be asleep.

"Wake up, Irene," Luna said.

Irene didn't move. Luna stepped closer and saw the blood and the blue hue of Irene's face. She turned away and then looked back, thinking maybe her eyes were playing tricks on her brain. Irene's entire chest was the same color as her red windbreaker.

October 2003

PARTY, Saturday, @ 2100 hrs
Hosted by Luna and Owen

Owen and Luna. Luna and Owen. Their names said so often as one, like twins or a romantic couple. Outsiders could never figure out what it was. Friends would often ask what their deal was. The truth was they were just friends. That's not to say there was never any attraction. They'd each thought about it. But neither of them wanted to mess with what they had. Whatever it was had become essential to their lives. The pair had been inseparable since the day Owen stuck his fingers in Luna's mouth.

One year and one month later, Luna and Owen were hanging out in his dorm room in Watson Hall. Luna was chomping on potato chips and watching Owen iron his shirt. She provided a running commentary, as if she were observing a sporting event.

"You're really taking your time between the buttons, aren't you?" Luna said.

"Don't get chips on my bed," Owen said, eyes focused on his chosen task.

The iron fired steam like a dragon, Luna thought.

"Any knucklehead can de-wrinkle the shirttails, but your sleeve work is mighty impressive. I give you an eight out of ten," Luna said.

Owen regarded Luna, who was lounging on his bed, wearing

threadbare jeans and a ratty old T-shirt that read "Camp Sunshine." She had this way of making herself at home in his space, which somehow made him feel more at home.

"Is that what you're wearing?" Owen said.

Luna checked her outfit, then turned to Owen, with an expression of wild confusion.

"What the hell kind of question is that?" Luna asked. "You can see what I'm wearing, right?"

"I can."

"I'll confirm that what you're seeing is probably at the very least a close approximation of what I'm wearing, taking into account any weird visual anomaly and perceptual errors."

Owen shut off the iron. Luna pulled the cord from the socket.

"Shall we?" Owen said as he checked his watch. Luna threw on her satin smoking jacket as she and Owen stepped into the hallway.

"Mason!" Luna shouted when she saw her friend leaving a room just a few doors down.

Mason spun around, startled. "Oh, hey, Luna."

Mason and Owen nodded at each other. Once, Owen had tried to talk to the guy. He asked Mason what he did when he wasn't smoking pot. *Dude, that's like a really personal question* was Mason's response.

Mason was exclusively Luna's friend at the time. Owen was convinced that it was because Mason had weed. He always had weed. He even smelled like it. In a good way, Luna thought; in a bad way, Owen thought. Most people called Ralph Mason just Mason, since it was generally agreed that Ralph sounded like a grandpa or something you did after a drinking binge. Mason was a math major with crooked teeth and a haircut that always began with a comma on his forehead. It was pure coincidence that Mason lived in Bing Hall, commonly known as Bong Hall.

"What are you doing here?" Luna asked.

"I'd rather not say," Mason said.

"You're coming to the lab party, right, Mason?" Luna asked.

"Maybe. I can't commit to anything right now," Mason said

quite earnestly. Mason liked to live in the present. He rarely committed to anything that might take place in the future.

Luna found this quirk endlessly amusing. She was always trying to get Mason to pledge himself to a future endeavor.

Mason, let's go see that Wim Wenders film on Saturday.

Mason, will you study with me tomorrow?

Mason, will you meet me at the dining hall in fifteen minutes?

Mason, promise me you'll go to sleep later tonight.

Mason's answer was always some variation of the theme: *We'll see. Let's play it by ear.*

But then Mason broke one of the primary tenets of his life and said, "Hey, Luna, can I talk to you later?"

"What's up?" Luna asked.

"Later," Mason said. "When you have time."

"I don't know," Luna said. "Let's play it by ear."

She finally understood Mason's resistance to making plans.

WHILE INVESTIGATING THE bowels of Markham University one night, Luna and Owen found the perfect party venue—a defunct laboratory with a faulty lock in the basement of the Life Sciences building. The lights had all burned out, but the pair found that replacing just a few bulbs gave them the ideal moody lighting for a midterm bash.

Owen draped the walls with abandoned art from his oil-painting class, while Luna pasted arrows from the archway outside the building, down the staircase, and through the hallway to direct the partygoers to the not-so-secret location.

When the clock struck nine, Owen suggested they crack the good bourbon before the early birds showed up. They toasted with plastic tumblers. Owen hid the bottle just moments before Amber, Bobbi, and Casey arrived. Owen called them the ABCs and was under the impression that they were inseparable and somehow identical, which was simply not the case.

Amber Klein was a lanky blonde who always seemed to speak at a volume two clicks above necessary. Her roommate, Bobbi Schwartz, had the shiniest black hair Luna had ever seen and a slightly wandering eye. The eye thing mostly made her look like she was suspicious of everyone. Casey Carr had unruly blond hair and equally unruly breasts. The only common denominator was that the three women lived in Avery Hall.

Owen didn't care for any of them back then, but Luna liked Casey and would always try to get her alone. Having grown up in a cult, Casey had some hilarious anecdotes about commune life. Plus, she was freakishly smart, enough to make Luna want to know why she was slumming it at Markham. She didn't ask, of course, because when you ask questions, you invite them in return. As for the A and B: Amber had an irrepressible crush on Owen, which manifested itself in embarrassing drunken displays of desperation. Bobbi played Amber's sidekick—a sinister one, Luna thought. Bobbi always encouraged Amber to *go for it,* knowing Amber would embarrass herself. Casey tempered Bobbi, always trying to keep Amber in check and restore some dignity. As predicted, shortly after her arrival, Amber found her way to Owen and began flirting with abandon.

Soon, others arrived: first Ted, Owen's neighbor in Watson Hall. Ted was just six months shy of being able to procure beer on his own. He had big calloused hands from summer construction jobs and a thick Jersey accent. Drunk Luna always wondered what those hands might feel like on her body, but she could see that other women had the same idea and was never able to get him alone.

Another dozen or so coeds of various degrees of acquaintance to Owen and Luna arrived before midnight. Owen controlled the music with a handful of CD mixes assembled just for the festivities. Luna had veto power and would remove any disc from the player when Coldplay came on. Owen took to pressing the SKIP button when he'd see her approach, mostly because she had a habit of ejecting a disc and snapping it in half.

"*Why?*" Luna would say every time she heard her nemesis, as if the popularity of the band was among the great mysteries of the universe. Owen barely liked Coldplay; he just liked seeing Luna's focused passion against them.

When Scarlet Hayes entered the party, the room quieted for just a second. From the moment Scarlet arrived on campus, people—mostly men—took note. It wasn't just the long legs, plump lips, and shiny auburn hair, which had to be a dye job to match the name. Scarlet had swagger, a seeming confidence uncommon among women of her age. The swagger turned out to be fake, but it was attractive all the same. She was also nice. Everyone thought so back then. Turned out, that was fake as well.

Scarlet first rested her gaze on Luna, then stealthily clocked Owen's location. She sat on the table next to Luna and put her arm around her.

"Hey, Luna. How are you doing?" Scarlet asked.

"I don't know. What have you heard?" Luna said.

Luna was stoned. Very, very stoned.

Luna heard something ringing. It sounded just like Owen's phone. *This is going to be a thing,* Luna thought, *people ringing all the time.*

"Is that you?" Scarlet asked.

"Never," Luna said.

"It's me," Scarlet said, reaching into her purse and answering the call. "Hi, Mom. I can't talk now. I can't hear you. I really can't hear you. I'll call you tomorrow. Didn't hear that either. I'm saying goodbye now."

"Owen has one of those," Luna said. "Doesn't it bother you, people being able to contact you all the time?"

"Sometimes it's a drag," Scarlet said. "My mother calls a lot. If I don't answer, she keeps calling. But once, I got lost driving home from the city, and all I had to do was call my dad and he gave me directions."

Luna was about to suggest getting a good set of maps, when she spotted Owen, cornered by Amber and Bobbi. His panic was on full display.

"You should save him," Luna said.

She said it because she saw the way Owen's eyes glazed over into lust whenever Scarlet was in range. She said it because she saw how Scarlet wasn't entirely Scarlet in front of Owen, as if she was holding back, pretending that she felt nothing. She said it because watching the charged energy between them made her uneasy. A girlfriend would alter the essential ingredient of their relationship. Luna struggled to imagine whether the new recipe would even work.

"Why don't *you* save him?" Scarlet said.

"Because he wants you to," Luna said. "You like him, don't you?"

"Not sure. I need more data to decide."

"Then go collect some."

Scarlet eyed Luna suspiciously and jumped off the table.

En route to Owen, Scarlet passed Ted. Ted took Scarlet's seat. His thigh brushed against Luna's. She felt a rush of heat. Luna took a sip of her drink. She had a sense that she wasn't experiencing time in the usual fashion, because after the next sip, the drink was almost dead.

"Would you look at that," Luna said. "I need a refill already."

"Don't go anywhere," Ted said.

"Where would I go?" she said.

Luna looked over at Owen and Scarlet. The ABCs were in retreat. Scarlet and Owen whispered in each other's ears as if they were in a loud concert hall.

Luna didn't notice Mason until he hopped onto the table next to her. They exchanged heys. Luna quickly remembered their appointment for a later conversation. She wanted it done, whatever it was.

"What did you want to ask me, Mason?"

"Uhhh," Mason said.

Briefly, Luna thought it had slipped his mind, which meant it wasn't the subject she feared.

"Not here," Mason said.

Luna felt a mild stabbing pain in her gut. It was indeed what she feared.

Outside, the air was crisp and had the faint odor of caramel corn. Luna had heard about people smelling burnt toast before they stroked out. Was she having a stroke? She decided she was too young. There had to be another explanation.

The campus had an abundance of katsura trees, which emitted a burnt-sugar scent after the leaves had fallen.

"What's up, Mason?" Luna said.

"Did you ever live in Colorado?" Mason asked.

Shit, Luna thought. *He knows. Wait, does he?* Was he confirming a known fact or merely trying to substantiate a theory he'd stumbled upon?

"Yeah, why?" Luna said.

Mason had hoped that once he broached the subject, Luna would make it easy on him. Luna pictured Mason, weaponless, trying to rob a bank through the power of suggestion.

Hey, guys, got any money in this vault?

Luna thought, *If you want the goods, use the gun.* She waited to see what Mason would do, thinking he'd let it go. But then he showed his weapon. He didn't aim it, just let it sit there as a quiet threat.

"Was Luna Grey always your name?"

October 8, 2019

———

Luna wasn't sure how long she'd been standing over Irene's body. Her face felt hot. When she touched her cheek, it was damp with tears. Vultures circling overhead reminded her that she needed to do something. Or at the very least stop crying over the crime scene. She jogged down the craggy incline onto the asphalt drive that circled the grounds. She followed the drive to the south exit and ran as fast as she could to Owen's house. She pounded on his door until her knuckles screamed.

Owen opened the door holding a cup of coffee, his face set hard, ready to reprimand whoever had the audacity to interrupt his morning. His expression softened when he saw Luna's ruddy face.

"What happened?" he said.

Luna stepped inside the house, catching her breath. The landline, resting on a table in the foyer, reminded her that there was something she had to do.

"What?" he said, ducking to make eye contact.

"Irene," Luna said, voice cracking as she tried to speak.

"No," Owen said.

"I'm sorry. I'm so sorry," said Luna.

"No," he said again, shaking his head. "Where is she?"

"Dover Cemetery. By that tree."

Owen raced outside in his robe and slippers. Luna wanted to chase after him, but she remembered how things were supposed to be done. She picked up the phone and dialed 911.

. . .

OWEN RAN TO Dover Cemetery, found Irene, and tried to shake her awake. She was cold and stiff and he quickly recoiled, fought hard not to vomit. He staggered back, caught his breath, and collapsed onto the ground by a nearby headstone. There he waited until he heard the sirens. Luna showed up a short time after that. She wished she had warned Owen about contaminating the crime scene; then again, he should have known.

Two state troopers were first to arrive on the scene. One had gray hair; the other looked too young to drink. The gray-haired trooper asked Owen to step away from the victim. *Victim.* The word sounded strange to Owen, as if the trooper was calling his wife by the wrong name. Owen moved to the side and sat down on a bench next to Luna. The younger trooper asked who discovered the body.

"I did," said Luna. "I went for a run and found her."

Luna didn't mention that Irene had been missing for twenty-four hours before she found her.

Neighbors began to assemble right outside the gates. After about thirty minutes, an unmarked police car purred along Dover Cemetery Drive. A coroner's van followed soon after. Two plainclothes detectives—a middle-aged woman and an almost-middle-aged man—got out and covered the distance from the street to the deceased.

Detective Margot Burns nodded at the older trooper. Margot couldn't remember his name, so she waited until her partner, Detective Noah Goldman, introduced himself.

"Trooper Mike Dale," the gray-haired cop said, extending his hand to Margot's partner and tipping his hat to the lady detective. The hat-tipping, she remembered that. She was going to have to establish herself as lead. Otherwise, Dale would address all information to Noah.

"Break it down for me," Margot said.

"Female, approximately thirty-five to forty," said Trooper Dale.

"Deceased. Been there awhile. Body is cold. Looks like GSW. Too much blood to tell if it's multiple bullets. No bullet casings near the body . . ."

"Who are they?" Margot said, nodding at Owen and Luna.

"The guy in the robe is the husband of the deceased," said Dale. "Owen Mann. He says the victim, his wife, is Irene Boucher. There's no ID on her."

"Was she carrying a phone?" Margot asked.

Mike Dale ticked his head to the side. His partner, like a well-trained dog, hurried over with an evidence bag containing Irene's phone. Noah took the bag and slid it into his pocket.

"Who's the jogger?" asked Noah.

"Luna Grey. She found the body," Dale said.

"Ms. Grey and the husband know each other?" Margot asked.

"Neighbors, I think," said the trooper.

Margot observed the bathrobed man and the jogger and took note of their proximity on the bench. *Just* neighbors don't sit that close to each other.

"More than neighbors," Noah said.

"I call dibs on the widower," Margot said.

OWEN AND LUNA stayed out of the way, huddled together on a bench next to a moss-drenched mausoleum. Owen watched the two detectives converge upon them. Luna knew exactly what Owen was thinking before he said it.

"I don't think I can go through this again," Owen said.

Luna was thinking the same thing.

October 2003

O wen watched Luna and Mason escape the party. He thought about chasing after them just to be sure that Luna wasn't so drunk that she'd hook up with the sad dude. But Scarlet was right there being Scarlet. Owen and Scarlet left the party soon after and made out on a bench under the light of the moon. She tasted like strawberry Jolly Ranchers and vodka, and she smelled like cotton candy. Her skin shimmered as if it were aglow from the inside.

Like drunk, lusty men often do, Owen oversold his affection. He told Scarlet she was the most beautiful woman he'd ever seen. He told her he thought he could fall in love with her—he didn't mention that he was already in love with this furry jacket she wore that felt like his childhood cat, Oscar.

Scarlet thought this might be the best night she'd ever had. Owen tried to remind himself that he shouldn't fuck her. It was Scarlet who suggested they go back to her dorm. Her roommate had a boyfriend in town and she usually spent the weekend at his place. Owen reminded himself again that he shouldn't fuck her.

Among the cheap plywood furniture and threadbare carpet, Scarlet lost some of the glow of the moonlight. For the briefest moment when she turned on the unforgiving fluorescent lights, Owen saw spots on her cheek and noticed that her lips were chapped and peeling. It didn't help that she was a slob and he smelled the faint odor of dirty laundry. But then she dimmed the lights and tossed off her shirt. And he forgot the warnings he had given himself. He fucked her and told her he loved her breasts.

Scarlet heard only the word *love*.

The next morning, while Scarlet was in a deep vodka slumber, Owen dressed in stealth and made a French exit. He didn't look back as he opened the door and laced up his shoes in the hallway. When Owen emerged from Avery Hall into the bright morning sun, he felt an adrenaline surge worthy of a man who'd just pulled off a prison escape. He purchased two coffees at the campus café, the Mudhut, and strolled kitty-corner across the quad to Blake Hall, Luna's dorm.

Luna, half awake but still hoping for a few more hours' sleep, heard Owen's three assertive knocks on her door. She didn't respond, thinking he'd go away. After the second, louder set of knocks, she sat up in bed and said, *"What?"*

"I brought you a latte," Owen said through the door. "Can I come in?"

Luna made Owen wait long enough that he considered leaving. When Luna finally opened the door, it appeared as though her right eye had got stuck in a wink. One eye down, she turned her back on Owen and began stumbling around her room.

"My contact lens dried up. That always happens when I smoke weed. Do you see my eye drops?"

Owen spotted the small bottle on Luna's nightstand and passed it to her.

"You shouldn't sleep with them in," Owen said as Luna shoved the tip of the dropper into her eye. "That's not how you're supposed to—"

"It's eight A.M. on a Sunday!" Luna said as she blinked the drops into her dry eyes.

"Sorry," Owen said, delivering the coffee.

Luna sipped the latte, which was excellent. But she knew if she drank the whole thing she'd never go back to sleep. She cut herself off and crawled back under the covers.

In bed, Luna closed her eyes and remembered the previous night.

She recalled sitting on the stoop with Mason when he was still just Mason, the chill guy who always had pot on him, and then she remembered the conversation that changed their entire relationship. She felt at once exposed and caged.

Owen took a seat on the floor when it became clear Luna wasn't going to kick him out.

"Where did you go last night?" Luna asked.

"Where'd *you* go?" Owen countered.

Luna had pocketed a lie for that very occasion. "Mason and I took a weed break. Your turn."

Luna enjoyed asking questions when she already knew the answers. It gave her a pleasant power buzz. Owen sipped his coffee and cleared his throat. More scraps of the night assembled in his mind.

"You don't want to know," Owen said with a mixture of pride and regret.

"Casey told me you left with Scarlet. How'd that go?"

"It wasn't anything. We hung out," Owen said.

"No sex, right?" said Luna.

Owen answered with silence.

"Did you sneak out of her room before she woke up?" Luna asked.

No reply.

"Dick move," Luna said.

Owen nodded, agreeing.

"I need more sleep," Luna said, regretfully eying her coffee on the nightstand.

"Can I stay?" said Owen. "I won't bother you."

"Be quiet," said Luna.

Luna drew the covers over her head and feigned sleep. She could rarely fall into slumber when another person was around, but there were still many substances fighting to clear out of her system. She rested her eyes for ten minutes. And then for a good fifteen she was asleep. Owen read a local rag that Luna had picked up for movie showtimes. He skimmed an article about the importance of cleaning your gutters at the end of fall. Then he thought he should use his time more wisely and plucked the philosophy reader from Luna's shelf.

An envelope slipped out. A business envelope, addressed to *Luna "Grey"*—last name in quotes—the original address covered with a forwarding label. The letter was opened with a neat slice across the top. A small piece of rice paper rested inside. Owen would have put the letter back if it weren't for the quotes.

Luna heard the rustling of papers but figured he was reading the *Markham Gazette*. Owen checked over his shoulder, saw the slow rise and fall of Luna's duvet. He quietly removed the paper and unfolded the sharp creases. There was no greeting or salutation, just four words written in clean box letters.

YOU'RE GOING TO HELL.

Owen read the note again. There was no logical explanation for why Luna would save a cryptic message with the suggestion of future damnation. Nor could Owen work out a probable motive for the missive itself. An enemy? An unhinged ex? Both seemed wrong. Maybe it was a joke. An inside joke? Yes, that was it. He checked the postmark date. It was only a few months back. If he had come upon the envelope in a more innocent fashion, he would have asked Luna about it, but that was out of the question. Once, Owen had searched the outside pocket of Luna's backpack for a pen. You would have thought he'd broken into her room and read her diary, the way she reacted.

It should be noted that Luna did not keep a diary.

There was a knock at the door—specifically, two loud and two soft knocks. Owen felt like a hammer had hit his heart. He shoved the letter back in the envelope and clamped the book shut.

"Hey, Luna, are you in there?" Mason said from the other side of the door.

Owen turned to Luna. She peered from beneath the covers and put her finger over her lips. She and Owen remained as still as possible. Mason knocked again, with the same two-loud, two-soft pattern.

"Luna, it's Mason. You awake?"

The doorknob wiggled but didn't budge.

"Luna, don't worry," Mason said, just above a whisper. "I won't tell anyone."

Mason shuffled away. Luna felt light-headed.

"Well, now," Owen said, smiling broadly. "I don't even know where to begin."

"It's not what you think," Luna said.

"Then what is it?"

"Nothing."

"You don't vow secrecy over nothing. Come on, Luna, spill it."

"Nothing to spill," Luna said.

"Did you guys fool around?" Owen asked.

"No."

"You sure? Maybe a little over-the-shirt action. You can tell me. Who am I to judge?"

"Stop it, Owen." Luna refused to make eye contact. She got out of bed and began tidying up the already tidy room.

"We all make mistakes," Owen said. "You were stoned *and* drunk. That's the exact recipe for bad decisions."

"I said stop."

"Wait. Do you like him, like him?" Owen said.

Luna spun around and glared at Owen. She had an expression of anger so electric, Owen would later imagine that she had flames in her eyes. But despite the look of fury, her voice remained measured—disturbingly so, Owen thought.

"You will stop. Now," Luna commanded.

Anyone else would have found Luna terrifying in that moment.

"That was amazing," Owen said, beaming. "Do it again!"

Luna fought back a smile, her fury extinguished. It was almost embarrassing how quickly her mood shifted. Only Owen could do that.

"I have an idea," Owen said. "Let's get out of here."

"Out where?"

"Who cares where we go? We'll have an adventure."

"I need a shower," said Luna.

"Shower. Then adventure."

OWEN AND LUNA had no plan or destination in mind. Owen got behind the wheel and Luna navigated according to some vague directional whim.

Right, left. Straight. Keep going straight. Stay on this road no matter what. It's going to take us somewhere.

They stopped for coffee in Rhinebeck. Owen insisted they go to the café that had a line out the door, because clearly that's where the good coffee was. While the pair were queued up, Luna noticed that every time she moved, Owen closed the gap between them, standing way too close, as if he was blocking her back from the light. Luna could feel him there hovering. She scowled. Generally Owen respected her space but never when they were in line.

"What are you doing?" Luna asked.

"What?" Owen said.

"Why are you always right there? You have a space problem."

Owen took a step back. "No. *You* have the space problem. You get really jumpy when people stand behind you. I figured I was better than a stranger. That's why I do it. Remember when you shouted *spaceman* at that guy when we were waiting to take our school ID photos?" Owen said, laughing.

"I said, 'Space, comma, man,'" Luna said.

"I know. But it wasn't clear to him," Owen said. "Or anyone else."

Luna, recalling all the times Owen had played bodyguard to her neuroses, smiled and punched him in the arm. "That's weirdly nice of you."

"It's for the greater good," Owen said.

Luna thought about it, sighing, exhausted by her own neuroses. "I've got a lot of things, don't I?"

"You do," Owen said. "It's so awesome."

Owen and Luna ordered drip coffee, deciding not to wait for anything fancy. They strolled down Market Street, searching for something to do that was both diverting and inexpensive. They soon realized that nothing fit the bill. They returned to the car and kept driving.

Owen checked on Luna out of the corner of his eye. She was gazing out the window, lost somewhere else. She was so inaccessible in that moment that Owen felt lonely.

"What are you thinking?" Owen said.

He'd never asked that question before. His last girlfriend asked that question so often, he'd had to admonish her to quit. *That* question was, in fact, a secondary reason for their breakup.

"Huh?" Luna said.

"You looked like you were thinking something specific."

"I think when you think, it's always specific at the time."

"Well, what was it, specifically, in that moment?" Owen said.

Luna wasn't going to answer that question. There were certain questions she never answered. For instance, if someone called her and said, *What are you up to?* Luna always said, *Nothing,* even if she was most definitely up to something. If someone inquired about her academic performance, she would tell them her average was a solid B/B-, even if she scored all A's that semester. When questioned about her general well-being, she responded like someone living out her final decade. *I'm still here.*

But the question *What are you thinking* always got under Luna's skin. It seemed that whenever she was asked that question, she was thinking something so private and shameful that she couldn't possibly ever share. Caught unaware, she always responded with cheap lies. *I was thinking what a beautiful day it is; I was thinking about how I should shave my legs this week; I was thinking about making a dentist appointment.*

Luna was generally against lying, considering her past. Although she didn't take as hard a stance as Kant. Some questions, Luna thought, invited a lie. Although she didn't lie to Owen.

"I don't think that's any of your business," Luna said. "It's my favorite thing about my brain. No one else is in it or has access to it. It's mine alone."

Owen was accustomed to girls offering themselves up on a plate to him. He loved how Luna, even after a year of deep friendship, remained a puzzle.

"So, what are you thinking now?" Owen said, like a lowbrow reporter.

"That you're even more annoying than I thought you were," Luna said.

Owen laughed. "I love you, Luna," he said. "You know. Not in a weird way."

The words surprised Owen. He didn't realize until they were uttered that they were true.

"I know," Luna said.

She couldn't remember the last time anyone said they loved her. At least not anyone she wanted to say it. She felt the same but couldn't offer those words. Her reticent nature had iced over years before. The thaw would take some time.

"What are *you* thinking?" she said.

"I was thinking that I wish we were twenty-one so we could kill the afternoon in a dive bar."

That was partially true, although he had been thinking many things in the few minutes of silence after he spoke. He was thinking about the cruel note he found in Luna's philosophy reader; he was thinking about the best way to cool things down with Scarlet; he was thinking about what might have transpired between Mason and Luna; and he was thinking about how she didn't say *I love you* back.

For the next several hours, Luna and Owen took a walk along the river, ate cider doughnuts, and visited a tourism info booth, hunting for any form of amusement. They were surrounded by people decades older who were thrilled by the sight of a dead leaf.

"Is that what happens when you get older? You get more and more excited by smaller and smaller things?" Owen asked.

"I hope so," Luna said.

Later, staring at a local map, Owen and Luna realized they were only an hour from Sleepy Hollow. Neither had been before. They took their time making their way down. They stopped at a diner that looked like an Airstream. In Tarrytown, they walked along the river until it was dark. It was after nine P.M. when Owen and Luna found themselves roaming the cemetery, searching for Washington Irving's grave. Owen tried to recall details from the famous story that he was so sure he'd read. Luna could only remember the cartoon's pumpkin head. Owen tried to scare Luna a few times, ducking behind a headstone, nothing fancy. Luna spooked easily, Owen noticed. He had never detected that trait before. The rustle of leaves, even the sound of her own shoe crunching gravel, could cause her to start. At one point in the night, Owen disappeared behind a gravestone, and when Luna looked back and saw nothing, she experienced a wave of fear so powerful, she began to see stars and had to steady herself on another gravestone, which was slick and slimy, causing her to scream and recoil from the unexpected tactile sensation. Then she became angry.

Luna fought hard to keep all her emotions, even joy, under the radar. But when an unruly emotion surfaced, it was merely an opening act. Anger was always the headliner.

She yelled Owen's name as if he was a mile away. "Where the fuck are you?"

Owen hadn't heard that tone before. He'd seen a flash in her eye but nothing tangible. She always managed to tamp it down.

The anger-management classes Luna had been forced to take in high school had taught her well. Counting to ten, if you're committed to it, drains the momentum from anything. Luna often counted to ten when any feeling struck her. Even elation.

Owen raised his arms above the gravestone, as if someone had a gun trained on him. "I'm here. I'm sorry."

Luna silently counted to ten as she caught her breath. Owen approached her cautiously, as if she were a stray dog baring its teeth.

Then he pulled her into an embrace. Luna tried to shake him off at first, as punishment, but then she gave in. Owen could feel Luna's fear as a quiet vibration in his arms.

"I'm sorry," he said.

"You're an asshole."

"I know," Owen said.

Luna broke away and summoned that steely guard that hovered around her body like the moon's corona. Owen could've sworn he'd seen its physical return. He was about to ask her a question—one he thought important—when a beam of light blinded them.

Before the officer spoke, Luna heard the static on his radio.

"Sir. Ma'am. This cemetery is closed after ten P.M."

Owen turned to approach the officer, prepared to offer his apologies for their trespass, when Luna whispered, "Run!" and booked it out of the graveyard, down Bellwood to Hunter Avenue, where their car was parked. Owen followed Luna's lead and chased after her. Luna reached the car ahead of Owen and shouted, *"Unlock, unlock!"* As soon as Owen clicked his remote, Luna jumped into the driver's seat. Owen, at a more leisurely pace, climbed into the car and handed Luna the key.

Luna turned the ignition, released the parking brake, gunned the engine, and took off up Riverside Drive before Owen had buckled his seatbelt. Soon, they were safely back on Route 9, heading north. For the next fifteen minutes, Luna continued to check her rearview mirror for flashing red lights.

"I think we're safe now," said Owen.

Luna tried to keep her gaze on the road ahead of her.

"That was . . ." Owen said, searching for the right word to describe what happened.

He went with *weird*.

Luna shrugged and acted like it was no big deal.

"Why did you run?" Owen asked.

"I don't know. It seemed like the right move," Luna said.

"Running from a police officer seemed like the right thing to do?" Owen said.

"At the time."

"You do know that when you run, you look guilty."

"We already looked guilty," said Luna.

Owen thought that an odd position for a white woman to take.

"He was going to ask us to leave. That's all," Owen said.

"I didn't want to take that chance," said Luna.

"Do you have a criminal record or something?"

"No," Luna said, after a brief pause.

"There's something you're not telling me," Owen said.

He wasn't going to press Luna for what that something was. But he wanted her to know that he knew this thing was there.

"There's always something I'm not telling you."

October 8, 2019

————

Owen was taken directly to the Deerkill station in his bathrobe and slippers. Underneath the robe, he had on a ratty T-shirt and pajama bottoms adorned with cigar-smoking rabbits. Later, he'd have vague recollections of being fingerprinted and photographed and relieved of his paltry attire. A woman in protective hospital gear put his pajamas and robe in a plastic bag and gave him gray jersey sweatpants and a sweatshirt in exchange. Another man or two could have fit inside those sweats. The odor suggested one or two had. Owen wanted to ask if they had any other clothing options, but he was too exhausted to make the effort. Someone else showed Owen to the men's bathroom. At the sink, he waved his hands in front of the sensor until water flowed. But the water kept stopping, as if he were invisible. Owen switched sinks, washed his hands repeatedly. He wasn't sure what he was trying to clean off them. The male detective, Noah Goldman, leaned in to check on him. Owen was wiping down the sink, trying to clean up the mess. He needed a shower. Goldman took him to an interview room, disappeared, and returned with a warm cup of coffee, packets of creamer and sugar on the side.

"You need anything?" Detective Goldman said.

Owen shook his head. He was cold and wanted a blanket, but he didn't want the kind of blanket that would be lying around a police station.

"My partner will be with you in a minute," Goldman said, stepping into the hallway.

Goldman joined his partner in the adjacent room. Margot was watching the man on a monitor. Owen wiped his face with the back of his hand. Margot leaned in for closer inspection. Those were quality tears, she thought. It takes a special talent to summon that much actual fluid from the lacrimal gland.

Margot Burns entered the interview room, dropped her notebook and coffee on the bolted-down table, and asked if she could get Owen anything. He was hunched over, on the verge of shivering. He had a sour taste in the back of his mouth, and his tongue felt like stucco. The list was too long. He wouldn't know where to begin.

"No," Owen said.

"I'm sorry for your loss," Burns said.

Her tone was sincere, not rote, which made it worse for Owen. He found himself coming in and out of a daze. Each time he resurfaced, he had to tell himself it was real. Irene was dead.

"It is Tuesday, October 8, 2019. Eleven hundred and five hours. Detective Margot Burns interviewing Owen Mann."

Burns pointed to a camera mounted in the high corner of the room.

"We're being recorded. That's as much for your protection as mine," the detective said.

Owen peeked at the camera, turned back to the detective, and then looked at the camera again. He'd been advised of his rights when they arrived at the station. He didn't think he needed a lawyer, though he also knew he might not be at his most rational at a time like this. Ultimately, the thought of dragging things out any longer than necessary was too repugnant to bear. He'd talk. Carefully.

"Did you hear me?" Burns asked.

"Yes. We're being recorded," Owen said.

Burns opened her notebook and casually leaned back in her chair.

"Were you and Irene legally married?"

"Yes."

"She never took your name? She always went by Irene Boucher?"

"Yes."

"How long have you been married?"

"Um, four years," Owen said.

"How long have you known each other?"

"Five years, maybe."

"That was quick."

Owen wasn't sure how to respond so he said nothing.

"What was Irene's occupation?"

"She ran a nonprofit arts education program."

"Was that a full-time job?"

"Her employees handle most of the day to day. She'd go in a few times a week, I guess."

"When was the last time you saw your wife?" Burns asked.

"I'm—I'm not sure," Owen said.

"Did you see her yesterday?"

"No. When I woke up she was gone. I thought she went for a run."

Burns leaned back in her chair, squinted slightly with a head tilt. "Your wife left for a run *yesterday* morning and never came back. Weren't you concerned by her absence?" she said.

Owen didn't like the way the detective raised an eyebrow, as if he was already her prime suspect.

"No. I don't know. She left sometimes. It was something she did."

"So, it was not unusual for your wife to be gone for a twenty-four-hour stretch without alerting you to her whereabouts?"

"No."

"No, it wasn't unusual? Sorry. The double-negative confusion is my fault. So, was the disappearance unusual or not unusual?"

"Not unusual," Owen said.

"Now, that's unusual," Burns said.

"I guess," Owen said.

He stared at the floor, focusing on the speckled pattern of the

THE ACCOMPLICE / 43

linoleum. The image of Irene's blood-drained face kept flashing in front of him.

"If your wife didn't come home at night—or at all—where would she go?"

"A hotel or motel. She wasn't gone overnight that often."

"But it happened enough that you weren't concerned."

"I was a little concerned. But that was mostly this morning."

"Would these . . . disappearances happen after a fight?"

"We didn't really fight."

"Really?" Burns said. "So, if you weren't fighting, then why the extended departure?"

"We both liked our space sometimes."

Margot nodded, trying to convey understanding. "I get that. But why wouldn't she leave a note, so you wouldn't worry?"

"I don't know. We didn't do that," he said.

"So, again, when was the last time you saw your wife alive?"

Owen had gone to bed late on Sunday. Irene was already in bed, talking in her sleep. Owen enjoyed Irene's somniloquies. She always sounded like she was giving directions to a jerk. Thinking about it, he almost laughed.

"Sunday night," Owen said.

"How did she seem?" Burns asked.

"Asleep," Owen said.

"So, you and your wife shared a bed."

"Of course."

"Let's go back to yesterday morning—Monday—when you first noticed your wife wasn't home. What time did you wake up?"

"Around nine or ten."

"What did you do after you woke up?"

"I drank coffee and read the paper."

"How long did that take?"

"About an hour or so."

"And then what did you do?"

"I took a shower."

"After the shower . . . ?"

"I went to work."

"Where is your work?"

"St. Michael's College. Art Department."

"What do you do there?"

"I teach. Painting."

"So, you're an artist?"

"I guess. I was. I dunno. I teach," Owen said.

That was a loaded response, Margot thought. "You arrived at St. Michael's around what time?"

"After eleven. Before noon. My first class was at one P.M."

Owen watched as the detective jotted down Owen's hazy schedule.

"I assume someone saw you on campus?" the detective asked.

"Sure," Owen said.

Owen was always surrounded by clusters of students, although he couldn't recall a single interaction that day until class.

"Your wife was in bed when you went to sleep. When you woke up, she was gone. And you assumed she went for a run?"

"Yes."

"What time did your wife normally go running?"

"In the morning. Before eight."

Owen felt a dull pounding in his head, with the rhythm of his heartbeat.

"When did you realize that your wife probably wasn't still jogging?"

"When I left for work."

"Did you try to call her?"

"Yes, several times."

"And at no point were you concerned about her silence?"

"Not really," Owen said. "We weren't the kind of couple who communicated all the time."

"That's an understatement," the detective said.

Owen, more than most men in his situation, was cognizant of the optics.

"Can you write down the names of anyone who might have seen you yesterday?" Burns said, sliding a notepad in front of Owen.

"Sure, okay."

Owen stared down at the blank page. He felt a tightening in his chest.

"What am I doing?" Owen said.

"The names of anyone who saw you yesterday."

Owen struggled to recall a single name. Even Amy hadn't dropped by his office. Then he remembered his classroom. "I had the one o'clock painting class. There's an Alison and an Oliver. I can't remember all their names. We haven't been in session that long. I need my roster."

"You can email it later," Burns said. "How long was that class?"

"Two hours. One to three."

"So, you arrived at the campus before noon. And you taught from one to three. What did you do after that?"

"I returned to my office. Answered emails for a while. I left at four-thirty to meet Luna for a drink."

"That's Luna Grey? The woman who found your wife's body?"

"Yes."

LUNA ARRIVED AT the station an hour after Owen, having been allowed to go home and take a quick shower and change. Sam had already left for work. She knew he was in surgery, so a call was out of the question. She tried to compose a text but couldn't figure out how to condense what had happened into a concise message.

It was Noah Goldman, the younger male detective, who met Luna when she arrived. He greeted her with a smile and a warm handshake. *This is the good cop,* Luna thought. Goldman offered Luna some coffee and cautioned her about the quality. She accepted it because she knew she'd need something to do with her hands.

The chair Goldman had given her was lopsided. She remembered reading somewhere that an unbalanced chair was part of an interrogation technique. She thought about asking for a new one while things were still friendly.

Goldman thanked Luna for coming in and asked her to go over the events of that morning.

"I went out for a run around eight-fifteen. I saw Irene at the cemetery maybe ten minutes later."

"Is Dover Cemetery a common running area for locals?"

"No. Most people use the river trail. It's flat."

"But you and Irene used the cemetery?"

"Yes."

"Would you ever go running together?" Goldman asked.

"We used to. Not much recently. I didn't like running with her. She was too fast."

"Did Irene always go to the cemetery at the same time?"

"She wasn't on a schedule, but she was fairly consistent."

"And how often do you go running?"

"Not that often."

"So, it was just a coincidence that you went for a run this morning?"

"I texted her yesterday—was it yesterday? Yes. I texted her to see if she wanted to go running this morning."

"I thought you didn't like running with her?"

Luna recognized that her story wasn't adding up. She wasn't saying anything that was untrue and yet it read like a lie. "I thought if I made a plan, maybe I could trick myself into it."

"Got it," Goldman said. "Did you make a plan with Irene?"

"No. She didn't answer that text. Owen messaged me this morning and asked if I'd heard from Irene. That's when I went out for a jog, thinking that maybe Irene was already at Dover."

"Okay," said Detective Goldman. "You went out this morning. What did you do right after you found the body?"

"I ran straight to Owen's house and told him. Then I dialed 911."

"From Mr. Mann's house?"

"Yes."

"You didn't have your phone on you?"

"No," Luna said.

"Mr. Mann's home is about a half mile from the cemetery, correct?"

"Yes."

"Where's your house?"

"Three Locust Street."

Goldman retrieved a street map and smoothed it out on the table. He clicked his pen and circled the cemetery and then circled Owen's house.

"Can you show me where your house is on this map?"

Luna pointed to a spot across the greenbelt, a quick shot from the cemetery.

"Here?" Goldman said, pointing with his pen.

"Yes," said Luna.

Goldman inked another circle. "So," he said. "You find the body here, but instead of running home, which is less than a quarter of a mile, you run past your home to Mr. Mann's house. Mind if I ask why?"

"His wife was dead. I thought he should be the first to know."

Luna clocked the flickering fluorescent lights with a scowl. She tried to remember if she'd taken her meds that morning. Detective Goldman, good cop, left the room to warm up Luna's coffee.

When he returned, Noah noticed that Luna had slipped something—a piece of cardboard or a pack of gum—under the chair. He couldn't hear the wobble as she crossed her legs. Most people, guilty or innocent, don't fix the wobble. It stuck in his head.

Noah cleared his throat and consulted his notes. "When was the last time you saw Irene?"

"Yesterday morning. She dropped by for a cup of coffee. I assumed she was on her way to Dover," Luna said.

"How long did she stay?"

"About five minutes."

"What did you talk about during those five minutes?" Goldman asked.

"There were rambling topics. I think I mentioned Leo Whitman because I was helping him hire a new assistant."

Luna made a quick decision to leave out the part where Irene told her about Owen's affair.

"You're talking about Leo Whitman, the artist?"

"Yes. He's Irene's stepfather, or was. Her mother passed about eight years ago."

"Were Irene and Mr. Whitman close?"

"No. But they were in each other's lives. He's had some health problems and doesn't have any family of his own. Irene helps him as much as she can. It would be good to tell Leo before it's on the news."

"Her name hasn't been released. How did Irene and Owen meet?"

"They met at a party for Leo. Irene asked Owen to teach a few classes in her arts program."

"When was that?"

"They met five years ago. Married a year later."

"Was this their first marriage?"

"It was Owen's first, Irene's second," Luna said.

"Irene had an ex-husband?" Goldman said.

"Yes," Luna said. "He lives in Boston. I think he's a financial adviser. Or something with money."

"Do you know his name?"

"I think his name is Carl. I'm not sure. She always referred to him as her ex."

"Was their divorce contentious?"

"I don't think so. He remarried quickly, if I recall. That troubled her some. Made her wonder how invested he was in the first place," Luna said.

"Let's get back to yesterday morning," said Goldman. "Do you recall what Irene was wearing?"

"The same clothes that—"

The image of Irene in her redundantly red windbreaker locked in Luna's mind. She felt a rush of heat and the pressure of tears fighting to escape. She couldn't explain why she didn't want to cry in front of the detective. It certainly would have made her appear less guilty. She then felt ashamed for thinking about how she might look to the detective. But when you're being questioned by authorities, your primary goal is to stop being questioned.

Goldman saw that she was fighting tears. He bought that her emotions were legitimate. He just wasn't sure of the root cause.

"You okay?"

"I was the last person to see her alive, wasn't I?" Luna asked.

"That seems likely," Goldman said. "Besides her murderer, anyway."

OWEN BEGAN TO shiver in his hideous sweats. He wrapped his hands around the cold coffee. He took a sip that he knew he'd regret. But he had to do something.

"Did your wife have any enemies?" Burns asked.

"No," Owen said.

"How about friends?"

"She didn't need a lot of people. She found them draining."

"I see," said Burns.

"There's something you should know," Owen said.

"What's that?"

"I was having an affair. You were going to find out eventually. Thought I'd save you the trouble."

"Thank you."

"I didn't kill my wife."

Burns clicked her pen and poised it over a pad of paper. Owen wondered why the detective bothered to take notes when they were being recorded.

"Now, this woman," Burns said, "that you'd been sleeping with. Was that Luna Grey, the jogger who came upon the body?"

"What? No. That—no. It's not like that. Luna and I are old friends. Just friends."

"Always?"

"Always."

"Can you give me the name of the woman you were seeing?"

"She has nothing to do with any of this."

"I understand. But I'll still need her name."

Owen paused for a long moment. "Amy Johnson."

Burns slipped a piece of paper and pen in front of Owen and asked him to write down Amy Johnson's address and phone number.

OWEN FOUND LUNA sitting on the steps of the police station. She'd been released an hour earlier and waited for him. In the interim she'd turned on her phone to a storm of buzzes, alerts, and dings. She scrolled through her recent callers—Whitman, Sam, Whitman, Sam, Maya, Casey, Sam, Whitman. She couldn't phone any of them until she consulted with Owen.

Owen sat down on the stoop next to her, ridiculous in his voluminous sweats. Luna reached into her pocket and pulled out a pack of Marlboro Lights and a book of matches.

"Here," she said. "I figured you'd need it. Today at least."

"Probably tomorrow as well."

"You have a week. Then you quit," Luna said.

Owen lit his cigarette and took a drag.

"I'm so sorry," Luna said.

"I know."

"I loved her too," she said.

When she said it, she hadn't realized how much she meant it. It had taken some time for Luna to warm to Irene. She had to learn to love her, but she did. Quiet tears slid down her cheeks.

"What am I supposed to do?" said Owen.

"I don't know. Mourn, plan the funeral."

"I think I'm a suspect," Owen said.

"The husband is always a suspect," Luna said.

"Who would kill her?"

"It could have been a stranger."

"Why would a stranger shoot a jogger running through a cemetery?"

"I don't know. People do terrible things to other people, and sometimes there's no reason for it. At least no reason that you can understand," Luna said.

Owen took another deep drag on the cigarette and experienced a head rush, followed by nausea. He put his head between his knees.

"You okay?" she said.

"Did they ask you about Markham?" Owen said.

"They don't know. Not yet," Luna said.

"They will," Owen said.

"Yeah. They'll know everything soon enough."

October–December 2003

Scarlet had been patiently waiting for Owen to call since the morning after they'd slept together. When he didn't, Scarlet decided there was no reason that she couldn't call him. She called three separate times before he answered. When he did, she asked Owen if he wanted to hang out sometime. He said, "Sure, sometime," but refused to make an actual date. A few days later, Scarlet ran into him at another party. Both drunk, they left the party together and went back to Owen's dorm. Soon after they had sex, Owen told Scarlet to get dressed. He'd walk her home. She wanted to stay the night. Owen explained that he couldn't possibly sleep through the night sharing a twin bed. Roughly the same scenario happened two more times.

After the third time, Scarlet sought Luna's counsel.

"I probably shouldn't have fucked him that first night, right?"

Luna never wanted to play anyone's confidante. Secrets were generally perceived as barter, and Luna could never reciprocate.

"I know he likes me, because we keep hooking up. Why won't he make a regular date with me?"

"I don't know," Luna said.

Oh, she knew. She'd gotten Owen's side of the matter. Luna hated the way Owen used Scarlet. And she hated that Scarlet let him. They were both idiots as far as Luna was concerned. But Scarlet was so obviously at a disadvantage, Luna wanted to even the playing field. That's why she helped her.

"Sit down," Luna said, guiding Scarlet onto the edge of her bed. "Listen to me very carefully. Owen needs to be off-balance. He likes people to be puzzles. If he's solved you, then he's no longer interested."

"So what am I supposed to do? Be mysterious?"

Luna hated the sound of that, a woman changing her ways to please a man. But it was the correct advice for Scarlet's endgame.

"Don't be anything you're not. But don't tell him everything that's on your mind. Wait, stop. This isn't good advice," Luna said, again recalibrating. "If you have things on your mind that you want to express, you should say them."

"No, this is great," Scarlet said, already setting in motion a plan of action. "He doesn't have to know everything I'm thinking, right?"

"That's my motto," Luna said.

If Scarlet was going to adopt any of her advice, Luna hoped it was that.

Scarlet played with her hair incessantly—scooping it behind her ears, grasping it in a ponytail and dropping it back down, twirling it around a finger and draping it over her shoulder. The touching, the stroking, the fidgeting, began to annoy Luna so deeply she had to stare at a distant wall.

"I have a paper to write," Luna said, eyeing the door, hoping that Scarlet would get the hint.

"What do I do if he doesn't call?" Scarlet asked.

"Wait him out," Luna said.

"So I shouldn't sleep with him again. At least not the next time he calls?"

"Yes. No. You should do what *you* want to do," Luna said.

Luna felt a medley of uncomfortable emotions, including annoyance and jealousy. She was disappointed in herself for feeling hostile toward Scarlet. To compensate, she offered another, more specific piece of advice.

"If you sleep with him again, make sure you leave first."

Over the next two months, Scarlet repeatedly came to Luna seeking counsel. She'd listen to Luna for a while and follow her advice to a T. Then she'd get comfortable, thinking that her relationship with Owen had finally found its footing, and slip up. Luna eventually gave up and told Scarlet to listen to her gut, just be herself. That was a good rule of thumb in general, but it wasn't going to improve matters with Owen. Scarlet's surprise visits to Owen's dorm had increased in frequency. Her availability, as far as Owen was concerned, was limitless. Owen spent more time than usual at the library or in a local café just so he wouldn't be home for Scarlet's increasingly common drop-ins.

WITH A WEEK left before winter break, Owen hoped to limit his Scarlet interactions. His dorm was no longer a safe place, and he'd grown tired of the unforgiving chairs in the library. Owen waited for Luna as she filed out of the Walter Hughes Humanities Building. Luna had just taken her Ethics exam, her brain still in the classroom. She didn't even see Owen until he was standing right in front of her.

"What are you up to now?" Owen asked.

Luna didn't want to answer the question. She glanced at her watch, just to buy time. "I got a thing," she said.

"What kind of thing?" Owen said.

Luna should have known better than to offer a vague answer. Owen could never rest on an ambiguity.

"What is it with you and specifics?" Luna said. "I have an appointment. I'll be gone for a few hours."

Normally Owen would have kept pressing for details, but he had other priorities. "Can I borrow your room key?" he asked.

"Why?"

"I'm tired. I really need to take a nap," Owen said.

"Who's stopping you?" Luna said.

"Scarlet always drops by in the afternoon, and I need some *me* time."

"Did you really just say that?"

"I did," Owen replied, turning up his palm, waiting.

"You've been seeing Scarlet for how long now?"

"We're not seeing each other," Owen said. "It's very casual."

"Here's the problem with having occasional sex with a woman for over two months," Luna said. "She starts to think you like her, because it's very unlikely that she would repeatedly hook up with someone that she doesn't like. Now that you have that information, maybe you'll think before you fuck."

"I appreciate that insight," Owen said. "Can you help me out?"

Luna was trying to figure out the best way to say no, but Owen pressed on. He was desperate.

"Luna, I just want to be alone. I don't want to talk about meaningful things. You more than anyone should understand that."

Luna took in a big breath and let an absurdly long sigh.

"Is there a problem?" Owen asked.

"I don't like people in my space when I'm not there."

Owen tried to recall if he knew this about her. Had he ever been alone in her room? He knew she was anti-snooping, but those were different things, right?

"I'm just going to rest in your bed, on top of your covers."

Luna was aware that denying the request might appear suspicious, so she reluctantly handed over her keys. "Take off your shoes and don't touch anything."

"You're the best," Owen said, kissing her on the forehead.

As Luna watched Owen jog back to the dorm, her gut twisted into a tight knot.

OWEN HAD FULLY intended to nap. He removed his shoes and lay on top of Luna's duvet. He closed his eyes, hoping that sleep would come. It did not. He sat upright and decided to study. He fished through his backpack for his French book and sat on the floor, translating a short passage about a trip to Greece. When his pen ran out of ink, he opened the drawers in Luna's desk. He knew very well that he was searching for more than a pen, but in some part of his brain, he could still insist on the innocence of his trespass.

In the bottom drawer, Owen found an old Adidas shoebox. After checking that Luna's door was locked, he removed the box from the drawer. He knelt on the floor next to the desk and opened the lid. Inside were a baggie of weed and a pipe. Owen returned the box to the drawer. After that, he fully committed to his search.

Owen understood that breaching Luna's privacy was the kind of transgression she was unlikely to forgive. He could only manage one flimsy rationalization for his behavior, which was decidedly out of character: He told himself that he was worried for Luna's safety. That was true, to a certain extent. But that wasn't all of it. Owen knew that something had happened in Luna's past. If he knew what it was, it might explain why she'd never told him.

Owen stood on a chair and rummaged through everything on the top shelf of her closet. He checked between the mattress and box spring. He peered under the bed and found two dusty pieces of luggage. Inside the smaller suitcase was an old cigar box that held about a half dozen letters, sent to Luna at a Colorado address.

The envelopes were all cleanly sliced open, which Owen experienced as a subconscious invitation. He chose a business-sized envelope at the top of the pile and removed the paper, which was folded in thirds. The letter was typed, with no return address, and postmarked November 2001.

Dear Ms. Grey,

I do not know if my letters have ever reached you. If they have, I wonder if they've meant something. If you've taken my advice and sought the help of the Lord. If you ask, if you pray, HE will forgive you. You were young and led astray by evil. I hope by now you have found your way back to the light.

I have prayed for my family and I have prayed for your family. Enough time has passed that I've found that I can forgive. I hope you can forgive yourself.

God bless,
Sharon Wells

Owen felt sweat beading on the back of his neck despite the chill in the room. One more letter, he told himself, and then he'd put the box away. As Owen searched the stack for a meatier envelope, the letter that would provide a full narrative, there was a quiet knock on the door.

He returned the letter to the cigar box, put it back in the suitcase, and slid it back under the bed. He got to his feet and scanned the room for anything askew.

"Luna, you in there?" a man's voice said from the other side.

Ted, Owen thought. He couldn't decide if he should remain mute or answer the door.

"Luna, I can hear you," Ted said.

"Hey," said Owen, swinging open the door.

"Hey," said Ted, stepping back, startled. Annoyed. "I was looking for Luna."

"She's not here," Owen said.

Ted was getting a bad vibe from Owen, but he wasn't one to let a bad vibe stick. He opened his backpack and pulled out a brown bag wrapped around a bottle.

"Cesar went on a liquor run," Ted said.

"Did Luna place an order?"

"Nah, she never has money for booze. I just thought I'd share."

"That was nice of you," Owen said.

Ted ignored Owen's tone, which was guarded and unfriendly, and pretended not to notice the weird way that Owen was blocking the door.

"So, you want some?" Ted said.

"Why not?" Owen said as he backed away from the door and let Ted inside.

A drink to calm his nerves was just what Owen needed. Ted was the price he had to pay for free booze. Ted passed the bottle to Owen.

"Maker's Mark. Nice," Owen said as he unscrewed the cap and lifted the bottle to his mouth.

"No, dude, let's be civilized," Ted said, as he plucked two shot glasses out of the pocket on his backpack.

Ted sat down on the floor and placed the glasses next to his feet. Owen took a seat next to him and poured two shots. The men clinked glasses. Ted said, "Cheers"; Owen said, "Skål."

Mason passed Luna's room and peered through the open door. "Hey," said Mason.

"Hey, Mason, come on in," Ted said.

Owen didn't think that was such a good idea.

"Where's Luna?" Mason asked.

"She had a thing," Owen said.

"She doesn't like people in her room when she's not around," Mason said.

"It's okay. I got her permission," said Owen.

"Mason, want a shot? I think I got another glass in here somewhere," Ted said, fishing through his backpack.

"Nah. Alcohol is poison," Mason said as he hovered in the doorway.

Owen wanted Mason to leave, but Ted invited Mason to take a load off. Mason decided to stay, figuring Luna would come back eventually. He also felt protective of the personal space that he knew Ted and Owen were breaching.

"So, you and Scarlet," Ted said, joining their names as if they were a well-established couple.

"We're just hanging out," Owen said.

Ted had heard otherwise but was only interested in the subject as a gateway to another topic. "So there's nothing going on with you and Luna?" Ted asked.

"We're pals, that's all."

"Cool," said Ted, pouring Owen another shot.

Owen drained the glass. Ted generously poured him another.

"You have a thing for Luna?" Owen asked Ted.

"I think she's cool," Ted said.

Owen wished Mason would leave. He was just sitting there, silently following the conversation.

"She is cool," said Owen. "Don't you agree, Mason?"

"She's got her good side and her bad side," Mason said. He adored Luna but couldn't shake his noncommittal ways.

Ted ignored Mason and returned his attention to Owen. "Dude, you're like her best friend. Give me something."

"Huh?"

"What do I need to know?"

"She's a girl," Owen said. "Ask her questions. Ask her lots and lots of questions."

Owen briefly caught Mason's confused expression. Mason knew what Owen was saying was bullshit, and he let Owen know he knew, but he didn't rat him out.

"HEY!" LUNA SHOUTED from the shadow of her door. "What the fuck?"

The three men scrambled to their feet. Mason took something out of his backpack and stashed it in the pocket of the army jacket Luna was wearing.

"I just came by to bring you that," said Mason as he made a quick departure.

Ted foisted on Luna the half-empty bottle of whiskey. "For you," he said as he slipped out of the room.

Luna dropped the bottle on her desk, then took Mason's weed out of her pocket and stored it in her dresser drawer.

"So many admirers," Owen said. "How can you possibly keep them all satisfied?"

"Keys," Luna said, holding out her hand.

Owen fished in his pocket and handed them over. He tried not to look as guilty as he felt. Luna tried not to look as angry as she felt.

"They just came by. I didn't invite them in," Owen said.

Luna opened her door wide to encourage Owen's departure. It took Owen a moment to get the hint.

"Ohhh. You want me to leave."

"I need some *me* time," Luna said.

October 8, 2019

Detective Burns gazed out the grimy window of the Deerkill police station and carefully observed Luna and Owen chatting on the front steps. Owen was smoking. Burns, who had a good nose, hadn't detected the odor of even a casual smoker during the interview. Trauma often caused people to return to bad habits. So did fear. And guilt. Luna had to have bought the cigarettes for him. Luna was not smoking. So, Luna had anticipated his need. There was something intimate about that.

Detective Goldman approached his partner, carrying two fresh mugs of coffee. He followed Burns's gaze out the window. "ME confirmed that Irene died yesterday. There's no point in testing the husband's pajamas."

"Right," Burns said. She took a sip of the piping hot coffee and winced.

"You going to tell me what you're thinking?" Noah asked.

"I don't think anything yet," Margot said.

Margot's first partner, now retired, had tunnel vision. He always trusted his gut and never let go. She came to realize that his gut was more about his psychological biases than anything else. If he wouldn't like someone in day-to-day life, he was more prone to like them for murder. Margot's takeaway from five years with the man was to keep her mind open until the weight of the evidence was too much to bear. At times it came off as absurd, like you had to beat her over the head with the truth. Still, she stood by her process. This annoyed the shit out of Noah because she would frequently ask for his early impressions. Just by answering the question, he was failing her test.

"What's your read on those two?" Burns asked.

Sometimes Goldman would refuse to answer on principle, but then Margot would keep asking.

"I think that whatever those two are, it's not normal," Goldman said.

Burns nodded. She was thinking the same thing.

LUNA'S PHONE BUZZED relentlessly as she drove Owen away from the Deerkill police station. Owen retrieved Luna's mobile from her purse and read the messages as if they were his own. Luna didn't mind, these days. The only secrets she currently had were the thoughts in her head.

"You haven't told Sam?" Owen asked, having noted the impatient tone of Sam's texts.

"He was gone when I got home after—I didn't want to tell him before a surgery. What if he fucked it up? I'd always wonder if it was my fault the patient walked with a limp the rest of their life."

"I'm going to tell him you're alive. That's all. He heard a jogger was murdered, and I bet he thought it was you."

"Shit, you're right," said Luna, glancing at her phone as she hit the brakes for a stop sign. She grabbed the phone from Owen and quickly knocked out a text.

Driving. Will call soon. I'm fine.

"We should be the ones to tell Leo," she said, passing the phone back to Owen.

"Let's get it over with now."

"Don't you want to go home first? Put on some normal clothes?"

"For a man who wears pajamas all day? No."

LUNA HAD PROMISED Leo she'd drop by that morning to help him review résumés again.

Leo swung open the door and said, "You're three hours late."

Leo was wearing his work uniform. Boxer shorts and a moth-eaten T-shirt. A long silk robe pulled the outfit together. Luna wasn't sure if he wore the robe all the time or when he was expecting company.

"Leo, I'm sorry. It was unavoidable," Luna said.

"Wasn't expecting Owen," Leo said, studying Owen's bizarre ensemble.

"Can we come in?" Luna said.

The trio entered the house. Luna sat Leo down on the couch while Owen disappeared into the kitchen and returned with three glasses and a bottle of Wild Turkey.

"What's going on?" Leo said in a bracing tone.

Owen refrained from responding, reminded himself that he had to behave the way a man in mourning behaves, although he struggled with the notion that one must impose outside rules of performance on personal conduct. *Like the last time,* he thought. Grief would be so much easier if you didn't have to spend your time worrying about whether you were doing it right. Owen sat down on the couch and poured the bourbon.

"Something happened," Luna said.

"What is it?" Leo asked. "You're scaring me."

There was a dramatic tension in the air, which Leo enjoyed. Life in the last few years had become dull. Owen slid a glass in front of Leo. Luna was waiting for Owen to break the news, while Owen thought Luna would do it. Owen finished his drink and poured another. He cleared his throat impatiently.

"You want me to do it?" Luna said.

"I just thought you were going to," Owen said.

"No. This is something you have to do," Luna said.

As Owen tried to find the right words, words that might soften the blow, Leo exploded.

"For fuck's sake!" Leo said.

"Irene is dead," Owen said quickly and flatly to get it over with.

Leo took a quick breath, like a gasp. "What? When?"

"Her body was found this morning. I think she died yesterday," Owen said.

"Her body? Where was she?" Leo asked. His questions were logical and reasonable, but there was aggression in his tone.

"She went for a run at the cemetery yesterday. She was shot. I found her . . . this morning when I went for a jog," Luna said.

"Where is she now?" Leo asked.

"At the morgue," Luna said.

Leo covered his face and began to sob. Luna was surprised Leo could cry so freely. She only knew Irene's version of her relationship with Leo. Sure, Leo was technically Irene's stepfather for a few years, but Irene's picture of their relationship was icy, at best.

Owen poured another drink.

"Slow down," Luna said to Owen.

"Back off," Owen said.

"Who on earth would kill Irene?" Leo asked.

"I don't know," Luna said.

"Did she say anything?" Leo asked.

Luna and Owen exchanged a look. Leo was in his late sixties. His health had been deteriorating recently. Perhaps he was developing dementia of some kind.

"Leo, Irene is dead," Luna said. "She died . . . yesterday, I think."

"I know that," Leo said. "I just wondered if she'd said anything before, about . . . oh, I don't know . . . someone giving her trouble."

"No," Owen said. "Why do you ask?"

Luna's phone buzzed in her pocket. *Sam,* she remembered. She had to contend with Sam.

"I have to go home," Luna said.

"Me too," said Owen.

"Please don't leave," Leo said. "I can't be alone right now."

Luna and Owen shared a silent exchange. Neither wanted to deal with Leo, but it was better to keep an eye on him than leave him to his own devices.

"If you get dressed, you can come with me," said Owen.

LUNA PULLED HER car in front of Owen's driveway. Leo stumbled out of the vehicle and shuffled up the walk.

"Don't be long," Owen said. "I can't—"

"I know," Luna said.

As Owen walked up to his front door, Luna spotted a bouquet of white lilies sitting on the porch. It unnerved her that the news was already out. She thought perhaps they'd have a little more time before the neighbors would begin to converge with their casseroles and condolences.

Luna drove straight home, which took all of two minutes. As she stepped out of her car, the weight of the morning set in. Her whole body ached as if she'd aged a decade. She felt like she could sleep for days. Sam was sitting in the kitchen in his scrubs, waiting for her, poised for a fight.

"Let me explain marriage to you," Sam said.

"Wait—" Luna said.

"You don't get to disappear for six hours—"

"Please stop—"

"We're not Owen and Irene," Sam said. "If they want to vanish on each other, that's their business. I won't live like that."

"Irene is dead," Luna said. "I found her body when I went for a run and spent the morning at the police station, being questioned."

Sam flinched briefly. Then he tilted his head and squinted, as if he misunderstood.

"What did you say?" Sam asked.

"Irene is dead," Luna repeated. "She was shot while jogging in Dover Cemetery."

"Shot? Who shot her?"

"They don't know."

"They? Who is they?"

"The police," said Luna.

"Why didn't you call?" Sam said.

"I was being interrogated," Luna said. "I'm sorry. I got here as soon as I could."

Sam stared at his feet. His eyes turned glassy. That was about as much emotion as you could get out of him, Luna had learned early in their relationship.

"I think I need to go to bed for a few minutes," Luna said.

Exhaustion came over her suddenly. She could barely stand on two feet. Sam nodded. Luna climbed the stairs to the bedroom, closed the blinds, kicked off her shoes, and crawled under the covers with her clothes on.

OWEN SET LEO up with a bottle of bourbon and headed upstairs to take a shower. He kept seeing Irene's blood-drained lips, the gray hue of her cheeks. He cried in the shower and stopped when he shut off the water. Owen dried off and changed into a pair of clean pajamas and a robe.

He heard a television on downstairs. Leo was drifting off in front of an old movie, snoring quietly. Leo had imbibed more that afternoon than he had in years. Owen poured another drink as he debated the various ways he might get the old man out of his house.

When the doorbell rang, Owen felt like a hammer was beating on his heart.

Leo opened his eyes and lifted his head and shouted, "I'll be right there," as if he was in his own home.

Owen looked through the peephole. "*Shit,*" he muttered, loud enough for the person on the other side of the door to hear.

"Owen, it's Maya and Greg."

Owen was too tired to play the I'm-not-home game. He swung

open the door to find Maya Wilton standing on his porch with a large casserole covered in aluminum foil in her hands. Greg, her husband, stood a few steps back to her left, like the second-in-command.

"Owen, I'm so sorry," Maya said, her face weirdly contorted into a cartoon of sympathy.

Owen was still trying to figure out if there was a way to keep Maya outside when she shoved the dish into his hands, not just invading but attacking his personal space. This caused Owen to take a step back, leaving room for her entrance. Owen looked at Greg, who shrugged. Owen had no idea what the shrug was intended to convey. Greg rarely said anything. But unlike most people who use words sparingly, he hadn't developed superior forms of nonverbal communication.

Maya squinted in the dim light. "You think maybe we should open the drapes, get some light in here?" she said as she circled the living room, opening drapes and flicking on every switch until the house was as bright as an operating room.

LUNA'S PHONE BUZZED against her dresser. Three texts in succession from Owen.

Where are you?
Please come back here.
Maya & Greg here. Make them leave.

When Luna checked the clock, she realized she'd been out cold for at least an hour. She rinsed with mouthwash, applied deodorant, and jogged down the stairs. Sam was stretched out on the couch, cycling through channels on the TV. She couldn't remember the last time she saw him killing time like that.

"I'm going to go back over to Owen's. Okay?" Luna said. "I left him with Leo, and now the neighbor—you know, Maya—is there, offering her condolences. I need to get rid of her."

Sam almost smiled. "You're good at that," he said.

It wasn't a dig. It was a genuine compliment.

WHEN LUNA ARRIVED, she found Owen cornered on the couch by Maya, who was gripping his hand and offering her mixed bag of condolences.

She's in a better place now.

If there's anything I can do, I'm here for you, Owen.

They'll get the sick bastard and string him up by the balls. I promise you that.

Luna nodded at Greg, who returned the look with an embarrassed smile. Greg always seemed confused by his wife's behavior, as if she were an alien with entirely different customs from his.

Luna stood by the open door and said, "Maya, it was so nice of you to drop by."

"Of course," said Maya. "You must make sure you stay nourished, Owen."

Owen nodded, afraid that any words could encourage a longer stay.

This fear of Maya, of her company, had begun when Owen and Irene first moved into their house on Vine Street. Maya dropped by with a plate of brownies to welcome her new neighbors and offer them the lay of the land. Irene was out shopping while Owen unpacked. Maya began to provide an accounting of every retail establishment in the neighborhood along with their relative pros and cons, including the personality quirks of the proprietors. Owen tried his usual tricks for encouraging a guest's departure. He had a certain way of saying *thank you* that was remarkably finite, and he found *okay, then,* to work quite well with sensitive types. But none of his usual tricks had any effect on Maya. She stayed for two hours and twenty minutes.

Owen knew he could rely on Luna. Her gift for swiftly dispatching visitors had only improved with age. When her first strong suggestion of a departure fell on deaf ears, Luna approached Maya, gently detached the hand that was gripping Owen's arm, and led her to the front door.

"Thank you, Maya and Greg, for your kindness. Owen needs his rest now."

"Of course," Maya said, as she was led outside the front door. Maya was on the brink of another paragraph of condolences, but Luna interrupted.

"We'll see you later," Luna said, shutting the door and clicking the deadbolt.

"Thank you," Owen said.

Luna scanned the room. "Where's Leo?" she asked.

Owen checked the kitchen. Luna opened the sliding door to the backyard and leaned out. They shouted his name a few times. Eventually, he answered from the top of the stairs.

"I'm here, for fuck's sake," he said. "Please stop shouting."

Leo snailed down the steps on his titanium knees.

"What were you doing up there?" Luna asked.

The first floor of the Mann-Boucher house had everything a guest might need. Only the master suite and Irene's office were upstairs.

"I was looking for a book I lent Irene," Leo said.

"What book?" Owen said.

"The Hockney coffee-table book. I'm sorry. It's precious to me."

"You could have asked," Owen said.

"You were busy with that woman," Leo said.

Owen's phone chirped and then the doorbell rang. Luna winced at the competing sounds. Owen turned to Luna, his eyes wide in panic. *What now?*

"I'll get it," Luna said.

It was Sam, still wearing his scrubs. Sam always claimed that he wore them because it was easier than assembling another outfit, but Owen wasn't buying that bullshit.

"Hey," Sam said to Luna. "I thought I should—"

"Right," Luna said.

Owen had noticed that soon after Sam and Luna met, they began to speak in an inelegant shorthand. Sure, husbands and wives often finished each other's sentences. But this was different. He thought they sounded like frat boys agreeing to a previously conceived plan.

Sam drifted past Luna and approached Owen. The two men hugged awkwardly.

"I'm so sorry, Owen," Sam said.

"Thanks, man."

"She was a good woman," Sam added.

Sam's tone was soft and sincere, which was incredibly rare. Luna took notice. He was really trying, she thought.

"I should call a car," Leo said.

Owen breathed an audible sigh of relief.

"Yeah. Get some rest," Luna said.

"I'll drive him," Sam said.

Leo appeared stunned by the offer. "I wouldn't think of it. I've got this app on my phone," Leo said, fumbling with his phone and glasses.

"Put your phone away," Sam said. "I said I'd drive you."

Leo sank his phone back into the pocket of his jacket. "That's very generous," Leo said. His words and tone were mismatched.

"Yeah," said Luna, surprised.

After Sam and Leo departed, Luna and Owen compared notes.

"That was weird, right?" Owen said.

"Yes," said Luna.

She wasn't sure which element was the weirdest, Sam offering the ride or Leo not wanting to accept. Sam was Leo's doctor. A few years ago, he'd replaced both of Leo's knees in close succession. Leo had always seemed fond of Sam.

Owen's phone buzzed on the coffee table. As Luna handed it to him, she saw the name *Amy* on the screen.

"Amy? That's her?"

Owen nodded.

"Did you tell her?"

"Not yet."

"Tell her before the police do," Luna said.

"I will."

"And do not text anything you don't want the police to read," Luna said.

"I know."

"You don't think—"

"No, Luna. She didn't do it."

"Okay," Luna said. "If you're sure."

"I'm sure," Owen said, although his conviction had already weakened.

December 2003

———

"Luna, what do you want to be when you grow up?" Owen asked.

Luna was sprawled out on her bed, smoking a spliff that Mason had sweetly shoved under her door that morning. It was just one day before winter break. Luna had taken her last final that morning; Owen, yesterday afternoon.

"Good," Luna answered.

What kind of answer was that? Owen thought. "You're already good," he said.

"I'm not. But I'd like to be. One day."

"I meant, what do you want to do with your life? You never talk about that," Owen said.

"Because I don't know."

"What did you want to be when you were a little girl?"

"A firefighter or a horse trainer. Frankly, both of those jobs still sound awesome."

"You really don't think about this stuff?"

"Not often."

"One day you'll need a job, and there are so many awful jobs."

"Maybe I'll be a drug rep," Luna said. "I hear they make a lot of money."

"Dude, you can't be serious," Owen said.

Two quiet knocks were followed by two more quiet knocks.

"I'm not here," Owen whispered.

"Come in!" said Luna. They were in her room, after all.

It was Ted. Owen had his own secret knock with Luna—three loud in quick succession—and wondered when Ted had joined the club. Luna adored her knocking system. It was like call screening for visitors.

"Hey," said Ted to Owen.

"Hey," Owen replied.

That was generally the extent of any Owen-Ted conversation those days.

"Scoot over," Ted said to Luna as he climbed onto the bed next to her. Luna passed Ted the joint. He took a hit and offered it to Owen, who shook his head. The whole passing-joints-around-with-unsanitary-abandon really got to Owen. Had none of these people heard of influenza, mono, or even the common cold?

"What's up, Luna?" Ted said.

Despite Owen's misguided advice, Ted soon learned that Luna was not interested in probing questions or deep conversations. If she wanted to tell you something, she told you. Ted generally kept his inquiries vague, unless they were in bed together. He had all kinds of questions for Luna when they were having sex, mostly guidance-focused. Luna didn't mind those.

"I was just asking Luna about her post-college career plans," Owen said.

"I'm going to be a drug rep," Luna said, as if it was a lifelong ambition. In fact, the more she thought about it, the more it seemed like a reasonable career goal.

"Shut up," said Owen.

"I would totally buy drugs from you," said Ted.

"You always know the right thing to say to a girl," said Luna.

"How about you, Ted? What's your plan?" said Owen.

"MBA, then some finance job. Make a shitload of money and retire early."

"And what will you do when you're retired? Play eighteen holes of golf every day?"

"Ultimate Frisbee," Ted said in all seriousness.

Owen caught Luna's eye and gave her a familiar look: *You're really fucking* this *guy?* Luna returned her gaze to the ceiling, because the ceiling didn't judge her.

"How's Scarlet?" Ted asked Owen, to remind him who his girlfriend was.

"She's good."

"Where is she now?" Ted asked. He had no qualms about giving Owen the third degree.

"I have no idea. We don't keep tabs."

Luna didn't like it when Owen and Ted spoke to each other. Their conversations always sounded like water simmering before the boil.

"I am a firm believer in extraterrestrial life," Luna said.

OWEN LOADED UP his car for the drive to his family's house in the Berkshires and dropped by Luna's room to say goodbye. Luna, still in her pajamas, had a thousand-piece puzzle scattered on top of a flattened cardboard box on her floor. She had just matched a corner piece to its vertical mate.

"I wasn't sure I'd see you this morning," Owen said.

Luna got up from the floor and gave Owen a warm hug. "Have a great holiday. See you in 2004."

Owen saw no evidence that Luna was prepping for a trip. Her room was as tidy as ever and there was no suitcase in sight.

"What time is your flight?" Owen said.

"What flight?"

"Aren't you going to Ontario for the holidays?"

"What gave you that idea? I'm staying here," Luna said.

"In the dorm?"

"Yes."

"Why aren't you going to your mother's?"

"Because I don't want to. And I lost my passport. Besides, I want to stay here and relax."

"What will you do for Christmas?"

"We'll have a group meal in the dining hall for all the squatters. Plus," Luna said, as she displayed the contents of a cardboard box, "my mother sent a care package. I've got all kinds of junk food, presents to open on Christmas. And Casey let me borrow the first three seasons of *Buffy the Vampire Slayer,* Mason gave me five joints, and Ted brought me two bottles of red wine and some bourbon. That reminds me, I need a corkscrew. My point is, I am set to have a most excellent and chill Christmas break. I might even get a small tree to make the room more festive."

While Luna was speaking, Owen sat down on her bed and rummaged through her sad box of Christmas goods. There were candy canes, bags of jelly beans and nonpareils, and a stuffed ferret in a poorly stitched Santa suit. The idea of Luna alone on Christmas morning unwrapping a new pair of socks or underwear filled him with unspeakable sadness.

"No way. No way," Owen said.

As Owen got on the floor to retrieve Luna's suitcase, he worried that she'd grow suspicious. He removed the suitcase that did not have the cigar box.

"What are you doing?" Luna said.

"You're coming with me," Owen said, as he unzipped the suitcase.

"No. I'm staying here," Luna said.

"You pack or I will," said Owen.

Luna briefly wondered how Owen knew where she kept her luggage. Then she had other concerns, as Owen began opening her drawers and randomly tossing clothes into the suitcase. He knew she'd quickly intervene, since she hated anyone touching her things.

"Owen, please stop. I want to stay here."

Owen didn't know whether this was Luna's true preference. The idea of his best friend being alone in a dorm room for more than two weeks was unacceptable.

"I don't care what you want," Owen said.

Owen rifled through Luna's shoulder bag and took ownership of her wallet and keys.

"You have an hour to get your things together," he said. "And then we'll hit the road."

LUNA WAS SURPRISED by how adamant Owen had been, that he cared so much about her, he wouldn't leave her despite her aggressive protests. The truth was she didn't want to be alone. The truth was also that she didn't know how not to be. About an hour into the drive, Luna's seesawing emotions flipped from gratitude to panic.

Owen, behind the wheel of his hand-me-down VW Jetta, had thought they were done with the conversation when Luna started in again.

"I'm not sure this is a good idea," Luna said. "Maybe there's a bus stop or a train station nearby where you can drop me."

"Relax, Luna. You'll love it there. I promise. It's on a lake. It's really beautiful. It's quiet and the food will at least be better than dorm crap."

"Listen, Owen. I've changed my mind. I'm sorry."

Owen pulled the car over at the next rest stop. "Tell me your specific concerns. I'll see if there's a solution."

"I have insomnia," Luna said. "And I don't want to wake anyone, but—"

"You'll take the downstairs guest room. It has its own private bath, a direct exit outside, and it's right near the kitchen if you need to make tea or something in the middle of the night. What else?"

"I don't know," Luna said, shaking her head.

Owen tried to anticipate the rest of her worries. "They won't ask too many questions. They're warm and friendly but a tad self-absorbed. If they inquire about your mother, just say she's on a cruise. They'll never ask a follow-up question. Guaranteed. They'll probably give you a hug—well, my mom will—when you arrive, but they won't otherwise invade your space. They're not the kind of people who get really close to you when they're talking. Nor do they make excessive eye contact. They won't test you on your knowledge of art or old films. If you need to leave the room at any time, just say, *I'm beat.* Yawn if you feel you need to sell it more. Then go to your room. No one will think anything if you need some *me time.*" Owen said the last part with a smirk. "What else? Everyone knocks before they enter a room—Mom had to learn that the hard way. The only warning, maybe, is that sometimes they drink too much and get a little messy. But that won't affect you. Is there anything I haven't thought of?"

Luna remained silent. The answer was no. At least, not at the moment. Luna was of two minds regarding the entire trip. Half of her still wanted out. The other half knew that being alone would be easy, predictable, dull, and, at times, deeply depressing. Owen's plan at least offered the hope of something else.

Owen knew that Luna's silence meant the fight was draining out of her. "Okay?" he said, starting the engine.

"Okay," Luna said.

"That's the spirit," Owen said, mocking her dull tone.

He pulled the car back onto the road. Luna rested her eyes, exhausted already by the day. Owen blasted Coldplay to wake her up. She smacked his stereo with the palm of her hand.

"Did you warn them I'm coming?" Luna asked.

"I called my mother while you were packing," Owen said. "She was delighted to have another woman in the house."

"Did you tell Scarlet?"

"No, I did not. Because Scarlet is not my girlfriend, and therefore I am not required to keep her abreast of my schedule."

During the rest of the drive, Luna gazed out the window and spoke only a few words here or there, generally answering a question or inquiring about their current coordinates. Outside, the trees were bare, and patches of snow, even a few snowbanks, lay muddying on the ground.

78 / LISA LUTZ

. . .

OWEN AND LUNA arrived at their destination just before dusk. The house was massive by Luna's estimate. She wondered how an architect might describe it. She'd say it was like a giant brown box with enormous windows. The lake was right there, behind the house. You could see it through the trees. The last glints of sun reflected off it. They even had their own boat dock, with an old rowboat parked at the ready. She made note of the rowboat as a possible means of escape.

Owen followed Luna's eye line and commented: "The town on the other side of the lake is farther than it looks. If you want to make a run for it, take my car. I'll leave the key by the front door."

"Get the fuck out of my head," Luna said.

Owen laughed. Luna regarded the house yet again.

"So, is this a time-share situation?" Luna asked as Owen parked his Jetta next to a BMW 3 Series, which was parked next to a Range Rover. There was also a Prius, which both comforted and confused her. Was the Prius an apology for the Range Rover?

"No," Owen said. "It's our vacation home. We're here most summers and holidays."

"You said your family was comfortable. Not rich," Luna said.

"They're here!" a woman's voice shouted.

Owen's mother, Vera, ran out of the house in the direction of her son. When they embraced, Owen picked her up and spun her around. She kissed his forehead, then each cheek twice, and took a step back to give him a look-over.

"You need to eat more," she said.

"*You* need to eat more," Owen said.

It was definitely Vera who needed to eat more. Vera's clothes hung loose, but you could still see bones jutting out here and there. For years Owen had assumed it was genetic. It wasn't until his brother made a comment about Vera starving herself for decades that Owen realized she had worked hard for it.

"You must be Luna," Owen's mom said. "I've heard all about you."

Luna politely extended her hand. "Nice to meet you, Mrs. Mann."

"Don't you dare call me Mrs. Mann. I'm Vera."

Vera ignored Luna's hand and gave her a quick kiss on both cheeks.

"We're so thrilled to have you here," Vera said. "Come out back. Your dad is tending to the barbecue."

Vera gripped Luna's suitcase and marched toward the house. She was stronger than she looked, Luna thought. Owen and Luna collected the rest of their luggage from the trunk and followed Vera inside.

The main floor was wide open, with a skylight and wood floors and a vaulted ceiling.

"Say hi to your dad, and then we'll get you settled."

They dropped their luggage in the foyer and crossed through the kitchen and out to the back deck, where Owen's father, bundled up in a hat and overcoat, stood by the grill. The dad, Luna thought, looked like a coarser, more masculine version of his son. He was fit but like a rugby player, with a suspicious tan for December.

"Tom!" Vera said, alerting her husband to Owen and Luna's arrival.

Tom dropped the tongs by the grill and gazed over at Owen. Tom smiled broadly, as if there was no sight in the world that could make him happier than Owen.

Tom pulled Owen into an embrace. He held on longer than Owen, who seemed to pull away. But there were so many details knocking around in Luna's mind that she wasn't sure she perceived everything as it was.

"Dad, this is Luna."

Tom continued smiling. Luna extended her hand yet again. Tom appeared to be debating whether a hug was in order. But he decided that a grown man ought not to invade a young woman's space until they were better acquainted. He gave her a warm double-handshake.

"Glad you could make it," he said.

"Thank you. Thank you for . . ." Luna trailed off, unsure how to phrase it.

"Of course. We're thrilled to finally meet the famous Luna," Vera said.

Luna gave Owen the side-eye, but he refused to give anything back.

"It's freezing out here," Vera said. "Follow me."

Vera led the way as the foursome returned to the living room. Tom noticed the luggage by the front door and gathered three pieces in his arms.

"Vera, where do you want them?" Tom asked.

Luna noted some kind of unspoken exchange between husband and wife. Vera shrugged and Tom nodded in agreement.

"We're not prudes," Vera said. "It seems silly to put you in two separate rooms when you're just going to sneak around at night anyway."

Luna felt confused and a bit embarrassed.

"Do they think I'm Scarlet?" she asked.

"No," Owen said.

"Who is Scarlet?" Tom asked.

"Owen's girlfriend," said Luna.

"Scarlet?" said Vera.

"Let me simplify," Owen said. "Luna and I are just good friends."

"Oh, I'm sorry. I thought . . ." Vera said, trailing off. Then she turned to Luna. "We've just heard so much about you that we assumed—our mistake."

Luna wondered what Owen could have possibly said about her.

"Either way, they can share a room," said Tom, returning his attention to the grill.

"I was going to put Luna in the downstairs guest room," Owen said.

"Oh. Okay. Whatever you think. The bed is made," said Vera.

Owen picked up Luna's suitcase, strolled through the living room past the den, and opened a door tucked away in the far corner of the house. Even Luna had to admit the room was perfect. It had a queen bed that looked incredibly comfortable. Owen dropped Luna's suitcase by the closet and closed the bedroom door. There was a simple deadbolt, which he latched and unlatched for effect.

"Check this out," Owen said. "I know how much you love locks."

After the lock demonstration, Owen opened the bathroom door. Luna hadn't had her own bathroom since she left for college. It even had a bathtub. Owen then strode across the room and opened the French doors to a small private deck.

"And your own exit," Owen said. "In the morning, check out the view."

"Thanks," Luna said.

"Don't thank me," Owen said. "I dragged you here for entirely selfish reasons."

Luna couldn't tell if Owen was serious or in jest. "Oh yeah?"

"I can't be alone with these lunatics," Owen said as he walked out of the room.

Luna unpacked and waited until she heard Owen's voice downstairs. When she emerged from the bedroom, she found Vera standing behind an old tiki-style bar shoved in the corner of the mid-century-modern living room.

"What are you drinking?" Vera asked her guest.

"Water is fine," Luna said.

"Wa-ter," Tom said, sounding out the word as if for the first time. "What is this water you speak of? Do you know, darling?"

"Never heard of it," said Vera.

Luna turned to Owen for an explanation.

"You can have a real drink here," Owen said.

Vera refilled her own glass with vodka and a splash of soda. Luna noticed that both Owen and Tom tracked her movements as if keeping mental score.

"We don't card in the Mann household. Because, really, what's the difference between nineteen and twenty-one?"

"Actually, studies show that the prefrontal cortex doesn't have nearly the same capacity at age eighteen or nineteen as it does at twenty-five," said a young man, about twenty-five, who had just entered the room. He was flushed and sweaty from exertion. He removed his gloves and headlamp.

This was Griff, the brother, Luna thought. He was clearly one of them, although the resemblance to his father wasn't as obvious as Owen's.

"Have you been spelunking?" Owen said.

"Went for a hike. I couldn't wait any longer. You were supposed to be here hours ago," Griff said.

The two men—or boys, or whatever age their prefrontal cortex suggested—gave each other bear hugs, as if it was a competition. The older brother won, thought Luna.

"Ouch," Owen said.

"College has made you soft," Griff said.

He probably thought everyone was soft. He looked like the kind of person who couldn't survive a day without vigorous physical activity. He wasn't built with the symmetrical muscles of a gym rat. But he was solid, tan, his face a bit too drawn for someone still in the glow of youth. One of his other notable features was a rather impressive scar along the side of his left eye, which made the lid droop just a bit.

He turned to Luna and smiled. It was an odd half smile, as if part of his face were fighting it.

"Hey, I'm Griff."

Griff didn't claim any knowledge of Luna or lack thereof. He simply extended his hand.

"Luna," she said, shaking his hand.

"We're drinking," Tom said.

"Of course you are," Griff said.

"What are you having?" Tom said.

"Water first," said Griff, heading into the kitchen and pulling a pitcher from the counter.

"That water again," said Tom.

"Must be a new thing," Vera said. "We should probably look into it."

"Maybe buy stock," Tom added.

"Luna drinks anything," Owen said, just to end his parents' embarrassing bit.

"I like you already," Vera said. "But, please, be more specific. We have wine, beer, bourbon, and I do make a mean martini."

"I'm having red," Owen said to Luna, as he uncorked a bottle.

"Okay. I'm good with that," Luna said.

"Hey, Dad," Griff said. "You got something on the grill?"

"I HOPE YOU like your steak well done," Tom said, once the overdone food was served.

As it turned out, Luna was the only one at the table who genuinely did.

"I told you I'd take care of the grilling," Griff said.

After guzzling two tall glasses of water, Owen's brother had finally cracked a beer.

"I didn't know when you were coming back," Tom said.

"I think it was safe to assume that I'd be back before nightfall, which even with a four P.M. cocktail hour gives us plenty of leeway."

"No point arguing over burnt steak," said Vera. "I got an excellent tart from that bakery in Pittsfield, so none of us will starve tonight."

Owen drained the open bottle of wine into Luna's empty glass without asking whether she wanted more. He retreated to the pantry and returned with two more bottles of red. By the time the meal was over, Luna felt more saturated than satiated.

Vera served their dessert out on the deck. They had heat lamps. One was aimed at the back of Luna's neck. Owen noticed the way she was looking over her shoulder, annoyed. He knew the lamp was pissing her off before she did. Owen demanded they switch sides. Luna preferred her new seat, even though it was cold. She excused herself to retrieve her coat. Owen's mobile phone, which sat charging on the kitchen counter, started to ring. Luna flipped the phone open to see who was calling. Maybe it was important. Or maybe she was too buzzed to make a thoughtful decision. She didn't recognize the number on the screen. She was about to close the phone when Owen appeared beside her.

"What are you doing?" he said, taking the phone from her hands.

"I don't know," Luna said.

Then, a tinny voice saying hello emanated from the phone. Luna and Owen both recognized it and froze in panic. If he hung up, Scarlet would just call back. Owen shook his head at Luna, silently asking her why the hell she'd answered. Luna wasn't sure how to mime her status as a mobile-phone Luddite. Owen reluctantly put the phone to his ear. Luna knew she'd fucked up. And yet she was still surprised by Owen's expression. She hadn't seen that level of anger before. She watched nervously as he handled the call.

"Hi, Scarlet," Owen said. "Sorry about that. Yeah, that was Luna. I'm in the Berkshires. Yes, Luna came with me. . . . It was last minute, that's why I never mentioned it. . . ."

Owen disappeared into the den. Luna returned to the guest room and grabbed her coat. When she returned to the kitchen, Griff was gulping water again. He removed a glass from the cupboard and poured one for her.

"Drink up or you'll regret it tomorrow. Most mortals can't keep up with my folks."

Luna downed the tall glass in a series of thirsty gulps. Griff smiled, impressed.

"Well done."

"Thanks," said Luna.

She could hear snippets of Owen's conversation in the den. He was on the defensive. His tone bounced around among placating, unnerved, sweet, and righteous.

"Who's Owen talking to?" Griff asked.

"His girlfriend," said Luna.

Griff's eyes focused on the ceiling, then back at Luna. "I'm confused. Who are you?" Griff asked.

"Owen and I are just friends. And Scarlet isn't exactly his girlfriend. I shouldn't have said that."

"Why did you?"

"She's his quasi-girlfriend. He's not comfortable with labels, but they're—you know."

"I see," said Griff. "Sounds like Owen is in the doghouse."

"It's my fault," Luna said.

"Care to elaborate?"

"I accidentally answered his phone—I don't have one of those things."

"Where does this Scarlet live?"

"Connecticut."

Griff strolled over to the den and knocked on the half-open door.

"Dude, invite her up here for a few days," Griff said to his brother. He said it loudly enough that the person on the other end of the line would most definitely be able to hear.

Owen shot dagger eyes at Griff, who, in return, smiled with wicked innocence.

Luna, however, was no longer paying them any mind. Outside on the deck, Vera was straddling her husband on the chaise longue, her hands wrapped tightly around Tom's neck.

Vera's face was beet red, tears streaming down her cheeks. "You disgust me," Vera said.

Her rage was so palpable, Luna felt it in her own gut.

"Fuck," Griff said as he opened the sliding glass door and pried his mother off his father.

Luna returned her gaze to Owen to see if he was paying attention. Owen didn't notice a thing. He continued to pace back and forth, talking on his phone.

"Hello. Are you still there? Yes, I'm here. It's fine. . . . It's fine. It would be *great* to see you," Owen said. He said the words Scarlet wanted to hear, but he refused to make them sound sincere.

Outside, Vera was crying, and Tom said, "One day you'll actually kill me, and then you'll be all alone and no one else will have you."

"Shut the fuck up, Dad," Griff said.

Griff shut the sliding glass door, avoiding eye contact with the houseguest.

Luna grabbed a half-open bottle of wine and her glass and retreated to the guest room. She opened the door to the deck and listened. The sounds of the water lapping against the shore mostly drowned out the domestic dispute on the other side of the house. *This is why rich people need so much space,* Luna thought. Although she was aware that space would never have saved her family.

Luna felt uneasy and alone and homesick for her abandoned dorm. She sat on the deck in her coat and hat and drank the wine until it warmed her and she felt like maybe she could fall asleep. She went back into her room, put on her pajamas, and crawled into bed.

Owen checked the call time on his cellphone. Sixty-five minutes. Almost 20 percent of his monthly call plan.

"Look, Scarlet, my battery is about to die, and my mom really wants the family to watch . . . uh, *The Sound of Music* together. I know, I know. I'll text you the address. Yeah, I can't wait. Me too. Bye."

Owen had heard some kind of family scuffle during the call, but it had quickly died down. When he surfaced, the house was quiet and Griff was sitting by the fire with a beer.

"What did I miss?" Owen said.

"Mom strangling Dad."

"Again? Is there a full moon?" Owen said.

"That's your reaction?"

"They had too much to drink. They'll be fine in the morning. They always are," Owen said.

"Until the next evening when they get plastered and one attacks the other like a rabid dog."

"Dude, you need to relax. They're fine," Owen said.

"You might want to have a chat with Luna about how your parents act out *Who's Afraid of Virginia Woolf?* every night."

"She saw?" Owen asked.

Griff nodded. Owen walked down the corridor and knocked on Luna's door. She didn't answer.

"Luna, I know you're awake."

Luna opened the door just a crack. "Hello," she said.

"You okay?"

"Yes."

"Want to talk about it?" Owen asked.

"Do you want to talk about it?"

"Nah."

"How's Scarlet?" Luna asked.

"She's coming here tomorrow."

"That's good," Luna said, trying to summon any enthusiasm. "I'm surprised you invited her."

"I didn't," Owen said.

"Ah. I see," Luna said. "Sorry about that."

"It's not all your fault. I mostly blame Griff."

"Yeah, me too," Luna said.

Owen followed the family script. He yawned and said, "I'm beat."

"Good night, Owen," Luna said.

October 9, 2019

L ate the next morning, Owen finally responded to Amy's texts
and made a plan to meet her for a hike at Poets' Walk in Red
Hook. As Owen opened the door to leave, he found the male
detective standing on his porch.

"Detective?"

"Goldman, in case you forgot," Goldman said. "Good morning."

"Do you know something?" Owen asked. "Do you know who
murdered my wife?"

"No. I'm sorry. Nothing yet. I do need to talk to you, though. I
was hoping you might come back to the station with me."

"Uh, I already talked to your partner."

"We have a few more questions. Do you mind?" Goldman asked.

Owen wasn't sure how to proceed. His phone was buzzing in his
pocket, but he could hardly tell the detective that he was heading
out to see his mistress.

"Also," Detective Goldman said, "I have a warrant for any
phones or computers in your residence."

OWEN'S HEAD THROBBED under the heavy fluorescent lights, and
his mouth still carried the cloying taste of metabolized whiskey. He
was sweating from his hangover, but the sweat made him appear

edgy, and he worried that Goldman would interpret his discomfort as guilt.

He was afraid he was going to vomit, and he worried about how that might look. And then he was angry that he cared. His wife was dead. If she'd died of natural causes, he could behave in any manner whatsoever.

"When can I have her back?" Owen said.

"Pardon?"

"My wife's body. I have to have a funeral. Wait, can you have a funeral without a body?"

"You can, but the body helps," Goldman said, regretting the phrasing. "Did you know what she wanted? Burial or cremation?"

"Definitely not cremation," Owen said.

Then he realized it was Luna who couldn't get past the part where your body is put in a fifteen-hundred-degree oven. Logically, she understood that she would no longer be a sentient being, but the idea just got to her.

"Actually, I don't know," Owen said. "Maybe it's in her will somewhere. When can I—when will she . . ."

"The coroner isn't done with the autopsy. Give it a few days. By the weekend maybe."

Owen nodded, already overwhelmed by the prospect of making arrangements. This was the sort of thing Irene would have done. The longer they were married, the less capable he became with administrative tasks.

"If you don't mind, I need to go over your timeline once again," said Goldman.

"It's the same as what I told your partner. And it was recorded, right?" Owen said.

Owen didn't want to tell the cops two different stories, but he wasn't sure that his current memory would jibe with his first interview.

"Yes," Goldman said. "But we have a confirmed time of death now, so I need to go over it again."

"Oh," Owen said. "When did she die?"

"Monday morning. She stopped by Luna's before she went for a run."

"Right," Owen said.

"Luna was the last person to see her alive and the first person to see her dead," Goldman said.

"Aside from the killer," Owen said.

Goldman was hoping to get a reaction out of Owen, but he couldn't read the guy. All Owen could think about was the drinks he and Luna had shared while his wife's body was growing cold.

"Something come to mind?" the detective asked.

"Nothing important. I was thinking that the whole time I was texting her, she was already dead."

Owen heard a familiar buzz and tapped his pocket, thinking it was his phone. Then he remembered that he'd given it to someone in a uniform. Goldman checked his own mobile device and thumbed a quick text. Owen was late to meet Amy. She'd be texting the phone that was in police custody. She'd be angry. *Fuck,* he thought.

"I told your partner I was seeing someone," Owen said.

"Yes," Noah said.

"Um . . . I was going to meet her this morning . . . now. And I didn't text her that I wasn't coming so, um, she's going to be calling my phone, which you guys have. She's waiting for me, and she doesn't like to be ignored."

"Does anyone?" Goldman said.

"Guess not," Owen said.

"I'll ask my partner to get in touch."

AN HOUR LATER, Owen and Goldman had reviewed Owen's whereabouts for the forty-eight hours bookending Irene's murder, and Owen couldn't ignore the fact that he was clearly a suspect. Perhaps their only suspect. He could have stopped the interview anytime. He could have, and probably should have, asked for a lawyer, but he felt an oppressive inertia that inhibited any sensible proactive decisions.

"Okay," said the detective. "So then you went to your studio at St. Michael's College. You taught a class, answered emails, painted, did whatever. Then, at five P.M., you met Ms. Grey at the Halfway House and you stayed for a few hours. You were home by eight P.M. In bed by eleven, and your wife was not home. You assumed she was at a motel freezing you out, since she hadn't replied to any of your calls or texts. You slept through the night, and Ms. Grey came by your place Tuesday morning at approximately eight-thirty with the tragic news."

Owen felt the heavy-saliva warning a brief few seconds before he doubled over and emptied his guts into the trash bin. Goldman had experienced a sympathetic vomiting reflex once decades ago, and that was enough. He got the hell out of the room. A few minutes later, after Owen's stomach had quit turning inside out, Goldman returned with a can of Coke in hand.

Owen put the trash bin by the door and sat back down. "Sorry," he said.

"No problem. Sure you want to go on?" said Goldman, sliding the soda across the table.

"Yeah. Thanks," said Owen, cracking the lid.

The purging, followed by the sweet carbonation, made Owen feel almost human again. Goldman put the trash can in the hallway.

"When was the last time you and your wife had sex?"

Owen, briefly, considered the question. Then he became distracted by the idea of his vomit sitting in a police-station hallway.

"A week? No. I don't—maybe two, I think," Owen said.

"Two weeks? Are you sure it wasn't more recent?"

"No. It was definitely more than a week. Why are you asking?" Owen said.

Owen was getting annoyed. The question felt invasive, like it had been asked just to fuck with him.

"Standard question," Goldman said.

· · ·

WHEN GOLDMAN WAS finished with Mann, he found his partner at her desk, cross-checking calls from the past three months on Irene's cellphone.

"Got anything?" Goldman asked.

"Ms. Boucher was overpaying for her phone plan, that's for sure. There are about four numbers in regular circulation. But compared to your average middle-aged woman—no, compared to any phone I've ever looked at—the call history is remarkably light. There is something, though," Margot said, drawing a page from the stack of phone bills and pointing to a highlighted number.

"Irene called this 215 number thirty times in the last three months. It's to a prepaid phone. And she's had more communication with that number than her husband's. And no texts. Weird, right?"

"I take it you tried the number?" Goldman said.

"Straight to an automated voicemail," Burns said.

Goldman examined the call list before and after Irene's murder. The number in question phoned Irene twelve hours after she passed. But there was no call in the twenty-four hours preceding her death.

Reading his mind, Burns said, "There's no unusual call pattern with the mystery number around the murder. You get anything new from Mann?"

"Yes," said Goldman. "Didn't the ME tell you he found seminal fluid?"

Margot nodded. "He did."

"Wasn't the husband's," Goldman said.

December 2003

———

The next morning, Luna smelled coffee brewing and heard what sounded like idle chatter in the kitchen, but she wasn't sure who was making the chatter. She opened the French doors and stepped outside, feeling a blast of cold air off the shimmering lake. The rusty rowboat was tied to the dock. She would have done just about anything for a cup of coffee—other than venture into the kitchen to be caught alone with Vera and Tom.

Luna heard leaves rustling in the woods and spotted Griff running back to the house. He waved and slowed down, approaching. She thought about running back inside to spare them the discomfort of talking about last night. But that would look weird. She made a split-second decision to pretend nothing had happened.

"Hey," Griff said, catching his breath.

"Hey," Luna said. That single syllable sounded less casual than she'd planned.

"You okay?" Griff said.

"Yeah. You okay?" she said.

Griff stood in front of her and tilted his head to the side, like a confused child. "So, that's how you want to play it?"

"I don't know," Luna said. "What would you prefer?"

"I don't like pretending," he said. "It's a version of lying."

"Right," said Luna.

"Do you have any questions?" Griff said.

"Does that kind of thing happen often?" said Luna.

"It does."

"Owen never mentioned it before."

"He grew up with it. Thinks it's part of a normal or passionate relationship. Or something like that."

"Huh. You don't think that."

"No, but I didn't have an older brother around to distract me. What are you doing outside? It's cold."

"I didn't know where to go," Luna said.

"You were afraid to go into the kitchen alone?"

Luna nodded.

"It's safe now. I'll meet you in there."

BY THE TIME Luna entered the kitchen, the whole family had gathered. Vera was making waffles while Tom whipped up a batch of scrambled eggs. Owen sat at the table, sipping a latte and reading the paper. Griff, finding only dregs in the coffee maker, admonished his brother and then cleaned out the carafe to start a fresh pot.

"I hope you like waffles," Vera said.

"Or eggs," said Tom.

"I like both," said Luna.

"Did you sleep all right?" Vera asked.

"Yes," Luna lied. "Very well, thank you."

"You slept late," Owen said.

"The room was comfortable and quiet," Luna said, without mentioning the hour she'd spent hiding out, fully awake.

"What are we doing today?" Vera asked Owen and Luna.

"I don't know," Owen said.

"Scarlet's coming today, right?" Vera asked.

"What's Scarlet's ETA?" Tom said. "Scarlet. That's a helluva name."

Owen smiled broadly at Luna, just to hide his annoyance. *Whatever happens is your fault,* his expression suggested.

"She said she was going to hit the road around one, so I figure three o'clock or so," said Owen.

"Luna, give me the 911 on Scarlet," Vera said.

"The 411," said Tom. "You use 911 for an emergency; 411 is for information."

"I think she knew what I meant," said Vera, with a whisper of the prior night's dark cloud.

"She's great," Luna said. "You'll like her. She's beautiful and nice and smart."

"Can't wait," Griff said.

"Maybe we should invite Ted up too. He's in Jersey, isn't he?" Owen said. "That's not too far."

"While we're at it, let's invite Mason and the ABCs," Luna added, calling his bluff.

"Mason and the ABCs. That sounds like a band, doesn't it?" said Tom.

"Mason is Luna's pot dealer," Owen said, ratting her out as payback for answering his damn phone.

"Well, then, let's *definitely* invite Mason," Griff said.

"What are the ABCs?" Vera asked.

"Mom, I think the waffles are burning," Griff said.

Breakfast was served. Luna watched as the Mann family chatted aimlessly, ate with gusto, and made her believe, once again, that they were whole.

While food was being consumed, Griff revived the lost topic: "So who or what are the ABCs?"

"Just some lame girls," said Owen.

"You don't like Amber just because she has a crush on you and doesn't hide it. And you don't even know Casey. Sometimes you're mean and way too judgmental," Luna said. She immediately regretted it, remembering her audience. "Sorry," Luna mumbled. Then she was angry that she apologized.

Griff broke the brief but tense silence. "You're right," said Griff. "Sometimes Owen is mean and judgmental."

"I'm going to have to agree with you there," Tom said pleasantly.

"Mom, do you have anything to add?" Owen asked.

"Poor Amber," said Vera.

"What about B?" Griff said to Luna.

Luna shrugged. "Bobbi *is* kind of a bitch."

WHEN SCARLET ARRIVED that afternoon, she walked right past Owen and hugged Luna first. The move felt false and calculated, and it got under his skin. Scarlet then turned to Owen, kissed him on each cheek, and said something like *So lovely to see you.* She'd never greeted him like that before, and he wondered how much performance he was going to have to contend with. He also wondered how long she was planning on staying.

Owen introduced Scarlet to the rest of his family. His dad tried to give him a high five when Scarlet's back was turned, but Owen left him hanging. Vera nodded her approval of the striking young woman. Griff, on the other hand, seemed not to notice or care that Scarlet was hot.

Vera and Tom claimed to have some shopping left to do in town. Vera set out a spread of salty and sweet snacks and a pitcher of sangria.

"Call me on my cellphone if you need anything," Vera said.

As soon as she left, Owen poured four glasses of sangria.

Scarlet picked up her glass. "To good friends."

"To oblivion," Owen said.

"To my liver," Luna said.

Griff laughed and said, "To Luna's liver."

Scarlet chugged her sangria and locked eyes with Luna. "Let's go outside for a minute," she said.

Owen and Griff watched the two women step out onto the deck and close the door behind them. Words were being exchanged, but nothing that could be discerned through the glass.

"What's going on here?" Griff said.

"I don't know," Owen said. "But she shouldn't be here with Luna."

"Why not? Your best friend and your girlfriend should get along, especially if they're both girls," said Griff.

Owen forced himself to turn away from the glass door. He took his drink over to the fireplace, fed the fire, and stoked the kindling.

"I just don't trust it," said Owen.

"Trust what?"

"Forget it."

"Do you even like Scarlet?" said Griff. "If you have a girlfriend, you're supposed to like her, not just think she's hot."

"She's not my girlfriend. I have made that clear on numerous occasions. And I do like her. Sometimes. Then, other times, she seems desperate and a little pathetic."

"Having feelings doesn't make someone pathetic," Griff said.

"No, that's not what I'm saying," said Owen. "I don't have a clue who Scarlet is."

"Maybe you should try to get to know her, since you're sleeping together."

"Let me clarify," Owen said, keeping the volume down. "I think that Luna coaches Scarlet about how to be around me. She's telling her what to do and what not to do, so that I like her more."

Griff laughed uproariously. "Are you suggesting that Luna is Scarlet's Cyrano?"

"It sounds crazy when you phrase it like that, but kinda."

Griff turned and watched the women outside. They sat right next to each other, backs to the men, on the steps of the deck. Luna's face was turned in profile and she was speaking. Scarlet was nodding slowly, like someone gathering and processing information. The scene certainly fit with Owen's claims.

When Luna and Scarlet reentered the house, Owen tried to catch Luna's eye, to silently gather some intelligence. Luna refused to meet his gaze.

"Everything cool?" Owen said, overtly fishing.

"Yes," said Scarlet. "Everything is cool."

"What were you talking about?" Owen asked.

"Girl stuff," said Scarlet.

"Why don't you give Scarlet a tour of the house," Luna said to Owen.

"I'd like that," Scarlet said.

Scarlet wanted to seem grateful, but sometimes she thought Luna was helping her just to look better in Owen's eyes. The night of the party, when Scarlet and Owen first hooked up, Scarlet thought she had Owen. *Really* had him. Every day since, she was convinced that Luna was stealing more and more of him away from her.

"This way," Owen said, walking up the stairs.

The tour was quite brief. One flight of stairs and straight into Owen's bedroom.

When Owen shut his door, Griff turned to Luna and said, "Interesting. I always start in the kitchen."

WHILE OWEN AND Scarlet were presumably having sex, Griff suggested that he and Luna take a walk. To be clear, it was a hike, not a walk, which Luna figured out within half a mile. Her legs were burning and her lungs had taken a beating. It wasn't that Luna was particularly out of shape. Griff's pace was relentless.

"Can you slow the fuck down?" Luna finally said.

"Sorry," Griff said, slowing down and then stopping for a water break. "I'm not used to company."

"Ever?"

"On hikes."

Griff offered Luna his water bottle.

"Thanks," Luna said.

She sat on a fallen tree trunk and caught her breath. When she finally had a moment to look around, she almost smiled. The cold woods were stark and stunning. The trail never lost view of the lake, with the bright and blinding water. Luna's nose was running from the temperature and exertion. She wiped it with her sleeve.

Griff took a seat next to her and riffled through his pockets. He handed her a tissue.

"Be civilized," he said, teasing.

"What a gentleman," Luna said. She blew her nose, balled up the used tissue, and shoved it back in Griff's pocket.

"That's disgusting," Griff said, laughing.

"Thank you," Luna said.

"So, you and Owen . . . ?" Griff said, trailing off.

Luna knew what he was getting at. "Never," she said. "What was he like as a kid?"

"Popular and . . . maybe a little lonely. So, the same, I guess."

An unusual combination, but it made sense to Luna. She had noticed that Owen was slow to warm to people. Not with her, but that could have been more about the circumstances of their first real encounter.

"Were you guys close growing up?"

"I'm five years older. That's a big gap when you're kids."

"Yeah," Luna said.

She braced herself for a reciprocal question, composing in her head an answer that would preclude any follow-up questions. All that wasted anxiety for naught. Griff remained silent, watched the sun duck behind a mob of nimbus clouds. Luna could feel the temperature dip.

"We should go. It's getting cold," Griff said.

They still had a mile to cover before they reached the house. By the time Griff and Luna reached the back deck, the tips of Luna's fingers were numb.

Vera, Tom, Owen, and Scarlet were sitting in the living room with drinks in hand. Griff waved at the cozy foursome as he and Luna kicked off their muddy shoes. Owen marched over to the sliding door and opened it.

"Oh, good," Tom said lightly. "We were just debating whether to call search and rescue."

"Lost track of time," Griff said.

Owen ignored his brother, while he and Luna shared a silent conversation. Her eyes clocked Scarlet watching them. Luna lifted a single brow, asking how things were going. Owen responded with a mild expression of panic. She nodded slightly, understanding yet unsympathetic. Griff watched, fascinated.

Luna took a hot shower to warm up. She found a giant terrycloth robe in the bathroom—like in fancy hotels, Luna noted. She wrapped her head in a towel and thought about climbing into bed for a nap. It was exhausting being around strangers all the time.

Owen used his secret knock.

"What?" Luna said.

"You decent?"

"Yes."

Owen entered the room. "Help me," he said.

"You need to help yourself," Luna said.

She had no idea what he was talking about, but her statement was valid nonetheless.

"I can't have her here the whole weekend," Owen said.

"You should have thought about that before you—you know."

"We didn't," Owen said.

"Really?" Luna said.

"Yes."

"I'm proud of you."

"We made out a little, but I was mostly trying to talk to her, to tell her we weren't a thing."

"How'd that go?"

"Not well," Owen said. "I need to know exactly what to say to end the relationship without any drama. She can be kind of crazy."

The previous night's strangling episode shed new light on Owen's fear of conflict. Then Luna wondered if Owen's attraction to Scarlet was partially oedipal. She decided it was better not to ask.

"Tell me what to do," Owen said. "What do I say to her?"

"I wouldn't say anything. Not right now."

"What are you not saying?" Scarlet said from the frame of the half-open door.

"Scarlet, what's up?" Owen said.

"Your mom wanted to know what Luna wanted to drink," Scarlet said, smiling with dead eyes.

"Something hot," said Luna.

"What were you guys talking about?" Scarlet said.

Owen conjured up a lightning-fast lie. "Luna found out that Mason and Bobbi hooked up."

"What? No way," said Scarlet.

"Yeah, no way," said Luna, deadpan.

"No one can know," Owen said.

"Can you two get out of here while I get dressed?" Luna said.

WHEN LUNA RETURNED to the living room, Vera abdicated her seat by the fire and handed Luna a brandy with hot water and honey. Tom and Vera continued to ply their guests with alcohol. Then dinner was served, followed by dessert. And then more drinks.

Griff saw the headlights of a car on their private drive. "You expecting company, Mom?" he said.

"Shit," said Tom, spilling some of his drink on his shirt.

"Is that Barb and Bill?" said Griff.

Owen rushed to the pantry and filled his arms with snack food.

"Save yourselves," said Vera as she ushered Owen and Scarlet down the basement steps.

Griff took Luna's arm and said, "We better go too."

"Who are Barb and Bill?" said Scarlet.

"Neighbors," said Owen.

"Are they dangerous?" Luna asked.

"No. But they could literally bore you to death. And there is no way to escape them," said Griff.

"TRUTH OR DARE?" Griff asked with the enthusiasm of a bank teller.

"Dare," said Luna.

"You *never* play truth," Scarlet said.

The quartet had been in the basement for an hour. Luna had expected to find one of those finished rooms with a pool table, a flat-screen TV, comfortable threadbare furniture, and maybe a well-stocked bar. But it was a musty storage area, loaded with crumbling boxes and cast-off furniture and a noisy water heater. The defectors were growing restless. Luna heard laughter from the floor above and wondered if the neighbors were really that bad. Or perhaps the Mann parents had fortified themselves enough to endure any kind of company.

The basement did, however, hold a stash of wine, of which the four had already availed themselves. Owen was uncorking the second bottle when Scarlet's genius idea struck.

"Let's play Truth or Dare," she said.

Her suggestion was met with silence. Griff began to wander the room, searching through boxes.

"I think we might have Risk or Monopoly," Griff said.

"Noooo," said Scarlet like a whiny child. "That's boring. Let's have some fun. You in, Luna?"

"Sure," Luna said, despite the warning she felt deep in her gut.

"See, Luna wants to play. Owen and Griff? Don't be buzzkills."

The brothers made eye contact and shrugged. *What's the harm?*

Scarlet had an unusual system of play. All four members of the quartet would draw cards. The low card was the victim and the high card the commander. They'd played five rounds without anyone exposing his soul or performing a life-threatening stunt. One more round couldn't hurt, could it? They drew cards, yet again. Griff got the high and Luna the low cards.

It was Griff's turn to deliver the challenge. "I dare you to go upstairs, introduce yourself to Barb and Bill as . . . Barb Billings, and ask for the time," Griff said.

Luna left for her mission without a word.

What Griff hadn't calculated into his amusing dare was how long Luna would be entangled upstairs with the garrulous neighbors. As they waited for her return, Scarlet grew bored again. She tried to hold Owen's hand, but he disengaged under the pretense of getting another drink.

Griff wanted the night to end. He didn't enjoy seeing his brother like this, and he felt sorry for the almost-girlfriend. Also, he got the feeling that Luna was wary and that Scarlet, despite her smiles and feigned warmth, had fangs with Luna's name on them.

Luna returned from her mission and collapsed in exhaustion on one of the beanbags. "It sounds like a simple question," Luna said, "but in the hands of Barb and Bill . . ."

"I apologize," said Griff. "Shall we call it a night?"

"It's only nine-thirty," Scarlet said.

"If we go upstairs, we'll have to engage," said Owen.

Scarlet shuffled the deck and placed the cards in the middle of the floor. They chose their cards and flipped them over.

"King," Scarlet said with a smile.

Griff saw Luna's face drop when she glanced at her card. He swapped cards with her. Luna smiled at him with gratitude. She placed an eight of diamonds faceup. Griff showed a two of hearts. Owen had a jack of spades.

Scarlet could sense an electric charge between Luna and Griff, which pleased her until she saw Owen watching them. Scarlet thought Owen looked jealous. It was like a gut punch. Scarlet, drunk and insecure, could no longer camouflage her hostility.

"Nice try," Scarlet said to Luna. "But no card swapping."

"I think we should call it," Owen said.

"When I get the high card? No way."

"Last round," Griff said.

"Truth or dare," Scarlet said to Luna.

Luna didn't want to go on another upstairs mission or take any other whimsical directions from Scarlet. "Truth," she said reluctantly.

"Truth," Owen said, leaning forward and steepling his fingers like a villain. "Luna Grey is going to tell the truth."

"*My* question," Scarlet said.

Owen's amusement quickly shifted to concern when he noted Scarlet's greedy expression. Scarlet made a show of pondering her question. In truth, she didn't have to think too hard.

"Go for it," Luna said, sheepish and impatient.

"Who is sending you hate mail and why?" Scarlet asked.

The silence that followed wasn't a simple lull in conversation. It was like a void, as if all the oxygen had been sucked out of the room.

Luna felt ice-cold and turned white as a sheet. Owen's face morphed into a mask of pure hate. Scarlet caught a glimpse of his expression and turned away. She bit hard on the inside of her lip to mask the pain she felt inside. Griff prepared for the tidal wave that was about to break.

"You fucking bitch," Owen said.

A tear slid down Scarlet's cheek. She stumbled to her feet and raced up the stairs.

Luna kept her eyes on the rug. She knew that Owen was the only person she had ever left alone in her room. Digging deep enough to find the letters was enough of a violation. But he'd told Scarlet. That was a betrayal.

"Go after her," Griff said to Owen.

"Luna, look at me," Owen said.

Luna looked up. "Go after her," Luna said. "I'm fine."

Owen left. Luna sat as still as possible and willed herself not to cry. Griff took her wineglass, washed it out in the bathroom sink, and refilled it with water.

"Hydrate," he said.

Luna gulped down the water. Griff refilled the glass.

"You probably want an explanation," Luna said.

"No, I don't," said Griff.

"Why not?"

"Because I know who you are."

October 9, 2019

L una had already texted Owen a few times Wednesday morning. She hadn't thought to check the tracking app, assuming he was still asleep. After a few hours, she grew worried and walked over to his house. His truck sat in the driveway. Luna rang the bell and put her ear to the door. Nothing. An engine purred behind her. Luna turned and saw a red Mini Cooper taking a slow roll down the street. The car paused for a moment in front of Owen's place and proceeded to the end of the block. A brown-haired woman sat behind the wheel.

As Luna walked back home, she phoned Owen's number again. This time, a female voice answered.

"Luna," said the woman.

"Did I call the wrong number?" Luna said, checking the screen.

"This is Detective Burns. I apologize for the confusion. We're processing Owen's phone. I saw you were calling."

"Where is Owen?"

"We have him here," Burns said.

"Are you arresting him?"

"For what?"

Luna felt like she needed a lawyer for the impromptu conversation. Then she realized that so did Owen.

"Would you mind coming down to the station?" Burns asked. "I have just a few more questions. I promise it will take no more than ten minutes."

. . .

Leo Whitman had been expecting a call from the police. When they did phone, he was as accommodating as he could be. As far as Leo was concerned, no one knew Irene as well as he did.

Whitman sat in an uncomfortable metal chair under hideous fluorescent lights, sipping from a cappuccino he'd grabbed on the way to the station. A tall, handsome woman in a gray suit entered the room. Leo loathed pantsuits, but this detective almost pulled it off. She sat across from him with her own mug of coffee.

"Thank you for coming in, Mr. Whitman."

"Of course. Anything for Irene."

"How did you know the deceased?"

"I was married to Irene's mother. Chantal Boucher passed in 2011."

"So, you were Irene's stepfather?"

"Technically, I suppose. I hardly took on any paternal responsibilities. Irene was a grown-up when Chantal and I wed."

Margot opened her notebook and wrote Leo's name at the top. He was wearing a remarkably cloying cologne. She was curious if his sense of smell was impaired.

"Do you have allergies?" Margot asked.

"Excuse me?" Whitman said.

His neck straightened like a turtle's, and his eyes registered confusion and offense.

"Not important. What was your relationship like with Irene, if not like a daughter?"

"Let's say more like a little sister."

"Interesting," Margot said. "How did you and Chantal meet?"

"She was a collector."

"An art collector?" said Margot.

"It's unlikely I would become intimately acquainted with a doll collector or vintage-car enthusiast," Leo said.

As the detective jotted down a few notes, Leo noticed her bare ring finger. *Divorced or lesbian?* he wondered, unable to conceive that she might have simply remained single.

"How would you describe Owen and Irene's relationship?"

"Average," he said.

"Could you elaborate?"

"They were hardly star-crossed lovers. I suspect they made decent-enough roommates and they had a few things in common."

"Like what?"

"Lack of ambition. And a somewhat modest way of life."

Leo's cologne was getting to her. It felt like it was burrowing down the back of her throat.

"What did you think of Owen?" Margot asked.

"I thought he was a nice-enough fellow."

"Did you approve of their marriage?"

"It wasn't my place to approve. I wasn't her father."

"How well did you know Luna?" Burns asked.

"Where there's Owen, there's Luna," Leo said.

"What does that mean?"

"They're *very* close."

"How close?"

"Oh, I don't think they were ever an item. If you're asking whether Owen had affairs with other women, well, that's another story."

He had to work to get that into the conversation, Margot thought. It wasn't a natural transition.

"Did Owen have someone on the side?" Margot asked.

"You're the detective," Leo said.

Margot couldn't decide whether Leo was trying to help the investigation or throw Owen under the bus. "What was Irene's relationship with Luna like?"

"They were friendly, I suppose. Irene was a generous woman."

Detective Burns sharpened her gaze. "What did Irene's generosity have to do with their friendship?"

"I merely meant that Irene didn't hold a grudge," Leo said.

"A grudge? About what?"

"Her wedding. I think it's safe to say that Luna ruined that day."

AN HOUR LATER, Luna was sitting in the same interview room. The smell of Leo's cologne lingered.

"Thanks for coming in," Margot said. "My partner told me you were in between jobs, so I'm assuming it's not a great inconvenience."

"No," said Luna. "It's not."

"How long have you been unemployed?"

"About a year."

"What did you do?"

"I was a drug rep at Nyteq," Luna said.

"Really? A drug rep is sales, right?"

"Yes," Luna said.

"You don't seem like a salesperson."

"That was the conclusion we all came to."

"What made you work for Nyteq?"

"I needed a job. A friend was working there and put in a good word. It paid well and the hours were flexible."

"Why did you leave?"

"The company was downsizing. I took the buyout because I could afford to. They were going to fire someone."

"And you don't have to work. Your husband makes a good living?"

"I want to work," Luna said. "There are limited opportunities in the Hudson Valley."

"You and Owen have lived in the same general area since college, right?"

"Not exactly. Owen lived in Manhattan for a few years. But it was too expensive, and he was offered a teaching job at St. Michael's."

"Doesn't Markham have a better art department?" Burns asked.

"Markham wasn't hiring," Luna said.

"Do you think he came back to the area because you were here?"

"I think it helped that he had a friend nearby."

"Would you say that Owen is satisfied with his career?" Burns asked.

Luna shrugged. She'd met few men who were satisfied. Few women as well. Was she satisfied? She wouldn't know how to answer that question. "I think he imagined a different life. But he accepted the life he had."

"You guys seem really close. Am I wrong?"

"We are close," Luna said. "But we're not cover-up-a-murder close."

"Understood," Margot said, reviewing her notes.

"Do you have any suspects?" Luna asked.

"Not exactly."

"That was not a definitive *no*."

"How close were you and Irene?" Burns asked.

"We were friends. I don't know how to quantify our closeness."

"Were you and Irene as close as you and Owen?"

"No," Luna said. "But I did love her."

An old memory came to Luna. Irene looking down on her, in her wedding dress. A smile where a frown should have been.

Luna, caught in the memory, refused to blink, hoping the tears wouldn't spill out. She'd always hated crying in front of people. There was that ancient courtroom illustration, her face scrunched up like an ugly doll. The artist had been deliberately vicious.

Burns saw genuine grief. But grief and guilt can commingle.

"Would Irene have told you if something unusual had been going on in her life?" the detective asked.

"Unusual how?"

"Like if she was seeing someone?"

"Having an affair?" Luna asked, mind whirling.

"Something like that," said Burns. "Or maybe she was just thinking about it. Or talking to someone an awful lot."

"Was she?" Luna said.

"I don't know. I'm asking you."

Luna knew the detective was lying. There *was* someone. Luna couldn't imagine who that could be.

"If she was, she didn't tell me about it," Luna said.

"Would she have? Did she confide in you about other things?"

"Yes. But I was Owen's friend first. If she was cheating on him, I guess she wouldn't have told me."

"Did you know about Owen's affair?"

"Yes," Luna said.

"Who told you about it? Irene or Owen?"

"Irene told me," Luna said.

"She confided in you," Burns said. "And what did you do?"

Luna could see the trap coming but couldn't escape it. "I told Owen."

Burns jotted something in her notes. "No question where your true loyalty lies, is there?" Burns said.

"I'm not sure that's fair," Luna said.

"Okay. Cards on the table," said Burns. "You don't doubt Owen, not at all? There's no chance in hell that he killed his wife?"

"No chance in hell," Luna said, her voice solid as steel. "No one wanted Irene dead."

"Someone did," said Burns.

Irene, March 2005

Chantal Boucher had phoned Irene that morning with the "wonderful" news. She was engaged. Again. It would be her third wedding. Irene, knowing that her mother was incapable of remaining single, had hoped Chantal might meet a banker or a doctor or anyone with a fat wallet and unimpeachable motives. Alas, the fat-wallet guys seemed partial to the young, skinny-legged girls.

"Leo and I are flying to London on Saturday. Call the service in for another cleaning."

"Leo? That's his name?"

"Leo Whitman. He's a painter. I've heard him described as a post-post-Impressionist."

When Irene didn't respond, Chantal added, "He had a series of nudes at the Tate Modern a few years ago."

"I've heard of him," Irene said. She was thinking about how a friend from college once described Whitman's nudes: like Renoir using a 1970s *Playboy* centerfold as a subject.

After an extended bout of silence, Chantal said, "I know. Another artist. I clearly have a type."

"How long have you been seeing each other?" Irene asked.

"Long enough," Chantal said. "Call the service for Friday morning and don't make any plans this weekend."

. . .

IRENE TRIED TO clear her head with a long walk. Occasionally she'd take photos on the sly. She always kept a camera in her bag, a vintage Olympus Trip 35 with red skin. It had been her father's. She worried sometimes that she looked like a tourist. But her manner was more amateur spy. Once she'd snapped a picture of an unsuspecting pedestrian, she'd stash the camera in her bag and briskly walk away. That day, someone behind her shouted "Hey." The tone was angry. She assumed it was her last photo victim. It was not. She jogged around the corner and slipped into her local pub, the Three Legs.

Irene sat down at the bar and looked over her shoulder. She was safe. Tessa, the bartender, served her a G&T.

"And how are we today?" Tessa asked.

Irene appeared to be considering the question. After a moment, she said, with a Scottish accent, "It's a sair ficht for half a loaf."

"No. No," Tessa said with her own real Irish accent. "No Scots today. There's a couple pissed Glaswegians at the end of the bar."

Irene spotted two twentysomething men slipping off their barstools, telling each other to feck off. Tessa's suggestions were more for her own sanity than Irene's safety.

"What shall it be, then?" Irene said with a Received Pronunciation, but more old-time aristocracy than BBC News.

"Can't ya be yourself today?"

Irene could not, would not, be herself. Especially not on that day.

"Can't," Irene said, sticking with the posh accent. "But I'll take requests."

"Yorkshire, then," Tessa said.

Irene appeared to be visualizing the act of putting on a coat. Then she spoke. "Phoebe from Sheffield. Ey up," Irene said.

Tessa nodded. "Don't know why you can't use your own name."

"Where's the fun in that?"

Irene left after one drink. She could have easily gotten blotto, but she was afraid of what she'd do after that. She'd been staying in the London apartment for almost nine months, ever since she graduated from Vassar. Sometimes she was lonely, although she was rarely alone. Word had gotten out back home, and soon every acquaintance she'd ever had was inviting themselves for a visit. Eventually, Irene shuttered the doors of the Boucher Boardinghouse and claimed to be backpacking across Europe. She screened all her calls.

Irene passed a hair salon on her walk. It wasn't one of the swanky ones her mother frequented, where you were greeted with a flute of champagne. A woman leaned against the brick wall, apron on, hair like a rainbow, smoking a cigarette. Irene turned back and regarded the smoker.

"I like your hair," Irene said, using her regular voice.

"Thanks. You American?"

"Canadian," Irene said. Then: "I'd like to make an appointment."

"What are you doing now?"

The next thing Irene knew, she was wrapped in a smock and Fiona was painting her brown hair with bleach. Irene's scalp felt like it was on fire.

"The price we pay for beauty," Fiona said. "Fucked-up world we live in."

It was hours later when Fiona finished. She wrapped the towel around Irene's head and returned her to the chair. As she combed out the platinum-blond hair, Irene caught her reflection in the mirror.

"Fuck," Irene said, floored.

"Jesus, you look gorgeous," Fiona said.

When women went blond, *that* was the transformation they were going for but rarely achieved. For some women, the color didn't do a whole lot. For others, like Marilyn Monroe and Carole Lombard and the customer sitting in Fiona's chair, it was a game changer. A stunning transformation. If Irene had walked out of the salon, she would have turned heads.

But Irene was clearly not pleased. As she stared at her reflection, her eyes began to water.

Fiona could feel pain coming off the woman like heat.

"You're gorgeous," she said. "Why are you upset?"

"I look like . . . old pictures of my mother."

Fiona thought maybe the mother was dead. "Can't have that, can we?" Fiona said.

An hour later, Irene's hair was cobalt blue. When Irene saw her reflection, she resembled neither her mother nor herself. Relieved, she smiled at Fiona.

"Thank you. I love it."

At the age of twenty-two, Irene imagined a lifetime ahead of her. She would have done so many things differently if she knew she had only fourteen years left.

December 2003–March 2004

"Who am I?" Luna asked.

When Griff said that he knew who she was, Luna allowed for the possibility that he was speaking of her character in general. Luna wasn't foolish enough to drop her cover until she knew for sure it was blown.

"We studied your case in law school," Griff said.

Cover blown, Luna felt like she was sinking into the floor. "Is that really a thing?" Luna asked. "Do all law schools have me on their curriculum?"

Griff, hearing the panic in her voice, said, "No, no. It was just a small segment in a legal ethics class."

"Did you tell Owen?"

"I didn't tell anyone," Griff said. "And you don't have to worry about Owen asking now. He feels too guilty."

"You think I should tell him, don't you?"

"That's up to you," Griff said.

Hours after the disastrous game of Truth or Dare, the house was quiet. The neighbors had finally departed; Vera and Tom were in a deep alcohol-induced slumber; Griff tossed and turned; and Owen and Scarlet were in his bedroom, unambiguously awake. Owen had apologized for his harsh words, but the contrition felt hollow, because so were his feelings. Owen couldn't remember a moment when Scarlet wasn't crying. The tears felt deliberate, unnecessarily punitive, like nails on a chalkboard. Owen was certain that Scarlet would quit if she lost her audience. He went downstairs, gulped water, took a glass to Luna's room.

Owen knocked and said, "I know you're awake." Luna opened the door and crawled back into bed. He delivered the tumbler of water and climbed into bed next to her. Owen closed his eyes and gulped oxygen. He rubbed his temples. He allowed his body, tensed for hours, to uncoil.

"Do you hate me?" Owen asked.

"I don't hate you," Luna said. "I'm disappointed."

Owen was startled Luna would use the parental-shaming word.

"That hurts," Owen said, wincing for show.

"Good," Luna said, satisfied.

"I'm exhausted," Owen said.

"You have to leave," Luna said. "If she finds you here, she'll— I don't know. Be careful. She hates me now too."

Owen slept on the living room couch. He woke before dawn. It wasn't the kind of couch that invited sleep. He was in the kitchen, making coffee, when Scarlet turned up, standing in the doorway, stony-faced, raccoon-eyed. She resembled a character in a horror film. It wouldn't have seemed incongruous if she had a knife in her hand.

"Hey," Owen said.

"Hey," Scarlet said. "I'm going to go."

"Okay. You good to drive?"

"Think so."

"You want some coffee for the road?"

"Nah," she said.

"Can I get you anything?" Owen asked.

"No," she whispered, walking toward the front door.

Owen could feel the anticipation of freedom. Once she left, the world would be right. Scarlet opened the door. A blast of cold air entered the house. She turned back.

"She's not so great, you know," Scarlet said. "The only reason you like her is because you don't know her."

Owen stared at his feet, afraid of what he'd say or do. His anger rose so intensely that his face flushed with heat and rage. In his head, he was screaming, *Get out, get out, get out.*

"Don't make this about Luna. Okay?" Owen said.

"Good people don't get hate mail. Think about it," Scarlet said.

Owen heard the creak of the floorboards on the stairs. He looked up. Griff loped down the stairs in his robe and pajamas.

"Good morning," Griff said, sounding pleasant enough.

Scarlet forced a smile. "Morning. Sorry about last night."

"You leaving?" Griff asked. The delivery was casual, but Scarlet could hear the warning in his tone.

"Yes."

"Great. Let me walk you out," Griff said.

Scarlet wasn't ready to leave. She had more to say. Much, much more. But Griff stood in the foyer, waiting for her.

"Got everything you need?" Griff added.

Scarlet gazed at Owen one last time.

"Bye," Owen said.

Griff followed Scarlet as she walked to her car. She turned back and said sharply, "I can take it from here."

Griff stopped where he was and waited until she got into her car. "Drive safe," he said.

Griff returned to the house. He and Owen waited until they heard the engine of Scarlet's car fade away. Owen exhaled. Griff closed the front door.

"Thanks, man," Owen said.

Griff put his arm around his brother. "So, what's the lesson we learned from this fiasco?"

"Dude, you interrupted my call and invited her here. You remember that?" Owen said.

"Yes," Griff said. "That's the lesson I learned. What did *you* learn?"

Owen delivered the answer he knew his brother was suggesting. "Don't sleep with people you don't really know. Okay?" Owen said, with the full knowledge that that was an edict he would not be able to strictly follow.

Luna woke up shortly after. She joined the brothers in the kitchen, her eyes scanning the room.

"She left about an hour ago," Owen said.

Luna sank into a kitchen chair, relieved. Owen delivered a cup of coffee.

"So," Owen said. "What's the plan for today? I still think we can turn this trip around."

Luna stayed with the Mann family for ten more days, bringing in the new year. Scarlet didn't call again. There were no more late-night incidents with Vera and Tom. Griff showed Luna how to use a chain saw and let her cut down the Christmas tree from their backyard. No one was precious about the tree-trimming. Tom couldn't find the box of ornaments. They used whatever was on hand. They strung jujubes instead of popcorn and hung a few key-chain flashlights, which Vera had purchased as stocking stuffers. It was the best Christmas Luna had had in years. Not that it had much competition.

LUNA HAD GROWN so accustomed to being a guest in the Mann house that the drive back to campus filled her with dread. She thought for sure Owen would mention the letters on that drive. When he didn't, she imagined it was possible to put the whole thing behind her. She also imagined that 2004 would be a Scarlet-free year. She was disabused of that notion within just a few days of returning to Markham. Scarlet showed up at Luna's dorm with a white lily in lieu of an olive branch.

Luna tried to politely send Scarlet away. "It's not a good time."

"You have to let me apologize," Scarlet said, gently shoving her way into the room and plopping down on the floor. "I'm sorry about mentioning the letters. I was drunk. Confused. He's so hot and cold. It's like whiplash. But why was he so angry? And what is this big secret?"

Luna was stunned that Scarlet had the nerve to ask about the letters. And was that even an apology?

"Have you heard the legal metaphor *fruit of the poisonous tree*?" Luna asked.

"Uh, I don't know," Scarlet said.

"I didn't tell Owen about the letters. He went digging through my stuff and found them. That's not cool. He shouldn't have seen them in the first place. Because of that, I don't think I need to tell you anything. And the fact that you asked is fucked up. Whatever is between you and Owen has nothing to do with me," Luna said.

"You're right. Sorry," Scarlet said. "I won't ask again."

"Thanks," Luna said.

"So, are we still friends?" Scarlet asked.

"Sure," Luna said, defeated.

The response was purely one of self-preservation. Keep your enemies close, that kind of thing. Luna hoped she and Scarlet could manage a surface-friendly acquaintance deal. But then Scarlet just kept turning up like she'd always done before. And, like before, it felt easier—safer, really—to just let her in.

A WEEK OR so into the new semester, Owen and Casey were hanging out in Luna's dorm when Scarlet showed up. Casey invited her in. When Scarlet saw Owen, she hesitated, thought about leaving, but decided to play it cool instead. She sat on the floor next to Casey and asked about her holiday. Scarlet nodded at Owen as if he was an afterthought. Owen understood why Luna was allowing Scarlet to remain in her orbit, but he would not do the same.

"Well, I'm going to get a slice. Later," Owen said.

He moved fast. Luna locked the door after him.

"You see that?" Scarlet asked. "He won't even look at me."

Luna sighed very loudly, trying to convey how tired she was of the Scarlet-Owen conversation.

"Do you really like him that much?" Casey asked Scarlet.

"I did," Scarlet said.

"Why?" Casey asked.

"We were good together."

"When, exactly?" Casey pressed. "When he was drunk and you were in bed? I hate to break it to you, but they all seem in love for somewhere between three and five minutes."

"Tell me what to do," Scarlet said.

"Back off for a while. Maybe start seeing someone else," Casey said.

"You're right!" Scarlet said. "Genius. He'll get jealous."

"I think you should move on," Luna said.

"You're right," Scarlet said. "That's exactly what I'm going to do."

"Got any liquor in here? I need a drink," Casey said.

Casey could sense the tension. She didn't need a drink but thought it might help Luna.

Luna took a bottle of vodka from her mini-fridge and poured shots. The girls drank. Scarlet, who hated hard liquor, followed her drink with a chaser of nauseated sounds. Casey scowled. Luna rolled her eyes. Scarlet stretched out her legs and arms in a luxurious yawn and rested her back against Luna's bed, as if she was planning to stay awhile. Luna's anger roiled quietly.

"Mason and Bobbi. Can you fucking believe that?" said Scarlet, remembering Owen's gossip from the Berkshires.

"What are you talking about?" Casey said.

"I heard they hooked up," said Scarlet.

Casey, visibly stunned, began to shove her books into her backpack.

"It's just a rumor," Luna said to Casey. "Don't leave."

"Bobbi must have told you about it," Scarlet said.

"I got a thing," Casey said. "Anyway, gotta roll. See you later, Luna. Scarlet."

Casey departed. Scarlet waited until the sound of her footfalls faded away.

"That was weird, right?" Scarlet asked.

Luna briefly lost control: "You need to get a fucking life."

MASON WAS SUBLIMELY baked a few hours later when he decided to confront Owen. The three lazy knocks on Owen's door were pure stoner percussion.

"It's open," Owen said.

Mason opened the door and peered around the corner like a stagehand beckoning the headliner. "Hello?" said Mason.

"Hello," said Owen.

Owen was nestled in the corner of the room with a book. It took Mason a moment to spot him.

"I was looking for you," Mason said.

"You were looking in the right place," said Owen.

Mason thought Owen sounded hostile, but sometimes pot made him paranoid. For a moment, Mason forgot why he'd dropped by.

"Was there something you needed?" said Owen.

"Yes. Yes. Dude. Dude. *Why?*" Mason said. He was more animated than Owen had ever seen him.

"I'm going to need a few more details to answer that question," said Owen.

"Why are you telling people that Bobbi and I hooked up?"

Owen's memory clicked into gear and he shifted from smug to contrite. "Oh, man, I'm so, so sorry," Owen said. "Let me explain."

OVER THE NEXT few months, Scarlet did everything she could to make Owen jealous. She hung out or hooked up with anyone remotely attractive. She assumed the gossip engine at Markham would take care of the rest.

The gossip engine worked just fine. Owen was served breaking news on every one of Scarlet's hookups. What Scarlet didn't understand was that Owen was *done*. There was no part of him that wanted her anymore.

Luna said only one thing to Owen on the subject: "If you fuck her again and ice her out, I—I will lose all respect for you."

Owen agreed. He couldn't fathom a situation in which he'd sleep with Scarlet again. But Scarlet wanted closure. At least that's what she told herself. What she really wanted was to see Owen and make him want her again. It wasn't so much that she missed him or had been happy with him. She simply wanted to win. She wanted to hook him one last time and then release him into the sea with a nasty piece of metal in his mouth.

Scarlet waited. One week, two, three weeks passed, and she got no more than a nod of acknowledgment if she passed Owen in the quad. She told herself that she'd be patient. That he would eventually come back.

By the time midterms rolled around and the threat of spring break loomed, Scarlet and Owen hadn't been alone in a room together for more than two months. Her grades slipped, her friendships began to fade, because her Owen obsession was exhausting for anyone in her company. At first, Scarlet blamed herself. She'd stare into the mirror and count her flaws. But self-loathing wasn't enough. Scarlet needed another receptacle for her rage.

Owen had learned his lesson with Scarlet. He eventually understood that he couldn't open the door even a crack. Every few weeks, despite Scarlet's best efforts, she'd get drunk enough to send him a text. Owen had ignored every one of those texts, until the night of March 5.

Scarlet returned home from a party where the only guy who remotely interested her was chatting up another girl. Drunk, weak, and defeated, Scarlet texted Owen.

Hey.

After ten minutes without a response, Scarlet texted again.

why won't u talk 2 me?

Five minutes later, Owen replied.

You have to stop, Scarlet. It's over.

Scarlet felt a rush of adrenaline. He'd finally replied. She had to see him.

She had to give him a reason to see her.

October 10, 2019

———

T he desks in the bullpen were set up in pairs—formidable steel squares headbutting each other. It was the end of the day on Thursday. Detectives Burns and Goldman had worked twelve-to-fourteen-hour days since they'd been assigned the Boucher murder. Burns watched Goldman's entertaining but fruitless interview with Amy Johnson, while Noah screened Margot's far more compelling interrogation of Leo Whitman. When she glanced up from her screen, Margot caught Noah smirking.

"What?" she said.

"If I watched this without sound, I could tell the exact moment you turned on him. And the other way around," Noah said.

Margot lifted up her earphones. "He went out of his way to throw Mann under the bus. You notice?"

"Yes," Noah said. "It was an inelegant transition."

For a cop, Margot had an unusual response to snitching behavior. She preferred pulling evidence out of a witness. When it came too easily, like they were enjoying it, trying to point a spotlight on someone else, that got under her skin.

"He's not the shooter," Goldman said.

"Why?" Burns asked.

"Did you notice his hand tremor?"

Burns shook her head. Noah beckoned her over, queued up the right part of the video, and hit PLAY. Margot's hair brushed against his neck as she watched. He didn't ask her to move.

Onscreen, Leo's right hand shook slightly. He would occasionally open and close his fist and the tremor would calm.

"Tremor is in the right hand," Goldman said. "That's what he used to hold his coffee. Not impossible, but unlikely he could make the shot."

"Jesus," Margot said, squinting at the screen.

"What?" Noah said, trying to spot what Margot was seeing.

"Why didn't you tell me about my roots? Do they look that bad in real life?" Margot said.

Noah palmed his laptop shut. "I need a drink. You?" he said.

Margot checked the time. Her daughter was out until nine or ten and her son had a sleepover.

"Yes," Noah said. "You need a drink."

BURNS AND GOLDMAN had been partners for two years. At first Noah found Margot terrifying. Well, first he found her attractive. Then terrifying. He wasn't sure he wanted a female partner. He'd had a woman training officer right out of the academy. Granite-hard, eyes that could slice you down the middle. Trooper Sally Wright. She'd come up when female cops were still a novelty, when they had to be Teflon to survive. Noah was afraid Margot would be the same. He wasn't Teflon; closer to particleboard. He soaked up everything, letting it warp him, become part of him. The days with Wright had worn him down. He figured out fast that Margot was different. He'd anticipated a dark side, but it never showed. Margot even had a family, and they all seemed pretty solid. Although the husband was gone now. Divorced, not dead, she had to explain when she first mentioned his absence. Her children were already teenagers. The girl sixteen, the boy fourteen. Noah had been over to their house now too many times to count. Noah used to talk about Burns to his psychiatrist. He was using his shrink as an expert witness, trying to gain understanding of Margot's character. She's sane but not boring. She's a good cop, without any demons. How is that possible? When the shrink suggested they discuss his feelings toward his partner, Noah stopped mentioning Margot's name in his sessions.

Noah was holding the door to Don's Oasis when Margot got a call.

"It's Bloom," she said. "I'll meet you inside."

Bloom, Irene's attorney, had been on vacation in the Bahamas when Irene was murdered. It had taken three days to get in touch with him.

Noah ordered two pints and found a table in back. Ten minutes later, Margot entered the bar. After her eyes adjusted to the dim light, she joined Noah at the table, quickly jotting down a few notes before she indulged in drink.

"Did you ask him why he went to the Bahamas during hurricane season?" Noah said.

"I didn't ask. But he told me. His brother-in-law, Arthur, a notorious skinflint, booked the travel. Big family vacation. I think he would have preferred a hurricane to the nightly meals."

"Any surprises in the will?" Noah asked.

"His office will messenger a copy," Burns said, glancing down at her notes. "He did say that the estate would be hard to estimate because half of it was art that hadn't been appraised in recent years. The gist is that about two-thirds of her estate, most of her art, goes to charity. The rest is divvied up among family members—including two distant cousins."

"The house?" Noah asked.

"She left him enough to pay off the house," Burns said.

"They had a mortgage?" Goldman asked.

"The house is in Owen's name and he paid the mortgage."

"That's odd. Why?"

"Maybe she didn't want him to get too comfortable. Bloom said he won't know until everything is liquidated. Rough estimate, the total estate was worth ten million. Owen would get less than a million after taxes. . . ."

"And if they divorced?" Goldman asked.

"Owen signed a prenup. He'd get the house and whatever was left on the mortgage. It's about a five-hundred-thousand-dollar motive for murder."

"He had access to more money with Irene alive," Noah said. "When was the will drawn up? Maybe he didn't know about it?"

Burns shook her head. "No, Bloom said he knew. Irene took care of it right after they married."

"Life insurance?" Goldman asked.

"Nope," Burns said, shaking her head again. "But people have killed for far less."

"The incentive for murder tends to have a proportional relationship to the overall estate. You wouldn't murder an oil tycoon for fifty grand, right?" Goldman said.

"I'd need at least a million for murder," Burns said, deadpan. "I've got to put two kids through college."

"We're missing something," Goldman said.

"Let's go over it one more time before I'm too drunk to follow," Burns said.

Goldman opened a file on his phone and reviewed the basics. "A victim shot once with a 9mm weapon from at least ten feet, probably closer to twenty. There was no weapon at the scene, no footprints, no cameras on Dover Cemetery, and, as far as we know, none of Irene's friends or family were gun owners. The shooter would have had to have some practice, right?" Goldman said.

"He or she knew what they were doing. Irene was likely jogging at the time, a moving target."

"It was planned. Shooter follows her, waits until she's in an isolated locale. Or an accident? Maybe some kid is using the cemetery for target practice?" Goldman suggested.

Margot shrugged. It was possible, she thought, but unlikely.

"Let's go over alibis again," Margot said.

"Carl Hendricks, the ex-husband, was on vacation in California. I talked to his wife, who confirms. And I have digital confirmation of their plane tickets. Irene's nonprofit had a few employees. All of them can be vouched for, and I'm not seeing a motive there. None of them seem to've had a personal relationship with Irene. And, as far as I can tell, she was well-liked. Whitman says he was home alone but probably couldn't have made the shot anyway. Amy Johnson said she was home in bed. She sent me a selfie of her in bed. It wasn't for the date in question, so I'm flummoxed as to why she sent it."

"She was flirting," Margot said, laughing. "Just out of curiosity, would you date a woman like her?"

"She's only twenty-three," Noah said.

"Not answering my question."

"No."

"Are you confirming that you're refusing to answer my question or was that a no-you-wouldn't-date-her?"

"I would not date someone like Amy," Goldman said.

"Wow. So judgmental, Noah," Burns said, smirking. Quickly, back to business: "Why would Owen risk his marriage for someone like Amy? What is it about her?"

"I don't know."

"Come on," Margot said. "Explain the appeal."

"I don't like it when you ask me to explain men to you, like I have special insight into lascivious behavior," Noah said.

"Fine, don't answer," Margot said.

"Luna and Owen don't have alibis. According to the timeline, Luna was the last person to see Irene alive," Goldman said.

"Right. She's the last person to see Irene alive, she finds the body. She doesn't call the police. She runs to Owen's house and tells him. He goes to the crime scene, contaminating the evidence."

"It's convenient," Goldman said.

"What do they get out of it?"

"Freedom. Some money," Goldman said.

"Maybe it isn't about money," said Burns. "Or money is just part of it."

"Then what?"

"Maybe he wants to see if he can get away with it."

"Maybe he's done it before?" Noah said.

Burns nodded, thinking. "It's hard to ignore that incident at Markham. What are the odds?"

Burns stared at her empty glass, trying to decide if she should get another. Noah went to the bar and got another pint.

"I'll drive you home," he said.

Burns smiled in appreciation. "Best partner I ever had."

Goldman felt pleased and embarrassed. "So, back to the Markham thing," Goldman said. "Are you suggesting that maybe they're in this together?"

"No. Not necessarily," said Burns. "But if Owen did it, Luna knows."

MARGOT ENTERED THE station the next morning a walking hangover cliché—coffee in hand, sunglasses indoors, cautious gait.

"You're the worst partner I've ever had," she said.

"Please take off your sunglasses," Noah said.

Margot tossed the glasses onto her desk. "Happy?" she said, revealing bloodshot eyes.

"You only had three pints, right?"

"Give it ten years," she said. "You'll see."

Noah's hair was a bit damp, and Margot noted the faint scent of baby shampoo.

"Did you go to the gym this morning?" she said.

Noah had and still arrived an hour before Margot.

"Course not," Noah said.

Noah had already skimmed through a third of Owen's emails, along with a printout of his search history for the past three months.

"What are you working on?" Margot asked.

"Mann's emails and search history," Noah said.

"Anything of interest?" Margot said.

Noah wasn't sure how to answer. He hadn't reviewed enough of the material to provide an educated opinion. Margot understood his reluctance, but she wanted his gut.

"Tell me," she said.

"We're not going to find a smoking gun here."

"Because he was smart and didn't leave evidence?"

"If he was deliberately keeping his computer clean, I don't think there would be so many emails between him and his girlfriend. Also, if I thought someone was going to be searching my computer in the near future, I'd at least clear out the porn-site search history."

"You're no fun."

"Hypothetically," Noah added.

"Tell me the truth. How much porn would I find on your laptop?"

Noah shook his head. "No. Not talking about that."

"I can't decide if you're genuinely square or a closet perv."

"Which would you prefer?"

"I really don't know," Margot said, then, recognizing the imprudence of their conversation, "I shouldn't talk to you like that. I apologize."

"Apology accepted," Noah said.

"Because if a male superior inquired about his female partner's porn-viewing habits, that would be . . . highly inappropriate. If you want to report me, I'll understand."

Burns's mobile rang. She answered.

"Detective Burns," she said into the phone. "Okay. Thank you. When? Right. Goodbye."

Margot ended the call and turned to Noah. "They released the body last night. To Mather and Sons. There's no service planned," she said.

"Nothing?" Noah said.

"No."

"Where is she being buried?"

"Cremated," Margot said.

Noah seemed confused, then troubled. "Owen said in our interview that Irene didn't want to be cremated, and then he cremates her?"

"Doesn't mean anything," Margot said.

"Doesn't it?"

"What does that get him?" Margot said.

"I don't know," Goldman said. "But you can't exhume ashes."

March 2004

———

At three forty-five on a Friday afternoon, Casey showed up at Luna's dorm room with a six-pack of beer. Luna was about to crack open a can when Casey told her to wait fifteen minutes, explaining that it was a bit early. Luna questioned her logic, prompting Casey to ask what logic had to do with any of it. By the time Luna had teased out Casey's full (and utterly arbitrary, in Luna's view) position on the matter—one shouldn't consume alcoholic beverages between the hours of twelve and four P.M.—the fifteen minutes were up. Over the next two hours, Luna and Casey polished off three beers apiece and started on a bottle of bourbon that Luna had stashed in her closet. A conversation about recent movies morphed into a game where one person would describe the plot of a film and the other would try to guess the title.

"A small country goes bankrupt and is in debt to a wealthy woman who installs the next president," Casey said. "Meanwhile, spies from neighboring countries are trying to stage a coup."

"*The Manchurian Candidate*," Luna said.

Casey appeared stunned for a brief moment and then exploded into laughter. "No," she said. "Oh my god, that was amazing."

"What was it?" Luna asked.

"*Duck Soup*."

When Mason, Ted, and Owen joined them at around six, the two were plastered. Casey was still laughing so hard about *Duck*

Soup that she couldn't manage to articulate what was so funny. Mason asked Luna if Casey was stoned, Luna said no, and Casey left the room to pull herself together.

Luna tried to explain Casey's condition, but since she didn't fully understand it herself, all she could say was "I think I need to see *Duck Soup*." At eight, after four solid hours of drinking and an unknown quantity of weed, Luna kicked everyone out of her room and fell asleep with her clothes on.

A few hours later, she was awakened by an annoying dinging sound that seemed to repeat every few seconds. Luna stumbled out of bed and hunted for the noise. She spotted Owen's phone on the floor, just under her bed. She thought about calling his dorm to let him know where he'd left it, but she figured Owen already knew and would probably come around sometime the next morning. Luna checked Owen's text messages, in case he was using someone else's phone to locate his mobile. That's when she saw Scarlet's texts.

Hey.
why won't u talk 2 me?

What Luna didn't know was that Owen hadn't responded to any of Scarlet's communiqués in the last few months. He'd delete them as soon as they popped on his screen. Luna had always believed it was the unpredictability of Owen's affection and disdain that unhinged Scarlet. A clear, immutable *no* could spare her months or years of pain and embarrassment. It took Luna and her drunk fingers five minutes to compose the message.

You have to stop, Scarlet. It's over.

Luna sent the message without a moment's hesitation. She thought that would be it. Then there was that annoying ding, along with another message.

someting importan I hav 2 tell you.

As Luna tried to formulate an even stronger sentence conveying utter disinterest, Scarlet sent another message.

Luna has a secret. A secret u wan 2 now.

Every remaining ounce of Luna's sympathy was gone. She punched out another message.

She told me. Let it go.

Five minutes later, Owen's phone dinged again.

u don know. If u knew, u wood not lik her

Luna, furious and frantic, replied again.

Stop. Stop. Fucking stop. Get a life.

A moment later, another message came in. Luna replied again, followed by another message.

meet at black budd in 30 min

You're drunk. Go to bed.

30 min Or I tell

Luna deleted the entire exchange and threw the phone back on the floor. She shut her eyes hard and tried to stanch the flow of tears. Then she stopped fighting and let the tears flow until she was drained.

Luna remembered the joint she'd stowed in her winter coat for emergencies. This was indeed an emergency.

She poured a shot of leftover booze and lit the joint, taking a long, slow drag. It tasted stale, but maybe it would slow down her careening mind. She couldn't help it. She dug out the cigar box with the letters. It was overwhelming, seeing them all at once. She reminded herself that they had accumulated over seven years.

Over time, some of the letters had diminished in power. The quasi-religious condemnations of her soul no longer packed the same punch as they once did. But when she reread all of them, the impact was like driving full speed into a concrete wall.

Luna didn't so much fall asleep as tip over onto the floor. When she woke for the second time, it was one A.M. She heard a light tap on the door, whispers outside her room. The memory of the past few hours flooded back, and Luna's adrenaline kicked in.

She crawled across the floor into her closet. She could wait until campus was silent, pack a bag, and be gone for good. But she had very little money and no safe place to crash.

The knock repeated, and Casey's comforting voice came through the door.

"Luna, wake up," said Casey. "You have to come outside and look at the moon."

Casey liked the moon. Since full moons had more moon than any other, she was partial to those. Also, Casey was determined to document any evidence of full moons altering human behavior. It troubled her greatly that more studies were not done on the subject.

Luna crawled over to the door, trying to decide whether to speak or keep hiding. The threat hadn't fully arrived. She could at least answer and buy some time.

"No moon for me," said Luna, her mouth a kiss away from the doorframe. Despite her name, or because of it, Luna was willfully indifferent to planets beyond Earth.

Luna thought she sounded normal.

"But what if it's the last moon?" said Casey.

"Fuck the moon," said Luna.

Casey heard it that time, the wobble in Luna's voice, the precipice of tears. Casey wasn't going to leave now, no matter what kind of moon the sky had to offer.

"Open the door," Casey said.

Luna tried to ignore her. Casey began knocking. Quiet, steady beats like a woodpecker on the job.

"I can do this all night," Casey said. "I have titanium knuckles."

Casey wouldn't stop. Of that, Luna was certain. She scrambled to collect the letters spread across the floor and unlocked the door. Luna crawled into the small empty space between her bed and her dresser. She snatched the near-empty bottle off the floor and pulled the blanket from her bed. She covered herself and her hate mail with it.

"Thank you," Casey said, entering the room. She shook her right hand, which stung from the pounding. "As it turns out, I don't have titanium knuckles."

Luna said nothing. She uncapped the bottle and drank, even though she was already feeling queasy. Focusing on her physical discomfort seemed far superior to the sick shit that was going on in her brain.

"Gimme some of that," Casey said, mostly to get the bottle out of Luna's possession.

Casey took a couple of heavy swigs. She never made a face after drinking booze straight. When Luna wasn't overcome with dread, she would marvel at Casey's strong disposition.

"This isn't about Ted. I know that," Casey said.

"No," Luna said, extending her hand for the bottle. She didn't so much want to drink it as hold it for comfort, like a degenerate's teddy bear.

"I can keep a secret like no one else," Casey said.

"How about Mason?" Luna asked. "Can he keep a secret?"

Casey had been spending some time with Mason. The fact that his name came up when Luna was clearly distraught caused her some concern. *This,* whatever had caused Luna's turmoil, couldn't possibly be about Mason.

"What does Mason have to do with anything?" Casey said, her voice on guard.

It was all going to come out anyway, Luna reasoned. She wanted to be the one to tell Casey, if Mason hadn't already.

"He knows my secret. I thought maybe, because you two are— what are you two?"

"That's still to be determined," said Casey. "Well, I guess he can keep a secret, if that means anything to you."

"Good to know," said Luna.

Casey was, by nature, a patient person. She sat with her hands folded, resting her eyes, until she heard papers shuffling. She turned to Luna, who handed her a yellow and battered newspaper clipping. It was a piece about the murderer John Brown. Casey had a vague memory about the trial, or at least about the second one. Casey skimmed the piece, her memory refreshing. Luna was always re-ferred to as the sister.

Luna searched Casey's eyes for that look—the hate, the horror, the realization when someone discovers they've been sharing space with an accessory to murder. Technically, an accessory after the fact, although Luna couldn't be that generous with herself. But Casey gave away nothing. She was trying to imagine what she would have done in the same situation. She couldn't answer honestly. No one can.

"Say something," Luna said.

Casey crawled next to Luna and got under the blanket with her. "That's a hell of a thing to live with," Casey said.

"I got pretty good at not thinking about it," Luna said.

"So, what happened tonight?"

Luna felt under the bed for Owen's phone. She checked it again. Not another word from Scarlet. "Scarlet knows."

"How?"

"Don't know," Luna said. "She's been texting Owen. Wants to

tell him about me. But I have his phone and I deleted her messages. Which was stupid. She's going to tell everyone now."

"The hell she will. Let's call her," Casey said, scrolling to Scarlet's number on Owen's phone.

"Don't," Luna said.

"Too late," Casey said, as she pressed the SEND button.

Luna vomited in her trash can while Casey listened to Scarlet's phone go to voicemail.

"Hmm, maybe she's over it," said Casey, ending the call.

"Doubt it," Luna mumbled.

Casey got up, dropped the phone on Luna's desk, and pointed at the trash can. "You done?"

"Yeah."

"I'll be right back," Casey said.

It was past two A.M. when Luna next checked the time. Scarlet's discovery had retreated in her mind. Front and center was a spinning room, which felt like a horrible ride she'd taken at an amusement park years ago. You stood inside a round chamber and it spun faster and faster, flattening you against the wall. Even if you wanted to vomit, the centrifugal force would likely keep it inside you.

Casey returned with water and crackers, which Luna devoured by the fistful.

"You look like Cookie Monster," Casey said.

Luna heard only the word *monster*.

OWEN WOKE TO a loud banging on his door. He checked the clock by his bed: nine A.M. Saturday morning, if he remembered correctly. It was socially acceptable to sleep until at least eleven on a Saturday or Sunday.

"Come back during business hours," Owen said.

"Scarlet, are you in there?" said a female voice, which Owen identified as either Amber or Bobbi.

Owen tossed the covers over his head. He thought they would

go away if he ignored them. They did not. There was knocking and more knocking. Female voices shouted Owen's name, then Scarlet's name.

"Maybe he's out," said Pete, Owen's RA.

"He just told us to go away," said A or B. "This is important. Do you have the key?"

There was further conversation, which Owen couldn't decipher. Then another knock landed, duller but more powerful.

"Owen, open up," said Pete.

"Seriously?" Owen mumbled.

Pete couldn't decipher Owen's words. And he hated using his key. No matter how many times he asked if someone was decent, he always found them indecent.

Pete knocked again and said, "Is Scarlet with you? Her friends are worried."

"She's not here," Owen said.

"We should call the police," A or B said.

"Dude, open the door," Pete said.

Owen stumbled out of his bed and threw on his robe. He opened his door and spewed dragon breath on A, B, and Pete.

"For fuck's sake, she's not here," Owen said.

"Then she's missing," said Amber.

"Missing?" Owen said. A and B could find drama in anything, he thought. "She probably went home with a guy or something," said Owen.

"No one has spoken to her in twelve hours. Have you heard anything?" Bobbi asked.

"Have you tried calling her?" Owen said. *Twelve hours,* Owen thought. He'd be furious if anyone started hunting for him after twelve hours.

"She's not answering. Are you sure you haven't heard from her?" Amber said.

Owen heard an accusatory tone in her voice. He was becoming increasingly angry that Scarlet was still his problem when they were never really together.

Owen turned around and scanned his room. He riffled through papers on his desk. He tried to remember the last place he'd used his phone, but he needed coffee for that kind of complicated mental backtracking.

"I need to find my phone. And I really need a cup of coffee," Owen said.

"So you haven't heard from her?" Bobbi asked.

"No," Owen said.

"You should tell your RA. There's a procedure," Pete told the girls, although he couldn't remember if there was one or not.

"If you hear from her, tell her she needs to call us immediately," said Amber.

WHILE OWEN WAS taking a shower, he remembered hanging out in Luna's room with Mason, Casey, and Ted the night before. He'd probably left his phone at Luna's. Post-shower, Owen strolled down to the dining hall, stuffed a banana in his pocket, and got two cups of coffee. He walked across the quad to Blake Hall, climbing two flights of stairs to Luna's floor. He felt mildly fatigued when he reached the top landing. *I'm too young to be this out of shape,* he thought.

Owen was more than slightly peeved to find Ted loitering outside Luna's door.

"She in there?" Owen said.

"Not answering," Ted said.

Owen figured Luna was ignoring Ted and took a seat on the floor by her door.

"So, you're just going to wait?" Ted asked.

"I've got nothing better to do," Owen said.

"I bet Scarlet could use a cup of coffee," Ted said.

"Then why don't you bring her one," Owen said.

"I'm not with Scarlet."

"Neither am I," Owen said.

He was so fucking tired of having to explain that to people.

"You're not with Luna either," said Ted.

"No one is with Luna," Owen said.

Luna had confided in Owen that she was bored with Ted but hadn't figured out the right way to end things. Owen tried to explain to her that men weren't quite as invested in a breakup narrative, but Luna was still searching for the kindest way out. So far, she hadn't figured out anything better than not answering her door.

"Later, dude," Ted said, walking away. He decided then and there, he wouldn't come back.

Luna was crouched by the door, listening to the entire exchange. When Ted was out of earshot, Owen told Luna the coast was clear, and Luna unlocked her door.

Owen entered with the two cups of coffee stacked on top of each other. He passed her the cup silently. The warmth between her hands took some of the edge off her overall queasiness.

Owen remembered the banana and placed it on Luna's desk.

"You're a saint," she said.

"Your exit plan has commenced," Owen said.

He was referring to Luna's relationship extraction.

"Huh?" Luna said. "What are you saying?"

Her brain was ready to loop everything back to Scarlet's threat. Was she supposed to run, to leave school? Was this the end of the half-decent life she'd carved out for herself?

"With Ted. Just pull the trigger, will you? I'm tired of seeing his Neanderthal forehead."

Luna reached for Owen's phone, which she'd shoved between the mattress and box spring. She checked it one more time for a new text. The battery was almost dead. She might have a reprieve of another few hours if she played her cards right. But what was the point?

"You left this here."

"Yeah, that's what I figured," Owen said, noting the absence of messages. "Scarlet is MIA. A and B woke me up this morning looking for her."

"She didn't go back to her room?" Luna asked.

"No. I'm sure she's with a guy. She can't survive without male attention. She goes fucking crazy."

"She texted you last night," Luna said.

"I don't see any texts."

"I deleted them."

"Why? What did they say?"

"Remember the hate-mail thing?" Luna said.

"Yeah."

"She said she wanted to tell you something about it. She wanted you to meet her someplace."

"Did Scarlet say where?"

"Someplace called Black Budd?"

"What the fuck's that?" Owen asked.

"I thought you'd know. Like an in-joke or something. But she was drunk. So was I."

"Black bud. Are you sure you're remembering that right?"

"Yes. Two Ds. I need to tell you something."

"What?"

"I think I'm going to be sick."

Luna was ready, she thought, to come clean on every last thing. But first she needed to vomit. Luna reached her trash can just in time. Owen had been through this with her before. She liked to be sick alone. She didn't want anyone holding her hair or rubbing her back. Owen took Luna's water bottle and filled it at the end of the hall. When he returned to her room, she was barely conscious on the floor next to her bed. He managed to wake her enough to relocate her to the bed. He emptied the trash can and put her water bottle on her nightstand.

"Luna, you awake?" he asked, sitting on the edge of her bed.

"Yes," she mumbled, eyes closed, curled up in a ball.

"Hydrate. Sleep. We can talk tomorrow."

That morning, 911 dispatch got a call from a pay phone in the town of Deerkill.

"There's a girl who might be missing named Scarlet. You'll find her near Black Oak Bluff. She said she was going to hike there."

"May I ask who is calling?" the operator said.

The line went dead.

O wen and his mother regarded the wall of urns. At first he wasn't going to get one, since the plan was to scatter the ashes, but it felt weird keeping the remains of his wife in a cardboard box for any duration. Owen thought Irene would want something simple, but each urn seemed more ornate than the last. She probably would have preferred the box. He honestly didn't know. They'd never had that conversation.

"I'm surprised she wanted to be cremated," said Vera. "She didn't seem the type."

"What's the type?" Owen asked.

"Agnostics, cynics, people who want their remains transported to inconvenient locations, and the poor," said Vera.

"You've given this a lot of thought," said Owen.

"She's a woman of means, is all I'm saying. Doesn't her family have a mausoleum somewhere?"

"No. And her mother was cremated. That's all I have to go on."

Vera's cellphone chirped in her pocket. She quickly pulled it out and answered. She spoke in a barely audible whisper, even though she and Owen were the only two people in the room. "Hello. Oh, good. Okay, dear. See you soon."

"Who was that?" Owen asked.

"That was your brother," she said. "He's running late. But he'll make it later tonight."

If it were up to Owen, he would have kept his family out of the whole thing. It was Luna who'd insisted that he call his mother, and Vera who'd insisted on calling Griff. Vera would sometimes go months or years not speaking to Griff, but they seemed to have been in communication more recently. Owen wasn't sure what had changed. Maybe Vera had forgotten the original cause of their rift. If she had, Owen could see her forgiving Griff's other filial misdemeanors. Whatever the reason, Owen was grateful to have Griff back on Mom duty. Vera was on the decline. Owen didn't want to shoulder that responsibility alone.

While Owen was at the mortuary with his mother, Luna swung by a liquor store and purchased jumbo bottles of vodka, bourbon, and gin. She also picked up paper plates, disposable cups, and a couple of bags of ice. After dropping off the wake provisions, Luna returned home. She found Sam upstairs, packing a suitcase.

"Going somewhere?" Luna said.

"Driving down to Philly tonight."

"You just saw your mom."

"She broke her wrist, Luna."

"Two weeks ago. And she's fine."

"Normal people see their parents more than once every two years."

As Luna was deciding how to respond, Sam said, "Sorry. I wasn't trying to be a dick."

"I understand. But the wake is tonight. Can it wait?"

"The wake is a bunch of your friends standing around Owen's house, drinking, in the vicinity of Irene's ashes. There's nothing ceremonial about it. It's a sad party with only your friends in attendance. I think I can miss that without anyone noticing. You don't need me, right?" Sam said.

It was more of a challenge than a question. And he was right. His absence wouldn't be felt. Then again, Sam's mother wouldn't have felt his absence either. She had been diagnosed with Alzheimer's five years past and hadn't recognized Sam in two.

"Mason and Casey will be here this evening. Did you—" Luna said.

"Yes. I cleared out the guest room," said Sam.

The only person who might notice that Sam was gone was Casey. Luna figured she would demand an explanation. But an explanation was easier than having Sam stay at home. With him gone, they wouldn't have to sleep in the same bed. Luna assumed that possibility was at least one factor in his decision.

"See you when you get back," Luna said.

"We should—"

"I know," said Luna.

LUNA'S DOORBELL RANG just after four o'clock. Such sounds had always irked her, but this time she felt a tiny rush of adrenaline, followed by a deeper wave of guilt. Despite the tragic circumstances, Luna couldn't deny that she was really happy to see the two people on the other side of the door.

Luna hugged Casey first. She was always surprised by how aggressive her friend's hugs were. They lasted longer than most people's. Then Mason stepped in and gently kissed Luna on the cheek. He touched her shoulders lightly and vaguely leaned in.

Luna often wondered how Casey and Mason's mismatched affection worked in a marriage going on ten years, but they seemed to have sorted it out.

"It's really good to see you guys," Luna said, picking up a random piece of luggage and leading the way past the kitchen to the office/guest room on the first floor.

The bed was made with military corners, Sam's belongings tucked away in some mysterious location.

"Let me know if you need anything," Luna said, exiting the guest room.

Casey dropped her bag by the bed, riffled through her purse, withdrew a pack of almonds, and handed them to her husband. "Mason here is going to eat these nuts and take a nap. I will have an adult beverage," Casey said on her way out of the room.

"Maybe I want an adult beverage," said Mason.

"After your nap," said Casey, closing the door behind her.

The dynamic of Mason and Casey's marriage offended Owen's strong notions of autonomy in relationships. It seemed mothering and decidedly unsexy. Luna argued that it was simply a preemptive effort to keep their relationship copacetic. She had, in fact, seen how Mason could unravel when he was overtired and his blood sugar plummeted.

In the kitchen, Luna mixed a negroni for Casey without inquiring what she wanted. She poured herself the dregs of a mid-shelf bourbon bottle.

"Sam at work?" Casey asked.

"He won't be here for the wake. I guess that's what we're calling it. Or 'a gathering with liquor near an urn,' as Sam calls it."

"Where is he?" Casey asked.

"His mother has been ill for a while. He needed to see her again."

"Did he?" Casey said, sipping her drink and delivering a probing gaze. "You're having issues, aren't you?"

"Most of the time I find your bluntness comforting," Luna said, "but today I need you to back off."

"Duly noted," Casey said, raising her glass. "To backing off."

"To backing off," said Luna.

THE GUESTS AT Irene's half-assed wake were mostly neighbors and a few old friends of Irene's mother. The absence of attendees who were genuinely close to the deceased was notable, especially in a house that size. People loitered and drank, and a few casual acquaintances, mostly from the neighborhood, caught up with one another.

Owen was grateful to have old college friends around to save him from the people he didn't know and didn't care to know. Several times, Mason had to rescue Owen from Maya or one of the ten or so elderly people in attendance whose connection to his dead wife he could not establish. To be fair, he hadn't tried. (They were, in fact, the more-mobile residents of Green Pine Senior Living, where Irene played cards once a week.)

Luna could never figure out how or why Owen's disdain for Mason had faded. But the two had been solid for years. Mason's first job was coding at a start-up that paid mostly in stock options. It went public after three years. He took the next year off to marry Casey and travel.

Then he and Casey invented an app called Sherp (short for Sherpa, he explained) designed to talk users through hallucinogenic (and occasionally cannabinoid) drug experiences. While the app was indeed used for that purpose, it was its unintended use for a wide range of psychological challenges—from childhood tantrums to general anxiety disorder—that made it wildly successful.

After the second windfall, Mason and Casey adjusted to their wealth, spending money almost as fast as they were earning it. There were times when even Luna was put off by Casey and Mason's excesses. When the couple purchased a six-bedroom house in Chester County, Pennsylvania, Luna asked how many children they were planning on having, suggesting that four was the minimum for a house that size. When she commented to Owen about the environmental footprint of such extravagance, he noted that Mason had plans to install solar panels. Luna remained baffled by Mason and Owen's post-college friendship. But it made her life easier, so she didn't question it. It didn't hurt that Mason and Casey were ardent supporters of Owen's work. In fact, there were a number of years when their patronage kept him afloat.

A few hours into the wake, it was Owen's turn to rescue Mason from Maya. Maya had asked the *what do you do* question, which Mason had unwisely answered by telling her about his and Casey's most recent venture. The company name was Belcopa. In a nutshell, they made sugar pills, which doctors could use in placebo therapy. Mason was accustomed to questions whenever he explained their business model, but there was not enough time in the day to field Maya's endless interrogatives.

"My husband takes Lipitor. Are you saying that we could be paying for something that has no pharmaceutical value?" she asked.

"Of course not," Mason said. "It's mostly used for pain."

"That sounds unethical," Maya said.

"You know what's unethical?" Mason said. "Overprescribing highly addictive and lethal pain meds."

Owen put his arm around Mason and nudged him in the direction of the backyard.

"Your wife needs you," Owen said. "She's outside."

Casey was, in fact, in the kitchen, discouraging Vera from using the microwave to heat a lasagna. Vera, already deeply intoxicated, wobbled on her one-inch heels. Luna kept suggesting that Vera eat something, until Vera snapped back, "There's nothing here I'd eat."

"Why don't you go outside or something," Casey said to Luna. "You're making me nervous."

"*I'm* making you nervous?" Luna said, ticking her head slightly at Vera.

"Yes," Casey said. "Go. Everything is under control."

Luna knew Casey could handle things in the kitchen, so she made her escape. She navigated through the crowded living room and slipped out through the sliding glass door.

A golden retriever bounded up to Luna and wagged his tail. Luna had no idea who the dog belonged to. Its fur was incredibly soft. She wanted to take the dog home with her. Why didn't she have a dog?

"Hey, Luna," said a male voice that triggered a familiar surge of heat and nerves.

Luna turned around and saw Griffin Mann. His hair was wet. He smelled like soap. A few more lines were etched deeper into his forehead, but he was mostly the same. He leaned forward and hugged her. His sweater felt even softer than the dog. She had to restrain herself from petting it.

"When did you get here?" Luna asked.

"Just a few minutes ago. Sorry I'm late."

"Where are you staying?"

"My boss has a weekend home in Hyde Park. It's just twenty minutes south. We come up here a lot. It's very dog friendly," Griff said.

"Wow. I didn't know you were coming," Luna said.

"Is that okay?"

"Of course," said Luna. "You should be here. It's been ages."

"Yeah," said Griff.

It was like seeing a ghost. She felt prickly and numb and vaguely dizzy. She hadn't seen Griff in fourteen years. Luna stared into the distance while she performed the mental calculations to confirm that it had been that long. To Griff, it looked as if all she wanted was to get away from him.

"It's good to see you," Luna said. Eventually.

"Is it?" Griff asked.

"Yes," Luna said, finally looking him in the eye.

They were both transported briefly to another time, a better one. Then a worse time. Luna's throat felt dry. She was almost too parched to speak. She was afraid that if she went inside, Griff would disappear. Then Casey returned from the kitchen with a pitcher of water and glasses.

"Thank god," Luna said.

Casey placed the tray on top of a table. She glanced over at the man Luna had been talking to. "Griff!"

"Casey, wow. Hi."

"Shit. I haven't seen you since . . . I don't know," Casey said.

"It's been a while," Griff said, not wanting to summon the memory of his father's funeral.

Griff and Casey hugged. As Luna guzzled a glass of water, Griff saw the woman as she was fifteen years ago, chugging beer the exact same way.

Casey leaned over and whispered in Luna's ear, "Owen needs to talk to you."

"I'll be right back. Don't go anywhere," Luna said, mostly to Griff.

Luna spotted Owen near the front door. He beckoned Luna toward the garage. The two had a cramped meeting between two parked cars and a wall of dusty boxes.

"Listen," Owen said. "Amy, my Amy, drove Leo to my house—I just saw him get out of her car. What is he doing?"

"I don't know," Luna said.

"Does he know her?" Owen said. "Or is he fucking with me?"

"Owen, relax. I'll deal with him," Luna said.

Luna found Leo at the bar, fixing a drink.

"Luna, my dear, what are you drinking?" Leo said.

"Nothing at the moment," Luna said. "How'd you get here?"

"The bar? I took a long stroll from the couch."

"No," Luna said. "How'd you get to this house?"

"By car. How else?" Leo said.

"Did someone drive you?"

"Oh yes. I finally hired an assistant. Since I knew I'd be drinking, I thought I'd avail myself of her services."

"What's her name?"

"Amy Johnson," Leo said. "You reviewed her application. Don't you remember?"

Now that he mentioned it, she did. Luna hadn't, however, considered the possibility that the two Amys were one and the same.

"You wouldn't even interview her last week. What changed?"

"I reconsidered," Leo said.

Luna wasn't buying it. She knew Leo hired Amy because of her connection to Owen. Luna would have asked Leo how he found out, if they weren't at a wake. Luna roamed the house, searching for Owen. She passed by Maya, who was refreshing the ice bucket.

"Owen's upstairs," Maya said. "You were looking for him, right?"

"Yes, thank you," Luna said.

Luna found Owen lying on top of his bed, resting his eyes and hiding out.

"I talked to Leo," Luna said.

"What did he say?"

"He hired her as his assistant. She was one of the applicants I pulled for him to interview a few weeks ago. I'm sorry."

"And it's just a coincidence that he hired her?"

"I'm too drunk to think about it. Come back down and talk to your guests. It's weird if you don't. We can discuss the Leo problem tomorrow."

Luna left Owen alone to regroup. She descended the stairs and wended her way through the balmy living room, returning to the brisk air outside. The golden retriever jumped up on Luna as she closed the sliding door behind her. She couldn't remember the last time anyone was that happy to see her.

"Down, Sam," Griff said.

Casey smirked and repeated the name. "Sam? Your dog's name is Sam?" Casey made eye contact with Luna.

"Yeah, why?" said Griff.

"That's Luna's husband's name," Casey said.

Luna was petting the energetic retriever. She thought about Wally, a mutt she had as a child. Wally always seemed to feel exactly what she felt. Griff's dog was wonderfully oblivious.

"That was his name when I got him," Griff said. "I swear."

"I believe you," Luna said. "Did you even know I was married?"

"Yes. Congratulations, by the way."

"Thanks," Luna said.

"Is he here? I'd like to meet him."

"He's not here. Had to visit his mother—"

"Speaking of mothers, how's yours?" Griff asked.

"The same," Luna said.

Griff started to laugh. "Still remains the single weirdest day of my life."

Griff was recalling a day nearly fifteen years earlier. It was the kind of memory that you couldn't shake, but, like any memory, you couldn't trust it either. It was so vivid and insane. Luna, present at the same moment in time, would see it from an entirely different vantage point. Still, *insane* was a fair descriptor.

"I'm sorry. Again," Luna said.

"Come on, don't apologize. One of the best days too. Well, the next day," Griff said.

Back in the house, the guests were slowly dispersing. Owen spotted Leo fading out on the couch. He wanted him gone. He stepped outside to track down Luna. She and his brother were doubled over laughing like no time had passed. How could it be that easy? he wondered. How could Luna look so damn happy at Irene's wake? Owen walked over to them. The smiles and laughter immediately ceased.

"Sorry to interrupt," Owen said. "What should I do about Leo? I don't want him sleeping here."

"Where's he's staying?" Griff asked. "I can give him a ride."

"No," Luna said quickly, aggressively. "We wouldn't do that to you. We'll call him a cab."

Griff noted Luna's use of first-person plural. They were still *we*. He marveled at the indestructibility of their bond.

"We should probably be going," Griff said. His *we* included a dog.

"No. You're staying. He's staying, right?" Luna said.

Owen forced a smile. "Yeah, dude, you should stay."

By midnight there were only five people left. Casey and Mason stayed because they missed their friends and the inebriated nights of their youth. Luna stayed because Griff was there and she wanted just ten minutes alone with him. Griff wanted the same thing. And Owen forced himself to stay awake to make sure they didn't take another moment to revisit the past.

March 2004

In all likelihood, Scarlet's body would have been found hours earlier if not for a number of errors on the part of both campus authorities and local police. To begin with, there was no established
protocol for communication. When Deerkill PD got the 911 dispatch to search at Black Oak Bluff, they didn't know that Markham
police had received a report of a missing student. And the trooper
who took the call interpreted *base* as the beginning of the Black
Oak Bluff trail, not the bottom of the cliff. The trailhead was at least
a hundred yards from where Scarlet's body lay.

By midnight on Friday, Scarlet's mother knew something wasn't
right. Her daughter always answered her calls and replied to texts.
After a sleepless night and a series of unanswered calls and questions, Mr. and Mrs. Hayes arrived at Deerkill station Saturday afternoon to light a fire under the local PD. It did the trick. The Deerkill
captain called the state police for assistance. A Detective Miles Oslo
with the BCI was assigned to the case. As soon as Oslo arrived in
Deerkill, he dispatched two officers, instructing them to walk the
entire Black Oak trail if necessary.

Scarlet's parents had been at the station a few hours when they
heard the news of their daughter's death. Mrs. Hayes didn't break
down; she didn't crumble or wail or scream. Her eyes watered, but
she spoke evenly, without a crack in her voice.

"I know who did it," she said.

. . .

THE FORENSICS TEAM didn't arrive until after dusk. A tent had been erected to shield the body and evidence from the rain that afternoon.

Scarlet's body lay at the bottom of a twenty-foot cliff. The ME's preliminary cause of death was a subdural hematoma from the fall, though he couldn't rule out other injuries. Detective Oslo, after notifying the parents, had slipped out of the station. The coroner didn't require an official ID at that point, since the deceased had been carrying her school identification card.

Oslo arrived at the base of Black Oak Bluff, spoke to the ME, and ducked under the tent to look at the deceased. Her body was twisted like a rag doll, her right knee bent inward, foot jutting out. She was wearing a gray peacoat over a short black dress with tights. The girl wore high-top Converse, no tread. Her tights were pulled down to just below her knees. She was splattered with mud and blood. Oslo asked the usual questions—cause of death, signs of struggle, sexual assault. Then he nodded at Craig, the campus officer, to walk with him up the path to the overlook. Oslo's Florsheims sank deeper into the boggy ground with each step. Craig followed behind, stopping several times along the way to catch his breath, marveling at Oslo's lung capacity. The trail narrowed as they snaked along it. Oslo stopped at the top of the overlook, where some murky footprints remained. The path was no more than four feet wide. He began snapping photos of the ground and what looked like a rain gutter, about four inches wide, carved in the mud. Next to the gutter was an imposing yet suicidal-looking oak, rooted precariously on the edge of the bluff.

"Any chance she jumped?" Officer Craig asked.

Oslo shook his head and directed the officer's attention to the mud gutter. "Looks like a heel, trying to get purchase."

"So maybe she slipped?" Craig said.

Craig and all the campus police desperately wanted the death not to be a homicide. If an accident was a headache, a suicide was a migraine. And a murder would be more like a brain tumor. Specialists would have to be called in.

"Maybe. Or she was pushed," Oslo said, as he aimed his flashlight down at the craggy rocks below the bluff.

Oslo and Craig made their way down the path as Scarlet's body was bagged. A young man in a coroner's windbreaker jogged up the last few yards to meet them.

The windbreaker guy delivered a baggie that appeared to be filled with mud. "Found a phone about ten yards from the deceased. Battery died. But it could be hers."

OWEN WAS ASLEEP when the police came. It was Sunday, after all. The knocking on the door intruded into his dream and twisted it into a gestapo-style home invasion in which he'd been accused of unspecified crimes. Later, Owen would remember only a fragment from the dream, a feeling of bottomless guilt, a sense that his conscience was truly unclean. He'd gone to sleep wearing earplugs—there had been an impromptu hallway party the night before. The knocking sound was muted just enough that Owen didn't wake up until the police were inside his room. His RA had given the key to the cops.

"Owen Mann?" said a large man in uniform.

As he came to, Owen noticed that the man in his room had a gun. There was another, older guy in a uniform standing behind him. It was like his gestapo dream had taken a pedestrian tangent.

"What's up?" Owen said.

He was trying to keep himself calm. To an outsider, he looked remarkably, ridiculously calm.

"I need you to come with me," said the guy with the gun.

"Where?"

"Deerkill station."

"Train station?"

"Nope. Police."

"Why?"

"Your girlfriend was found dead last night," said the older cop. Students began to spill into the hallway. *What happened? Scarlet's dead. Scarlet Hayes? Yes. Oh my god.*

The cops let Owen put on a pair of pants and a sweatshirt. Owen wasn't being arrested, so there were no handcuffs and no perp walk, but the way people looked at him as he followed the two men with guns out of the dorm, there might as well have been.

"Is Scarlet really dead?" Owen asked on the drive to the station.

"Yes," said the cop behind the wheel.

The news of Scarlet's death evoked some feeling in Owen, but there were too many other emotions, all vying for attention, canceling one another out. What remained was an oppressive depression mixed with caffeine withdrawal.

"What happened?" Owen asked. "How?"

"We thought you might know," said one of the cops.

That's when Owen's nerves took over.

THE NEWS BEGAN to spread across campus as soon as the police knocked on Owen's door. An hour later, Scarlet's death of a likely subdural hematoma had become a slit throat; the suspicious death was now a sex crime and murder.

Luna remembered feeling it first, the way the news came to her. It wasn't spoken; it was a collage of sounds that evoked a feeling. Like the chatter of an audience right before a movie begins, but instead of quieting when the screen went dark, the volume slowly increased. Shrill voices saying, *Oh my god.* Random swear words. Then there was a loud knock at the door, not a secret knock.

Luna crawled out of bed and opened the door. It was Casey. She had an expression that Luna had never seen before. It was like fear combined with a mild flu.

"Have you heard?" Casey said.

Luna could only imagine that her secret was out. She felt like a hand was squeezing her heart. She thought she might vomit again and swallowed sour saliva. "Heard what?"

"Scarlet is dead."

"'Dead,'" Luna repeated.

The word didn't make sense at first. Luna had prepared for other unfortunate news. Not this. Not death. Not Scarlet.

DETECTIVE OSLO HAD instructed the officers to bring Owen Mann around to the back door of the Deerkill precinct, but they instead marched him right through the front door, past the waiting area, where Scarlet's mother and father had been sitting all night. A woman Owen had never met charged at him, screaming, "What did you do? What did you do?"

Owen felt her hands grasp at him. Then more pulling and pushing. Men were shouting. The woman, screaming. A door opened and Owen was shoved into a long corridor. Another man in uniform led him into a smaller room with walls made of tiles and holes. None of it felt real except the sick twist in his gut.

"Detective Oslo will be with you in a minute," the officer said, shutting the door.

Owen's throat burned, his head throbbed, and his tongue felt like gravel. He knew there were things he should be thinking about, but he was too tired and hungover to form coherent thoughts. All he could do was look around and take in details of the room. As he was observing the patina of handmade grooves that lined the desk, which was bolted to the floor, Detective Miles Oslo entered, knocking on the way in. He was tall and wiry—the opposite of the pudgy slob in a rumpled suit Owen had expected. He had the hollowed-out cheeks of a long-distance runner, his face splattered with freckles. His hair was almost red but sun-bleached closer to blond. Oslo explained that Owen wasn't being arrested, that they were just having a conversation, which he would be recording. He placed a digital recorder on the table and pressed a button.

"Your neck okay?" Detective Oslo asked.

"What?" Owen said.

"Got a little scratch," Oslo said.

"Who was that woman?"

"Scarlet's mother. I apologize. You were supposed to come in the back door."

"How did she know who I was?" Owen asked.

"She'd seen photos."

"From who?"

"Who do you think?"

Owen thought for a moment that he might vomit. He hadn't fully processed what was happening. The detective asked Owen if he needed anything.

"Like what?" Owen said.

He wasn't sure what he could ask for. Owen had smoked a fair amount of weed the night before.

"Water or coffee?" Oslo said.

Owen wanted both, but he didn't think he could ask for that. "Coffee, please," Owen said.

Detective Oslo stepped out. Owen looked around the room. There were pockmarked panels on the walls. A mirror. Owen's reflection startled him because it didn't look like him. He turned away, thinking that there might be someone on the other side.

To be fair, in the quiet moments when he could truly consider Scarlet's death, Owen felt a deep sadness. However, he was in a police station, in a room that smelled like sour sweat and stale coffee, and he had a basic understanding that a part of his life was over, the good part. It was hard to feel anything other than the panic of his current predicament. He'd had it easy so far. It would never be that easy again. He experienced his first true moment of nostalgia, thinking back just one week.

Owen's phone buzzed in his pocket. It was Luna. He told her where he was. He had more to say. He wanted her to call his brother. But then the tall man came back inside. What was his name? He said it, but Owen couldn't remember.

"I have to go," Owen said to Luna, obediently ending the call.

. . .

DETECTIVE OSLO QUESTIONED the kid for about another hour. Owen explained that he and Scarlet were not together, despite views to the contrary. Oslo thought the kid looked sad but not sad enough.

Based on Scarlet's phone records and the ME's report, she died between eleven P.M. Friday night and two A.M. Saturday morning. Oslo asked Owen to detail his activities from Friday evening into early Saturday morning. Owen was alibied for the first half of that time. Then, Owen claimed, he was in his room, alone. The campus police could check his key card for entry, but that would only prove where his card had been.

"Did Scarlet understand that you were broken up?" Oslo asked.

"We barely spoke this year, so yeah," Owen said.

"Did you fight recently?"

"I was trying to avoid her. So no."

"When was the last time you had sex?"

"Last year. Maybe November," Owen said.

"Long time to hold a torch for someone," Oslo said.

Owen wanted to ask for a lawyer, but the thought of figuring that out was too overwhelming. He'd have to tell his parents and they'd have to find a lawyer and then everyone would come to town. It was a lot of trouble. Owen wasn't sure it was necessary.

"How did she die?" Owen asked.

Oslo had been waiting for him to ask. He'd been interviewing the kid for over an hour. You'd think he'd want to know, unless he already did.

"Can't say," Oslo replied.

"Where was she found?"

"Black Oak Bluff. You familiar with that trail?" Oslo asked.

"Yeah," Owen said.

Oslo noted a slight change in the kid's manner, his pallor taking on a greenish tinge. Owen shifted in his chair.

"So, you've hiked that trail?"

"Sure."

"Did you and Scarlet ever go there together?"

"Once," Owen said.

"When?"

"A month or two ago, I guess," Owen said. "I was trying to get away from her. She hated hiking. I just wanted to be alone. I thought it was the one place I could go where she wouldn't follow. It was freezing that day."

Oslo looked friendly, understanding. But Owen sensed that it was an act. He pondered his empty cup. The coffee was horrible. His bladder was about to burst and yet he still wanted more coffee.

"Can I use the bathroom?"

"Sure," Oslo said. "Down the hall on the right. If you don't mind, leave your phone."

"My phone."

"I can get a warrant, if you'd prefer. But I'm going to need it eventually."

Owen was planning to text his brother from the bathroom. He had come to the conclusion that he needed a lawyer. Probably. Well, he wasn't sure. He had to piss so badly, he couldn't think straight. He dropped the phone on the table and made a beeline for the door.

After Owen used the facilities, he stepped into the empty hallway. He spotted a pay phone and thought about calling Griff, but he didn't have any change on him. He didn't know how long he'd been standing there when the detective opened the door and leaned into the hallway.

"Just a few more questions, Owen."

Owen, defeated, slunk back to the interview room. Oslo had another cup of coffee waiting for Owen. He needed the kid to wake up a bit. He was too sedate, which made him hard to read. Owen took a sip of coffee and winced in pain from the heat.

"Who is Luna?"

"A friend."

"A friend of yours?"

"Yes."

"Not a girlfriend?"

"No."

"Were Scarlet and Luna friends?"

"Yes," Owen said without conviction.

"Were they?"

"They were. Then . . ." Owen said, trailing off. He wasn't sure how to describe what they had become.

"Then what happened?"

"Why are you asking about Luna?" Owen said.

"Because in the last hours of Scarlet's life, she had a single-minded focus on Luna. So, Owen, help me out here," Detective Oslo said. "What the hell was Luna's secret?"

E veryone woke up rough in Luna's house. No one, however, rougher than Mason. Luna found him the next morning stumbling through the kitchen, opening and closing drawers, hunting for something.

"What are you looking for?" Luna asked.

Mason froze, stared at Luna, and gripped the kitchen island for balance. "I forgot," he said.

Casey emerged from the guest bedroom and took her husband's hand, guiding him, like a senile patient, back to the bed.

"Lie down before you vomit," Casey said.

Casey asked Luna for an Alka-Seltzer and dropped the tablets into a large tumbler of water. She delivered the fizzy beverage to her husband's bedside, shut the door, and returned to the kitchen. Luna made a pot of coffee. While they waited for it to brew, they talked about the night before, trying to conjure up memories lost to booze.

"What's the deal with Leo? I remember him from the wedding. But I sensed some strange vibe."

"I'll tell you if you promise to not say anything to anyone."

Casey nodded her acquiescence. "If you only knew the kind of secrets I've kept."

"Owen was sleeping with someone," Luna said.

"And . . ."

"You're not surprised?" Luna said.

"I'm surprised that you're surprised," said Casey. "Now, what's the deal with the old guy?"

"He's been looking for a new assistant. I offered to help."

"Why? You don't like him. No one likes him, come to think of it."

"If I helped, Irene wouldn't have to. That was the logic."

"Why would she have to help?"

"I don't know. She felt obligated. I can't explain," Luna said. "Anyway, each time I set up interviews, he canceled them. Then, this week, out of the blue, he hired Owen's . . . girlfriend."

"You mean mistress," Casey said.

"Yes," Luna said.

"This is a small town. She might have legitimately been the best candidate."

"Maybe," Luna said. She didn't want to get into it right then. "Do you have to leave today?"

"Afraid so. We have meetings all next week."

Luna poured two cups of coffee.

"How was it seeing Griff?" Casey asked.

There was no succinct answer to that question. It was so many things. Mostly, it was disorienting.

"It was—I don't know," Luna said.

A horrible retching sound came from the guest room.

"Think you'll see him again?" Casey said, ignoring her husband's purging.

"Doubt it," Luna said. "Is he going to be okay?"

"That's actually a good sign," said Casey. "He'll be fine in about thirty minutes. Well, not fine. But he won't barf in the car."

OWEN WOKE TO the smell of burnt pancakes. His brother was in the backyard, playing fetch with Sam the dog. As Owen watched Griff through his bedroom window, he felt a sharp ache. Guilt. He threw on his robe and headed downstairs. Vera was plating the brown disks as he entered the kitchen.

"Look, I made breakfast," Vera said.

"Thanks, Mom," Owen said. "Sleep well?"

"You know me," said Vera.

His mother, when drinking—which was most of the time—usually crashed early, woke in the predawn hours, and watched infomercials until daybreak.

Griff and Sam bounded inside from the backyard. The joy of a retriever was at such odds with the mood of the house that it made Owen laugh.

"Thanks for letting us crash here," Griff said.

"Yeah, totally. Thanks for . . . coming."

Vera opened the refrigerator and discovered an open bottle of prosecco. "Anyone want a mimosa?" she asked.

Vera drinking translated to Vera not driving home, among other unpleasant scenarios. Owen gave his brother a pleading gaze and Griff nodded in understanding. Despite all that had gone down between them, they could still fall back into their sibling shorthand.

Owen's mother mixed orange juice and flat prosecco. Griff stole her drink and gave it to Owen.

"Mom, when are you heading back?" Griff asked.

"I was thinking of staying the week. Breakfast is getting cold."

Owen panicked silently. Griff squeezed his shoulder and accepted the plate from his mom.

"I think Owen needs to be alone," Griff said.

Owen had a flashback to when they were kids and Griff would speak on his behalf, always more effectively than Owen ever could on his own.

I think Owen needs a ten-speed. It's time.

Owen could use more painting supplies.

Have you considered letting Owen walk home from school on his own?

Although Owen did recall a few occasions when Griff abused his position.

I think Owen needs a time-out.

Owen seems to be too attached to the television.

It was almost like a hypnotist's directive, the power of Griff's words back then. But things had changed.

"I didn't ask what you thought, Griff," Vera said, practically spitting his name.

Vera served Owen a plate of pancakes and washed the dishes as loudly as possible.

"Actually, Mom, I do need some time to figure things out," Owen said.

"Well, the weather is supposed to take a turn tomorrow. I suppose it would be best to drive while it's still clear," Vera said.

She didn't turn around. No one saw her eyes welling with tears.

As CASEY AND Mason's departure grew imminent, Luna's sadness deepened. She uncapped a beer.

"Morning drinking," Casey said, wheeling a piece of luggage to the door. "I'm so jealous."

"You want one?" Luna said.

"No. Alas, Mason can't drive when he's hungover. Sometimes I wish I hadn't married such a lightweight."

Mason, freshly showered, entered the room, carrying his laptop bag.

"Ready?" Casey said to her husband.

"As good as it's going to get," Mason said.

"I'm sorry to hear that," Luna said.

"Me too," Casey said, pulling Luna in for a hug.

"Ouch," Luna said.

Mason gave Luna one of his half embraces and a slightly damp kiss on the cheek.

"Are you missing a phone?" Mason asked Luna.

"No," Luna said.

"I found one under the bed. It's charging on the nightstand," Mason said.

"Come visit us. Soon, okay?" Casey said.

After her guests departed, Luna walked down the hall to investigate Mason's phone discovery. Her mission was aborted when the doorbell rang. Luna assumed Owen had escaped his mother. She was alarmed to find Griff standing on the threshold, rocking back and forth on his heels with Sam the dog panting by his side.

"Griff," Luna said. "Hi."

"I wanted to see you before I left," Griff said. "Can we come in? Or I can tie him up outside."

"You can both come in."

Griff unleashed his dog, who bounded into the house and began sniffing around. Luna and Griff strolled back to the kitchen.

"Nice house," Griff said.

"I had nothing to do with any of it," Luna said.

"What a weird thing to say," he said.

"Was it?" Luna responded, thinking it over. She always felt a little embarrassed of her wealth by association.

Griff paced around the kitchen island, trailing his fingers along the smooth marble. Two beers sat on the counter, Luna's and the one she'd cracked open for Casey.

"I'm not sure why I came here," Griff said.

"It's nice to see you," Luna said.

"Is it?"

Luna took a slug of beer. "Don't judge me."

"I'm not. Were you expecting someone or just getting the other beer ready?" Griff said.

"I opened it for Casey and then she left. Would you like a beer? This one or another one?"

Griff took a sip of Casey's would-be beer, then remembered that he too had to drive.

"I didn't know if I should come," he said.

"I'm glad you did," Luna said.

Griff nodded, satisfied. Then he walked back to the foyer, with Sam following on his heels. Luna wanted to tell him not to go, but she wasn't clear whether he was pacing or departing. Griff returned to the center of the house, reappearing in the kitchen. He had another question, or perhaps a statement, that he was on the precipice of speaking. But then, to Luna's great disappointment, he paced back toward the front door.

"I can't tell whether you're leaving or not," Luna said.

"Sorry. It's been a long time. I'm nervous."

"Me too," Luna said.

"There's something I need to ask you."

"Go ahead," Luna said.

She felt extraordinarily awake. Excited, really. Although if pressed, she couldn't think of anything good that he might want to ask her.

"Is there any chance he did it?" Griff said.

Luna, heart deflated, considered the question. She knew that Griff wasn't asking lightly.

Griff expected Luna to have a flash response: *No, no. Of course not.* When she paused, he wondered when she'd begun to doubt Owen—the first time or only recently.

"You think it's possible?" he said.

Luna snapped back to the present. "No, Griff. It's not possible," she said.

Irene, March 2005

Irene's timing was terrible, but it could have been worse. She could have done it the day of, while her mother was having her hair done, getting sewn into her lace gown. Irene had been debating what to do, whether she should say anything at all. She decided that if she didn't, she'd always regret it.

Chantal Boucher wanted a simple, relaxing night alone with her daughter. The next day would be long, chaotic, and, Chantal hoped, perfect. She wanted to reserve all her energy for her wedding day. Her third, and hopefully final, wedding. Irene and her mother were booked in a two-bedroom Gatehouse suite at the Stafford Hotel. It was Irene who'd suggested room service. It would be easier that way.

Irene devoured an entire plate of chips. Then she dug into a steak. Chantal tracked her daughter's consumption of everything.

"I was like that at your age," Chantal said. "Enjoy it while it lasts. Because it won't last. I swear I gained five pounds every year after age thirty."

They'd had that very conversation too many times to count. Irene was so tired of the way her mother, and even strangers, commented on her body as if it were their own. She was the object of envy and doubt. She was the kind of skinny that made many people question whether her food was staying down.

Irene followed up her steak with Veuve Clicquot. One flute down, then another. Chantal told Irene to pace herself and reminded her daughter of the nine-thirty A.M. appointment at the salon. Blue hair was forbidden at Chantal's wedding.

"I don't care what color you choose," Chantal said, "so long as it's one that humans had before the invention of hair dye. Do we understand each other?"

"I understand," Irene said.

Under different circumstances, Irene might have pushed back. But her hair was the least of her concerns.

"Mom, you don't have to marry him."

Chantal's lips pursed, her gaze sharpened. God, Irene hated the way her mother's face scrunched when she was angry. Chantal's darker emotions had a contagious effect on her daughter, emboldening Irene.

"Don't marry Leo. He's a creep. I know at least three girls from college that he slept with," Irene said.

"Oh god," Irene's mother said.

She wasn't shocked by Irene's statement but rather disappointed. In her daughter, not her betrothed.

"You can't trust him," Irene said.

Chantal crossed the room and picked up the hotel phone. She called guest services and asked to have the room-service table taken away. She told them not to knock. That she'd be asleep. Irene understood that Chantal was done with her. The conversation was over.

Irene threw on her jacket and slipped on her boots. "I'm going out."

"Why don't you stay at the apartment tonight? Then you won't have to worry about waking me," Chantal said.

"Sure," Irene said.

"I'll see you tomorrow," Chantal said.

"Are you sure you want me to be there?" Irene said.

"At my wedding? Yes."

"Why?"

"Because you're my daughter. What would people say if you weren't there?"

. . .

AFTER DROPPING HER luggage at the apartment, Irene went to the Three Legs. Tessa served Irene her usual gin and tonic while chatting with a boy or man Irene hadn't seen before. He was young and lean, wearing a plaid blazer and a striped tie. His almost-black hair, chin-length, was combed back and tucked behind his ears. His outfit, Irene thought, looked charmingly ridiculous. He was handsome, in a young, vaguely effeminate way. He couldn't have grown a beard if his life depended on it.

Tessa delivered a beer to the young man and said, "Hope it's cold enough for you."

"What?" the guy said.

"We don't get many Yanks in here," Tessa said.

"Not a Yank. Canadian," he said. "I'm from Halifax."

Tessa nodded and smiled. She served a drink to the blue-haired girl to his right.

"Owen from Halifax," Tessa said, "meet . . . uh—wait, remind me."

Tessa wasn't sure who Irene wanted to be that day.

"Phoebe from Sheffield," Irene said.

"Right," Tessa said with a subtle wink. "Phoebe."

"Hi, Owen," Irene said.

"Hi, Phoebe from Sheffield," Owen said. "I like your hair."

"Thank you," Irene said. "I like the way your jacket and tie are begging for attention."

"When you're done with that drink, can I buy you another?" Owen asked.

Irene finished her drink in one take. "Why not?"

They ordered another round.

"I've never been to Halifax," Irene said.

"Glad to hear it," Owen said.

October 13, 2019

G riff wished he hadn't asked the question. If Luna thought Owen was a killer, she wouldn't still be friends with him. He wondered if she'd tell Owen about their conversation.

"I shouldn't have asked. I'm sorry," Griff said.

"That's okay," Luna said.

A phone rang in another room.

"Is that you?" Luna asked.

"No," Griff said.

The ringing stopped. Then started again a moment later.

"One second," Luna said, retreating into the guest room. A cheap TracFone sat on the nightstand, a local number lit up on its screen. Luna pressed the CALL button and put the phone to her ear.

"Hello?" she said.

"Well, hello," said a male voice on the line. "Who is this?"

"You called me," Luna said.

"I did, didn't I? This is Detective Noah Goldman. Is that you, Luna?"

Griff stood by the door to the guest room and watched Luna make a plan to meet with the caller. Afterward, she stared at the phone for a remarkably long time, as if phones were new to her. To be fair, the phone didn't look like the kind people used anymore. It was clearly intended only to make calls. Griff asked Luna if she was all right. Luna nodded, then shook her head.

THE ACCOMPLICE / 173

"I have to go to the police station," Luna said.

"Now?"

"Yes," Luna said, searching for her shoes.

"What just happened?" Griff said.

Luna didn't answer. She was wondering if she could have another beer before she left. She finished Casey's beer and shrugged on her jacket. Then she opened a few kitchen drawers, looking for something. She grabbed two Ziploc bags and returned to the guest room. She emerged a minute later.

Griff didn't say anything until Luna took the key fob for the Audi from a row of hooks in the kitchen.

"What's happening here?" Griff said.

"That was the police. I need to see them."

"You're driving to the police station? You just downed two beers," Griff said.

"I think I'm sober," Luna said, not sounding sober at all.

"You want to chance it?" Griff asked.

Luna didn't care about anything at that moment. She couldn't muster enough energy to feel stunned, angry, or even mildly depressed. She had to wonder, again, if this was her fate. Whether it was punishment or just bad luck.

Griff also experienced a sense of history repeating itself. Once again, he was playing the adult, though all the children should have grown up by now. He blocked the door and extended his palm.

"Give me the keys. I'll drive," he said.

On the way to the station, Griff didn't ask Luna what had happened, why the police needed to see her in that precise moment. They hadn't spoken in fourteen years. He wasn't comfortable asking anything about her life, though he could have killed an entire day with his questions.

Griff parked in the station lot and suggested that he come in with her. But Luna told him to go, to spend time with Owen. And to get his dog out of her house before her husband came home.

"Okay, but don't—you know," Griff said.

"Don't confess to a crime I didn't commit?" Luna said.

"For starters," Griff said. "Just . . . speak as little as possible. Ask for an attorney if at any point they seem focused on you."

"This isn't my first rodeo," Luna said.

"Don't say that in there," Griff said.

Luna took a deep breath. When she exhaled, Griff noted a distinct yeasty fragrance in the air. He spotted a pack of mints in the cup holder and placed it in Luna's palm.

"Take these. All of them," he said.

TWENTY MINUTES LATER, Noah stepped out of the interview room and delivered the phone and a toothbrush to Margot.

"Wow," Margot said. "She just brought in her husband's toothbrush of her own accord?"

"She's being cooperative," Noah said. "I'm not getting the snitching vibe from her."

"Okay," Margot said skeptically. "What's the over-under on their divorce?"

When the mystery number was answered, Burns and Goldman thought that was a win. Luna bringing in her husband's DNA, that was too easy. Burns wasn't quite as excited about the new development as Goldman was.

When Noah returned to the interview room, he found Luna resting her head on the table, her arm shielding her eyes. She didn't lift her head when he entered. She didn't move. He thought there was a chance she was asleep. Burns once told him that innocent people don't fall asleep when being interrogated about murder. He wasn't sure if it applied in this situation, since Luna was low on the list of possible shooters.

Luna was not, in fact, asleep. The fluorescent lights were making her eyes blurry. She felt the familiar knock on the inside of her temple. The feeling of not being fully present. She had taken her meds and hadn't had a seizure in years. But she wanted to do whatever she could to avoid that possibility.

"Ms. Grey," Goldman said, "are you awake?"

"Of course," Luna said, keeping her head down. "Would it be weird if I asked you to turn off the lights?"

"Migraines?" he asked, flicking off the three light switches.

"Seizures. Rarely, these days," Luna said, lifting her head and adjusting to the welcome darkness. "But there's always a warning."

There was just one small window in the interview room. Outside, the sky was dull and overcast. The dim light made the room feel oddly intimate.

"Better?" Goldman asked.

"Thank you," Luna said.

Goldman took his seat. "We appreciate you bringing in the . . . uh—" Goldman began.

"Even if Sam's DNA matches what you found on the body, it doesn't mean he killed her," Luna said.

"No. It doesn't. But it helps. We could at least exclude your husband," Detective Goldman said.

"Right," Luna said.

"Where was your husband the morning of Monday, October 7?"

"He left for work before I woke up," Luna said.

"Around what time was that?"

"He usually wakes up before six A.M."

"Did he wake you?"

Luna paused before answering. "We don't sleep in the same room."

"Because of his early mornings?"

"That might be one of the reasons."

"Was your marriage in trouble?" Goldman asked.

"Clearly it was," Luna said. "But I'm not sure I would have said so before I answered that phone."

"So, how would you have described your marriage yesterday morning?" Goldman asked.

"I don't know," Luna said.

She felt an oppressive exhaustion wash over her.

"Did you fight?"

"Not often," Luna said.

"So, you didn't sleep in the same bed and you didn't fight," Goldman said.

He was getting a decent picture of the union.

"It sounds passionless, I know," Luna said.

Luna had to admit that their sex life had waned. Was that before or after Sam started up with Irene? She didn't know when they started up, so she couldn't say. The interview felt more like a therapy session than an interrogation.

"Was it?" he asked.

Luna wasn't going to offer intimate details of her marriage. To a psychiatrist she might have admitted that she and Sam were like friends with benefits who resided under the same roof. Weird, but efficient.

"It was always easy with Sam. I never had to explain myself. I think we had similar dispositions. I couldn't be around another person all the time. Neither could he. At least that's what I believed. Maybe he was lonelier than I thought. Whatever happened with Irene has nothing to do with her death."

"You sure about that?" Goldman asked.

"What's his motive?" Luna asked. "I don't see one."

"Maybe the relationship with Irene was the only good thing he had. Maybe she wanted to end it and he couldn't bear the thought of that."

"That's another man you're talking about."

"How do you mean?"

"You're describing a man who's out of control."

"Sam likes to be in control?" Goldman said.

Luna realized that her description of Sam was not helping his case. "Look, I gave you Sam's toothbrush because I knew you'd want his DNA. And I knew you'd have to look at him for this. Still, I don't think Sam did it."

Again, her conviction weakened the more she insisted upon it.

"Noted," Goldman said.

"Does this mean you're done looking at Owen?"

Goldman leaned back in his chair and looked Luna in the eye. People don't look you in the eye all that often. It can unsettle someone who doesn't want to be seen. But this time it didn't have the desired effect. Goldman felt like she was seeing him instead. Maybe it was the dim lighting. It had that strangely charged feeling of a first date. He immediately looked away and asked the first question that came to mind.

"Would you rather our prime suspect be your husband or your best friend?"

"I'd rather it be neither," Luna said.

"But if you had to choose—"

"Come on, Detective."

Goldman raised his hands, conceding the unfairness of the challenge. "Indulge my curiosity for a moment," Goldman said.

Luna nodded, bracing herself for the usual questions.

"Given Owen's history, have you considered the possibility?"

"It's not a pattern, Detective. A lousy coincidence, maybe."

"Maybe," Goldman said. "But if you were me, wouldn't you look twice?"

"Maybe," Luna said. "If you're looking at patterns, you should know something."

WHEN SAM UNLOCKED his front door, he fully expected to find his wife at home. The visit to his mother in Philadelphia was really just a brief reprieve from Irene's death and his domestic life. He hadn't had time to think about Irene or allow himself to feel something.

Sam announced his arrival. There was no answer, but he had a powerful sense of not being alone. He heard labored breaths first. Then he saw the dog. It was just sitting on his couch, breathing. It frightened Sam. He stepped back. The dog didn't move. Sam called Luna's name, but she didn't answer. Sam was not a dog person. He didn't know what to do. He stood in his living room, staring at the animal for about a minute or so. He'd remember the moment as being much longer.

At some point, he realized that the dog wasn't going to attack. He walked in slow motion over to the refrigerator and poured a strong Bloody Mary. Sam knew that it was only a matter of time before the police found out about him and Irene.

Sam heard someone fumbling with the lock. He assumed it was Luna. He guzzled his liquid courage, searching for the right words. She was really having some trouble with that key. He assumed she was drunk. He checked the time. It was just past two. It was early for Luna to be stumblingly drunk. The dog jumped off the couch and ran down the hall.

Then Sam heard a man's voice call his name.

"Owen?" Sam said, because what other man would be calling his name?

Sam peered into the hallway and spotted a strange man kneeling in his foyer patting the strange dog.

"Who the fuck are you?" Sam said.

Griff startled and rolled onto his backside. Sam the dog wagged his tail, thinking that Griff wanted to play. He jumped on top of his owner and licked Griff's face.

"Shit. Sorry. I thought the house was empty," Griff said.

"Doesn't answer my question," Sam said.

Griff was surprised that Luna had married a man like that. Granted, their first introduction wasn't under the best of circumstances, but Griff's first read was that he was a hard motherfucker.

Recovering from his surprise and quickly getting to his feet, Griff said, "So sorry. I drove Luna to the police station, and she told me to leave the keys in the house."

"Again. Who are you?"

"Right. I'm Griff, Owen's brother. Here for the . . . wake?"

Griff read Sam's expression. He sensed something, an internal calculation.

"*You're* Griff," Sam said.

"Yep," Griff said. "Would you like to see some ID?"

"No," said Sam, who wasn't just looking at Griff, he was studying him.

Griff dropped the car keys on the kitchen island and started to back away, like you would with a wild animal. "Sam, right?" said Griff.

Sam nodded. "Yeah."

"Nice to meet you," Griff said. "Again, I'm really sorry."

"Huh," said Sam. "It's good to finally put a face to the name."

It seemed odd in light of Griff and Owen's relationship and Griff and Luna's non-relationship that Luna's husband would have heard much, or anything, about him. But Griff wanted to leave, so he didn't ask for clarification.

"Well, thanks," Griff said.

"For what?" Sam said.

Griff shoved his hands in his pockets and shook his head, exhausted. "I don't know," he said, sounding defeated.

"I'm being weird, aren't I?" Sam said.

Luna had told him on one of their first dates that he had an extremely cold conversational style. She'd likened him to HAL from *2001*. Sam had been amused by the comparison, or by Luna's bluntness. He would be less amused now if he knew how often Luna and Owen mocked his affectless tone.

"A little," Griff answered. "No judgment. A strange man just broke into your home."

Sam nodded, agreeing. "She told me about you once," said Sam.

"Good things?" Griff said.

Sam's eyes squinted in confusion, then amusement. "You broke her fucking heart, man. No. Not *that* good."

Griff had backed all the way to the front door. His phone rang in his pocket, visibly startling him. "I gotta go," Griff said.

"Don't forget the dog," Sam said.

SAM WAS FAIRLY drunk when Luna returned from her third police interview. He showed no obvious signs of inebriation. A layman would never know. But Luna recognized the way his face relaxed, the jaw muscle resting, the molars taking a break from their constant grind.

"Hey. You're back," Luna said to her husband.

Luna was unsettled to find Sam home. Even though logic told her that he didn't kill Irene, his freshly won person-of-interest status, and her participation in it, made their reunion profoundly uncomfortable. Luna had made the bland statement because she had to fill the air, but she knew it was the kind of thing that got under his skin. Sam didn't believe in using words to state the obvious, or fill up silence, or attempt to ease discomfort.

"Your powers of observation are impeccable," Sam said.

Luna decided to give Sam the efficient conversation he craved. "Mason found your phone. Your secret phone, I mean."

Sam remained silent as he considered every possible response.

"Detective Goldman was trying to figure out whose number it was. He called. I answered."

"You gave him the phone, I take it," Sam said.

"Yes. I also gave him your toothbrush so they could test your DNA."

"They could have gotten that from the phone," Sam said.

"Good to know," said Luna. "So, you and Irene?"

"Yeah. I'm sorry, Luna."

Grief over Irene's death undercut emotions that would otherwise have been in the conversation. Luna and Sam both felt as if they were going through the motions of talking about infidelity. Still, they went through them.

Luna opened the refrigerator and retrieved another beer. "For how long?" Luna asked, uncapping the pilsner.

"About a year."

Sam paced around the couch, noting a few dog hairs trapped on a throw rug. Neither Sam nor Luna made eye contact during their entire conversation. As usual, they spoke concisely, using as few words as possible.

"Why?" she asked.

"Because she understood."

"Understood what?" Luna asked.

"How fucking lonely it is being married to you," Sam said.

The statement stung, but Luna had to concede that it was reasonable.

"I should pack," Luna said.

"Where will you go?"

"Not sure."

Sam was about to mention his brief meeting with the infamous Griff, but then the landline rang.

"Answer that. It's for you," Luna said.

Her tone was cold. Sam wondered if she was imitating him, if that was how he sounded to her. It was creepy, he thought. Sam answered the call. He could feel his blood pressure rise as his heart thumped, trying to sustain the oxygen level that his brain required.

"Hello," he said.

"Dr. Burroughs, this is Detective Margot Burns. We should talk."

March 2004

After Luna spoke to Owen, she phoned Griff at the Berkshires house. She and Griff had exchanged a few emails over the past few months. He'd mentioned staying at the Berkshires house over spring break. Griff immediately got in the car and drove to Deerkill. He arrived at the police station an hour after his brother's interview began and just a few minutes before it would come to its natural end. When Griffin Mann identified himself to the desk clerk, Mrs. Hayes went on a tear. Police had to intervene again. An officer ushered Griff down the hallway, where he was reunited with Owen. At which time, Detective Oslo patted Owen on the back and thanked him for his cooperation.

"Use the back exit," Oslo said. "We'll be in touch."

Owen caught his brother's disapproving gaze as they passed under the emergency exit sign.

"Dude, what part of asking for an attorney do you not understand?" Griff said.

"Chill," said Owen. "It was fine. He just asked a few questions. How'd you know to come?"

"Luna called right after she spoke to you," Griff said. "What did you tell him?"

"I don't know," Owen said. Once he stepped out of the interview room, he didn't want to think about it anymore.

Luna pulled up in Owen's car. Owen climbed into the back seat on the driver's side.

"Why don't you move up front, Owen? I have my car," Griff said. "I've got a room at the Motel 6. I'll check in and meet you back on campus later."

"I'm good here," Owen said.

He'd had enough of Luna that day. All he wanted was a quiet ride back to campus.

"Why don't you stay with Owen?" Luna asked Griff.

Motels, to her young, broke mind, were an expense reserved for family road trips and illegal assignations.

"Because Owen needs his space," Griff said, walking away.

"Do you want to drive?" Luna asked Owen, trying to catch his eye in the rearview mirror.

"No," Owen said.

Owen was silent for most of the ride. Luna took the main drag back to campus. Owen wished he had taken the wheel, because Luna was so goddamn slow. He rested his head against the cold window and closed his eyes. He was too angry to sleep. Luna wasn't sure what had transpired during the interview, but she couldn't help but feel as if Owen was paying for her crimes.

"There's something I need to tell you," Luna said.

Owen gave up on sleep, opened his eyes, and caught Luna's partial reflection in the rearview mirror. "Go ahead," he said. "I'm listening."

Luna confessed to Owen as she drove him back to campus. She told him who she was and detailed her text conversation with Scarlet. In the front seat, like a chauffeur, she never saw his reaction. Or the absence of a reaction.

Luna dropped off Owen at the quad, offering to park the car in the lot, a half mile away.

"Write down the parking space" was all he said when he got out of the car.

Luna parked and made a quick call from the pay phone outside the lot. She left a message at Griff's motel. Then she caught the bus back into town.

. . .

DETECTIVE OSLO PLAYED dumb. *Ms. Grey, is it? How can I help you? Yes, your name has come up in the investigation. I can't say much more. Should I know who you are? Why don't you tell me?*

Oslo had looked her up as soon as he saw her name in the text messages on the victim's phone. He contacted the president of Markham U. Apparently, Luna's birth name was on record because she'd had to explain her two years of homeschooling. But when the girl showed up alone at the station, Oslo wanted to hear the story straight from the source. He took Luna into an interview room and offered her a cup of coffee.

It had been seven years since Luna had set foot inside a police station. She was unprepared for the feelings it would evoke. At first it was mostly nausea, accompanied by a cold sweat. She understood that she was having a panic attack, but that awareness didn't help. She knew that the detective would look at her state and think, *Guilt, guilt, guilt.*

Oslo fetched a cup of water for the pallid girl.

"What can I do for you, Ms. Grey?" Detective Oslo asked.

"Were you the detective who was talking to Owen?"

"I was."

"Did you ask him about the texts on his phone?"

"Can you be more specific?" Oslo asked.

"Scarlet sent texts to Owen before she died," Luna said.

"Where did you get that information?"

Luna nodded and gulped water. She wondered if the detective had given her the cup to get her DNA. It didn't matter. She was thirsty. She could have drunk another gallon of water and still felt unquenched.

"I had Owen's phone. Did he tell you that?"

Oslo preferred to guide the conversation. He rarely answered questions that witnesses or persons of interest asked him. "Why don't you tell me what happened Friday night. Start at the beginning."

Luna told Oslo the whole story, how she had Owen's phone the entire night and was texting Scarlet as Owen. The detective eventually asked the question Owen could not seem to answer.

"So, Luna, what is your secret?"

Luna was ready to come clean. "My brother, my half brother, is John Allen Brown. You know, the guy who killed two girls in Colorado. Are you familiar with that case?"

He was.

"Would you mind refreshing my memory?" Oslo asked.

"When John was eighteen, he had a girlfriend. Her name was Susan James. She was seventeen. She disappeared on April 1, 1995. Her body was found in a shallow grave in a nature preserve near Denver. The police thought he did it, but the evidence was circumstantial. A few witnesses thought they saw a guy who matched his description nearby. My mother and father were out of town that weekend. A friend had let them use their condo in Aspen. John was watching me. He did that a lot back then. After John was arrested, he told the police that I was with him. The police brought me in and questioned me. I gave John an alibi for the whole weekend. They didn't believe me. They charged John with murder. There was a trial. I testified on closed-circuit TV. I told everyone that John didn't do it. That he couldn't have killed her. He was with me the entire weekend. My parents were out of town, so they didn't know one way or the other.

"I didn't want to believe he was a killer. I didn't want him to go to jail. So I gave him an alibi, even though I didn't remember seeing him that night. John coached me, told me what we did, what food we ate, what movies we watched. I think I started to believe his version. I had seizures sometimes and I wouldn't remember things. I thought that's what might have happened. I wanted to believe him more than anything. His story became my story. You know the rest, right?"

"He was found not guilty," Oslo said. "How long was it until he killed again?"

"Eighteen months. Her name was Lila Wells. She was also seventeen. She'd be twenty-four now if not for me. He thought he was being smart, picking a girl he didn't know. No one could put them together. But they found her body really fast. She was buried not far from Susan. I remember he cleaned his car. They found a movie ticket stub in her jacket pocket, and John worked at Sunset Cinemas in Cherry Creek. They brought him in. While John was talking to the cops, I told my mom that I thought that maybe he did it. I told her that I'd lied the first time—that I couldn't really remember anything. My mom got me a lawyer and they made a deal—I think that's what happened. He was sentenced to life without parole. My dad, who was John's dad, had died about a month after the Susan James trial. That's when my mom and I went back to using her maiden name. The point is, Owen didn't know any of it."

"You sure about that?"

"I didn't tell him until just now," said Luna. "Even if he knew, why would he hurt Scarlet?"

"To stop her from telling everyone. To protect you. Maybe you're protecting him now," Oslo said.

"Look, I was with him earlier that night, with other people around. I can't remember exactly when he showed up. I made everyone leave around eight or nine. I know where Scarlet's body was found. I can't imagine why he would go there or how she would have gotten in touch with him when I had his phone. Also, people kill for a reason, right? Unless they're like my brother and they kill because they enjoy it. I can't think of a logical reason why Owen would kill Scarlet. She was after *him*. He was trying to get away. He didn't go about it the right way, but just to get a girl to stop calling you—have you ever seen someone kill for that?"

"It would be unusual," Oslo said. "You're confident that he had no idea where Scarlet was Friday night?"

Luna wanted to swear on her life that Owen didn't kill Scarlet. She didn't think he did. But she'd learned the difference between what you want to be true and what is true.

"I don't know how he could have," she said.

"What about your brother? Did Owen know about him?"

"I never told him. He would have said something if he knew."

"How do you think Scarlet learned about your history?"

"I don't know, exactly. If you were familiar with the case and thought I might be that Luna, then spent a lot of time online, you might draw that conclusion. It's not easy. It takes time. My name isn't supposed to be out there, but there are a few determined bloggers. I don't know exactly how, but she got there."

"She sure went to a lot of trouble to expose your secrets. How'd you feel about that?" Oslo asked.

"I didn't like it. I didn't like Scarlet. But I didn't kill her. I don't even know if I have an alibi. You should talk to Casey Carr. She saw me later that night and she was sober. Well, she was more sober than I was, so she'd be able to give you a better timeline."

Oslo slid a paper in front of Luna. "Write down her number for me."

Luna gave the detective the number for Casey's dorm room.

"Question for you," Oslo said. "Why didn't you change your whole name? Might've made your life a lot easier."

"Maybe I didn't want it to be too easy," Luna said.

A young woman in uniform opened the door and leaned in. "Luna's lawyer is here," the policewoman said.

Oslo turned to the girl and smiled. "That was fast."

"I don't have a lawyer," Luna said.

Owen's brother walked into the room. Oslo did a double take.

"Mr. Mann, nice to see you again," Oslo said.

"How long have you been interviewing my client?" Griff said.

Griff gave Luna the what-the-fuck-is-wrong-with-you look.

"Not long," Oslo answered. "Isn't this a conflict of interest?"

"Look, I'm just trying to keep two morons from accidentally implicating themselves in a suspicious death that they know nothing about."

"Luna came here of her own accord," Oslo said. "I have just a few more questions."

"You don't have to say anything, Luna," Griff said. "In fact, it would be better if you didn't."

"That's okay," Luna said. "I think I'll stay."

October 13, 2019

Margot took Dr. Burroughs into the interview room while Noah reviewed the call history on Burroughs's secret phone.

Sam Burroughs wasn't what Burns had expected. Not that he was unattractive. He was tall, big, a rough-around-the-edges, traditionally masculine kind of guy. In short, the opposite of Owen. Burns gestured at the camera in the high corner of the room.

"We're recording this interview," she said.

"I assumed as much," he said.

Burns opened her notebook and clicked her pen to attention. "You had to know that your DNA would still be in the victim's body. Why didn't you come to us sooner?"

"You haven't had time to process the toothbrush," Sam said. "How do you know it's a match?"

The detective smiled and nodded. She'd have to be careful with Burroughs. "I have a hunch it's going to match. Am I wrong?"

"No," Sam said.

"You knew we'd find out about you eventually, right?" Burns said.

"Maybe," Sam said.

Burns thought he was avoiding eye contact. In reality, he was trying to make sense of a large brown stain on the wall.

"It would have looked better if you came in on your own."

Sam's focus turned to the detective. His eyes narrowed. He spoke just above a whisper. "I don't give a shit how it looks. I'm still getting used to the fact that she's dead. I was . . . sad."

Now that Sam thought about it, he was gutted. He hadn't had time to feel anything, to think it all through. He would never see Irene again. She wouldn't be there to commiserate. She wouldn't be there to—

"Were you in love with her?" Detective Burns asked.

"No. I don't think so. But we were close, and she meant something to me."

"How long had you and the victim been sleeping together?" Burns asked.

"Don't call her that. Say her name," Sam said.

"When did you and Irene begin sleeping together?"

"A year ago, maybe."

"Did you meet Irene through Luna?"

"No," said Burroughs. "The other way around. Irene used to bring Leo Whitman in for his appointments. I'd seen Irene a lot over the years. Always liked her. Then, one day, Luna drove Whitman to the appointment. I was trying to figure out who she was to Leo, why she was doing this favor for him."

"Did you ever find out?"

"The favor was for Irene."

"Can you elaborate?"

"When Irene's mother died, she left most of her estate to her daughter. There was a small trust for Leo. Chantal made Irene the executor of that so Leo wouldn't tear through the funds. Leo and Irene were not close. I got the feeling she really didn't like him."

"Do you know why?"

"Irene thought Leo married her mother for the money."

"So, Luna starts to bring Leo to his appointments, and that's how you got to know her?"

"I must have asked what she did for a living. She said she worked at Nyteq. I assumed she was using Leo's appointments to get face time with me, so I was expecting a hard sell. Then, nothing. Luna asked a few questions about Leo's care and they left."

"What happened after that?" Burns said.

"I saw Luna at the hospital cafeteria one day. She was chatting with a few doctors. I asked about her. She had quite a reputation," Sam said.

He almost laughed at the memory. Then he remembered where he was.

"How so?"

"Whenever you're around a true salesperson, you know it, right? They're all the same in some way. It takes a certain personality to do that job. Obviously, there are different versions of it. A used-car salesman and a Rolls dealer might comport themselves differently, but, ultimately, their energy is all about the attack. There's a vigilance to them. Imagine if you walked into a car dealership and said that you were looking to buy and the salesperson said, *Are you sure you need a new car? Have you considered buying used?* Or if you want to buy a car and you point to a particular one and the salesperson tells you about all its shortcomings."

"Are you saying that Luna had a rep for being a bad salesperson?"

"Unorthodox, at least," Sam said. "I ran into her a few weeks later. She offered to buy me lunch. I figured she'd at least put in a mention of Ciphyxa. That was a new pain med on the market. Instead, she wanted to talk about medical ethics. An orthopedic surgeon prescribes a lot of pain meds. The ones that work, as you know, are highly addictive. Luna asked if I would ever consider placebo therapy. She said she had friends who were trying to actually get a placebo pill on the market. She sent me links to a number of studies. I was aware of the efficacy. But the idea that a drug rep would even mention placebo therapy was so insane and . . . charming. I asked her out. We started dating."

"How long until you married?" Burns asked.

"A year," Sam said.

"A man in his mid-forties, first marriage. What made you jump in so fast?"

Sam rubbed his tired eyes and took a long, slow breath. "I don't know. Partly because being with her was a novel experience. It wasn't like any other relationship, and that made me think it was right."

"What was so novel about it?"

"She didn't care about the things women usually care about."

Burns focused her gaze at the man and smiled. "What do women care about?" she asked.

Sam often offended people. He could never quite figure out what he was doing wrong. "She didn't care that I had money or that I was a surgeon. Other women, they cared."

"How do you know she didn't care?" Margot asked.

"Not long after we started dating, I got her a bracelet. It had diamonds. I don't know. It was simple. Expensive. She was polite but firmly suggested I not buy her things in the future. I could also tell by the way she lived. I always got the feeling that she was burdened by objects. Buying stuff didn't appeal to her."

"I will refrain from commenting on your narrow view of women and jump to the next question. So, you married her because she was frugal?"

"I married her for many reasons. I loved her. Still do. We never fought about my character. She didn't mind that I needed to be alone, that I liked quiet. She was the same. She didn't ask much of me. Every woman I'd previously met wanted the big house and two children. But Luna didn't give a shit about any of it. And I was tired of dating, I guess."

"No kids?" said the detective. "So, you never wanted children?"

"I don't know. I figured I'd have them eventually. But Luna couldn't. And it seemed easier."

"She couldn't—meaning, you had tried?"

"No. She made sure she couldn't have children," Sam said.

"That's unusual, wouldn't you say?" said Burns.

"I think she thought that—well, you know."

Sam questioned whether he was giving the cops this information as a good citizen or a retaliatory husband.

"She was worried about having a child like her brother?" Burns asked.

Sam had assumed that they'd learned about Luna's past. He was grateful to have that detail confirmed. "She never said it outright, but I'm sure that was the reason," Sam said.

"When did Luna tell you about her brother?"

"Maybe six months in. She'd gotten a letter from the brother of one of Brown's victims. Luna couldn't figure out how the guy found her address. She was quite upset and considered moving. I suggested she move in with me. We got married about six months later."

"Did she get many letters of that nature?"

"No. That's the only one I can think of. Nothing since we've been married. The house and most of the bills are in my name."

"You and Irene. How did it begin?" the detective asked.

"Irene called the house, looking for Owen. He wasn't answering his phone. I called Luna and couldn't reach her. Irene came over. We waited. Started talking and comparing notes. We had a similar sense of being the third wheel in our own marriages. We kept talking and then—it just happened."

Sam looked at the detective and nodded slightly to convey that he was not elaborating any further.

"So much for the seven-year itch," Margot said.

"What?"

"You'd been married to Luna for just over a year at that point, right?"

"And?"

"Didn't take you long, did it?"

"Being both married and lonely is an uncomfortable combination," said Sam.

"Why were you lonely?"

"I'd—I'd never met a woman who asked so little of me. She

never needed to talk. She never burdened me with her problems. The only thing she ever wanted was sex. At first, it seemed perfect."

"Please don't tell me she was also a good cook," said Burns.

"No. Horrible."

"That's a relief. But still, she doesn't sound like any woman—or man, for that matter—I've ever met. People *need*. All of them. There are no exceptions."

"I agree," said Burroughs. "Most of her other needs were met by Owen."

"So, you're saying that the primary relationship in Owen and Luna's lives was not with their spouses but with each other."

Sam nodded. Close enough.

"When was the last time you had sex with Ms. Boucher?" Margot asked.

He lifted his cup of coffee, took a sip, scowled. "The Sunday before," Sam said.

"Where?"

"Motel 6, across the bridge."

"Sunday, what time?"

"Afternoon. Two or three."

"Who paid?"

"I did. Cash."

"Did you always pay?"

"Yes."

"What time did you leave your house Monday morning?"

"Six-thirty, maybe."

"Where'd you go?"

"I drove to Chambliss Medical Center."

"What time did you arrive?"

"It takes about a half hour."

"So you would have arrived at the hospital around seven? And then what?"

"I was in my office for a few hours. Then I had a surgery at eleven."

"Can anyone verify that?"

Sam shrugged. "Before the surgery? I don't know. I was in my office for a while. Then I did rounds. I probably got a cup of coffee. I don't know if there were cameras or witnesses. I'll let you figure that out."

Margot felt a slow ache build at the base of her neck. She rolled her shoulders to loosen up, which only made it worse.

"Can you write down the name of the contact person for your department?" Burns said, sliding paper and pen in front of him.

As Sam scribbled down the name of the contact, he asked, "You figured if you found the DNA, you'd find your killer?"

"That secret phone didn't do you any favors," Burns said. "Why'd you get it?"

"Have you ever sent a text to the wrong person?"

"Yes."

"Even if it's an utterly benign exchange, it's unsettling. You feel naked, exposed. I don't like to make mistakes. It was a simple way to be sure I wouldn't."

"But you didn't send any texts," Burns said.

"Yeah. It was too annoying on that phone."

Burns leaned back in her chair. She felt a nagging sensation of something unfinished. A question at the tip of her tongue. She traveled back through their conversation, trying to pinpoint the snag.

"Anything else, Detective?" Sam said.

"Did you kill Irene Boucher?"

"No. Why would I?"

"Motive is not always ruled by logic. And logic isn't always immediately evident."

"You're wasting your time looking at me," Sam said.

"Then who should I look at?"

"Isn't it always the husband?"

March 2004

———

Before Scarlet died, before Owen was called into a police station for questioning, before he settled for Markham U, and before he met Luna, Owen had a shine to him. Everyone saw it. If you'd asked anyone who knew him when he was young, they'd tell you he was going to be somebody. It was assumed that he'd be a working artist, maybe a famous one. There was no denying his talent. And he was handsome and charismatic. However isolated Owen felt, no one ever saw it. People liked him, wanted to be around him. He had nineteen years to get used to that feeling.

Right after talking to the red-haired detective, Owen returned to his dorm and slept. It was early evening when he finally got out of bed. He didn't notice the shift in his universe as he walked down the hallway to the showers, but it had already happened.

Just as the news of Scarlet's death had been disseminated and transformed, so had Owen's police interview. As far as anyone knew, it was not an interview but an arrest, in handcuffs, no less. If, during the first few weeks after Scarlet's death, you'd asked a student of Markham U what had happened to her, they would have told you that she was murdered by her boyfriend or ex-boyfriend, Owen Mann.

After his shower, Owen headed over to the dining hall. He'd made it halfway across the quad when he noticed the way some students would stop and stare. Once or twice, he'd wave or say hello. The moment he acknowledged their presence, they'd look away. Sleep-deprived, his mental reserves used up from the interview, he couldn't comprehend what was happening. He kept walking until he ran into Amber and Bobbi. He started to walk around them, but Amber stepped to the side, blocking his path. Then he saw the look in their red-rimmed eyes. Amber wore a sneer; Bobbi's hands were balled into fists. Amber got right up in front of him. She was so close he thought she was going to hug him, but she was just eye-fucking him. Still, Owen did not understand.

"What are you doing here, Owen?" Amber said.

"I was going to get some dinner," Owen said.

"Did you hear that?" Amber said.

"Yeah," said Bobbi. "He's getting dinner."

"I guess murderers have to eat too," Amber said.

"Do they?" Bobbi replied.

Owen wised up around that point. *Okay, I see what's happening. They think I killed her. What's the best way to deal? Walk away.*

Owen cut to his left, but Amber blocked his path. They reminded Owen of thugs he'd seen in black-and-white movies. It was utterly ridiculous.

"Where are you going?" Amber said.

"I just told you," Owen said.

Owen scanned the quad, looking for someone he knew, someone who might help him. There was a scattering of students around, but no friendly faces. Everyone watched like it was a show.

Owen turned around. Food wasn't worth this. He'd just go back to his dorm. This time, Bobbi blocked his path.

"I thought you were going to the dining hall?" she said.

"What do you want from me?" Owen said.

"What do we want?" Bobbi said, turning to Amber.

"A confession, for starters," Amber said.

"Get the fuck away from me," Owen said, as he walked back to the dorm.

"Or what?" said Amber, chasing after him. "Are you going to kill me too?"

. . .

AFTER TALKING TO Luna Grey, Oslo took a quick drive across town to the morgue to see the medical examiner.

"I have to wait for the drug panel," Dr. Frank Logan said. "But blood alcohol was point-one-five."

"On a Friday night, that's half the school. How about semen? Evidence of sexual assault?" Oslo asked.

Frank shook his head. "We'll have to wait for lab work, but I don't think so. There was some urine."

"What?"

"Probably hers."

"Takes some time to get DNA, right?" said Detective Oslo.

"If there is DNA," said Logan.

"You think he used a condom?" Oslo asked.

"I'm not sure there was any sexual engagement," Logan said.

A woman in her mid-twenties with the pallor of someone who spent far too much time indoors entered the room. She smiled at the cop and waited for Logan to introduce her. He did not.

"Her tights were pulled down and you're not sure there was any sexual component?" Oslo asked the ME.

Dr. Logan shrugged. He said he wasn't comfortable offering any hypothesis until he had all the evidence. Oslo noticed the pale woman's eyes darting back and forth between him and Logan. She had something on her mind. He wanted to hear it but was fairly certain that she wouldn't undermine Logan with an answer, if he asked directly. Detective Oslo turned to the woman and introduced himself.

"Hi. I'm Detective Miles Oslo."

"Janet Hahn, intern."

"Nice to meet you, Janet," Oslo said.

"Detective, I'll be in touch as soon as I have something," Logan put in.

"Right," Oslo said, and turned to leave.

The detective loitered in the hall. Janet emerged from the morgue a few minutes later.

"Hi, Janet," Oslo said.

"Detective."

"Is there a place to get coffee around here?"

"Not good coffee," Janet said.

"Show me," Oslo said.

He followed Janet through the corridor to the break room. It was empty.

"When I asked Dr. Logan what might have happened, you looked like—I don't know, like you knew something," Oslo said. "This case is all over the place. I don't want to be looking for a killer or a rapist if there isn't one. And, if there is, I need to know now."

Janet looked the detective up and down, the way men sometimes looked at her. She stopped herself and looked away. "Anyone ever tell you you look like Conan O'Brien?"

"Yep. All the time," Oslo said.

"You gonna get some coffee?" Janet asked.

"No," Oslo said. "You going to help me out?"

Janet looked at her shoes, debating.

"This is all off the record," Oslo said. "No one will know."

"I think she pulled down her tights herself," Janet said. "She'd been drinking, probably had to pee. There was some urine on her clothes. Tree bark on her peacoat, like she was leaning against the tree for balance. Granted, it's been raining, some things wash away, but there was no sign of sexual trauma or sexual activity, and there was only dirt under her nails. All her injuries appear to have been caused by the fall. That's what it looks like. Logan thinks so too. He prefers having all the data before he shares information."

"No signs of a struggle?" Oslo said.

"Not with man," Janet said. "Nature, yes."

"Don't ever talk to the police without an attorney present," Griff said to Luna as he drove her back to campus. "You should know better."

"That's why I left a message and told you where I was," Luna said. "If they were trying to stitch me up, I would have been there for hours."

"Stitch you up. Did you learn that in the clink?"

"I don't know. A movie?" Luna said.

"I don't want to have to keep saying this. Do. Not. Speak. To. The. Police. Without. A. Lawyer. Present. Got it?"

"Okay. But I think Detective Oslo believed me," Luna said.

"Doesn't matter. Don't do it."

"Let me break it down for you," Luna said. "What happened when I was a kid was that I lied, not that I didn't have good counsel. I don't lie anymore. At least, not about important things."

Griff made a right turn onto the road that led to the main campus.

"Left up ahead," Luna said. "This is a shortcut to the parking lot."

Griff guided his Prius onto a gravel road.

"I didn't kill her," Luna whispered. "In case you were wondering."

"For fuck's sake, Luna. I know that."

Griff didn't say anything else until he'd found a space in the four-level parking garage. Griff cut the engine. The car was already so quiet, you could barely tell.

"You're going to have to forgive yourself one day," Griff said.

Luna disagreed. She believed that she had to think about it. Every. Single. Day. Luna believed that part of her penance was never letting her guilt subside. And trying, whenever possible, to compensate for her sins. Her past, her secrets, had transferred to Owen like a virus. For the rest of his life he'd have some variation of her condition. She didn't know it that morning, when Owen was taken in. Or later, when she was talking to Detective Oslo. It became unmistakably clear ten minutes later, when she and Griff walked into Owen's dorm.

Murderer, painted red, fresh, and fragrant on his door. There was other graffiti in black, green, and purple Sharpie. *Killer, monster, evil,* and *redrum,* just because.

"Fuck," Griff said, as he scanned the hallway, looking for possible culprits. Luna said nothing, because she instantly and completely understood what was happening.

Luna pounded on Owen's door. "Open up," she said.

Griff was surprised how forceful she sounded.

"Owen," Griff said in a more modulated tone, "please open the door."

"Go away," Owen mumbled from the other side.

Luna kept up her knuckle-bruising racket. Griff tried to speak to Owen through the walls.

"Come on, man, let us in."

Some guy named Joe or Jim who lived next door peered out of his room and shouted, "Hey. Keep it down."

Luna lasered in on the guy. "Who did this?" she said, charging toward Joe or Jim.

"I dunno," the guy said, his ire muted by his fear of Luna and the look of boundless fury in her eyes.

"Luna," Griff said, turning her name into a word of caution.

Everything felt dangerous right then.

"Whatever," Joe/Jim said, shutting the door when Luna got too close.

Griff knocked on Owen's door again. Quietly. Luna started banging on other doors, random doors, shouting, "Open up. Who did this?"

"Luna, stop," Griff said. Then, pleading to the door: "Owen. Let us in."

It wasn't Griff's quiet appeal that prompted Owen to unlock his door. It was the sound of Luna, feral and dangerous. She could make it worse, he thought, and he didn't think he could live through worse.

Luna heard the deadbolt unlatch and stopped yelling. Griff was waiting for the door to open. But Luna knew they wouldn't receive a more overt invitation. She turned the doorknob and entered Owen's room. Griff followed. Neither of them could have imagined what they would find.

Owen's left eye was swollen shut. His nose was red and blue, small drops of blood trickling like a leaky faucet, his lip split and doubled in size. There were other injuries that they would learn about later, at the hospital. Two broken ribs, a mild concussion, and a fractured patella from something metal hitting his knee.

Luna's rage was so powerful, she felt like it could fuel two of her, maybe three. Her eyes darted around the small room. She checked the closet, searched the corners, even ducked down and checked beneath the bed.

Owen, eventually: "What the fuck are you doing?"

"Looking for a weapon," Luna said, as if that was the most obvious of things.

Griff felt like he was the only adult for miles, and the weight of that burden exhausted him. He knew he had to set a tone. "Luna, sit down. No weapons."

Miraculously, Luna listened. She sat in Owen's desk chair. Griff found Owen's suitcase on the top shelf of the closet. He opened it on the bed and told Owen to pack. Owen moved the suitcase to the floor and climbed under the covers.

"No," Owen said. "I'm too tired."

Luna started to pack for him. She figured he'd be gone for a few days, tops. Griff sat down on the edge of the bed and watched Owen pretend to sleep. He could always tell when his brother was faking.

"Who did this, Owen?" Griff said.

Griff repeated the question. Luna was watching, attentively waiting for an answer. Owen's eyes opened at half-mast. He shook his head and said, "Doesn't matter."

Then he looked at Luna for the briefest moment. She nodded slightly. An understanding was reached. Neither ever spoke of it outright, but they were very much on the same page and it all boiled down to this: What happened to Owen was ultimately Luna's fault. Luna accepted blame and would pay off the tab.

There was one problem with this unspoken contract: The two parties had very different ideas about the size of the debt.

October 13, 2019

O wen wanted nothing more than to be alone. Being in the empty house, without distractions, allowed his mind to wander. Naturally, it wandered to Irene. He'd been not thinking about her as much as possible, which he knew wasn't normal. He wasn't ready to think of her being dead. There were still times when he could almost pretend that his wife was just freezing him out and would be home in a day or two.

Owen showered, dressed, drank a flat mimosa, then another. When Amy texted him to see if he could come over to talk, he decided he should get that conversation over with, whatever it was. He texted her that he'd come as soon as he said goodbye to his brother.

The doorbell rang. Owen didn't bother checking the peephole, assuming it was Griff and Sam returning from their walk. Instead, he found Maya, hugging another casserole dish. Owen was glad to take it off her hands, but he did think it was overkill and worried that accepting the plate meant he also had to accept her company.

"You're being watched," Maya said. "There's an unmarked police car a few yards down."

Owen leaned outside to look. There was indeed a plain sedan parked across the street, with a man sitting behind the wheel. Owen realized that Maya had slipped past him and was already inside. Panicked, Owen rushed into the kitchen to find Maya elbows deep in the kitchen sink. There was still quite a mess from the night before.

"You don't have to do that, Maya. Our housekeeper will come later."

"I don't mind," Maya said.

"No, really, please don't," Owen said. "I was actually on my way out."

"Oh. I see," Maya said. "I'm all out of baking dishes. Doesn't your door have an automatic lock?"

"Uh, yeah?"

"You go. Do whatever you have to do. I'll just wash my plates and leave. That okay?"

"Okay," Owen said.

He grabbed his wallet and keys and left. He climbed into his truck in the driveway and was trying to decide where to go when he caught a glimpse of the cop car. How many mimosas had he had? He felt buzzed but not drunk. If there were no cops on his tail, he would have driven in his current condition without a second thought. Instead, he called an Uber and waited in the cab of his truck until the car arrived. He jumped out as soon as the Uber pulled up. The cop had to hustle to stay on his tail.

Owen knew that visiting his mistress after his wife's murder looked bad, really bad. But he wasn't really trying to evade the cops. He didn't want to put on a show. He was doing what he had to do. If the police wanted to watch, that was their choice. Amy lived in a spacious first-floor apartment in an old Victorian on Willowbrook Lane in Red Hook.

"*Two hours,*" Amy said, blocking the door. "I waited two hours at Poets' Walk for you."

That was the place they had agreed to meet on Wednesday, before Detective Goldman dropped by for another interview.

"I already explained," Owen said. "I'm sorry. This was the first chance I had to get away, and I think I'm being followed."

Amy let Owen inside, first peering onto the street to see the unmarked car with her own eyes. It was indeed there.

She softened a bit when she saw the state he was in.

"How have you been?" Amy asked.

Owen shrugged. "How do you think?"

"I'm sorry," Amy said.

"Thanks."

"Want a drink?"

Owen didn't need another drink. However, a drink was the only thing that sounded good to him. He didn't want to be there. Everything in Amy's apartment was a hand-me-down from her grandmother. It was all so oppressively floral. Amy opened a bottle of white wine and poured two generous glasses.

Owen took a seat on the couch. Amy sat right next to him, even though there was ample room on the other end. She was pushing hard for an intimacy that Owen didn't feel. He couldn't remember what they were like before. He could barely remember any conversations. They would drink, fuck, drink, and then he'd leave. But he also felt like he had to manage her, to make sure they were on the same page.

"What was she like?" Amy asked.

"Who?"

"Irene," Amy said. "Who else?"

"She was smart and beautiful and strange and ridiculously blunt," Owen said.

"What happened?"

"I don't understand the question," Owen said.

"When did things go wrong?"

"Your question is based on a faulty premise. Who says there was something wrong with the marriage?"

"If you're having sex with other women, the marriage can hardly be perfect," Amy said.

Owen didn't buy that theory. He loved his wife. He also enjoyed having sex with other women. He knew that he should have been up front about this character flaw—was it a flaw or simply a trait?—when he proposed to Irene or at least mentioned it before they married. But he'd convinced himself that he might be able to make monogamy work. He didn't say any of this to Amy. As far as Owen

was concerned, sharing intimate details about his marriage to another woman was a greater betrayal than adultery.

"I should probably go," Owen said.

"Don't go," Amy said as she kissed his neck and fumbled with
his belt.

Owen was too tired to resist.

WHILE SAM WAS being interrogated at the police station, Luna
packed a bag, loaded her car, and drove to Owen's house. His truck
was in the driveway, so she assumed he was home. She rang the
doorbell. Waited. Then Maya answered, breathless.

"Luna, what are you doing here?" Maya said.

"What are *you* doing here?" Luna said.

"Helping clean up."

"Where's Owen?"

"Don't know. He had to be somewhere. Would you like to come
in?" Maya asked, still blocking the door.

"No," Luna said. "I—I have to be somewhere."

Luna climbed into her car and texted Owen. Five minutes later,
when he didn't respond, she started the engine and drove. Luna
could feel the pressure building inside her. The need for an epic cry.
She didn't want to be sitting outside her house when it came. She
staved off the tears as she drove the ten miles along Route 9 to the
dubiously named Sleep Chalet. Luna asked for a room on the second floor and followed the balcony to room 209. Her key card
flashed red three times before the light turned green, the door unlatched, and she entered the dank, dingy room. But once inside, the
tears wouldn't come. There was one tear, maybe. But the thing that
needed to escape was taking hold inside her, festering.

Luna was about to text Owen yet again, when a text from an
unknown number popped up.

Hi Luna. Griff here. Have you seen Owen?

She promptly texted back.

No. He's not answering. You?

Luna saw the dots of a looming text. Then the phone rang, startling her. Same number. She'd given him her contact information when he drove her to the station. An unstable heady feeling—a young person's love or lust—came over Luna. She hadn't felt that way in years and didn't realize she could anymore.

She answered the call.

"Have you talked to your husband?" Griff asked.

The question felt loaded. How did he know about Sam and Irene?

"Uh . . . why?" Luna said.

"As you know, I left Sam—my dog Sam—sorry, that's obvious. I left him at your house when I drove you to the station, and so your husband came home to a strange dog and then a strange man, since I showed up shortly after that. I didn't know he was inside, so I used your keys to let myself in. I'm really glad he doesn't own a gun," Griff said.

Luna didn't answer. She was thinking about how epically bad Sam's afternoon must have been.

"He doesn't, does he?" Griff said, responding to Luna's silence.

Griff didn't like the idea of anyone with a gun, especially Sam.

"No," Luna answered. "I don't think so."

Luna couldn't say for sure. She was silent again while she tried to wrangle the many threads that occupied her mind.

"Can you tell me what happened now? What was the phone call about?"

Luna couldn't find a reason not to tell him. And she used to tell Griff things, most things.

"Sam was sleeping with Irene," Luna said. "That phone I answered—I'd never seen it before. Sam bought it to call her. Just her. The thing is, I never checked his phone. Ever. There was no reason for an extra layer of security."

"Shit," Griff said. "Does Owen know?"

"Not yet," Luna said.

It sounded like the line went dead. Luna wondered if he'd hung up because it felt like a funhouse-mirror version of history repeating itself. Luna, the common denominator, surrounded by murder suspects.

"Are you there?" she said.

"Yes," he said.

Griff didn't ask what he wanted to ask, but the question hung in the air anyway.

"You want to know if maybe Sam could have killed her," Luna said. "I don't think so. He had no motive other than keeping it a secret, and that wouldn't be much of a motive. Our prenup did not have a morals clause. If he killed her, it would have to be a crime of passion. He'd have to lose control. I can't conceive of what would precipitate that."

The logic was sound enough, but until the killer was identified, Griff didn't like the idea of Luna living under the same roof as the man.

"Either way, you should get out of that house."

"I did. I'm at the Sleep Chalet on Route 9."

"Sounds swanky."

"If the *swank* were onomatopoeic, then it would be," Luna said.

"What are you doing for dinner?" Griff said.

It was an impulse invitation. Her silence filled him with dread. Luna was silent because she wasn't sure what he was asking and she didn't want to embarrass herself.

"I haven't thought that far ahead," said Luna.

"Why don't you come over?"

"Not sure I'm up for a drive that long."

"I'm not in the city, remember? I'm staying in Hyde Park. That's, what, twenty minutes from you?"

Luna really wanted to accept the invitation, but the day had taken so many strange turns. She didn't feel steady enough to be alone with Griff. "I think I need a night in."

"I understand."

"How long are you staying here?"

"A week, maybe," Griff said. "I'd like to see you before I leave."

"Yeah," Luna said. "Me too."

Luna ended the call, paced around the small boxy room, and took long, deep breaths that sounded like a person sighing over and over again. It was something she did occasionally, which annoyed the shit out of Sam. Luna had a bad feeling the first time he'd jokingly commented on it. The second time, she began to worry about the state of their marriage. *You want me to stop breathing?* was her standard response. Luna couldn't bear the sound of Sam's eating. But she never told him not to eat.

Luna was about to text Owen again. She remembered the tracking app, and checked it instead. Owen was in Red Hook. Luna zoomed in on the map and read the street name. Willowbrook Lane. That had to be Amy's place, she thought.

Luna's phone rang. Sam. Luna debated whether to answer, then decided she should get everything over with as soon as possible.

"Done with the cops already?" Luna said.

She knew that was an aggressive way to answer a call. Too aggressive, probably.

"Where are you?" Sam asked.

"Out," Luna said.

"I got that. Are you coming home tonight?"

"No."

Silence. Then: "You can't really think I killed her."

She didn't. Not really. But she had a sense that she was missing something. Luna remembered having the same feeling when Scarlet died.

"I don't know what I think," Luna said. "But I'm not coming back. Call your lawyers. Have them draw up the paperwork. I'll sign whatever."

Sam knew he should be relieved that she was so easy. Another woman might have torched his world. As grateful as he was for a hassle-free divorce, it still infuriated him how little she demanded of him. He'd thought about it before, why she was that way. He always came back to the same thing. Guilt. He'd always interpreted it as guilt by association. But there were days, here and there, when he considered the possibility that he'd gotten her all wrong, that maybe her guilt was rooted in something far less forgivable.

AFTER AMY AND Owen had sex, Owen felt his depression return in deeper form. It was like being buried alive, he thought. He lay in Amy's bed, wanting to leave, but the idea of putting on his pants, locating his socks, and tying his shoes, felt like climbing Everest without oxygen.

Amy polished off her wine. Owen wanted to be alert later, for whatever was coming next, because he knew something was. It would be like that for a while. But the cheap wine seemed to excavate some of the dirt he was buried under. He drained his glass, then poured another. He nodded off. Then he woke up. Amy's naked body was draped over him. She whispered in his ear, "If you did it, you can tell me."

Owen bolted up and recoiled. "What the fuck, Amy?"

He crawled out of bed and searched the room for his clothes. He put on his boxers and jeans and prowled the room, hunting down his T-shirt, which he found under a chair.

"Don't leave," Amy said.

Owen threw on his shirt inside out. He grabbed his jacket and reached for the door.

"Owen. Look at me," Amy said.

Owen opened the door.

"Piece of advice," he said, keeping his back to Amy. "Don't get into bed with men you suspect of murder."

IT WAS DARK when Owen left Amy's place. He saw the unmarked car down the block. He was worried that if he gave her time to dress, Amy would chase after him, so he jogged a few blocks away, to a strip mall with a bar that he'd been to once and vowed never to go to again. Players, it was called. He ordered a bourbon and then patted down his pockets in a panic, thinking he'd lost his wallet. It was in his inside jacket pocket. He never put his wallet there. Had Amy been going through his stuff? He couldn't say for sure what had happened, why he suddenly felt panicked in Amy's company. But he had a sick feeling that Amy was trying to seduce a confession out of him.

Some of the men in the bar gave him the side-eye. They were all white men of a certain age, rough around the edges. Owen knew he didn't belong. Owen had always planned to live in Manhattan, but his career never took off the way he imagined, and he came to prefer the big-fish/small-pond scenario to the other way around. Owen drained the bourbon, tipped well, and strode out of the bar without looking back.

Owen knew he was being watched, followed, but there was an unspoken etiquette he'd always assumed was in play. Not that he'd been tailed by cops before. But he'd seen movies. The subject either goes about his day in oblivion or he aggressively acknowledges the tail by bringing the cops doughnuts and coffee. Owen strolled over to the unmarked car and waved. The cop rolled down the window.

"Hi. I'm, uh—"

"I know," said Trooper Hank Good. "Can I help you, sir?"

"You're following me, right?"

"Just making sure you're safe, sir."

"If you have to go where I go, can you just give me a ride?" Owen said.

Officer Good didn't particularly like the idea of playing chauffeur to a suspected murderer, but there was a certain logic to the request. He shrugged and told Owen to get in. Owen climbed into the back seat, like he was taking an Uber. Although he felt decidedly more like a perp, seeing the cage divider.

"Where to?" said Officer Good.

"The corner of Locust and Main," Owen said.

. . .

Officer Good pulled his car in front of Sam and Luna's residence. Owen thanked the officer for the ride and climbed out of the vehicle. He was sobering up and didn't like how it felt.

Owen rang the doorbell. It took a while for anyone inside to stir, but when he heard the footsteps approach, Owen realized that it was Sam. Owen's eyes darted around as he considered a last-minute escape. Alas, it was too late. The doorbell took his picture. How would he explain the ding and ditch?

"Shit," Sam said, after opening the door, clearly disappointed by the sight of Owen.

This confused Owen. It wasn't like Owen and Sam were buddies, but Sam was friendly most of the time. Owen thought Sam liked him as much as he liked anyone. Maybe the problem was that Sam suspected Owen killed his wife. At least that's what passed through Owen's mind during those first few seconds.

"Hey, man," Owen said.

"Sorry. Hi, Owen."

"Apologies for the interruption," Owen said. "Is Luna here?"

"No, she's not," Sam said.

"Oh, okay," Owen said.

Owen felt like his feet were stuck in cement. Sam was waiting to see some signs of rage or fear or something that made sense.

"It's been a really weird day," Owen said. He seemed drunk and spacey, but nothing else.

"Yeah," Sam said, nodding.

Owen was waiting for Sam to invite him inside. Then he thought that maybe Luna didn't want to see him, that Sam was playing guard dog for her.

"When's the last time you talked to Luna?" Sam said.

"I don't know," Owen said. "Yesterday?"

"Fuck," Sam said.

"Did something happen?"

"Yeah."

"Where is she? Is she back there?" Owen said, then shouted, "Hey, Luna, what's going on?"

"Owen, she's at a motel. She's not here."

Sam didn't want to be the one who told Owen, but he also didn't want Owen to get anyone else's spin on it. "Why don't you come in," Sam said, turning his back on Owen.

Owen followed Sam down the hall. There was a game on. Sam was always watching some sporting event, shouting at the TV. Sam muted the sound and offered Owen a beer.

Sam pointed to the couch and told Owen to relax. Sam was being nicer to him now, and Owen was grateful. Sam perched on the edge of a giant reclining chair. It was a fancy easy-chair kind of thing. Comfortable, with an interior mechanism so you could practically sleep on it, with every angle in between. And it wasn't an eyesore, like some others he'd seen.

"I didn't kill her. That's the most important thing you need to know," Sam said.

Sam's statement shook Owen's attention away from the stupid chair.

"Wait, what?" Owen said. "Dude, that's the last thing that would have crossed my mind."

"You were going to find out eventually," Sam said. "I was sleeping with Irene. The police know already. I talked to them today."

Once Owen heard the words, he still didn't get it. Not really. It took him a few long seconds to process the information. Then he had to say it out loud, to understand. "You and Irene? Really?"

"Yes."

Then Owen was angry. "What the fuck, Sam. Why?"

"I don't know," Sam said. "It just happened."

Owen couldn't move or speak. He just stared at Sam, which was making Sam incredibly uncomfortable.

"I thought I should be the one to tell you," Sam said. "Sorry. It's not like you were the most faithful husband."

Owen kept staring. Sam strode down the hall to the front door.

Owen didn't follow right away. Sam, impatient, opened the door and cleared his throat. Owen slowly got up and ambled toward the foyer. He felt unsteady, his psyche split between reality and dull hallucination. Sam noticed Owen's strange gait and lack of focus.

"You cool?" Sam said.

Owen thought Sam was asking if they were cool, if Owen was cool with Sam fucking his now-dead wife. Owen never liked the guy, never understood why Luna would marry him. If he had been more lucid, didn't have a potential murder charge on his back, he might have done something bold right then, like smash Sam's head against the front door. Instead, Owen merely stepped outside. It was for the best. He would have lost just about any physical match against Sam.

"Where's Luna?" Owen said.

"I told you. A motel. I guess we're splitting up."

"Sorry," Owen said.

Owen cracked a smile. He wasn't trying to be a jerk. He simply couldn't control his subconscious response to the news. Then he started to laugh. It was nerves, sleep deprivation, and day drinking. But to Sam, it read as pure cruelty.

"Fuck you, Owen," Sam said.

Even after he slammed the door, he could still hear Owen laughing.

March–August 2004

The official cause of Scarlet Hayes's death was a subdural hematoma. The district attorney, after two months of poring over witness interviews, forensic data, and autopsy reports, decided not to pursue any criminal action. Detective Oslo knew Mrs. Hayes would not be satisfied. There was no convincing the bereft mother that her daughter's death was a tragic accident. Mrs. Hayes would always believe that Scarlet was murdered by her ex-boyfriend, Owen Mann. And Scarlet's mother was not alone. Despite articles in the local paper and repeated statements from authorities that contradicted her narrative, the consensus on campus was that Owen was a murderer who got away with it.

Owen spent a night in the hospital after the assault. His parents came out and hired an attorney. A lawsuit was filed. Owen refused to return to campus. Arrangements were made for him to finish up the semester remotely. Vera and Tom decided that Owen and Griff would live in the Berkshires house while Griff studied for the bar and Owen finished his sophomore year. Luna offered to deliver classwork—notes, assignments, tests—from campus to the lake house on weekends. Casey was generous about loaning her car. *Mi Peugeot es su Peugeot,* she liked to say.

While Owen recovered from his wounds, Luna and Griff packed up his dorm room. As they carried boxes to and from Watson Hall, no one offered to help. Griff felt the tension, the simmering anger that hovered nearby. He'd never experienced that kind of thing before. Luna and he worked at a breakneck pace to get it over with. There was a lot of staring and hovering near the car. Luna kept reminding Griff that he had to lock it between loads. They were just about done, heading back into the dorm, when a beefy guy knocked shoulders with Griff.

"Sorry," Griff said, assuming it was an accident.

"Fuck you," the guy said.

Griff spun around and caught sight of the very large man. He was young, face budding with zits, but big enough to do some damage.

"Is there a problem?" Griff asked, not in that tough-guy way but earnestly.

The guy stood there sizing him up. Luna had a bad feeling. She yanked Griff's arm. Told him they had to go. *Now.* They rushed upstairs and locked the door to Owen's room behind them. They performed one final check of the closets, dresser, under the bed, took the last two boxes down the stairs, and loaded them into the car. The large man and a few of his friends were loitering near the driveway, watching them. As they approached, Luna leaned into the car and grabbed a tiny canister from her purse. Her palm wrapped around it, index finger hovering on the trigger. Luna, arm outstretched, waved the threat in front of her.

"Have you ever been pepper-sprayed?" she said, lunging forward, forcing their retreat.

Griff circled the car, opened the passenger door, and whispered to Luna, "Get in the car now."

She backed into the passenger seat, waving her arm back and forth. She only released her grip on the canister when she closed the door. Griff jumped into the driver's seat, hit the locks, started the engine, and quickly pulled out of the driveway, lead-footing it as soon as they hit the road.

As they drove off campus, Griff eyed Luna. She was still clutching the small bottle.

"What is that?" he asked.

Luna turned the nozzle, opened her mouth, and pulled the trigger. "Breath spray."

A minute earlier, Luna had been another person—tense, feral, capable of something Griff couldn't begin to imagine. He wondered if she could just put it in a box, like a sinister ventriloquist's dummy. It both impressed and unnerved him, which explained why, a few weeks later, when Owen thought Luna might be trying to kill him, Griff had a moment's pause.

WHILE OWEN STAYED at the Berkshires home, Luna returned to campus life. She was a pariah by association. She wondered how much worse it would get once her true identity became known. She waited for it, bracing herself, always prepared. But it never happened. As it turned out, there were only three people—alive, at least—in Deerkill, other than Owen, who could have broadcast her secret: Casey, Mason, and Detective Oslo.

Detective Miles Oslo made a call early on not to share Luna's backstory with the Hayes parents. They'd seen the text messages their daughter sent and questioned the detective about what this "secret" was, but Oslo assured them it was unrelated. This didn't satisfy Mr. and Mrs. Hayes, who threatened to hire an investigator. Oslo had a split second to think of something. He didn't have time to weigh the ethics or the consequences. He didn't enjoy lying to the parents of a dead girl, but he also knew that if Mrs. Hayes learned the secret that her daughter had threatened to expose, she'd likely find another suspect. Owen's life was already uprooted. Oslo didn't want that to happen to the girl. Not again.

"I'm not going to tell you what the secret was. All I can say is that it was not the kind of secret you kill over," Oslo said.

"How do you know?" Scarlet's mother asked.

Oslo was tired of fighting Mrs. Hayes. He had told her repeatedly that Luna was alibied for the night. Still, Mrs. Hayes kept pressing. So Oslo made up a secret. He told the Hayes parents that

Scarlet found out that Luna was gay and she was determined to let Owen know, because she thought that Owen was in love with Luna. Scarlet's mother questioned whether that was motive enough for Luna to kill Scarlet. Oslo said that he thought it was an unlikely motive and, again, reminded Mrs. Hayes that Luna was alibied. Resigned to the unsatisfying conclusion, and embarrassed that their daughter could be so cruel, the Hayes parents left Markham, never to return. They did, however, receive a significant settlement for their daughter's accidental death, because Black Oak Bluff was part of the campus and there was no signage to discourage nighttime hiking.

LUNA, DESPITE HER tendencies toward isolation, had found college more socially rewarding than she expected. Her world expanded significantly during the first two years. Luna had friends; she threw parties; she had fun. After Scarlet, it pared down suddenly, like the very end of a chess game. It was obvious who her friends were, because she had only three of them—Owen, Casey, and Mason. The latter two were now a couple and would remain so for as long as she'd know them.

Casey and Mason took a risk by staying friends with Luna and Owen. They weren't ostracized on Luna's level, but their world shrank too. Then it expanded again, and their college experience returned to something closer to normal. But Markham would always be a hostile place for Luna, though not once did she consider transferring. Being ostracized was status quo for her. She'd survive.

Even from the safe confines of his family's retreat, Owen wasn't surviving quite as well. During those first few weeks after he left Markham, he fell into a quicksand of depression. Owen killed most days in his bedroom playing Grand Theft Auto and taking extended naps. Griff cooked all the meals. Owen would get a plate, grunt, and return to his room, which was becoming more and more rank. Whenever Luna visited, Owen told her not to come, that she could mail his school assignments to him. In fact, most things could be emailed, but she kept coming back. When she was there, Griff was even more of a dick about making Owen leave his room. One time, Luna brought tabs of acid and suggested they take it. Griff got pissed off, started lecturing her about some guy in Pink Floyd who went insane. Then he confiscated the drugs. When Griff was hiding the contraband, Owen asked Luna what she was thinking.

"I heard it helps with depression," she said.

"I'm not depressed," he said.

"What are you, then?"

"Maybe you shouldn't visit anymore."

"Is that what you want?"

"Yes."

Sunday morning, Owen waited in his room for the sounds of Luna packing up to leave. She knocked on his bedroom door.

"I'm going soon," Luna said.

"Okay," Owen said.

"If this is my last visit, I want to go out on the rowboat," she said.

"It's freezing. You don't want to do that."

"Come on," Luna said. "Let's go."

"I'm not going anywhere, and you shouldn't either."

Luna and Owen went back and forth for a while. Until Owen shut the door on her. Luna kept knocking and saying that she'd leave if he went out on the boat with her. She'd never bother him again after that.

"Give me your word," he said.

"Promise," Luna said.

Fifteen minutes later, Luna was rowing them out into the middle of Pontoosuc Lake. Owen felt a strange energy coming off her. It made him feel unsteady and, frankly, a tad frightened. Her eyes were darting around; her mind was working on something. She wasn't admiring the sparkling blue water or enjoying the physical effort of maneuvering the small boat. It was an unusually brisk morning. Luna shivered as she rowed.

"Okay, let's go back," Owen said.

"No," Luna said, refusing eye contact. She regarded the oars. "These are clamped on?"

"Yeah. Why?" Owen said.

"I wondered what would happen if we lost the oars," she said.

Owen already had a strange vibe from Luna. Her comment only heightened the feeling.

"That's why they're clamped on, so you don't lose them," Owen said.

"I see," Luna said.

"I think we should go back," Owen said.

"I'm too tired," Luna said, releasing the oars.

Owen wasn't sure what her angle was, but he wasn't buying it. "Okay, I'll row," he said.

Luna stood up and jumped on the stern. If he didn't know better, he would have thought she was trying to flip the boat.

"Stop it, Luna—what the fuck," Owen shouted.

He half-stood, trying to reach the bow to rebalance the weight, all the while yelling, "What are you doing? Stop."

While Owen's center of gravity was elevated, Luna barreled right into him, tackling him into the water. The shock of the cold took his breath away. Once submerged, his temperature slowly dropping, it occurred to Owen that Luna might be trying to harm him, kill him perhaps. Adrenaline surging, Owen swam to shore, stumbled out of the water and up the banks to his house, not once looking back for Luna. He was colder than he'd ever been and utterly confused and somewhat frightened. Luna, not as strong a swimmer, barely made it back to shore before hypothermia set in.

Owen walked into the house, soaked to the bone, shouting for his brother.

"What the hell?" Griff said upon seeing Owen blue-lipped and drenched, shivering uncontrollably. "Where's Luna?"

Beyond the sliding glass door, Luna lurched toward the house, in even worse condition.

"Dude," Owen said to his brother, "she's fucking insane. She pushed me in. I think she's trying to kill me. I swear to fucking god."

"What?" Griff said. He was sure he misunderstood.

"I'm taking a shower," Owen said. "Keep her away from me."

Griff took a stack of towels from the linen closet and met Luna at the back door.

"What happened?" Griff said.

"Show-er," Luna said between chattering teeth.

Luna rushed into the guest room and took a hot shower. Griff ramped up the heat and started a fire. Luna was still shivering. She kept stomping her feet, like they were asleep. Griff gave her tea and blankets and told her to sit by the fire. He alternated between trying to warm up her feet and checking on his brother. Owen had followed up his shower with a hot bath. The door was locked. He wasn't taking any chances.

"You okay, man?" Griff said through the door.

"I'm fine," Owen said. "But get her out of here. She's insane. She pushed me in the lake. On purpose."

Griff returned to the living room. Luna, still feeling ice-cold, was getting dangerously close to the flames. He put an old wool cap on her head and sat next to her for warmth.

"How is he?" Luna asked.

"Fine. Owen says you capsized the boat on purpose. He thought you were—"

"What?"

"He's afraid of you, Luna."

Luna marveled at the inadvertent genius of her plan. "Is he really afraid?" Luna said with a smile.

Her pleasure at that news was disconcerting.

"Yes, Luna. He misunderstood, right?" Griff said.

"Fear. That was my next experiment," Luna said, followed by a full explanation of her recent actions.

Griff took Luna upstairs to Owen's bedroom. Owen was under an electric blanket turned up to high.

"No," Owen yelled when he saw Luna standing next to his brother.

"Just let her explain," Griff said. "It's kind of sweet, in its weird-ness."

Griff left them alone. Luna went to sit on Owen's bed, but he pointed at the floor.

"Stay back," Owen said. "Let me see your hands."

Luna's fingers were still numb. She wanted to keep them in her pockets.

"You have one minute," Owen said.

"I read somewhere that cold-water immersion can ameliorate depression. You haven't been normal since . . . you know, which is totally understandable. But because that whole thing was in some ways my fault, I wanted to see if I could help. Wake you up. I think maybe it worked. You're mad now. Before you were just in this fog. I wasn't trying to kill you. I just wanted you to feel better."

Owen gawked at Luna for a long moment. Then he said, "I'm not your fucking guinea pig."

"I know. I'm sorry," Luna said, still shivering. "I didn't think the water would be that cold."

Owen had clearly recovered far better than she. The self-sacrifice did not go entirely unnoticed.

Owen lifted the covers. "Get in."

Luna crawled into the warm bed. He turned on the television. They cycled through the stations for a while, searching for some-thing decent to watch. Eventually they landed on *Young Frankenstein*.

Griff heard his brother's laugh for the first time since he'd ar-rived. Later that night, Griff checked in on them. The pair was cozy under a blanket, fully recovered from the day's events. Credits played on the TV screen.

"Everybody okay?" Griff said.

Owen gently shoved Luna. "She was just leaving."

"I can take a hint," Luna said.

As Luna met Griff in the hallway, Owen told them to shut the door. Luna went downstairs and helped Griff tidy up in the kitchen.

"He seems a little better, right?" Luna whispered.

Griff placed his hands on Luna's shoulders and gazed into her eyes with an uneasy devotion. "You're . . . insane. And amazing," he said.

Griff kissed her on the lips. Luna felt light-headed. When it was over, Griff turned away, embarrassed.

"Good night, then," he said.

"Good night," said Luna.

Luna left the next morning without saying a word. She didn't want to give Griff a chance to tell her it was a mistake.

Owen always thought of the rowboat incident as the beginning of his recovery. Just like the way you thaw out after being submerged. Your fingers go numb and turn blue in the cold. Then you put them in front of the fire and it stings. For a while there, he'd felt nothing. Then he felt pain, and then the pain softened and he started to think about things he'd like to do. Going back to Markham was out of the question.

It was Vera who suggested Owen study abroad. Since it was too late for Owen to enter any official university program, Vera managed to make arrangements for Owen to have an apartment in London and take classes at Chelsea College of Arts. It would cost a fortune, but Owen's parents could afford it back then.

Luna still visited every few weeks, even during the last dregs of summer, when Owen no longer needed his class assignments. Griff was gone by then. He'd gotten a job in New York City and was apartment hunting.

As Owen packed, Luna read aloud from a Lonely Planet travel guide to London. She promised to mail Owen American sundries. She'd heard peanut butter was hard to come by.

"When's the last time you saw me eat peanut butter?" Owen asked.

"You'll want it when you can't have it."

"You have to visit," Owen said to Luna. "Promise."

Luna knew she'd be too cash-strapped to manage a trip, and she wouldn't lie.

"Have the best year. I'll be here when you come back," Luna said.

Owen and Luna promised to write every week. Luna had sent three letters to Owen before she heard back. He'd taken a photo of himself, glued it to a postcard of Big Ben, added an illustrated top hat and monocle, and scribbled a quick message on the back.

Wish you were here.

October 14, 2019

___

Owen woke up Monday morning reeling from his encounter with Sam and still waiting to hear back from Luna. Briefly, he thought it might have all been a dream. Not the part about Irene's death—that was firmly entrenched in his subconscious—but the part about Sam and Irene having an affair.

Luna returned his texts that morning, agreeing to meet him at the diner across from her motel. Luna found a booth in the back of the Lunch Chalet and ordered a coffee. When Owen arrived, Luna thought he seemed different. Older, tired. It had been only a week since they'd had that drink at the Halfway House and talked about Owen's "no one."

Owen immediately felt a chill coming off Luna. It didn't seem right, when she was the one holding out on him. The waitress breezed by, warmed Luna's coffee, and poured a fresh cup for Owen. Luna wasn't eating, so Owen ordered waffles—it seemed rude to take up a booth just for coffee. The waitress forced a smile, which came off as sinister. Luna busied herself doctoring her coffee, polishing a spoon.

"I went to your house. Late last night," Owen said, after the waitress had moved on.

Luna glanced up from her shiny spoon. She hadn't considered the possibility that Owen would be in Sam's orbit before she could tell Owen.

"Shit. He told you?" Luna said.

"He did."

"I'm sorry," she said flatly, without conviction. "You should have heard it from me."

"Why didn't I?"

"You weren't around," Luna said. "I tried to find you yesterday. Maya answered your door."

"How'd you find out? Or when? I guess I'd like to know both things."

"Mason found a phone in the guest room. He left it charging and it started ringing when I was—after he left," Luna said, editing out the detail about Griff being in her home. "I answered the phone and it was Detective Goldman. Apparently, Irene had been calling that number over the last several months. They'd been trying to find the owner. It was one of those pay-as-you-go phones."

"Sam had a burner just for Irene? Why?"

"I don't know," Luna said.

"It's pretty fucking suspicious, don't you think?" Owen said.

"They were having an affair and she was murdered. I'm not sure there's causality there. You should understand that more than anyone."

"Right," Owen said. His brain snagged on something Luna had mentioned a few moments before. "What time did you come to my house yesterday?"

"Around one or two."

"Are you sure?"

"It was definitely after one," Luna said.

In light of everything that had happened, she thought it was a strange detail to lock on.

"And Maya was still there?"

"Yes," Luna said. "Where were you?"

Luna could hear Owen's heel tapping under the table. His eyes darted back and forth without any focus.

"I just drove around," Owen said. "The point is, I left no later than eleven. What was Maya doing in my house for more than two hours?"

"I think she said she was cleaning," Luna said. "Who gives a fuck?"

"I do," Owen said. "She wasn't cleaning. I don't know what she was doing."

Owen was sure that Maya's behavior meant something, although he had no working theory. He wanted Luna to join in the brainstorming, to help him figure it out, but she seemed uninterested. He also wanted to tell Luna about Amy and how strange she had been, how he thought she might have been trying to trap him in a confession. He didn't say any of that because Luna's thermostat had shifted from icebox to sauna in no time at all.

"You want to tell me who you're mad at?" Owen asked.

"All of you," she said.

Luna wanted to leave. She wasn't hungry and the coffee was crap. She felt like no one was who she thought they were or who they were supposed to be. Learning about Sam and Irene was bad enough. Being angry at the person whose death you're currently grieving didn't cancel out either emotion. It somehow managed to heighten them both.

"I think Maya was searching my house," Owen said. "Isn't that weird?"

Luna, lost in thought, didn't answer. Owen waved his hand in front of her to wake her up.

"Did you hear me?"

"Why are you going on about Maya?"

"She's making me nervous. I'd kind of like to know what she was looking for."

"Remember when we installed an app on our phones so we could find each other?" Luna said.

Owen nodded, though he'd actually forgotten about the app.

"I couldn't reach you yesterday, so I checked the app to make sure you were okay," Luna said.

"Your husband was fucking my dead wife and you're angry that I went to see Amy?"

"Owen, they think you did it. It's almost always the husband. I guarantee, they're locked on you. Everything you're doing now, they're watching. They're going to keep watching you until they've got something to use against you. And they're probably going to keep watching me, because I found the body and I'm your friend. When you visit your mistress, you look guilty. There's only so much I can do to defend you, to be a witness to your character. I don't think you killed Irene. But from an outsider's perspective, I'm not the best judge. I lied for a murderer once; some people think I did it twice. I can't vouch for you this time. I can't help you. I'm not your alibi."

"What are you working on?" Burns asked her partner.

"I'm tracking Irene's cash withdrawals in the last three years." Noah spun around his laptop, showing Margot his Excel spreadsheet of cash withdrawals.

"That spreadsheet is a little bit like porn for you, isn't it?" Margot asked.

The answer was yes, but Goldman ignored the question.

"In 2016 through '17, she makes an average of five ATM withdrawals each year. Then, at the end of last year, she started withdrawing larger sums. One thousand, five thousand. It adds up to close to thirty thousand in the last year. All in cash. I contacted her financial adviser, Cliff Easter. He'd asked Irene about it, because he didn't like how it looked, and she told him she was buying art," Noah said.

"Can we verify that?" Margot asked.

"I reached out to the attorney. I'm going to get a look at her storage facility in a few hours. Get this: According to her attorney, there were no amendments to her will."

"So if she was buying art . . ." Burns said.

"Right," Goldman said, nodding. "Anything not designated in her will goes to the husband."

Margot threw on her coat and searched her desk for car keys. "Let me know as soon as you find anything. We'll need an appraiser."

"Where are you going?" Goldman asked.

"Albany," Margot said. "I want to talk to Detective Oslo. He investigated the Scarlet Hayes death."

"You think there's anything there?"

"I have no idea," Margot said.

MILES OSLO HAD retired from the New York State Police three years earlier. Now he worked very part-time as a private detective, running his casual business out of a sparsely furnished office in a decaying strip mall in Troy, New York. Oslo agreed to meet Detective Margot Burns to discuss the Scarlet Hayes case.

Margot found it both disappointing and suspicious that he didn't even have signage on his door. She rang the buzzer for unit four. A tall, extremely lean man with fading strawberry-blond hair answered the door.

After introductions were made and coffee offered, Margot sat down in an old leather chair in the shabby ten-by-ten-foot room.

"I know. This place is a shithole," said Oslo.

"I appreciate your time," Burns said.

Oslo moved a small file to the center of his desk. "I reviewed my notes this morning," Oslo said. "I'm afraid I don't have much more to tell you. Nothing stuck out. Back when I interviewed Owen Mann, he had an on-again off-again relationship with Scarlet Hayes. By all accounts, he was not the pursuer. While the death was unfortunate, all the crime-scene evidence suggested that it was an accident."

"Was there anything about the case that didn't sit right with you?" Burns asked.

"Sure," Oslo said. "A few things. When we were still getting heat from Scarlet's mother, I asked Owen if he'd take a lie-detector test. He declined right away, didn't even think about it."

"Any good lawyer would tell him to refuse," Burns said.

In the same situation, she wouldn't let her own son take a lie detector.

"I agree," Oslo said, nodding. "But I always got the feeling there was something he wasn't saying, like maybe he was protecting someone."

"Like who?"

"I don't know. It was just a feeling."

"Anything else?"

"Yes," Oslo said. "We got an anonymous call the morning after Scarlet disappeared, telling us where we could find the body."

"Where was the call made?" Burns asked.

"A pay phone in town. It could have been a hiker who came upon the deceased and didn't want to get involved. We'll never know."

"The trail was on public grounds?"

"Technically part of Markham, but anyone could hike there," Oslo said.

"Did you investigate the call?" Burns asked.

"There were no cameras near the pay phone."

"Fingerprints?"

Oslo pretended to consult his notes. "I'd have to get back to you on that."

"Didn't you think that the caller might have been the killer?"

"If I thought there was a killer, I would have considered that a possibility," Oslo said.

"What didn't sit right with you?"

"It didn't make sense that Scarlet made that hike alone. I thought maybe she was lured up there. And the call bugged me. But a lot of people are wary of cops. At the end of the day, we didn't find any evidence to dispute an unfortunate accident," Oslo said.

"Why did you close the case when you still had doubts?"

"The evidence pointed to an accident. And I didn't want Owen living with a cloud over him."

"Did you interview Luna Grey back then?" Margot asked.

"Luna Grey? What does she have to do with anything?"

Oslo hadn't thought about the girl until he'd pulled the file to refresh his memory.

"Luna was the one who discovered the body of Owen's wife. In fact, she notified Owen before the police," Margot said.

Oslo knew the brushstrokes of the case Burns was working. Still, his thoughts were spinning too fast to catch up. He wasn't expecting to hear Luna's name in reference to the open case.

"She and Owen are still friends?" Oslo asked.

"Yep."

"Huh. How'd she find the body?"

"Owen and Luna are neighbors. They live just a quarter mile from each other. Luna and Irene would jog at the same cemetery," Burns said.

"You know who she is, right?" Oslo asked. "Luna Brown-slash-Grey?"

"We do," Burns said. "It's hard to ignore her proximity to death."

"It snags your brain, doesn't it?" Oslo said.

"Yes. But repetition isn't necessarily a pattern," Burns said.

"True. And yet it's hard to resist imposing a pattern."

"The anonymous call about Scarlet. I assume you listened to the recording."

Oslo nodded. "Many times. I don't think it was Owen. Doubt it was Luna."

"Could you tell if it was a man or woman?"

"Woman, I think. Disguising her voice."

"That feels a little more suspicious than an innocent bystander," Burns said.

"I agree," Oslo said. "But people often act suspiciously whether they're guilty or not."

October–December 2004

Things had been shaky for a while in the wake of Scarlet's death. Luna was associated with Owen, who was still considered a murderer. If it hadn't been for Casey and Mason, Luna would have become a complete outcast. Because their friendship was given at their own risk, it felt generous. Luna was surprised when Casey and Mason suggested the three of them become roommates junior year. They found a two-bedroom, two-bath house off campus. Mason even visited Owen in London over Christmas break. Luna couldn't remember when those two had become friends. It seemed to happen when Owen was gone. She thought Mason probably wrote really great letters.

Luna missed Owen, for sure. But Griff filled the void, in a very different way. At first, Luna and Griff's relationship was a modern epistolary one—daily emails. Then long phone calls were added to the mix. Finally, Griff invited Luna to meet him at the Berkshires house for a weekend in October. Luna still couldn't tell whether he was courting her or not.

Luna borrowed Casey's car and arrived late Friday night. Griff greeted her with a kiss on the cheek. He kept offering her things from the refrigerator. When she asked for a beer, he stammered something about her not being of drinking age. Luna threatened to leave unless he gave her the beer. Then they sat on the couch, on opposite ends, watching television. Hours passed that first night. Nothing. Luna didn't think she could take any more of it.

"I'm going to bed," she said.

On Luna's past visits, she'd always slept in the downstairs guest room. That night she went to Griff's room on the second floor and climbed into his bed. Griff came upstairs about fifteen minutes later. Without commenting on her presence there, Griff got into bed and said, "Good night, then."

When Griff didn't make a move, Luna said, "Oh my god. Seriously?"

"Something on your mind?" Griff said.

"Are you planning on going into the priesthood or currently under treatment for a venereal disease?" Luna asked.

"*No.*"

Luna sat upright and said, "Did you invite me here to *not* have sex?"

"No. But I didn't invite you for the sole purpose of sex."

"You kissed me six months ago. Nothing since then."

"We haven't been alone until now."

"We're alone now," Luna said.

"You're right," Griff said.

He kissed her. She kissed him back. Griff suggested they try to take things slowly. Luna suggested they'd already done that. They had sex that night. Luna, who always, always slept alone, stayed in his bed and actually fell asleep. The morning light surprised her. When she looked over at Griff still in a deep slumber, she felt happy in a way she didn't think was possible. The guilt, however, would soon follow.

As WINTER BREAK drew near, Griff phoned Luna to invite her back to the Berkshires house.

"It'll be great," Griff said without any conviction.

"I can't. I'm visiting my mother."

"In Canada? How will you get there?" Griff asked.

"I'm thinking about driving, so I can stop at Niagara Falls on the way back."

"Niagara Falls?"

"Yes," Luna said. "Have you been?"

"Never," said Griff.

"You should go," Luna said. "It's totally worth it."

"Is that an invitation?" Griff asked.

Luna's silence told Griff that it was not.

"I'll only be gone three days, and most of it will be driving," Luna said.

"Did you say three days?"

"You keep repeating things I say," Luna said.

"You keep saying weird things. Why would you go home for only three days? Actually, one day, since two of those days you'd be driving."

"It's just how we do things. My mom has a new boyfriend. I don't want to get in the way."

"All of that sounds highly suspicious to me, but I'd still like to come with you," Griff said. "Besides, I have a car and you don't."

"Casey said I could borrow her car."

"I'm a good driver," Griff said.

"Wouldn't your parents want at least one of their sons around?"

"No," Griff said. "In fact, they might prefer an obligation-free holiday season."

"Interesting," Luna said.

"Multiple-choice question," Griff said. "You're not inviting me because: A, you don't want to spend three days with me; B, you don't want me to meet your mother; C, you're tending to illegal business across the border; D, none of the above."

"There's never an E," Luna said.

"What's the answer?" Griff asked.

"B, maybe," Luna said. "Or D. None of them were on the nose. I haven't seen my mom in a while. I don't know what you'd be walking into."

"How about I just come with you on the trip? I don't have to meet your mom. I can stay in a motel and watch movies. Then we'll go to Niagara Falls. It'll be fun."

234 / LISA LUTZ

"You won't miss your family?"

"Now you're being stupid," Griff said.

Once Luna agreed to the road trip itself, she knew she was agreeing to Griff meeting her mother, who was a true wild card.

"Did Owen ever tell you anything about my mother?"

"He said you don't see her that often."

"Anything else?"

"I don't think so."

"Before you change your plans, I want you to be prepared. It could be weird. Like, really, really weird."

THEY DROVE STRAIGHT through on Christmas Eve morning, stopping only for gas, bathroom breaks, a quick lunch at a Chinese restaurant in Buffalo, and, of course, the border. Griff did most of the driving, while Luna navigated from internet directions she'd printed that morning.

When they arrived at the London, Ontario, address, Griff was sure they were at the wrong place. The rambling ranch house was festooned with Christmas decorations. The eaves were dripping with lights, the lawn littered with elves. There was even a cheesy Santa sled, with reindeer, traversing the front lawn.

"Wasn't expecting this," Griff said.

He couldn't decide if the garish display was comforting or unsettling. Luna had claimed that she didn't know what to expect either and that talking about it would only cause stress. While they were still sitting in the car, Luna reached into her backpack and retrieved a bottle of Maker's Mark. She'd seen Griff drink it a few times and assumed he liked it enough.

"This is for you," Luna said.

Griff searched for a hidden card somewhere on the bottle.

Luna took the bottle, uncorked it, and handed it back to Griff.

"Drink," she said.

"Wait, is your mom a teetotaler?" Griff asked.

He was the driest member of the Mann family, but he couldn't imagine a Christmas Eve, especially under unknown circumstances, without some inebriation.

"I hope not," Luna said. "She wasn't the last time I saw her. Drink."

Griff took a swig. "Ready?"

"One minute," Luna said.

She removed a pill from a blister pack and swallowed it dry. Then she took an EpiPen from her bag. "You know how to use one of these things?"

"Why?"

"You just hold it against my thigh and press the button."

Griff had assumed that the prime source of weirdness that night would be Luna. He'd also assumed that her caginess was partly punitive, the price he'd have to pay for inviting himself along.

When the pair reached the front door, Luna took a couple of deep breaths before she rang the bell. Then Luna's mother swung open the door and smiled. She had short gray hair in a can't-be-bothered cut. Griff was too distracted by her Christmas sweater to notice anything else about her appearance. A bright-red knit thing with stuffed animals on it. That's what he thought until the stuffed animals started moving. A startled Griff yelped and stepped back, tripping on the stairs, falling on his ass. Luna turned around and offered her hand. She bit her lip to fight a smile.

After Luna helped Griff back onto his feet, introductions were made.

"Mom, this is my . . . uh, friend or something, Griff Mann. Griff, this is my mom, Belinda Grey."

"Mrs. Grey," Griff said. "Thank you so much for having me."

"Call me Belinda or Bee," Luna's mom said as she plucked the living creatures from her sweater and held them out for formal introduction. "And these are Luna's brother and sister, Lysander and Hermia. Say hello."

Griff couldn't tell whether Belinda was talking to him or the creatures, which he later learned were ferrets.

"Hello and hello," Griff said to Lysander, then Hermia.

Luna appreciated that Griff addressed each one individually, which would score points with her mother.

"Come in," Belinda said.

"I warned you," Luna mumbled as she and Griff entered the overheated house.

The smell hit them both hard—a musty odor that overpowered everything. Griff tried to make polite sense of it, not understanding that it was the natural odor of ferret. He thought that it might have been a combo of mold and something in the oven with the distinct aroma of game.

The couple followed Belinda down a long hallway, flanked by closed doors and walls adorned with a few family and mostly ferret pictures. Griff studied every photo with humans, searching for young Luna. He couldn't find her in any of them. At the end of the hall was the kitchen and living room. A lanky man in a ruffled apron hovered over the stove. He turned around to greet his guests. He had a thick helmet of brown hair speckled with gray.

"Beau, this is my daughter, Luna, and her *friend* Griff," Belinda said, adding a wink to the *friend* reference.

Beau looked at Luna and extended his hand. "Luna, nice to finally meet you."

"Yes. Nice to meet you," Luna said.

Then Beau and Griff shook hands. After one forced smile and two handshakes, Beau returned his attention to the stove. Griff thought that a guy in a frilly apron would be friendlier than he was. Four adults and two ferrets crammed into the small kitchen got awkward fast. Griff asked Beau what he was making. Cranberry sauce, Beau said. Griff asked for the recipe, because he couldn't think of anything better to say.

"Sugar, water, cranberries. They print it on the bag. It's not rocket science," Beau said.

Griff would always remember those words.

"Are you ready to meet the rest of the family?" Belinda asked Luna.

"Sure," Luna said, because it was inevitable.

Belinda walked back to the front of the house, indicating that Luna and Griff should follow. She opened one of the closed doors. Inside were at least six more ferrets, all of them in seasonal costumes. Griff counted two Santas, two elves, a snowman, and a tree. The odor that Griff first noticed when he walked in the door had become an unmitigated stench.

As Belinda rattled off the names of the costumed ferrets—Oberon, Titania, Demetrius, Puck—Luna began to wheeze.

"Oh dear," Belinda said. "I was afraid of this."

"I'm going to step outside and get some air," Luna said.

Luna raced out of the house like it was a burning building, drinking in clean, ferret-free oxygen. She reached for her inhaler and sucked down the medicine. Griff had taken out the EpiPen, waited for Luna to give him a sign. She held up her hand to hold him off.

"You okay?" Griff said.

Luna nodded. Her breathing improved. She took another hit on the inhaler. She and her mother exchanged a glance. Luna shook her head slightly. Belinda nodded her understanding and went back into the house. When she reemerged, Belinda was ferret-free.

"Sorry, honey," Belinda said. "I thought you might have outgrown it. I was allergic to cats when I was a kid."

"It's okay, Mom. Good to see you. Good meeting Beau."

"It's so good to see you," Belinda said.

No one said anything for a while. Griff and Belinda watched Luna breathe.

Then Belinda said, "Are you happy?"

Mother and daughter were standing three feet apart.

"Yes," Luna said. "You?"

"Very. You want to try coming back tomorrow?" Belinda asked. "I could do some vacuuming and maybe if you only stayed in the living room . . . We rarely let the kids in there."

"Better not," Luna said.

"Okay. I understand," Belinda said, relieved.

"We could meet somewhere," Griff said. "There's usually a few Chinese restaurants open."

Both women ignored Griff's suggestion.

"We gotta go, Mom."

Belinda took a hesitant step closer to Luna, like she was about to hug her. Griff couldn't figure out whether it was for show or not.

"I would hug you, but I don't want to make it worse," Belinda said.

"It's okay," Luna said.

"Well, I just feel terrible," said Belinda.

"Don't, Mom. We're going to Niagara Falls tomorrow."

"Oh, that's wonderful. That's wonderful. Have you been, Griff?"

"No," he said.

"You will love it."

They all stood there smiling and cringing inside. Belinda's body slowly turned back toward her house, as if by gravitational pull.

"You should probably go back in and help Beau with . . ." Luna said, giving her mother an out.

"Yes," Belinda said. "Thanks for making the drive. Nice meeting you, Griff."

"Uh-huh," Griff said.

He was so stunned by the turn of events that he couldn't summon his usual pleasantries.

"Love you, Mom," Luna said. Her voice cracked just a bit, but she recovered. "See you soon."

"Yes, dear," Belinda said. "See you soon."

Griff drove while Luna drank his bourbon and hung her head out the window, trying to clear the ferret dander from her respiratory system. They stopped at the first chain motel they could find. Luna jumped out of the car and raced to the motel office so she could pay for the room before Griff staked his claim on the bill. Griff unloaded the car, because Luna's breathing was still heavy. She'd packed two suitcases, which had seemed odd when he loaded the car, even odder at the moment.

Luna returned with the key and told Griff that the room was on the second floor. He asked which suitcase she needed. Both, she said.

Inside the room, Griff and Luna put their ferret-tainted clothes in plastic bags. After that, they showered and changed. Then they stripped the bed of the duvet, which they'd determined to have had a beyond-shady past. Luna sat back on the bed and finally filled her lungs without feeling like a sandbag was resting on her chest. She looked so relieved, it registered as pure joy. Griff couldn't decide if it was the air or the distance from her mother. He located the bourbon and poured two drinks into plastic cups.

"You okay?" Griff said.

"Question is, are *you* okay?" Luna asked.

"I'm confused. And a little worried about your breathing and wondering what we'll do for dinner. Most things are closed Christmas Eve."

Luna opened up the second suitcase, revealing a complete spread of charcuterie, cheese, chips, crackers, chocolate, wine, cookies, as well as plates, forks, knives, and plastic tumblers. A feast that would not require a flame or refrigeration. Luna passed the wine and corkscrew to Griff.

"Open that, will ya?" she said.

Griff reconsidered the events of that day and before. "You knew this would happen?" Griff said.

"I thought it was a distinct possibility," said Luna.

"Wow. Okay. Let's recap what went down today," Griff said. "We drive eight hours and cross a border to spend Christmas Eve with your mother and her cranberry-sauce-making boyfriend and we're at her house all of fifteen minutes because you have a life-threatening allergic reaction to her menagerie of ferrets."

"She only had two the last time I saw her," Luna said.

"Were you always allergic?"

"We moved to Canada when I was sixteen. She got two ferrets a few months later. She kept them in the basement back then and we had a system. I could manage. But then my aunt and uncle in Seattle invited me for a visit. They didn't have any kids. Or ferrets. It was easier to finish school in the States. My mother didn't argue."

"So, your mom knew you had this allergy and she still got more ferrets?"

"I haven't lived with her in years. It didn't really matter how many she had."

Luna placed a blanket from home on top of the bed and began organizing the spread. Griff uncorked the wine and poured two cups. He handed one to Luna and raised it for a toast.

"To this feast," Griff said.

"To Motel 6," Luna said.

"To ferret-free air," said Griff.

"To my inhaler," said Luna.

"To not having to stab you with an EpiPen."

"Yet," said Luna.

They tapped cups and drank.

"I'm glad you're here," said Luna. "I'm sorry it was so weird. I did warn you."

Griff didn't respond right away. His brain snagged on a detail he couldn't reconcile. "I'm confused," he said.

Luna knew what confused him, but she didn't feel like spelling it out. If his worldview prevented him from arriving at the obvious conclusion, wasn't it for the best? Luna built a small army of cheese-salami-olive crackers and delivered them to Griff, who deconstructed Luna's perfect stacks and ate the cheese and crackers first, then the olive-salami combo.

"You're eating it wrong," Luna said.

"Can we revisit the ferret experience briefly?" Griff said.

"What about it?"

"Remember the first two ferrets I met—your mom called them your brother and sister?"

"They're not actually my brother and sister. You get that, right?" Luna said, deadpan.

"Yes. But are *they* brother and sister?"

"I think so. If I remember correctly, they were the last two in a litter."

"And she named *sibling* ferrets after the lovers Lysander and Hermia? That's weird, right?"

"They've been fixed if that makes you feel any better," Luna said.

"It does. Sorry. I won't mention them again."

"Good," Luna said.

A few minutes later, Griff finally pieced it all together.

"Oh, I see," Griff said. "She doesn't want you to visit."

FERRETS AND FALLS were the theme of the holiday. The falls part did not disappoint. In fact, it more than made up for the disastrous ferret segment. Griff finally understood why Luna insisted they visit Niagara on the return trip. When you stood out on the walkway, gazing at Horseshoe Falls, at the overwhelming power of it, your own thoughts didn't matter. It was cleansing, in its way.

They walked up and down the promenade for hours in the bitter cold. It was too incredible to step away. Eventually they needed to warm up. Griff had booked the hotel. When they entered the room, Luna saw that it had a full view of the falls.

Griff ordered room service while Luna stood in front of the window, feeling so happy it started to turn on her. Happiness could easily shift gears into guilt or shame. She was on the precipice of the shift. Griff could see it happening. He stood next to Luna, put his arm around her.

"You think it's just going to be bullshit, a cliché, a tourist trap from hell," he said. "And yet it's—"

"It's all that and still the most beautiful thing you'll ever see," said Luna.

"You want to stay another night?" Griff asked.

"Do you?"

"I could stay here forever," he said.

October 15, 2019

———

Burns was still mulling over her interview with Oslo when she arrived at the station the next morning. Goldman's jacket was on his chair, but his desk was vacant. She found her partner in an unlit video room, staring at a frozen screen. On the monitor was a blurry image of Sam Burroughs in a hospital corridor.

"Have you alibied the doctor?" Burns asked.

"Not yet. We have him on camera at ten-thirty A.M. in the hospital corridor but nothing earlier."

"How'd he get into the building?"

"There's an entrance in back. I'm assuming he used that. Unfortunately, security is having trouble locating a file for Monday morning. That's either good luck or bad luck for the doc," Goldman said.

Margot sank into a chair and closed her eyes. "So many suspects and none of them good. I take it you didn't find anything in the storage unit?"

"Nothing that wasn't accounted for in the will."

"So where is the art that she was purchasing?"

"I don't think she was purchasing art," Goldman said.

"I really thought we had something."

"Me too," Goldman said. "Owen is either unlucky and a murderer or *really* unlucky and not a murderer."

Burns, without another word, gathered their files and walked into the conference room. Goldman followed with their coffees. He watched as Margot sorted witness statements into a grid across the table, which ran the length of the room.

"What are we doing, Margot?"

"Let's blank-slate it today," she said, cleaning up the dry-erase board.

She passed the pen to Noah because he had far superior writing and didn't mind the squeak.

"Irene's dead. What is our evidence?" Margot said.

It took Noah a moment to realize the question was for him. "Uh, we have the 9mm bullet, no murder weapon. But our shooter had to know how to shoot," Noah said.

"But what does the gun get us?" Margot said.

"Nothing. No one in the suspect pool has a registered gun. There was no gun found near the body or around the cemetery."

"We need that gun," Burns said.

"Maybe we should widen the search. Is there a lake nearby?"

Margot shook her head. "We're not getting the funds to drag every pond in a twenty-mile radius. Since no one had a registered weapon, we wouldn't be able to connect it to any of our suspects. What about the cemetery—does it mean anything?"

"Victim jogged there regularly."

"The killer knew her habits?" Margot said.

"He knew them or he learned them," Noah said.

"We think it's a he because it usually is, right?" said Margot.

"Can't rule out a female killer," Noah said.

"Let's go over our suspects one by one."

Noah printed OWEN MANN at the top left of the whiteboard.

"What does Owen get with his wife dead?"

Noah bullet-pointed:

- House
- Some money
- Freedom

"Freedom to do what?" Margot asked.

"To be with someone else," Noah said.

"But he was already doing that. And according to Luna, Irene knew about the affair. If she divorced him, how does he fare?"

"There was no morals clause in the prenup," Noah said.

"So, is he better off widowed or divorced?"

"There's no obvious winner," Noah said. "He's better off married. That's the crux of it."

"Okay. Who benefits if Irene dies?"

Noah printed Amy Johnson's name next to Owen's.

"She kills someone just to be with a guy who's not particularly wealthy on his own? It's a stretch," Margot said.

"Is it?" said Noah. "Remember that crazy astronaut lady? She planned to kill her new boyfriend's former girlfriend just to get rid of the competition. There was no other benefit, far as I know."

Margot had a moment of déjà vu. She'd had this conversation before.

"Have we discussed my astronaut theory?" Margot asked.

"I think I'd remember," Noah said, laughing. "I'd love to hear it."

"It's not Amy," Margot said.

Noah had never liked Amy for the crime, but he wanted to make sure they worked through each suspect to completion.

"She has no alibi," Noah said. "Said she was home when the murder happened, but she lives alone."

"The absence of an alibi means nothing. Here's the real reason: Women don't typically kill. But when they do, they generally fall into a few obvious categories. You've got the sociopath; she kills for a reason—money, love, et cetera. Then there's the self-defense killer, even if there's no immediate threat, which is generally a response to repeated abuse or a high-stress situation. There's also the mentally ill killer. Some kind of altered reality is involved. None of those apply here. If you have a woman who presents as normal in regular society and kills to clear the way for a relationship, which I think this would have to be, that woman is, I argue, a classic type-A high achiever. That's the kind of woman who works her ass off all the time. That's someone who believes there's nothing she can't accomplish if she sets her mind to it. That's an *astronaut*. Amy, on the other hand, attends a second-rate art school. She has no obvious ambitions or plans for when she graduates. If you look at the pictures in her social media accounts, there's always dirty laundry in the background. She's a slob. Does that sound like an astronaut to you?"

Noah scribbled a single bullet point under Amy's name.

• Not an astronaut.

"Moving on," Noah said. "The murder had to be premeditated. It was too clean."

"Maybe," Margot said. "Or it was a random shooting."

"For the hell of it, are there any astronauts in the mix? And does your astronaut theory apply only to women?"

"No," Margot said. "But there is a higher probability of astronauts in female killers than male killers."

"How about Dr. Burroughs?" Goldman asked.

"Burroughs is definitely an astronaut. He's the type of person who would think he could get away with the perfect crime."

Noah wrote ASTRONAUT under Dr. Burroughs's name.

"His motive is weak," Noah said.

"Correction. The motive we've so far managed to conceive of is weak," Margot said.

Noah wrote JEALOUSY under Owen's name. "Owen finds out about the affair and kills his wife out of jealous rage. Why doesn't he kill Sam?"

"I don't know. Because Irene betrayed him."

"It could be a jealousy-greed combo," Goldman said.

Margot took another pen and scribbled Luna's name in her messy script. The *L* looked almost like an *h*. She remembered why she wanted Goldman to do the writing.

"Maybe Luna found out about the affair and killed Irene?" Margot said.

Goldman wrote JEALOUSY under Luna's name.

"So, Luna brings in the husband's burner and toothbrush to deflect blame?" Goldman said.

The partners were exchanging hypotheticals but not buying any of it.

"Maybe," Burns said, unconvinced.

She paced over to the window and squinted at the blazing landscape. The kaleidoscope of colors would fade in just a few weeks.

"She's not an astronaut," Goldman said.

"Definitely not. Is there anyone else in Irene's orbit that we need to look at?" Burns asked.

"Her neighbor, Maya Wilton," Goldman said, writing her name on the side of the board. "I interviewed her briefly when we were canvassing the neighborhood. She claimed that she and Irene were good friends. Neither Owen nor Luna mentioned her at all. She seemed overly interested. After I gave her my card, she gave me her card. She said I should call if we needed any help."

"You should definitely call," Burns said. "Let's take a step back and look at motive from a wider view. Why do people kill?" she asked. "They kill as a misguided expression of love."

"They kill for greed," Noah added. "They kill because they lose control. They kill for jealousy and hate. But who hated Irene? No one, based on our interviews. Everyone loved her."

"Whitman didn't. He seemed to resent her, in a way. I'm not sure what it was, but something wasn't right with them," Margot said.

Goldman wrote Whitman's name on the board. "He hated that she got all Chantal's money," he said.

"Right. Maybe all those cash withdrawals were going to Whitman."

"How hard would it be to get his bank records?"

"We'd need more evidence. We can certainly bring him in and ask him about it," Burns said.

"Why would she give him the money? That's the question," Goldman asked. "She had already written him a check for fifteen thousand earlier this year."

"But why switch to cash? Was she trying to avoid the gift tax or hiding the gift?"

"What are you thinking? Blackmail?"

Burns worked through the possibility. "Whitman blackmails Irene about her affair with Sam. Then Irene finds out about Amy and Owen and decides it doesn't matter. She stops paying Leo off. Leo gets angry. Is that motive?"

"I don't know," Goldman said. "I'm not following the logic. If it's just revenge, it's a big risk to take. And he has the hand tremor, so he'd probably have to hire someone. It doesn't make sense."

Burns closed her eyes and rubbed her temples. "It doesn't. But murder isn't rational," she said. "I still want to dig deeper with Whitman."

Noah erased everything Margot had written in her messy scrawl and rewrote it in neat block letters. He took a step back, checking his work. Margot watched, amused by Noah's desire to tidy up a board that they would be erasing by the end of the day.

"You're almost an astronaut," Burns said.

"Almost?" Noah said, trying to decide whether he was insulted by the qualifier.

"Cops can't be astronauts. Too low on the food chain," she said.

March 2005

When Owen was in London, time moved faster than normal. It felt like being on one of those walking belts in an airport. He didn't look at it as regular life—more like an above-average vacation with mediocre food. But food wasn't that important to Owen. He did enjoy the pubs and pints, and he knew what grub to steer clear of. *Anything kidney. Why am I the only person who smells the urine?* Once settled, he began to write long letters to Luna, reciprocating her ambitious correspondences. Receiving something in the mail was such a thrill, he finally understood why Luna continued to use that form of communication. Owen didn't have as much patience for words, so he would often interrupt his letters with casual drawings that better illustrated the story. One was a two-paneled cartoon rendering of Owen catching a bus. In the first image, he shoves his way through the front door; in the second, after being scolded by a flatmate, he notices the queue and waits patiently in line for his turn with the other passengers.

Owen was hardly a monk that year. There were girls, all kinds of girls, too many girls to count. What he liked best about these girls was their accents. After that it was that none of them knew about Scarlet. He didn't have to fight any preconceived ideas people might have about him, other than being American, which he apologized for whenever possible. Later, tired of apologizing, he'd say he was Canadian. He decided on Halifax, because he liked saying Halifax.

Luna's letters were less informative about her day-to-day. She figured Owen wouldn't want to know about anything Markham-related. She thought he ought to know more about Halifax if he was claiming it as his hometown. She wrote a three-page letter including a serviceable history of Halifax and a collection of trivia to strengthen his story. *Did you know Halifax has more pubs per capita than any other city in Canada? Every August, Halifax hosts a busker festival. Lobster and scallops you can find in abundance, so don't get too excited if you find them on a London menu. Halifax scallops will always taste better.* Luna almost wished Owen had gone to Halifax instead of London. It sounded like a great place, and she wouldn't have to buy a plane ticket.

AFTER HIS MONTHS alone in the rambling Berkshires house with only his brother and Luna as company, it had taken Owen a few weeks to shake off the feeling that everyone hated him. He tried to remember, to repeat, to imprint in his brain, Luna's parting words of advice: *People don't know what you think they know.* On the whole, Owen thought that was good advice. However, some people did know about Luna.

It wasn't long before Owen had a small set of friends he could drink, hang, and frequent museums with. One night he made plans to meet a friend at the Three Legs in Camden Town. The friend couldn't make it and called the pub. Tessa, the bartender, delivered the message and kindly offered Owen a pint on the house. Not that he needed it. He was already blotto. Tessa accused Owen of being a Yank. He told her he was from Halifax. Then a girl with blue hair sat down next to him. It was the hair that got your attention, but the rest of her kept it. She was almost too striking, he thought. She was all cheekbones and long limbs and way too skinny. Some guys were into that. Owen didn't usually go for that type. It reminded him of his mother. But the blue-haired girl had other things going for her. The bartender made introductions.

"Owen from Halifax, meet . . . uh—wait, remind me," Tessa said.

"Phoebe from Sheffield," the blue-haired girl said. "Hi, Owen."

"Hi, Phoebe from Sheffield," Owen said. "I like your hair."

He wasn't lying. The hair grounded her appearance. It drew attention and deflected it. Phoebe figured out that Owen wasn't Canadian as soon as he said, "Hi, Phoebe."

"Never been to Halifax," Phoebe said with a heavy northern accent.

"Glad to hear it," Owen said.

"Tell me about it," Phoebe said.

"It's a great place to visit. We've got more pubs per capita than anywhere else in Canada."

"And, tell me, what do Halifaxians do for fun?"

"Haligonians," Owen said, delighted to have that correction on hand. "We drink. Wasn't that clear?"

"What's the population of Halifax?"

"Few hundred thousand," Owen said.

"Sport?"

"Hockey."

"What's your team?"

"I'm a Moosehead," Owen said.

"When you're rooting for your team, what team are you rooting against?" Phoebe asked.

Owen knew she was trying to trip him. "I give up," Owen said, dipping into a whisper. "I'm from Boston. Please don't tell anyone."

"No!" Phoebe said, feigning shock.

Having used the Canadian bluff herself, she didn't hold it against him. Still, she maintained her heavy northern accent and never suggested that they had a country of origin in common. She didn't want to be herself, especially that night.

Owen watched Phoebe devour another bowl of pretzels.

"Why don't we get some real food?" Owen suggested.

The new friends left the bar and found a chip shop down the road. Phoebe inhaled her order—so fast that Owen briefly wondered if she'd slyly tossed the newspaper cone of potatoes when he wasn't looking.

"That was impressive," he said.

"I know," she said. "What should we do now?"

"I don't know."

"Want to come back to my place? We've got a good liquor cabinet."

Owen hesitated. The *we* threw him. He thought she might be trying to get even with a boyfriend.

"No pressure. Just to hang," Phoebe clarified, noting his pause.

Owen asked about the first-person plural. Phoebe clarified that her mother owned the apartment but she wouldn't be home. Owen and Phoebe left the shop and headed back to the apartment. Phoebe picked up a couple of bags of crisps on the way.

"This is it," Phoebe said, nodding at a well-kept Edwardian structure surrounded by a wrought-iron fence. Owen followed Phoebe through a pristine foyer that had a couch and coffee table and then up two flights of stairs. She stopped in front of a door and put her ear to it, listening. Owen thought he might have heard a male voice inside. Phoebe said, "Run," in an urgent whisper, and they raced down the hall and took the stairs.

Outside, as they caught their breath, Phoebe apologized. "We can't stay there. Sorry," she said.

"Come back with me," Owen said. "My place is small, but I don't have any roommates."

"Okay," she said. She didn't know where else she'd go.

On the way to the tube station, Phoebe suggested they get one for the road. They dashed down a few whiskeys and then headed for the train. It was a thirty-minute ride to Owen's stop. The brightness of the train made them feel exposed. They hardly said a word. When they arrived at Owen's studio apartment, Phoebe asked if he had anything to eat.

Owen poured the bags of crisps into a bowl and reviewed the contents of his refrigerator. He offered to scramble eggs. She declined. Owen then crawled under his bed to retrieve a bottle of Macallan. He remembered hiding it there when he had a few friends over. He'd been tired and figured they would leave once he ran out of booze.

"What else have you got under there?" Phoebe asked.

"Just this," Owen said, uncorking the bottle and pouring two glasses.

"Cheers," she said.

They clinked glasses and drank.

"What were we running from at the apartment? Was that your boyfriend? Or your ex?" Owen asked.

"No," she said. "That was the bloke my mum plans to marry."

"Why'd we run?" Owen asked.

She topped off her glass, then his. "It's a long story," she said. "And fucking dull."

"Try me," Owen said.

She told Owen the whole sorry saga. It helped that Owen didn't react with horror or shock. He didn't judge.

"That was definitely not boring."

"Good to know," Phoebe said.

"You told your mother only part of the story," Owen said.

"I told her what she needed to know to make the right choice."

"Maybe she needed to know everything," Owen said.

Phoebe kept shaking her head. That was not ever going to happen.

"I can't do that," Phoebe said.

"Why not?"

"Because if I told her the whole truth and she still married him, I don't think I could ever forgive her."

Owen wrapped his arm around Phoebe. "I'm sorry," he said.

"Thanks," she said.

Phoebe reached for the Macallan.

"Haven't you had enough?" Owen asked.

"I haven't had nearly enough," Phoebe said.

Owen took the bottle away from her, replaced the cork, and rolled it back under his bed. "I think we've had enough."

"Now what are we gonna do?" Phoebe asked.

He kissed her, began to unbutton her blouse. Phoebe loosened his tie and freed the knot.

"Where are you from again?" Owen asked.

"Sheffield," Phoebe said.

"Really?" Owen said. His brain tripped over a recent memory. He thought the bartender said something else.

"Why?"

"Your accent is killing me."

Phoebe laughed. Not like she was dismissing a compliment but more like she thought something was funny. He liked her laugh almost as much as her accent. He didn't know what was so funny, though. It didn't matter.

They had sex. Owen remembered having a pretty good time. Most of the night was a blur. They both crashed sometime after two A.M.

Owen woke the next morning as Phoebe was rushing out. He recalled that she had the wedding that day. He wished her luck. She thanked him for his hospitality. Owen asked for her number. She scribbled it on the back of a coaster and kissed him goodbye. Owen waited a few days to call.

A woman with a slight French accent answered the phone.

"May I speak to Phoebe?" he asked.

"Sorry, wrong number."

October 15, 2019

G oldman thought he was just dotting a few i's when he rang Maya Wilton's doorbell. He could hear someone inside moving around. When Maya finally answered, she was wearing a coat and carrying her purse in one hand and a metal box in the other.

"Hello, Mrs. Wilton. Noah Goldman. We spoke a few days ago."

Maya stepped outside, handed the box to Noah, and locked the front door behind her.

"In my defense," Maya said, voice quivering, "I was planning on turning myself in."

"Good to know," Goldman said.

Back at the station, he put Maya in an interview room and delivered the box to his partner in the bullpen.

"What's this?" Burns asked.

"Maya Wilton gained access to Owen Mann's house two days ago and searched it. Then she stole this box, took it home, and watched YouTube videos on how to pick a lock with a paper clip. She thought I came to her house to arrest her. She was stunned when I let her sit in the front seat."

"What's in the box?" Burns asked.

Goldman lifted the lid. A messy pile of photos sat inside. "We should be grateful that she didn't find the murder weapon. No judge would have allowed it."

"I'll look through these," Margot said. "Make sure Maya is alibied for Monday morning."

Goldman returned to the interview room.

"Do I need a lawyer?" Maya asked when Goldman entered.

"For what?"

"I didn't realize until after I took the box that it might be construed as theft."

"Well, technically, it was theft," Goldman said.

"I know. I don't know what I was thinking," Maya said. "I've never done anything like that in my life. What could happen to me?"

"For stealing the box?" Goldman asked. "I wouldn't worry about it. Owen would have to press charges. To be clear, I'm only interested in finding Irene's killer."

"I did not kill Irene," Maya said. "I adored her."

"Good to know," Goldman said. "You said you found the box in Irene's closet."

"Yes. In the back. Behind a stack of shoeboxes."

"What were you looking for?" Goldman asked.

"Her diary. I thought it might be in the box."

"Seems like an inconvenient location for a diary," he said.

"Yes. But I couldn't find it anywhere else."

"Why were you so sure she kept a diary?"

"Because I gave her one for her birthday. I asked her if she was using it and she said she was."

"Maybe she was just being polite," Goldman said.

Maya felt like a fool. A deep sadness set in.

"I hadn't thought of that," she said.

"When you were looking for the diary, did you find anything else of interest?"

GOLDMAN FOUND HIS partner in the conference room. Burns had arranged a collection of photos in a grid on the long table. A middle-aged bride in a white beaded gown was the subject of the majority of the photos.

"I sent the neighbor home. I think she was overly interested in Irene but not a stalker or killer. What's this?" Goldman asked.

Burns showed Goldman the contact sheet for the photo array. "This camera roll is from 2005," Burns said.

"Who's the bride?" Noah asked.

"I'll tell you in a minute," Burns said, placing a photo in the middle of the table.

"Who is that?" Goldman said, leaning in for a closer inspection.

It was a photo of a woman in a lavender dress. The woman— barely a woman, rail thin, platinum blond—resembled an air- brushed ad in a magazine.

"Am I supposed to recognize her?" Goldman asked.

"Keep looking," Burns said.

Goldman studied the photo. Finally gave up. "I don't know. You tell me."

"That's Irene," Burns said.

Stunned, Goldman looked again. "No way."

It was like one of those ambiguous-image pictures. Sometimes you can't see the other figure until someone else shows you. Even after Goldman saw the resemblance, he didn't see it that clearly.

"That's really weird," Goldman said. "But . . . I'm missing some- thing. What does it mean?"

"Now look at the rest of the pictures," Burns said. "They're in order. I'm thinking Irene took the photos, because they're from her mother's wedding and Chantal Boucher is in most of them. That's the only picture of Irene. Check out the first picture."

Burns pointed at a three-by-five print of a young man sleeping.

"You know who that is, right?" Burns asked.

"That's Owen."

"Right," Burns said. "I just reread the interview transcript. He said he met his wife *five* years ago. The date on the contact sheet says 2005. That's fourteen years ago. Not five."

"Why would he lie about that?" Goldman asked.

"That's what I want to know."

To bring Owen back in, Detective Goldman had to lure him with new evidence. "We just want you to look at an old photo and give us context," Goldman said. "I promise it will take no more than ten minutes."

Burns and Goldman took Owen into an interview room.

The trio sat down around the table. Burns placed the photo of Owen in front of him. In the photo, Owen was young and sleeping.

"Have you seen this before?" Burns asked.

Owen picked up the picture. His brain was tripping over itself. "Where did you find this?"

"I'm afraid we can't say. Have you ever seen that before?"

"No," Owen said.

"It's you, right?" Burns asked.

"Looks like me. What's going on?"

"We believe the photo was taken by Irene."

"That's impossible," Owen said. "I met Irene five years ago. I couldn't be more than twenty in this photo. Where did you get this?"

Burns showed Owen the contact sheet. "These pictures were taken on a 35mm roll. They were time-stamped when they were developed in 2005. You're the first photo on the roll."

Owen's eyes had already jumped ahead to the wedding photos. "Can I see the rest?" Owen said.

Goldman arranged the photos on top of the table in their original order while Burns studied Owen's reaction. His confusion was profound, palpable.

"This is from Chantal Boucher's wedding to Leo?" Owen asked.

"Yes," Burns said.

Then Goldman dropped the one picture that included Irene, wearing a miserable expression and a lavender bridesmaid's dress. Owen picked it up and stared at it, baffled. With her hair blond rather than blue, Owen didn't place her at first. The memory of a booze-filled night had clouded over, like so many memories from that year. Slowly, the woman became more familiar. Pieces clicked into place. The girl from the pub. The blue hair.

"What was her name?" Owen said. "I don't understand. Why do you have a picture of her?"

"You know who that is?" Goldman asked, looking over at his partner.

Burns was studying Owen, trying to determine whether Mann's response was genuine.

"I can't remember her name. I met her in London. We hung out one night."

Burns turned to her partner, raised an eyebrow.

"That's Irene in the picture," Margot said.

Owen continued to stare at the photo, waiting for it to make sense.

"Oh fuck," Owen said. He stood quickly, knocking over his chair. He started to pace, but there was no room for it. "I don't understand."

"You didn't know that was your wife?" Goldman asked.

"No. I don't know," Owen said. "I need to go for a walk. I can't . . . move in here. I need to think."

Burns nodded at her partner.

"Let's get some fresh air," Goldman said. "I'll come with you."

There was a greenbelt behind the station with a short dirt footpath created by decades of cops trying to clear their heads. Owen followed the path, his mind racing, trying to rationalize the irrational.

"What does that photo have to do with anything?" Owen asked.

"Maybe nothing. Probably nothing," Goldman said. "You said that you met Irene five years ago and yet she had a photo of you from almost fifteen years back."

Owen nodded, staring at the ground. "Yeah."

"So you really didn't recognize her?" Goldman said.

"The woman in the photo was from Yorkshire. She had an accent. She had blue hair. And I met a lot of—of girls that year. I probably spent a third of my waking hours in a pub. It was one night out of hundreds, fourteen years ago. She looked completely different back then. Phoebe. I think her name was Phoebe. Well, I don't know why that matters. It was just a name she gave me."

"Do you remember anything else about that night?" Goldman asked.

The detective wasn't sure Owen had heard him. They rambled along the dirt path until they reached a muddy section. Owen stared at the soft ground and turned back. Then Owen spoke. "Are you sure those pictures are from Chantal and Leo's wedding?"

"Yes," Goldman said. "The date tracks. Although Whitman wasn't in any of the photos."

Owen stopped walking. He stood, hands sunk in his pockets, staring down. Goldman waited patiently for whatever memory was surfacing.

"I don't understand why she never—fuck," Owen said, turning to the detective. "She told me about him. When I thought she was someone else. She told me. Fuck."

"What did she tell you?" Goldman asked.

"She slept with him once. Phoebe—well, Irene—told me she slept with her mother's fiancé when she took a course from him at college. Before he was her fiancé. He pursued her mom, just a few years later. She was horrified. She tried to stop it, the wedding. She even tried to talk to the guy, and he pretended like it never happened. She knew that if she told her mother the whole truth, her mother wouldn't believe her."

"When you met Irene for the second time, in 2014, what did she tell you about Leo?"

"Nothing. Well, nothing about that. Every time Leo was around, you could feel this thing, this sickness. She'd told me that her mom and Leo had a difficult marriage. I figured Irene still resented Leo for how he treated her mom. I never thought anything else."

Goldman's phone buzzed in his pocket. The sound brought Owen back to the present, to his current reality.

"Did Leo do this?" Owen asked. "Did Leo kill her?"

It was early in April when Luna got the first call from the FBI agent. She'd returned home from class to find a series of Post-its from Casey on her wall. One said, *Listen to messages!!!* It was followed by a few more with arrows tracing a path toward the answering machine. The exclamation points and cuteness suggested something positive to Luna. When the message started playing, Luna's heart sank and her stomach churned.

Hello. This is Special Agent Paul Murdoch, FBI. I am trying to reach Luna . . . Grey. Um, hmm, the subject is a bit sensitive, so I'd rather not leave the information on a machine. If Ms. Grey could return my call at her earliest convenience, that would be greatly appreciated. This is regarding a matter in Colorado. You can reach me at . . .

Luna played the message three times before she jotted down the number. She picked up the phone, put it down, picked it up again, without knowing whom she wanted to call. She paced, did a few jumping jacks, ate oatmeal with chocolate chips, drank a beer. Then she came to the conclusion that if she just made the call, she could get on with her life. She took the landline into her bedroom. The cord stretched just beyond the doorway. She sat on the floor, her back to the wall, and dialed the number. A receptionist transferred her.

"Ms. Grey, Agent Murdoch here. Thank you for returning my call."

"Is John dead?" Luna asked.

Luna couldn't fathom another reason for the call.

"No, miss. Is this a good time? Are you able to speak freely?"

"I guess so," she said. "I'm getting scared."

"Nothing to be scared about, okay?" the agent said. "I'm going to ask you a favor. And you can say yes or no."

"Okay," Luna said.

"As you know, John Brown has been incarcerated at Sterling Correctional Facility for more than eight years now. I interviewed him a few weeks ago, and he suggested that he may have information about other murders."

"Murders he committed?" Luna said.

She searched her room for something to throw up in. The wastebasket was one of those dumb mesh ones.

"Possibly," said Murdoch. "We want to know, one way or the other."

"I don't understand," Luna said.

"He won't tell us where the bodies are," Murdoch said.

"What bodies?"

"This is where you come in. Mr. Brown has asked to see you. He said that if you came to visit him, he would tell you where he buried his other victims."

"There were more?" Luna said, her voice breaking, hot tears falling, something primal pulling her away from her body so she wouldn't be stuck in it. She was watching a version of herself on the phone with the FBI agent.

"Could be a ploy. But we need to know."

"What do you want me to do?" Luna said.

Murdoch could hear the shift in her tone, tears sopped up, a flatness entering her voice. "We'd like to fly you out and have you talk to him. If he did kill other women, those families would want closure. You would never have to be alone with him. You'd be safe. I promise. You can stop at any time if you're feeling uncomfortable. We can also arrange for you to talk to a psychologist, if that would help. Whatever you need."

262 / LISA LUTZ

"Have you spoken to my mother?"

"No," Agent Murdoch said. "Do you want to discuss it with her?"

"No. Don't call her. Please."

"You're an adult. It's up to you," he said, relieved.

There was a long silence. Murdoch could hear Luna's staccato breathing.

"How are you doing, Ms. Grey?"

"Okay," she said.

"Okay, you'll do it?" Murdoch asked.

She was going to finish the call, then vomit.

"I'll do it," she said.

FRIDAY MORNING, CASEY drove Luna to Albany International Airport.

"Does Griff know about your plans?" Casey asked.

"No," Luna snapped. "And let's keep it that way."

"Got it."

"I'm sorry," Luna said. "I'm just—"

"Stressed out about visiting a murderer in prison?" Casey said. "Hey, we've all been there."

When Casey returned home, Mason was on the phone with Griff. Mason had the expression of someone talking to a senile person. Griff had thought Luna was going to visit her mother in Ontario and had just called to say goodbye. Mason, who did not share Casey's steely adherence to secrecy, told Griff everything that Luna had not.

MURDOCH PICKED UP Luna at the airport Friday evening. He forgot how young twenty-one could look. He pictured this young woman sitting just a few feet away from convicted murderer John Brown, predacious and salivating, the Big Bad Wolf. When Mur-

doch dropped Luna at the Marriott—one of those giant business-
men's compounds—he felt uneasy, knowing that lesser wolves lay
inside. Murdoch offered to buy Luna dinner. She politely declined.

"Order room service," Murdoch said. "Anything you want.
There are movies you can buy. You might think they're too expensive. They're not. That's what movies cost in hotels. If you want to
watch three movies, go right ahead. Okay?"

"Okay," Luna said.

Murdoch confirmed that Luna had his cell number and reminded
her to call at any time. When he got home, he worried and phoned
her hotel room. She answered right away, assuaging his fears. He'd
been imagining her at the bar, drunk and alone and talking to god
knew who. The last thing he needed was the girl hungover when she
saw Brown for the first time in eight years.

MURDOCH HAD WARNED Luna about the long day ahead. It was a
two-hour drive to Sterling, Colorado. The agent had considered getting a hotel closer to the prison but decided against it. He thought
the girl would do better spending a night in a proper hotel, miles
away from John Brown. And he could use the driving time to de-
brief her. Agent Murdoch had two daughters, both much younger
than Luna, but that fact forced him to be on high alert for any precarious moments with John Brown. Luna seemed like a good kid.
He didn't like what she'd done for her brother, but he figured she'd
paid for it already. Murdoch worried about the psychological rami-
fications. Sometimes when you talked to someone who was truly
sick, some of that sickness could stick to you, like drifting ash after
a fire. He needed to be sure she was ready.

The drive felt longer than two hours. The Denver mountains still
had snow on their peaks, but they weren't driving in an especially
pretty part of the state. The landscape grew increasingly barren.
Murdoch kept giving Luna their ETA. *Just another hour. Thirty
minutes out. Almost there.* Luna saw the sign for Sterling Correc-

tional Facility, a cement box wrapped with barbed wire. Murdoch flashed his badge at the security checkpoint and pulled his car into the visitor parking lot. Luna watched the agent lock his gun in a small safe located in the trunk of his car.

Murdoch had his hand on Luna's shoulder as they walked down the stark hallway to the meeting room. Luna was suddenly thirsty. The fluorescent lights were so bright that Luna wished she could wear sunglasses. She hadn't had a seizure in a few years, but the conditions were ripe for one. A man in an orange jumpsuit was chained to a metal table. It took her a moment to realize it was John. Back when they'd lived under the same roof, when she thought she knew him, Brown was trim and handsome, in a way. Like a secondary character in a Western. The man before her had maybe thirty more pounds of muscle and another twenty of soft gut, not to mention the monk's pattern baldness.

John Brown grinned toothy and wide when Luna walked into the room. "Look at you, Taco, all grown up," he said.

Luna thought she was in the wrong room at first. Why was this big man calling her Taco? Her brain had worked overtime to erase him from her memory, but *Taco* did ring a distant bell. Then she recalled a night when she was a little girl. Maybe seven or eight. John was tucking her into bed and he'd wrapped a quilt around her, said she reminded him of a taco. He called her that maybe once or twice. She felt like he was using the nickname now for show, trying to trick Luna into thinking they'd had their own secret language.

Brown maintained his Cheshire Cat grin, waiting for Luna to join in on the happy reunion. Murdoch was impressed with the young lady's implacable demeanor. Agent Murdoch and Luna had talked about how she could best manage the situation. *Don't be afraid—we're with you—but even if you are, try not to show it. If you're not sure what to say, take a moment, think. There's no rush. If you need a break, ask for a break.* He also told her she didn't have to appease Brown.

"Remember," Murdoch had said, "John needs you there, nice or not. He will do whatever he has to, say whatever he can, to keep you in that room and not have to go back to his cell."

Luna checked the clock. She and Murdoch had agreed on limiting catch-up to ten minutes. John had many questions for Luna, most of which were off-limits. She would not reveal any specific details of her life. John asked if she was in college. Luna said she was, back East. Where? John asked. Nope, Murdoch said, staring the prisoner down.

"I heard you got a new name," John said. "Grey. Not very original, is it?"

He shouldn't have had that information. Murdoch considered ending the interview right there. It was possible that John Brown was bluffing, that there were no more bodies and he was just trying to do as much damage as he could from inside.

"Were there others?" Luna asked.

John ignored her question. The meeting was going to move according to his own pace. Agent Murdoch reminded John Brown that there was a clock on the reunion. He had forty-five more minutes, and then Luna was gone. There were other incentives—a different prison, his own cell, that kind of thing—but additional face time with Luna was off the table.

John Brown reminisced about a trip to the county fair where he'd let Luna eat three voluminous clouds of cotton candy. Then he held her hair while she puked pink until her guts were empty.

"Prettiest vomit I ever saw," Brown said, chuckling, trying to get Luna to join in on the laughter.

When she didn't laugh, his expression soured.

"You're not as fun as you used to be."

"Maybe your expectations for this reunion were unrealistic," Luna said.

Brown ignored the comment and began to reminisce about old pets. Bruno the cocker spaniel, Cleo the cat. "Did Bee ever meet an animal she didn't fall in love with?"

"Who's Bee?" Murdoch asked.

"My mother," Luna said.

"How is she?" Brown asked.

"Fine."

"What does that mean, 'fine'?" Brown said.

"It means I'm not going to tell you anything about her," Luna said.

"Remember that snake-squirrel she brought home? What was its name? Hermes? Something like that."

"Don't remember that," Luna said.

Her mother didn't get ferrets until their move to Canada, as far as Luna recalled.

"You don't remember that ferret?" Brown said.

"I don't."

"You couldn't breathe, Taco. We had to take you to the hospital."

Luna had a foggy recollection of a hospital corridor, the raspy sound of her own breath, fighting for air.

"Vaguely," Luna said. "I remember a stray cat causing that asthma attack."

"Trust me," Brown said. "It was Hermes, that filthy fucker. God, that thing stank."

"I don't remember," Luna said.

"It was my first," John said. "I did it for you. Then I found I had an aptitude for it."

It took Luna a moment to understand what he was saying. Her throat felt dry. Too dry to speak. She wanted to ask for water, but she worried that Brown would see weakness in that. He already had too much power, having just carved a new memory into her brain.

"The lights are bothering me," Luna said.

"Turn 'em off," Brown said.

"No," Murdoch said. "Luna and I will step outside for a few."

"Maybe I don't feel like waiting around," Brown said.

Murdoch knew he was bluffing. But he played along.

"You got something better to do? We'll be back in five," Murdoch said.

Luna sat down on the floor in the hallway and closed her eyes.

"Hanging in there?" the agent asked.

"Yes," Luna said.

Murdoch took a pair of aviators from his pocket and offered them to Luna. "Maybe this helps?"

Luna donned the sunglasses. "It's better," she said. "But it'll piss him off."

"That's okay. You're safe," Murdoch said. "So, what's your gut telling you? Other girls?"

Luna got to her feet. "I don't think so. But let's just make sure."

"Take those off," Brown said, when Luna walked in wearing sunglasses.

"John, it's time to get down to business. Luna has a plane to catch."

John refused to acknowledge Agent Murdoch. He wanted the man to go away and leave Luna alone in the room. He knew it would never happen, so the best he could do was pretend the lawman wasn't there.

"All these years, Taco—you couldn't have written at least once?"

"I didn't want to," Luna said.

"Did you get my letters?"

"Got them. But didn't read them."

"I bet Bee threw them away."

"No. It was my decision."

"That's okay," John said. "I forgive you."

"You forgive me," Luna said. "For what?"

"John," Murdoch said. "Let's get to business."

"You let me take the fall for everything."

"You killed them," Luna said.

"Sure, I did the heavy lifting. I was the bank robber; you were just the getaway driver. But we were a team. Admit that."

"No."

"You knew what you were doing when you lied to the police. I just want you to own that part of it."

"You're right, John. I knew I was lying. Then I was afraid to change that lie. I take some responsibility for Lila. But we were not a team."

"John," Murdoch said. "Were there others?"

Brown kept seeing his own reflection in Luna's sunglasses, which infuriated him. Luna could feel his anger. Her skin was prickly and cold.

"I think we should go," Luna said.

"You're not in charge here, young lady, I am. There are four corpses in unmarked graves and only I know where they are," Brown said.

"We can get a map. You could show us the general area," Murdoch said.

John held his gaze on Luna. "No. I'd have to be there myself to jog my memory. If you want to arrange a field trip, I'd be happy to show you."

"What's the general vicinity?" Murdoch asked.

"In the general vicinity of Denver. A place where there's land and dirt and you can bury someone without being seen. Doesn't narrow it down much, I know. Like I said, you need me to find the graves."

"What were their names?" Luna asked.

"Not sure I'm ready to answer that," John said.

"How about one?" Luna asked.

John Brown smiled, paused for a moment, and said, "Daria."

Luna took a breath, got lost in a memory. Then she turned to Agent Murdoch and whispered in his ear, "He's lying."

"You sure?" Murdoch said.

Luna nodded.

"What the fuck you two talking about?"

"How about another name?" Luna said.

John seemed stumped by the question. Luna saw the brief expression of confusion before it was replaced with resolute anger. "One at a time," he said.

Luna turned to Murdoch and shook her head.

"I think we're done here," Murdoch said to the guard.

While John Brown unleashed a stream of curses and railed about all the girls who would never be found, Murdoch ushered Luna out of the room and down the hallway, to a quiet place where she'd feel almost safe.

She took a moment to catch her breath.

"You okay?" Murdoch asked.

"I'm really sorry," she said.

"Don't be. If you needed to get out of there, I understand."

"There weren't other girls," Luna said. "He would have remembered their names."

"He said Daria," Murdoch said.

"He said Daria after a pause. He had to think about it. She was my babysitter when I was younger. He might have thought about killing her. But I'd have heard if she went missing or died back then. If what he's saying were true, he would have used the information sooner. He wouldn't have waited eight years to barter. He was waiting until I was an adult. This was his only way to get to me."

It made sense, Murdoch thought. "Does anything he said ring true?"

Luna shook her head. "No. I could always tell when he was lying. There's a way he squints a little, stares at you, dead in the eye. I knew back then. I was never innocent. I'm not saying I saw him do it, but I think I always sort of knew that maybe he had."

The girl appeared shaky and pale, Murdoch thought. Something was happening that he was ill-equipped to handle.

"You were eleven years old," Murdoch said. "Don't let old mistakes poison a new life. Let's get the hell out of here."

Murdoch and Luna stopped at a diner on the way back. Luna ordered a vanilla shake after Murdoch dissuaded her from the spinach salad.

"Did you tell your mother you were coming out here?" Murdoch asked.

"No," Luna said. "It's better if she doesn't know."

"The parent is supposed to protect their child. Not the other way around."

"Maybe," Luna said. "But I understand. Mom left me alone with him all the time. I think she felt guilty about that."

"When did your father pass away?"

"A month or two after John was found not guilty. Heart attack. If you see photos of him before and after the trial, he was like a different man. I think he might have suspected the truth. I'm glad he didn't live long enough to be sure about his son or to know what I did. That part would have killed him."

"This visit, it might stick with you for a while. Make sure you talk to people, okay?"

"Okay," Luna said.

"Have you or your mom gotten letters from Gregory Wells recently?"

"How do you know about that?" Luna asked.

"Your aunt mentioned it when I was trying to track you down."

"He used to write a couple of times a year. It's been a while. Did something happen to him?"

"He was hospitalized after a suicide attempt. He's been out for a few months. I just wanted to be sure they hadn't resumed."

"No," Luna said.

"Let me know if that changes."

Murdoch drove back to the Denver field office. Luna signed some paperwork there and talked to a shrink for a while. She promised to follow up with a phone session a week later.

Murdoch offered to buy Luna dinner. She said she was tired and wanted to order room service again. Murdoch understood. There were some days when the mere thought of hiding out in a hotel room at night, wearing a white robe and eating food on a tray, seemed like heaven.

Luna just wanted to get away from him before she fell apart. It was like she was holding off an avalanche. Once she returned to the hotel, she took cover in her room. She didn't know what would happen when she didn't have to pretend anymore. She waited for tears. There were none. She bent over the toilet, thinking she needed to vomit. Nothing. Instead, what she felt was like a poison going through her. Not enough to actually kill her, but enough to feel like a half death. It just stuck there, stagnant in her body.

She decided to go to the bar. Maybe another poison would mask the feeling of the first. She ordered a whiskey. The bartender asked for her ID.

"Happy birthday," he said.

It had been a week before, but she thanked him. Luna drained the whiskey and ordered another. The bartender nodded and gave her a look that said, *Let's be careful, now.* Luna thanked him for the second drink. He knocked on the bar. She'd never seen anyone do that before and wondered what it meant.

A businessman sat down next to her and smiled. He didn't give off a man-on-the-prowl vibe. It was more like *What's this kid doing alone in a hotel?*

"Business or pleasure?" the man asked.

Luna laughed. "You wouldn't believe me if I told you."

The businessman's curiosity was piqued. "Try me," he said.

Luna almost blurted it out; she thought it might lessen the poison sensation. She felt a presence on the other side of her. Luna's drink disappeared. Griff was standing there, finishing her whiskey. The bartender scrutinized the bold customer, debating whether he'd need to intervene.

"Miss, do you know this man?" the bartender asked.

Luna nodded. "I think so," she said.

The poison lifted, like Griff was the antidote.

October 15, 2019

———

"Let's recap," Detective Goldman said. "Owen tells us he met his wife five years ago. But we find a picture of him on Irene's camera roll from fourteen years back. When we show the evidence to Owen, he has a brain melt—a convincing one, I admit—and suddenly remembers that he spent a night with Irene in London back then. He also remembers a rather damning story she told that night. Do you believe him?"

"I think I do," Burns said. "Memories are flexible and unreliable. And he seemed genuinely confused."

"If we believe him," Goldman said, "all it tells us is that Leo is a creep. What does it give us for Irene's murder?"

"Not sure. But it does establish Leo's murky ethics. It's possible he thought he'd get something upon Irene's death. Either way, let's bring him in."

"You're going to enjoy this, aren't you?" Goldman said.

"Well, I won't not enjoy it."

An hour later, Whitman was sitting in an interview room with Detective Burns. Noah watched the proceedings on a monitor. Burns started the interview by asking for insight into Irene and Owen's marriage.

"I can't say I was hopeful about it, even at the beginning. Of course, not in a million years did I think it would end like this. God, her mother would kill me if she knew I let this happen," Leo said.

"You're saying that Owen and Irene's marriage was always rocky?" Burns asked.

"Indeed."

"In what way?" she said.

"The usual. Fights and infidelity."

"Both of them were having affairs? Or just Owen?" Burns asked.

"I'm sure you know more than I do," said Leo. "May I ask a question?"

"Go ahead."

"How common is it for someone to be shot in broad daylight without a single witness?"

"Not common," Burns said. "But the cemetery wasn't a heavily trafficked area."

"Can't you trace the gun through ballistics?" Leo said. "I'm ashamed to admit I've watched a few episodes of *Law and Order* in my day."

"The gun would have had to be used in a previous crime," Burns said.

"I see," Whitman said.

"What was Irene's relationship like with her mother?"

"Fraught. Well, more so when Irene was younger."

"Fraught how?"

"Chantal was conservative in many ways. She had some trouble with Irene's lifestyle."

"Lifestyle?"

"Nothing unusual. Late nights, drinking, smoking hash. I don't think she was into anything harder, if that's what you're asking."

"Tattoos?"

"She didn't have any tattoos," Leo said. Then, after a pause: "At least, I don't think so."

"Do you remember how they were getting on before your wedding?"

"There was definitely some tension," Leo said.

"About what?"

Leo took a moment to consider the question. Or pretend to consider it, Burns thought.

"Chantal didn't want Irene to have blue hair in our wedding photos."

"She had blue hair, did she?"

"Yes," Leo said, smiling, remembering. "She was something back then. Not that Irene wasn't an attractive older woman."

"I apologize," Margot said. "I'm not following. Who are we talking about?"

"Irene."

"She was thirty-six when she died," Burns said. "That's an *older* woman to you?"

"Older than she was, that's all I meant. Don't take offense, Detective."

Burns felt the lascivious tone that Owen had described. Mann's story was adding up, at the very least.

"How much money has Irene given you in the past year?" Burns asked.

"Pardon me?"

"We know that Irene gave you fifteen thousand in April. That's the limit for tax-exempt gifts," Burns said.

"Well, we are family," Leo said.

"Was she just being generous, or were you having financial problems? Doesn't have to be one or the other," she said.

"I think Irene felt guilty about the way her mother's estate was settled. I was married to the woman and she left virtually everything to her daughter."

"It was my understanding that Chantal established a trust in your name," Burns said. "What happened to that?"

"It was hardly anything," Leo said. "It kept me afloat a few years."

"When the trust ran dry, Irene continued to give you money," Burns said.

"She helped out now and again. It was the least she could do."

"How much did she give you in the last two years?"

"I don't know."

"Ballpark."

"Are you moonlighting for the IRS, Detective?"

"I'm trying to make sense of the numerous cash withdrawals Irene made in the last six months. If all of those funds went into your account, that's fine. As you said, you were family. But let's say she was giving money to someone else. Maybe there was an innocent explanation. Maybe not. Maybe someone was blackmailing her. Either way, we need to know. Would you mind giving us a detailed accounting of Irene's gifts or loans in the last two years? I promise we won't rat you out to the feds."

"Two years. I can barely remember last week," Whitman said.

"You can go home, review your records, and come back with the information," Burns said.

"I won't be able to do that overnight," said Whitman. "I'll probably have to contact my accountant."

"You need an accountant just to print out bank records?"

"I'm afraid I'm terrible with computer stuff."

"I'm sure your assistant could help you."

"Excuse me?"

"You hired Amy Johnson, right?"

"For a trial period. I'm not sure it will work out."

"Why not?"

"Myriad reasons, Detective. Are we almost done?"

"Did you hire Amy because she was Owen's mistress?"

"Of course not."

"What was your angle?" Burns asked.

Whitman got to his feet. "I'd like to go home now."

"Of course," said Burns. "Detective Goldman will drive you."

IN THE CAR, Leo sat frozen, like a side of beef. Some people got really still when they were scared.

"I love this time of year," Noah said, genuinely moved by the way the leaves revolted in beauty before they gave up and rejoined the earth.

Silence.

"What, it doesn't do it for you?" Noah said.

"I prefer the simple austerity of winter," Leo said.

"Huh. Interesting."

"You do understand that Irene giving me money is hardly a motive. In fact, it's the opposite of one," Leo said. "With Irene dead, so is my benefactor."

Goldman pulled up in front of Leo's house.

"I don't think you killed her," Goldman said.

Leo reached for the door. "I appreciate that. Thank you for the ride, Detective."

"Do you have a paper shredder?" Goldman asked, freezing Leo mid-exit.

"I . . . uh. I don't know," Leo said. He had one and decided it was best not to lie. "I think so."

"Don't shred anything. It won't help your case and it just makes us angry."

"Didn't you just tell me you thought I was innocent?"

"Of murder. Probably," Goldman said. "Now, blackmail, that's another story."

June–July 2005

Owen knew something was up with his brother and Luna before he left for England. It was funny how they were trying to avoid telegraphing their feelings when Owen could see it plain and simple. He didn't have a strong opinion about their budding relationship at the time. He had other concerns back then.

After the new year, Owen had received a letter from Luna detailing her insane Christmas road trip with Griff. Owen figured she just wanted company. He didn't think it was serious. Luna wasn't even twenty-one yet. Who meets their future spouse at that age? Not Luna. Griff emailed Owen after the trip to say he and Luna were dating. *I hope that's cool.* Then, casually, he told Owen about the crazy ferret trip. *And then her sweater came to life!*

Owen wrote Griff back a month later, saying he was happy for them. That wasn't strictly true, but he wasn't unhappy for them either. Owen didn't think it was serious until he heard that Griff had accompanied Luna to Denver. She'd mentioned it briefly in a letter.

So I flew to Denver to help the FBI investigate other murders that John Brown might have committed. That was weird.

Owen had to wait until his next phone call with Luna to learn that there were no other victims. On that call, Owen insisted on a few more details. Luna got as far as Agent Murdoch dropping her off at the Denver Marriott, then nothing. Silence.

"You still there?" Owen asked.

"Yes. Sorry," she said.

Luna wasn't prone to monologues. She always hated when people talked at her, so she was overly sensitive to taking a long turn in a conversation.

"Next morning, the fed picks you up at the hotel," Owen said. "Then what?"

"Hey, Owen," Luna said. "Do you mind if we skip this for now? It doesn't feel good."

"Shit. I'm sorry," Owen said. "You don't ever have to talk about it, if you don't want to."

"Thanks," she said.

He knew it wasn't rational, but it hurt him that Griff got to be there and he couldn't even get a summary.

As MUCH AS Owen missed many things that he could find only back home—Luna, the Berkshires house, driving, being a passenger in the correct seat—he'd planned to postpone his reentry as long as possible. Other than Luna, nothing was waiting for him back home.

But then, in June, Griff called. Their father was in the hospital. Stomach cancer. The oncologist had suggested that the best-case scenario was a few years.

The treatment plan for Tom was immediate surgery followed by chemo. When Owen decided to fly back, he didn't realize he was committing to a full summer of living in his childhood home. The contrast between Owen's freewheeling London life and sharing a suburban home with his parents at peak dysfunction was jarring, to say the least. Vera had no talent for caregiving and Tom was a crap patient. His physical discomfort fueled his temper, which rattled everyone in his wake, including the part-time nurse.

Owen made his father food, watched sports with him, and hid out when his parents fought. The good news was that, with Tom's condition, the fighting never got physical. Still, the words traumatized Owen. The arguments felt different with Tom's weakened, raspy voice. Eventually, Owen learned that he could snuff out a conflict if he just walked into it. It made for an uncomfortable moment or two, but then it was over.

His father was always in pain, always asking for his pills. Vera rationed them conservatively, giving Tom only the minimum dosage. She kept them in a lockbox in the pantry, which Owen found odd, since his father got winded walking ten steps to the bathroom. When Owen asked his mother about the lock, she launched into a lecture about the dangers of opioids.

Because he hadn't applied to transfer to another college or made any other arrangements for his future, Owen remained stranded in Boston with his mom. Griff came to visit every other weekend, giving him something of a respite. But even then, Owen had to fend off Griff's aggressive interest in his plans. One morning, Griff asked Owen if he was thinking about returning to Markham to finish his degree.

"Seriously, dude. You remember what happened there?" Owen asked.

"Yeah. But it's over, Owen. And you're going to need a degree to teach, which, let's face it, is probably how you'll make a living. Unless you're luckier than I think you are."

Owen winced. "Did you pay for douchebag school or go on scholarship?" he asked.

Vera breezed into the room and warmed her coffee in the microwave. "Boys, be nice," she said.

"All I did was suggest Owen return to Markham in the fall. It's easier than transferring credits."

"Half the student body thinks I'm a murderer. I'm not going back," Owen said.

He was stunned that he had to explain it to his family. Griff could tell that Owen's wounds were still exposed.

"Sorry," Griff said. "I thought your reputation would have been rehabbed after the police closed the case."

"People don't remember the two paragraphs in the *Markham Gazette*. They don't care that it was an accident, that Scarlet went on a drunken late-night hike, wearing a party dress and Converse sneakers. They remember that I was dragged off campus by two uniformed officers. They remember that I was the only suspect. For the rest of my life, that incident will hang over my head. I go for a job interview, all they have to do is google my name."

Griff nodded his understanding and didn't say a word after that. Owen took Griff's silence as a win.

LUNA AND GRIFF were still a couple and still in love, by both accounts. But there wasn't much time for them to be together. Griff's first year at the law firm required eighty hours a week. Before Tom's diagnosis, Luna would take the train to Manhattan every other weekend. Griff's visits home to see his dad cut into some of that. Sometimes Luna would meet Griff in Boston, see the entire clan, but she always felt uneasy in that house. It could have been the looming death, Luna's general discomfort with Vera, or the weirdness of being under the same roof as Owen while sleeping with his brother.

Then Luna found out she was pregnant. Her plan was to deal with it without telling a soul. Casey came home early one day and heard Luna crying.

"What happened?" Casey asked.

"I don't want to talk about it," Luna said.

"You're not pregnant, are you?" Casey asked.

It was a wild guess. Luna's shocked expression answered the question.

"Oh fuck. You are," Casey said. "Wait, are you sure? You should see a doctor." She sat down on Luna's bed, dispensing tissues.

"I'm sure."

"What are you going to do?" Casey asked.

"What do you think?" Luna said.

The answer was so plain to her, she couldn't believe Casey would even ask.

"Have you talked to Griff?"

Luna sat up in bed and glared at Casey. Casey winced under Luna's feral advance.

"If you say one word to anyone, I swear, Casey, I will—"

She didn't need to finish the sentence; the threat was established. Casey knew not to cross Luna.

"I won't say a word. Have you made the appointment?"

"A week from Monday," Luna said.

"Okay," Casey said. "I'll come with you."

Mason didn't know what the hell was going on. Casey had sworn her silence. Even if she hadn't, she knew Mason was a crap liar. But because of Mason's sensitive nature, he couldn't get used to the overall feeling in the house. There was so much pain behind Luna's door. Mason only wanted to help. Since Luna so rarely emerged from her room, Mason took to bringing her things. Coffee in the morning. Toast a few hours later. Soup or sandwiches around lunchtime. Water. He'd place a mug or plate next to her door and knock quietly, alerting Luna to the delivery. One of those times he was hovering near her door, he heard Luna on the phone.

"Why can't I do it now? It's my choice. What would I need to do to make it happen?" she said. "I can't wait eight more years. It's not about that. It's better for society—I understand what you're saying, but it's my body."

Mason spent the whole day trying to figure out what was going on with Luna. Then he had an idea.

"Is Luna donating an organ?" Mason asked Casey.

Casey inquired how Mason arrived at such a hypothesis. He explained the one-sided conversation. The eight-years remark stumped Casey as well. Mason insisted that's what Luna had said.

BY MID-JULY, OWEN, Griff, and Vera came to realize that the doctor's original prognosis was not just optimistic but unrealistic. In early August, Vera asked the doctor how much time Tom had. The doctor said six months. A week later, Tom was dead.

It was Owen who made the discovery. As usual, he got up, started the coffee, and walked down the hallway to check on his dad.

"Morning, Dad," Owen said, as he opened the door.

Owen sensed it right away. His dad was a loud breather, generally. Owen stepped closer to investigate. He poked his dad and jumped back. Tom didn't move. Then Owen saw the empty bottle of pills on the nightstand. Owen couldn't figure out how his dad would have gotten the pills, since they were locked up.

When Owen turned around, his mother was standing there. He startled. He felt his heart thumping. Why was he so jumpy?

"Mom," he said. "Dad's—"

"I know," Vera said. "He died last night. Doesn't he seem at peace?"

Owen wasn't expecting his mother to be so tranquil. It wasn't really her style. Owen stared, slack-jawed, and said, "What?"

Vera turned Owen around, so he was facing Tom. "See? He's no longer in pain."

"Okay," Owen said.

"Do you want some time alone with him?"

"Why?" Owen said, his voice cracking in panic.

"To say goodbye," said Vera.

"No. I'm good," Owen said, rushing out of the room.

Later, when his mother was meeting with an undertaker, Owen found the key to the lockbox and opened it. He found another prescription of Oxy. Only a few pills were left. He snapped a photo of the almost-empty bottle and another of the bottle on his dad's nightstand. Owen knew his mother was getting weekly refills. Doctors aren't stingy with pain meds in terminal cases. Owen suspected that Vera was keeping a few for herself. But it didn't track, when he thought about it. His mom had been unusually lucid. She wasn't even drinking that much. Owen could always tell when Vera was altered. He logged on to her computer—Vera used the same password for everything—and checked the prescription-order history. He cross-checked the orders against the spreadsheet they used to keep track of his father's meds. There was a surplus, which Owen couldn't find anywhere in the house. If you asked Owen to explain how he came to the conclusion that his mother had hastened his father's death, he couldn't tell you. He just *knew*.

Vera made the call to her older son, and Griff drove back to Boston late that night. Owen had just assumed he would bring Luna with him. When Griff walked in the front door, Owen hugged his brother then stepped outside, anticipating her arrival. The street was empty. Owen reentered the house.

"Where's Luna?" Owen asked.

"She had an appointment or something," Griff said. "She'll come out for the funeral."

OWEN WOULD REMEMBER the sound of the phone ringing more than anything. It wouldn't stop. Sometimes it felt like Luna was the only person who wasn't calling that house. Vera always answered the phone. Owen could hear all her conversations. His mom wouldn't shut up about how peaceful Tom looked. Owen was thinking, *You know who looks peaceful right now? You, Mom.*

At breakfast, he asked his mother if there would be an autopsy.

"Why on earth would they do that?" Vera asked.

"I don't know," Owen said.

"He had cancer," Vera said. Firmly.

The phone rang. Vera retrieved it and disappeared into the living room to take the call.

"The doctor said he had six months," Owen said to his brother.

"Dude, you don't get a countdown clock with a prognosis," Griff snapped.

"Fuck off, Griff. I'm just asking a question. Remember, I'm the one stuck here."

"Sorry," Griff said, genuinely contrite. He knew the summer had to have been hard on Owen. "I haven't slept more than four hours a night in . . . months?"

"You do look like shit," Owen said as a way of accepting the apology.

. . .

THE FUNERAL ARRANGEMENTS were set for Monday, just two days after Tom died. Noting the speediness of the arrangements, Casey asked Luna if the Manns were secret Jews.

Luna rented a car and drove on her own to Boston, made it just in time for the church service. She didn't even see Owen or Griff until after the service was over. Along with Casey and Mason, Luna returned to the Mann house, where Vera was hosting a small gathering with deli plates and, more important, an abundance of alcohol. The younger crowd hid out in Griff's childhood bedroom. Luna kept checking the clock. She couldn't drink, because she had to drive home and have a procedure the next morning. She was trying to figure out the earliest socially acceptable exit.

Luna was being distant, a bit odd. Both brothers noticed. Owen's generous opinion was that family gatherings were challenging for Luna. That she'd learned it was safer to be alone. She didn't know how to behave in a normal family. When Luna was late for the service, Griff wondered if she was sending him a subconscious message that she wanted to break up. He wondered if she was waiting for a socially acceptable time to do so. But then later, when the group was hanging out in his room, she held his hand and asked how he was doing, and everything seemed as normal as it could be. He relaxed briefly. Griff told himself that he was being paranoid.

An hour later, Luna said she had to go. It was late. Griff didn't realize she was driving back that night. He was so stunned that she was leaving, he just nodded and said, "Okay."

"Walk her to her car," Mason said.

Mason was drunk by then, but he had a few stubborn life rules. Walking a woman to her car or her home when it was dark out, even if that woman could probably manage self-defense better than he could, was one of them. He was a chivalrous feminist, Casey would tell people. It was one of his best qualities, she thought.

"I'm fine," Luna said.

"I'll walk you," Mason said, stumbling to his feet.

"Mason, sit down," Griff said.

Mason's ungainly dismount back to the floor broke the tension. Luna said her goodbyes to Owen, Casey, and Mason. Griff walked her out.

After they left, Owen said, "Something's weird."

"Yeah," Mason said. "Everything changes when your parents die. It's a lot to process, man. You gotta give yourself time."

Casey was disappointed in herself for not monitoring Mason's drinking better. The next morning was going to be a shit show.

"I was talking about Luna," Owen said. "She was weird today, right?"

"Yeah. She's been a little strange lately. I wouldn't worry about it," Casey said.

Mason leaned closer to Owen and tried to whisper, but he seemed to have forgotten how whispering worked. He was also putting an emphasis on random words, like he drew them out of a hat.

"I *overheard* a really weird conversation," Mason said. "Luna's conversation. *Well,* only one side. Luna's side. A *phone* call."

"Mason," Casey said, as a warning.

"What did she say?" Owen asked.

"I don't remember . . . exactly."

"He doesn't know what he's talking about," Casey said.

"I do know!" Mason said. He took some time to think about it. Then he became distracted by the carpet. He hadn't seen a proper shag rug in a while. Mason's brain finally circled back to Luna. "I think Luna is donating an organ. Or trying to donate an organ and they won't let her. That happens, right?"

Casey rolled her eyes and breathed very loudly.

"Let's get you some dinner," Owen said to Mason.

As Owen guided Mason down the stairs, Mason asked, "Did Luna tell you she was donating an organ?"

By midnight, all the guests were gone, the catering staff had cleaned up and cleared out, and Vera was asleep in bed. Casey and

Mason were in the guest room. Owen and Griff sat outside on the back deck. Griff had forgotten how quiet it could be away from the constant noise of New York City.

Owen kept thinking about the missing pills and Vera's part in Tom's slightly premature death. You couldn't say he was upset or angry. But he did want to know if his theory was sane or not.

"Do you think Mom was taking some of Dad's pain pills?" Owen asked.

"No. Weird question," Griff said.

"Why?"

"She can't take opioids. They make her vomit. We only need to worry about her drinking."

"How do you know that?" asked Owen.

"Remember when she had kidney stones? Maybe you don't. You might have just left for college. Dad told me about it. It was a nightmare for him. She was in extreme pain. When she took the pain meds, she started vomiting. He had to call an ambulance."

"Huh," Owen said.

He had no knowledge of that incident.

"Why are you asking about that?" Griff asked.

"I think maybe Mom killed Dad," Owen said. Casually.

October 15, 2019

————

Griff had planned to return to the city soon after the wake. Then, on Monday morning, he'd phoned his boss and asked whether he could stay on at the country house a few more nights. The boss was glad someone was getting use out of it, and most of Griff's work could be done remotely. While Griff was fond of the house, and Sam (the dog) was certainly having a fine time, he had only one reason for staying on. He couldn't stop hearing one line over and over again.

You broke her fucking heart, man.

Griff texted Luna again Monday afternoon. He asked about the dining situation at the Sleep Chalet. He was informed there was a Lunch Chalet across the street. He asked Luna if she'd like a home-cooked meal, and they planned a dinner for the next night.

OWEN CALLED LUNA after he left the police station. He was reeling after seeing the photo and remembering that night. He needed to talk, to make sense of things. Luna, however, wanted to have just one day away from Owen, one day alone with Griff. She said she'd call him tomorrow. She needed some space.

Owen texted Mason after that.

Weird shit is going on here. Mind warp kinda shit.

Sorry, man. In a meeting. Call you later?

Owen, desperate, texted his brother.

Where are you?

Still upstate. Get an attorney yet?

No.

Jesus, Owen.

Call you later.

Owen drove down to Rhinebeck to meet with Irene's financial adviser, Cliff Easter. The office was on the second floor above a health-food store. Owen climbed a narrow staircase and was greeted by a middle-aged man with shaggy brown hair. He wore a Grateful Dead T-shirt and an old green cardigan.

"Owen. Nice to see you. So sorry about Irene. Come in."

Owen followed Cliff into a modest office that was equipped with a mismatched collection of standard office furniture. It felt like a statement about how one should use one's money.

"Have a seat," Cliff said, after clearing a stack of papers from a beat-up swivel chair.

"Thanks," Owen said, sinking into the chair and rolling back a bit.

"I can't fucking believe she was shot," Cliff said.

Owen, so startled to hear someone say anything beyond the standard *sorry for your loss,* could only manage to blurt out, "Yeah."

Easter got right to it: "I know you've been in touch with Mr. Bloom. Probate should take under a year, depending on the timeline for the art auction. I assume there were no surprises."

"No," Owen said.

"Was she buying the art for you?"

"Excuse me?" Owen said.

"Irene had made a number of large cash withdrawals from her personal brokerage account in the last year."

"How large?"

"About thirty thousand, total."

"In cash? Why?" Owen asked.

"She said she was buying art."

"She wasn't," Owen said. "At least I don't think she was. And why would she pay cash?"

"I asked her that same question."

OWEN'S MIND SWIRLED with vague conspiracy theories as he sat in his car outside Cliff's office. There was no obvious reason why Irene would need large sums of cash. She wasn't the kind of person who hid money in a shoebox. Then again, Owen also hadn't thought Irene was the kind of person to have an affair. Or the kind of person who wouldn't remind you that you'd actually met them fourteen years ago.

Owen needed Luna. He texted her, waited five minutes, and texted again. Nothing. He drove to a pub nearby, parked, and entered the dim establishment.

Owen was halfway through his first beer, and Luna still hadn't replied. He knew she wasn't busy. Maybe she was driving, he thought. He remembered that Luna had recently tracked his location. He opened the app and saw her somewhere on Route 9. At first he thought she was at the Sleep Chalet, but the icon traveled south. In fact, Luna appeared to be heading right toward his current location. Knowing she wouldn't text while driving, he called. The phone rang four times and went to voicemail.

LUNA HEARD HER phone ringing as she drove to Griff's place. She stopped along the way to pick up a bottle of wine and noticed that it was Owen who'd called. She didn't bother to check the message.

Back on the road, her mind drifted to the past, to subjects she hadn't thought about in ages. The memories had a power that was both thrilling and deeply uncomfortable. At some point along Route 9, Luna noticed the car behind her. It was dark out, but Luna could still see that the headlights behind her belonged to an SUV. The driver kept a safe distance between them, which she noted because she always felt like people were either tailgating or damming up the roadway. The SUV also got her attention because Owen had mentioned his police escort. She wondered if they were now following her. Maybe the cops thought she and Owen were in on it together. She wondered when all of this would be over. Luna's GPS told her to turn left in half a mile. After the turn, she checked her mirror again. The SUV was gone.

Luna followed a narrow country road for half a mile. A full moon cast a glow over the heavily wooded lane. Her GPS told her she'd reach her destination in a quarter mile, then in eight hundred feet. Then it told her she had reached her destination. She spotted a reflector and a narrow private drive. Luna slowed to a crawl and made a sharp right turn onto an unpaved path. After a jostling ride surrounded by dense brush, she came into a clearing with a two-story yellow farmhouse lit up in the center.

Luna parked the car and killed the engine. Griff stepped outside and waited on the porch. Sam the dog greeted her as she strolled up to the house.

"Nice place," Luna said, handing over the bottle of wine.

Griff kissed her on both cheeks. His proximity conjured all kinds of long-forgotten feelings. As soon as they stepped away from each other, Luna heard an engine and felt bright lights on her back. She turned around and squinted at the high beams.

"Are you expecting someone?" Luna asked.

"It's Owen," Griff said.

"I didn't know you invited him," she said.

"I didn't."

"I'm going to open the wine," Luna said, entering the house.

As Griff waited for Owen on the front porch, Luna searched the kitchen, with Sam the dog on her heels. She rummaged through several cutlery drawers until she found the wine opener. Once Luna wrestled off the cork, she pulled three wineglasses from the cabinet. Owen and Griff joined her as she emptied the bottle of wine into thirds.

"I was calling you," Owen said.

"I was driving," Luna said.

She delivered two swelling glasses of wine to Griff and Owen. She raised her own goblet and said, "Cheers."

"Didn't know you'd be here," Owen said.

"Same," Luna said.

Owen didn't like how Luna was avoiding eye contact. Luna considered the odds that Owen had shown up at Griff's place because he saw her location on the app. She made a mental note to change the settings. No one needed to know where she, or her phone, was all the time.

"I'm sorry," Owen said. "Am I interrupting something?"

"No. Glad to have you," Griff said, trying to cover the disappointment in his tone.

Over a dinner of pasta puttanesca, Owen watched Luna pick sardines from her plate and casually toss them onto Griff's dish. Griff, with the same ease of familiarity, plucked olives from his dish and stacked them in a pile on Luna's salad plate. It was like watching them kiss, Owen thought.

Owen knew they didn't want him there. But he really needed to tell Luna what happened that day. He kept waiting for her to thaw out, remember who they were to each other. When Griff disappeared into the kitchen to find more wine, Owen finally caught Luna's eye.

"We need to talk. I'm freaking out," Owen whispered.

"About what?" Luna said.

Griff returned to the table with a freshly opened bottle of red and refilled the trio's wineglasses. Owen didn't want to have the conversation in front of Griff, but Luna wasn't making it easy on him.

"I went back to the station," Owen said. "The cops showed me this picture."

"You talked to the cops without a lawyer. Again?" Griff said.

"Not now," Owen said to Griff. Then, back to Luna: "They showed me a photo."

"What photo?" Luna said.

"It would make more sense if I could show it to you. They wouldn't let me take it."

"You really need to get a lawyer," Griff said.

"I heard you already," Owen snapped. "Sorry. It's complicated. Listen, this picture jogged a memory of me and Irene."

"What photo?"

Owen needed to present every detail about that night, the memories the photo sparked, but with Griff there, he rushed through the details.

"I met Irene before. She said her name was Phoebe."

"What are you talking about?" Luna said.

"It's really weird and hard to explain in one sentence or two," Owen said, stumbling over the series of events. "When I was in England, I met Irene. I didn't remember. She looked completely different. But I met her one night and she told me about Leo. He slept with her when she took a class with him in college. Then a few years later he married Chantal."

"You met Irene when you were in London," Luna said, trying to remember Owen's most recent trans-Atlantic trips. There hadn't been many. "When were you in London?"

"Fourteen years ago," Owen said. "You know, after Scarlet. I met Irene that year. She used a fake name."

"Why?" Griff said.

"I don't know," Owen said. Impatient, exasperated, he jumped to the next salient detail. "Irene told me things about Leo that night. It explains why they were so weird. Why she hated him so much. I think he was blackmailing her. And maybe she stopped paying him and he—"

"You think Leo might have killed Irene?" Luna said.

"Maybe," Owen said.

"Tonight he does," Griff said. "Tomorrow is a different story."

Owen turned to Griff, eyes narrowed. "Why are you being such a dick?" Owen said.

"Sorry. I don't want to start anything," Griff said.

"I can't believe you're still pissed about that," said Owen.

Luna's eyes toggled between the brothers.

"*Still,*" Griff said. "You accused our mother of murder."

"I thought *maybe* she did it. And I told you that in confidence," Owen said.

Luna saw a vein pulsing on Griff's forehead. He got to his feet. So did Owen.

"You know, Owen, it's deeply concerning how lightly you take the killing of another human."

Owen grabbed his coat and checked the pockets for his keys. "I'm going," Owen said.

Luna was drunk enough by then that she wasn't sure she was hearing things correctly. "What is going on with you two?" she said.

"He thinks I killed Scarlet," Owen said. "Right, Griff?"

"No, he doesn't," Luna said, turning her attention to Griff.

Griff exhaled and stared at his feet.

"Go on. Tell her what you really think," Owen said.

Griff leveled his gaze on Owen. "I think maybe you killed both of them."

Owen walked out as soon as Griff accused him of more than one murder. Another time, another year, Luna might have chased after Owen. Not that night. For one thing, she was too destabilized by the trajectory of the conversation to manage an exit. Then, when Griff suggested Owen might be a killer, she wanted to know how he came to that conclusion. Griff began cleaning up, bussing plates as if the goal was to split them in two. Luna sat in the living room, drinking more wine, trying to decide which questions to ask and in what order.

Her wine depleted, she entered the kitchen.

"You were angry," Luna said. "You don't think that."

"Yes," Griff said. No hesitation. "I think it's very possible."

Luna wasn't buying it. Griff rinsed and dried his hands and turned to Luna. He could tell he was losing her. After all her years of friendship with Owen, all that loyalty, Griff didn't expect to get through to her. At least not right away.

"I get that you don't want to believe it," Griff said. "But I know I'm not crazy."

"You don't draw that conclusion randomly. Tell me how you got there," Luna said.

Griff poured more wine, against his better judgment. He already felt a headache coming on. "That summer when Owen came back from England," Griff said, "I asked him about returning to Markham. He was angry at me for suggesting it. He said something about how no one cared what actually happened that night. Then he briefly mentioned Scarlet, how she was dressed the night she died. He knew what shoes she was wearing," Griff said.

When Luna didn't respond to that comment, Griff asked, "Did she have only one pair of shoes?"

"Maybe that detail was in an article somewhere," Luna said.

"No," Griff said. "It wasn't. It wasn't in any article anywhere. I read every last one. He knew she was in a party dress."

"She always wore miniskirts or dresses," Luna said.

"On a late-night hike? Why would you assume that? The answer is, you don't make that assumption. You know it because you saw it. He was there."

"Griff, I had his phone. I was communicating with her and even I didn't know where she went. The text was misspelled and basically gibberish."

"He had a phone in his dorm room, in the hall. There were other ways they could have communicated. How did he know what she was wearing if he didn't see her?"

"How do you know what he said was right?" Luna asked.

"Because I got the police report."

"When?"

"After he slipped up," Griff said. "When I asked him about it, how he knew what she was wearing, it got weird. He looked angry. Like I'd caught him in a lie. That's when I started to think he did it."

Irene, 2014

Chantal Boucher eventually came to realize that she'd married a lout. A money-grubbing, medium-talent lothario. But while Leo had been a truly terrible husband, he was an adequate deathbed companion. Near death, Chantal's sentimentality won out over spite. She simply couldn't bring herself to leave her husband penniless, though she'd witnessed the way Leo tore through his—and her—income. By all objective standards, Whitman had done well for himself as a young artist. If he'd had any discipline, he would have been comfortable for the rest of his life. Chantal did what she thought was best. She left some funds designated for her husband, making her daughter trustee, unwittingly forcing a life-long relationship that neither daughter nor husband would have desired.

At first, Irene would just give Leo what he asked for to make him go away. But once that money was gone, then what? He'd keep coming back. Irene started saying no, putting her foot down, forcing Leo to stick with a budget. Once she understood her power over the man, she noticed that wielding it—not abusing but managing it—was satisfying in its way.

When Leo had finished his latest dick-waving sculpture series, he wanted a proper fete for the unveiling. He'd given Irene an itemized budget, expecting to get a nice check in return. Irene told Leo that she'd arrange the party. She wasn't being punitive or parsimonious. Irene needed more donors for her arts-education nonprofit and knew that Whitman could likely bring in some fat-wallet patrons. Irene borrowed a friend's seldom-used studio for the gathering. It was a drafty old barn just south of Hudson, New York.

Irene recognized Owen the moment she saw him. He was simply an older, handsomer version of his younger self. Age had blunted his too-feminine features. And he still had that shiny, almost black hair. She'd never forgotten that night, the sex especially. She'd had only three partners up to that point. But that night was special. At least, she thought it was. She thought for sure he'd call. When he didn't, it hurt.

As Irene, now thirty-one, was debating whether to go over and reintroduce herself to Owen, she saw a woman sidle up next to him. *Wife or girlfriend?* Irene wondered. Either way, she felt more jealous than she should have. Irene cringed in private embarrassment. She shouldn't feel such things toward a man she hadn't seen in almost a decade. Irene kept watching Owen and the woman, who she'd soon learn was called Luna. She seemed out of place, Irene thought. Luna was dressed for an office—boots, skirt, blouse—but she had on a long military jacket over the professional ensemble. Maybe she worked at one of the local colleges, Irene thought. She definitely wasn't from the city. Her hair and makeup weren't right for that. Irene was good at spotting city dwellers among the upstaters. There was always a tell—an excess of cashmere, a physique too lean or too toned, professionally highlighted hair, or a ring that cost more than a car.

Whatever Owen and Luna were to each other, it wasn't casual acquaintances. It seemed unlikely they were a romantic couple, because they didn't greet each other with a hug or kiss. They stood right next to each other, in front of a floor-to-ceiling poster of Leo Whitman standing next to his piece. While the image measured over eight feet high, it wasn't to scale. Leo Whitman was about four foot six in the picture. Irene watched as Owen bumped Luna's shoulder. That was their first point of physical contact. Irene circled the room to get a different angle on them. Luna was squinting to read Leo's pompous mission statement.

"Is this considered good?" Luna asked.

"It's considered big," Owen said.

"Is it solid?"

"That would be impossibly heavy," Owen said. "It's just alumi-num siding. The whole thing probably weighs a couple hundred pounds."

"What do you think is inside it?" Luna asked.

"Nothing," Owen said.

"I can't tell you how disappointing I find that," Luna said.

"Why? What do you want inside it?" Owen asked, grinning.

"Candy," Luna said.

"Like a piñata?"

"Yes. Then I'd give a chain saw to a child and let them slice open the tin. Actually, I'd probably put a sardine lid on it—you know, the kind that you roll back with a key. It would take at least four kids to muscle off the tin—"

"Why do you keep bringing kids into this scenario?" Owen asked.

"I thought they'd be the most keen on the piñata angle," Luna said.

Irene laughed. Owen and the woman looked over at her. Irene blushed in embarrassment.

"Sorry," Irene said. "I'm a chronic eavesdropper."

"Who isn't?" Luna said with an open, friendly smile.

"I don't believe we've met," said Owen.

Irene stifled a laugh. "I'm Irene Boucher," she said, extending her hand.

"Hi. Owen Mann, and this is my friend Luna Grey."

He wouldn't call her a friend if they were more than that, right?

"A pleasure," Irene said, shaking Owen's hand, then Luna's.

There were so many things that Irene wanted to say. None of them felt quite right.

"I need a drink. What can I get you?" Luna said to Irene.

"That's very kind of you," Irene said.

"It's free," Luna whispered.

Irene laughed again. "Red, please," she said.

Luna left them alone. Irene thought it was on purpose. Owen was smiling at Irene. Flirting, she thought. He must recognize her. She was waiting for him to say something.

"So, what would you stick inside our tin piñata?" Owen asked.

"Dynamite, perhaps," Irene said. "Or anything explosive."

Owen smiled broadly. They were of like mind, he thought. "Not a Whitman fan?" he said.

"Not in the slightest," she said.

"Beautiful *and* wise," he said.

Okay, Irene thought. *The game is up. Let's get to this.*

"You look familiar," Irene said. "Have we met before?"

It felt like an inside joke. Or maybe a game of chicken, where they both waited for the other one to admit it. Owen smiled and shook his head.

"No," he said. "I'm sure I'd remember that."

OWEN ASKED IRENE out the night they met for the second time. Irene thought she'd tell him on the first date, but she couldn't find the right moment. On the second date, it was going so well that she didn't want to break the spell. After that, it just felt wrong. Irene liked what she and Owen had in the present. If she reminded him of that night, he'd be reminded of other things that happened, things she'd told him. Their relationship wouldn't fully exist in the present, which was virtually flawless, but also in the past, which was not. By the time she was in love, Irene had decided that Owen didn't have to know. Ever.

It was Owen who'd wanted the wedding. Irene, after the hassle of disentangling herself from her first husband, figured she wouldn't do it again. She wanted a modern coupling, based on the shared understanding that they'd last as long as they weren't making each other miserable.

Six months after they'd moved in together, Owen said, "If you wanted to get married, I'd be cool signing anything."

Irene had no idea what he was talking about. Owen meant he'd sign a prenuptial agreement. He'd assumed that Irene hadn't broached the subject because she had more money and, by extension, more to lose.

After a year passed and Irene had not once mentioned marriage, Owen wondered if she wanted out. It was this uncertainty that provoked Owen's sudden openness to the idea.

"Do you want to get married or break up?" Owen said one night, after a few too many drinks.

"If that was a proposal, it stunk," Irene said.

"Well, what would you say if I did propose?"

Irene then enlightened Owen on the parameters of a proposal she would accept. She insisted on sobriety, an element of risk (no asking ahead what the answer would be), and a ring at the ready—*no blood diamond, no diamond, you're an artist, make the damn ring.*

Owen forged a white-gold band and proposed, on bended knee, on a weekend hike to Stony Kill Falls. He assumed that Irene's desire for a traditional proposal meant she also wanted a traditional wedding. As they began to plan the day, it became abundantly clear they were not on the same page. Irene had notions of courthouse nuptials or a tiny backyard affair officiated by a friend. But when Owen began to draft his guest list and brainstorm wedding venues, Irene realized that he wanted a ceremony, a celebration. Since it was Owen's first wedding—hopefully, his last—she wouldn't deny him that.

IRENE AND OWEN'S June wedding day was a disaster. It began ominously enough, with a record-breaking storm. They'd rented a house with a converted barn for the ceremony and party. The unseasonably heavy rain caused a small leak in the roof, which required a reconfiguration of the seating arrangements. Irene watched from a dressing area in the adjacent house as her guests trudged across an open field under an awning of umbrellas and took cover in the barn. She stressed about lightning strikes and waited for a call from her matron of honor, an old college friend who, Irene would soon learn, had been sidelined by food poisoning and was unable to manage the two-hour drive to the venue.

Leo arrived early, making himself at home on a plush sofa in Irene's dressing room. An outsider might think he was being supportive and fatherly. For years Irene had managed him, avoided being alone in his company. Even Leo wasn't aware of Irene's implacable hatred. Leo experienced the world through his own internal thermostat. The outside temperature didn't matter. Leo availed himself of the guesthouse because the barn was drafty and Irene was all alone.

"Why don't you go upstairs and have a drink with Owen," Irene said to him.

Irene hadn't hired anyone to do her hair or makeup. She sat at a dressing table, applying eye shadow. She saw Leo in the mirror, standing behind her. He put his hands on her bare shoulders.

"Good god, you're so tense," Leo said.

"I'm fine," she said, trying to shrug loose his hands.

She wanted to say, *Stop touching me, you disgusting pig,* but she didn't have the nerve. She couldn't figure out why her natural bluntness was dulled around him. Her psychiatrist suggested it was connected to her mother's response when Irene tried to tell her the truth.

Leo stopped massaging her shoulders, but he wouldn't move. He stood right behind her. She could see the strain of the buttons on his dress shirt.

"Cold feet?" Leo asked.

"Could you get me some tea?" Irene said.

There was a knock on the door.

"Come in," Irene shouted.

Luna leaned in. "You need anything? Owen sent me to get more booze."

"Luna, come in. Please," Irene said.

"Actually, if you could get Irene a cup of tea," Leo said, "that would be wonderful."

His hand was back on Irene's shoulder. Irene was trying to catch

Luna's gaze through the mirror, pleading with an expression of sheer panic. At least, that was her goal. She couldn't tell if Luna had registered it or not. When Luna turned around and began to walk out of the room, Irene's heart sank.

The next thing Irene knew, Leo was shouting, "Oh god, what's happening?"

Irene spun around to find Luna lightly convulsing on the floor. It was only a few seconds, then Luna went still.

"What's wrong with her?" Leo said, annoyed.

"Go get help," Irene shouted at Leo.

He didn't move. He stood there, gaping at Luna.

"Leo," Irene said. "Go get Owen."

Leo ambled out of the room and slowly climbed the stairs, grunting in pain with each step.

Irene knelt on the floor next to Luna, who suddenly opened her eyes, wide-awake. Irene, stunned, fell back on her haunches. Luna sat up and put her finger to her lips.

"Are you all right?" Irene whispered.

"I'm fine," Luna said. She jumped up and closed the door, securing the lock. "I was faking it. I had a bad vibe and I couldn't figure out how to make him leave."

After a moment of confusion, Irene said, "You faked a seizure?"

"I did. If I misread the situation, I apologize."

"No. Thank you," Irene said. Her eyes watered. "I can't believe you did that. That's one of the nicest things anyone has ever done for me."

"Great. Because I haven't gotten you guys a wedding present yet."

Irene pulled Luna into a tight hug. "Thank you," she said.

"Anytime," Luna said. "You want to tell me what's going on?"

"No. Not today," Irene said. *Not any day,* she meant.

THE SECOND, REAL seizure occurred post-ceremony. The photographer had wanted a few casual shots of the groom with his female best man. Luna loosened her tie and the first button on her dress shirt. She felt like someone had finally quit strangling her. The photographer had to use a flash in the dim lighting of the barn.

Leo, looking on from the crowd, didn't notice how different the second seizure was from the first. But he did have something to say on the subject.

"How is that woman allowed to operate a motor vehicle?"

October 16, 2019

———

Luna was too inebriated to drive back to the Sleep Chalet, but she had to get out of that house. She needed to be alone with her thoughts, to untangle the night's events and the memories that had gotten snarled up with them. She took an Uber back to the motel, made a slurry of instant coffee, and opened her laptop, running searches on Scarlet Hayes for half of the night.

In the morning, she woke up lying on her laptop, fully clothed. Her eyes were blurry, her throat dry, and she wasn't even sure where she was. Some, not all, of the details came back to her. After a shower and a trip to the lobby for fresh coffee, Luna returned to the motel room and reread the articles in her browser history. There was not one mention of what Scarlet had worn the night of her death.

Then the motel phone rang, startling Luna.

"Hello," Luna said, tentatively and with a vaguely disguised voice, in case she needed an out.

"Luna, it's Griff."

"Hi," Luna said.

"I texted you this morning," Griff said. "Did you get it?"

"No. I think my phone is off."

Luna searched the motel room for her phone.

"I just took Sam to the dog park. I'm not far from you. Want a ride?"

"To where?" Luna asked.

"To the house," Griff said.

Luna felt like she was missing something. "Uh . . ."

"Don't you want your car?" he asked.

"Oh, right," she said. More details returned. "I can get an Uber."

"I'll pick you up," Griff said, quickly ending the call.

Sam the dog was reluctant to relinquish his shotgun position, so much so that Luna suggested she take the back seat. Griff got out of the car and physically removed his giant retriever. Five minutes on the road and no one had said a word.

Luna had many questions. She started with one she thought she could manage. "What was that thing about your mom last night?"

"After our dad died, Owen told me he thought Mom might have hastened Dad's death. He was angry when I asked her about it. What did he think I was going to do?"

"What did she tell you?"

"She neither confirmed nor denied," Griff said. "But she was stung by the accusation. That was the end of our relationship for many years."

"I'm sorry," Luna said.

The subject of Vera was easy compared to everything else they needed to discuss.

"Why aren't you asking about Scarlet?" Griff said.

"Griff, I don't know that I'm ready to be convinced. It would change my whole life," Luna said. "I love him. He's my best friend. He's my family. He's all I have."

Griff felt a familiar stab of jealousy. "When I met your husband, he said he'd heard about me," Griff said.

"Did he?"

"Yes."

"Isn't that normal? We tell partners about our pasts."

Both of them understood that the conversation was dangerous, but neither knew where the land mines lay.

"Why'd you tell him I broke your heart?"

"Because you did," Luna said. "I don't blame you. I understand."

Griff felt a sudden surge of anger. He'd never seen her as the kind of person who could reimagine history so far from the truth.

"You ended it. You ended everything," he said. "You just disappeared. Then you sent a text, said that it wasn't working, something like that. I tried to call. I don't remember everything. I know it was over. You made that clear."

Luna rummaged through her memory banks, trying to make sense of Griff's narrative. It didn't jibe with anything she could recall. There were many moments of her life that felt fuzzy, but there were some things she couldn't forget.

"I didn't send that text or anything like it," Luna said.

Griff felt as if he and Luna were having conversations in different realms. For fourteen years he'd wondered what had happened, why Luna had suddenly lost interest. He'd worked so hard to get over it—it never occurred to him that he hadn't.

"Are you sure? It was a long time ago."

"Yes, I'm sure."

"Fuck."

Griff turned off the main road and continued along the canopy of trees. He pulled onto the gravel road and parked the car. He opened the back door and released Sam, who ran off into the distance. Luna and Griff got out of the car and silently followed Sam as he trotted off past the house. They strolled through a wooded area to a clearing with a small pond. It glimmered like a disco ball.

"This is what I remember," Griff said. "My father died and you just disappeared, like you didn't care at all. I was calling you. Maybe not that often. I was working long hours. I reached out one night. You sent that text. I gave up. I figured Owen had confided in you after I asked him about Scarlet. I always believed that you sided with him, that you couldn't have both of us in your life."

Rationally, Luna understood that memories were shape-shifters, but she couldn't help but feel betrayed by that idea.

"I didn't know any of that," Luna said.

"Did something else happen?" Griff asked. "It seemed like you wanted out before the funeral."

Luna wasn't sure she should say anything. Was there any value in digging up the past?

"You need to tell me the truth," Griff said. "I'm starting to feel like a puppet in my own life."

"I had to get an abortion. The next day," Luna said.

Griff took a step back. His face went slack. It was impossible to read.

"I'm sorry," Luna said. "I don't know what you would have wanted or said—"

"You should have told me," Griff said.

"Maybe, but it wasn't about you and me. It was only a few months after Denver, after seeing him. All I could think was that I had his DNA. I could never, ever have a kid. I was coming to terms with that, trying to figure out a way to deal. The only thing I could think of to feel better was to have that surgery to—"

"What? You did that?"

"Not back then. I was too young. I couldn't find anyone. I just had the abortion. The whole thing messed me up. I didn't want to tell you, because you were dealing with your dad. Then Owen and I were talking and he said you'd want kids and I knew I wouldn't have any."

"You see any kids, Luna?" Griff said, angry.

Luna was still trying to make sense of it all. "We hadn't spoken in a while. I sent you a text when I was starting to feel better. I figured you were done with me, but I wanted to be sure. I thought maybe you were just busy. I think I texted you and asked if you wanted to talk. You replied. I remember. It was something like We don't have to be friends."

"That was a week after you ended it."

"How did I end it?" Luna asked.

"You sent me a breakup text. Something like This isn't working. I tried to call you and you wouldn't answer. It was a long time ago. I don't remember all the details, but you definitely broke up with me," Griff said.

"I didn't send that text," Luna said.

Luna felt nauseous. Griff's anger surged. Both had drawn the same conclusion.

"Are you sure?" Griff said. "Because if you didn't—"

"Fuck," Luna said, wiping a tear from her eye.

"You believe me now? Owen did this. You see that, right?"

"I don't know," Luna said.

"He didn't want me in his life anymore. I doubted him. He was worried that my doubt was contagious. He was okay without me. He wasn't okay without you," Griff said.

If Luna believed Griff's accusation, it wasn't just a blight on Owen's character. Luna would have to reckon with her own role in the matter. Had she given an alibi to yet another murderer? She dug in her pockets for her keys and stumbled toward her car. She could hear her own breathing, like she was wearing earplugs. She felt faint and couldn't decide if she needed more or less oxygen.

Luna had, once again, been forced to reconfigure her image of Owen. She finally had to accept that she'd gotten him all wrong. Liar and manipulator didn't necessarily signal murderer, but she couldn't stop herself from making that mental leap. It was the first time in her life she'd ever really doubted Owen. The doubt crept into everything.

Griff kept saying Luna's name. He felt invisible. Luna opened the car door, then turned back to Griff.

"Do you really think Owen has it in him? You think he killed her?"

"Which one?" Griff said.

O wen suddenly became the golden child—or, perhaps, the only child—after Griff accused his mother of murder, manslaughter, or illegal euthanasia. Whatever it was, Griff wanted to know. He hadn't bothered tiptoeing around the issue. He'd asked point-blank. And based on Vera's defensive response, her conscience was not clear. What was clear to Vera was that Griff was a monster for accusing her of such a thing. How dare he? Even after Griff explained how his suspicion came about—from Owen—Vera's ire remained focused on her elder son.

The brothers' dispute didn't arise from a misunderstanding. They understood each other just fine. Their conflict was based on two different worldviews.

Owen's: *Let's say Mom did kill Dad. It sucks, but what are we gonna do about it? Turn her in? Dad was about to die anyway. And maybe she didn't want him to suffer.*

Griff's: *WTF? If Mom killed Dad, that's not okay. I'm not suggesting we call 911 and have her taken away in cuffs, but we should, at the very least, get to the bottom of it and make sure she knows that offing people isn't okay.*

OWEN DIDN'T HAVE a solid post-London plan. He thought about applying to art schools as a transfer student, but they all required letters of recommendation. He couldn't even imagine reaching out to anyone from Markham. After two months under the same roof as Vera, Owen's priority was just getting out of Boston.

Tom had left both of his sons some money. It was intended for college but wasn't contingent on it. Mason suggested Owen move into the off-campus house with Luna, since Casey's parents had bought a rental property for her to share with Mason. Owen wasn't thrilled with the idea of returning to the general area of Markham U, but it was still a far better option than staying where he was. And he did miss his friends, the few he had left.

OWEN MOVED BACK to Markham in August. He expected Luna to be more enthusiastic when he offered to take over the lease. While Luna did rally the night Owen moved in, she couldn't summon much energy after that. Owen and Luna had been living together for a few weeks when he realized that her dark cloud wasn't lifting. Owen watched Luna sleepwalk through her life. She barely went to class, watching TV half the night, staying in bed most of the day. Owen couldn't work out what had happened with her. He knew from watching his mother that depression could strike randomly.

Owen also knew that if something didn't change, she was going to fail out of Markham. He went so far as to go to her professors, claiming she had mono and asking for extensions on her assignments. He started gently waking her up at more reasonable hours, quietly reminding her how much money it would cost to redo a semester if she failed all her classes.

Casey was the only person Luna would talk to. When Casey dropped by, Owen could hear the women whispering behind Luna's door. Whatever was going on with Luna, Casey knew. And Owen knew better than to ask Casey about it. She'd never tell. All of Casey's secrets were sealed up like a can of soup. He used to like that about her.

. . .

Frugal to her core, Luna forced herself to do the bare minimum. She'd make it to class a few times a week, shower occasionally, and cut herself off from TV after two A.M. Casey and Owen convinced her to see a shrink. She started taking meds. The progress was slow, but Owen noticed incremental changes. Most of Luna's energy was devoted to not failing. She didn't have much left for Griff, and she didn't want him to know the state she was in. Every single time he suggested Luna visit him, she declined. The few times Griff offered to visit, she firmly said no.

Owen had been in the Hudson Valley just a month when Vera summoned him back home. She'd decided to put the family house on the market and gave her sons a week to clear out the junk in the garage and all their childhood crap from their bedrooms. Owen and Griff arranged to meet over the weekend while Vera escaped to a friend's house on Martha's Vineyard. She would not, under any circumstances, be under the same roof as her elder son.

Griff had expected to see Luna at the house. At least, that was the plan they'd made when he spoke to her a few days before. When Owen arrived, sans Luna, Griff was visibly upset. Griff finally realized that something wasn't right. He asked Owen for advice. Owen told Griff to give Luna some space. The advice was not given with any sense of malice. Owen legitimately thought that's what Luna needed.

The brothers worked through the weekend, trashing memories. Neither Owen nor Griff mentioned the subject of Vera and the missing pills. Griff had already been punished for asking, and he still had no means of getting a real answer. But there was another question lurking in the back of his brain. If he didn't ask Owen, it would always be there. Griff took the opportunity when they were alone, since he wasn't sure when he'd get another chance.

The brothers were sorting boxes of files—taxes, bills, contracts, all of the boring shit that proves you exist. Griff had a separate box for the paperwork they needed to keep. Everything else got thrown into an aluminum bin. Griff and Owen had planned a bonfire for later that night.

"You know how Luna had your phone the night Scarlet died?" Griff asked, wading into the subject without a shred of delicacy.

Owen stopped sorting and glared at his brother, silently conveying, *Why the fuck are you talking about this shit now?*

"Yeah," Owen said impatiently.

"So . . . did you see her the day she died?"

"Who?"

"Scarlet."

"Why are you asking?"

"Just curious," Griff said. "When someone dies, you usually remember your last interaction with the person. Do you remember?"

"She waved at me from across the quad," Owen said. "I ignored her."

"The day she died?"

"No. Maybe a few days before," Owen said.

"Are you sure?"

"Griff," Owen said. "What the fuck?"

"Sorry," Griff said. "This summer, you said something about what Scarlet was wearing when she . . . died."

Owen waited for Griff to continue. Owen understood that he needed to be cautious. In fact, he had more sense of caution with his brother than he'd had with the police.

"How did you know what she was wearing?" Griff asked.

Owen shrugged, shook his head. "I don't know. Maybe I guessed. We went out for a while. I knew what clothes were in regular circulation."

"You guessed right," Griff said.

Owen sensed the presence of a trap. "How do you know?"

"It's in the police report," Griff said.

Owen thought he might vomit. He wondered if Griff was recording their conversation. He heard a siren in the distance and briefly considered that Griff was working with the cops. It all became clear. Griff thought he killed Scarlet. Griff thought his own brother was a murderer.

"Sorry, Officer," Owen said. "My lawyer has advised me not to answer any more questions."

All Owen could think about was getting away from Griff and staying away. It felt dangerous being around that suspicion yet again. The fact that it was Griff made it almost unbearable. Owen packed up his car and trashed all his childhood crap that he was previously undecided about. He drove away before the bonfire, without another word to Griff.

When Owen returned to Markham, he expected that Griff would have spoken to Luna, poisoned her against him. She was already in bed. Owen wasn't sure if she was sleeping or avoiding him. The next morning, she knocked on his door. He assumed they were about to have a talk. Instead, Luna asked Owen if he wanted to go to a movie. *Duck Soup* was playing at the local revival house.

"I really need to see it," Luna said, sounding more burdened than enthusiastic.

Owen was surprised on a number of fronts. Luna wasn't accusing him of murder and, after a summer of melancholy, she was suggesting an activity outside the house. He didn't want to question it.

There was only one other person at the matinee. Owen and Luna never got a good look at him. He arrived shortly after the lights dimmed and left as soon as the words *The End* popped up on the screen. The man had clearly seen the movie before, probably more than once. He would laugh in anticipation of a joke or bit. Owen was on the fence about whether the man was more annoying or amusing. He glanced over to check on Luna a few times. She didn't laugh until Harpo Marx showed up in the film. And she was sending texts, which was unlike her. She had stringent rules about phones on in a theater. He worried that she was texting Griff, but after she laughed a few more times, he knew that couldn't be the case. Afterward, Owen suggested getting a beer. She agreed.

Walking home, tipsy and loose, Luna felt like she did in the old days, before Griff, before Scarlet.

"I've been worried about you," Owen said.

"I know," said Luna.

Owen wanted to root around for the origin of Luna's funk, but he knew enough to wait until she offered the information, which she did a few blocks later.

"If I tell you something, you can't ever tell Griff."

"No problem," Owen said.

The brothers didn't talk much, even back when they did talk.

"I was pregnant."

Owen stopped in his tracks and turned to her. "Shit. Did you—"

"Yeah. Keep walking," Luna said. Luna found it easier to have the conversation without making eye contact.

"When?"

"Day after your dad's funeral."

Owen revisited that day, revising his memory with this new piece of information. "That explains some things," Owen said. "I'm sorry. Are you okay?"

"When it happened, it got me thinking about things. Things I hadn't considered before and, uh, you know . . ."

"Actually, I don't know," Owen said. "I need a few more details."

"John Brown and I have the same father. Same DNA. I kept imagining what it would be like to have a kid like him. I . . . couldn't imagine. Well, I could, but it seemed worse than anything. Worse than death. I panicked. Thinking about it made me sick. I called a clinic. I wanted to get the surgery so I wouldn't have to worry about it."

"Jesus, Luna, you didn't do that, did you?"

"No," she said. "They wouldn't let me. It's hard to find people who will do it. Even if they do, they won't agree to it unless you have a medical reason or are over thirty-five. One doctor told me she'd consider it if I waited eight years. I got an IUD for now."

"Good," Owen said. "Because you do know that the odds of you having a child like your—you know."

"Stop. Stop," Luna said. "You don't understand. I'm not having a kid. Ever."

"You might change your mind," Owen said.

"I won't," said Luna.

"Have you talked to Griff about this?"

They were too young to have such conversations, Luna thought. It was the kind of topic that made it sound like you were rushing things.

"No," Luna said. "I think I'm afraid to."

Luna wasn't the sort of person who thought much about the future. But she thought about it then. If she and Griff had a fundamental incompatibility, wouldn't it be better to end things sooner rather than later? Luna was the kind of person who'd want to get pain out of the way.

"He wants kids, right?" Luna asked.

"Of course," Owen said.

Owen didn't know anything for a fact. But it was hard to imagine Griff not following the traditional trajectory of life.

"He'd make a good dad, wouldn't he?" Luna said.

"Yeah, he would," Owen said.

Another week passed. Griff and Luna hadn't spoken, as far as Owen knew. The next weekend, Luna was locked in her bedroom, fighting inertia and trying to finish a philosophy paper due on Monday. She'd even left her phone in the kitchen to avoid distractions.

When she went to bed Sunday night, her phone was still on the kitchen table. Owen knew she'd need it in the morning, so he plugged it into the charger. That's when he saw Griff's text.

Why won't you call me back?

Owen stared at the text for what felt like hours. When he replied, it seemed like the most natural thing to do.

Owen typed: Sorry. Been busy.

Griff: Can u talk?

Owen: No.

Griff: tmrw?

If Griff hadn't just accused Owen of murder, it was unlikely that he would have made such a bold move. But he saw an opportunity that he might not have again. One that could solve the one lingering problem in his life that he didn't think he could get over.

Owen typed: This isn't working.

He waited twenty minutes for a response. Luna's phone rang. Griff's name popped on the screen. Owen silenced the ringer and sent the call to voicemail. His heart started racing. Then another text came in.

Griff: Is this about Owen?

Owen typed: No. I don't want to do this anymore.

Griff: You want to break up?

Owen typed: Yes.

Owen deleted all texts exchanged that day and the notification of Griff's call. He hung on to the phone for the rest of the night, waiting for Griff to send one final message, leave a voicemail, make one more attempt at repairing the relationship. Owen was split in two regarding his own behavior. One side experienced the natural guilt and fear of doing something so utterly wrong. The other side was so angry at Griff that he just didn't care. Owen didn't think Griff and Luna would last anyway. If they were over, really over, he might save her some future heartache. That's what he told himself.

It was so simple. Too simple, Owen thought. For months after, he was afraid of being caught. With time, he recognized the depths of his betrayal. One thing comforted him, though. If they were meant to be together, it shouldn't have been that easy to break them up.

October 16, 2019

—————

As Luna drove away from Griff, she scrolled through the past seventeen years, revisiting key memories, reconfiguring them with a new set of parameters.

Sending that text was so calculating, such an extreme betrayal, that it briefly eclipsed the whole murder thing. That text changed her life, Griff's life. Why? What was the point of it? Because Owen liked having Luna all to himself? The leap from liar to murderer isn't easy or obvious, but lying was a crime that Luna could deal with head-on.

When she showed up at Owen's front door, her cheeks ruddy from tears, her eyes narrowed in rage, he couldn't register what was happening. His brain was still tripping over his forgotten night with Irene. What it meant. Why she never told him.

"I'm so glad you're here," Owen said, turning back inside his house, waiting for Luna to follow. "I got a copy of the picture. You need to see it."

He picked up his phone and found the photo.

"I know," Luna said, pacing back and forth in his living room. "I know what you did. Griff told me."

It took Owen a moment to get out of his own head, his own skewed timeline.

"What did I do?" Owen asked.

He wasn't sure what Griff had told her. He didn't know whether to confess or deny.

"You—you broke us up," Luna said. "You sent a text from my phone."

Owen had dreaded this moment for so long. He should have been more prepared. "Let me explain," Owen said, even though he wasn't sure he could.

"How could you do that?"

"You were twenty-one. It was going to end eventually."

"That wasn't for you to decide. Why'd you do it?"

"I don't know. There was a lot going on back then. I thought I was doing you a favor."

Luna was trying to get a read on Owen's behavior. He was explaining, but it was all matter-of-fact. Sometimes you're too tired for panic. That was the stage Owen had reached.

"You didn't feel guilty?" Luna asked.

"Not that guilty," Owen said.

What Owen would have said if he'd had time to think about it was that Luna thought too hard about being good. Thinking about being good didn't make you good. Sacrificing individual happiness didn't make the world a better place.

Luna felt dizzy, an anger so intense that she almost understood a murderous urge. Was that how it worked?

"How did you know what Scarlet was wearing the night she died?" Luna asked.

Owen shook his head, disappointed. He wasn't sure until that point how much past dirt Griff had kicked up. "Who's asking? You or Griff?"

"I'm asking," Luna said. "How did you know?"

"One conversation with Griff and now you think I'm a murderer?" Owen asked.

"Why won't you answer the question?"

"Because you're not asking me what you really want to know. If you're going to accuse me of something, have the fucking balls to say it."

"Fine," Luna said. "Did you kill Scarlet?"

"No," he said.

"Did you kill Irene?"

Owen wasn't expecting that. Clearly, Griff had gotten into her head.

"You're the only murderer in this room," Owen said. "You're still Luna Brown, and at least one girl would be alive if it weren't for you."

Owen felt like an asshole. Not once in their entire friendship had he picked at the scabs of her past. But Luna didn't care anymore. There are only so many blows you can absorb before you stop feeling the individual punches and all the pain melts together.

Luna turned around and stumbled toward the front door. Everything was coming out wrong, Owen thought. Watching her leave, Owen wondered if this was really the end. To lose Irene and then Luna, in less than two weeks. He wasn't sure he could handle that. But he also wasn't sure if he loved Luna enough to forgive her for the accusation.

Luna opened the door. The day was so bright, you could see the dust particles in the air. She stepped outside, blinded by the sun and her own tears. She walked down the steps to the street. She didn't see the man standing behind his car until he shouted at her.

"Luna Brown," the man said.

That's what she would remember later—hearing the name she'd tried so long to escape, twice in one day.

She turned in the direction of the voice, squinting. She heard the shot before she saw the gun or hit the ground. Her perception of time went askew. Like each individual moment was on a card and then those cards were shuffled. She stared at the last card, diagonal stripes of cirrus clouds on a bright-blue sky.

MAYA WILTON CALLED the police as soon as she saw the suspicious man park outside her house. Maya had been staring out the window when Luna drove up and came to a stop with her front right tire against the curb, the back left fender jutting into the street. There was hardly enough room for two vehicles to pass. Maya was about to step outside and have a word with Luna when she noticed a Chevy SUV pull up at the curb. The driver was male. Maya had a sixth sense, she later explained. She could feel bad energy. The man just sat behind his wheel, watching Owen's front door. She couldn't see his license plate, so she stepped outside and walked down her block to take a quick photo in case she needed it later.

Maya estimated that about five minutes passed before Luna emerged from Owen's house. There was yelling. Maya strained to make out the words. The strange man got out of his car. His hair was so greasy it looked like a pile of garter snakes. Maya heard a gunshot and then saw Luna collapse on the sidewalk. She realized that the strange man had a gun. Maya ducked behind a neighbor's shrubs and dialed 911. The man with the gun scanned the sidewalk, climbed into his car, and drove away. Maya told the 911 operator to send an ambulance and provided a description of the perpetrator, reading off the license-plate number from her photo. While Maya was alerting the authorities, Owen knelt down over Luna, screamed for help, and tried to stop the bleeding.

TROOPER MIKE DALE heard about the incident at the Owen Mann residence over his radio. A female victim, in her mid-thirties, shot in the chest. A witness claimed that a middle-aged man in a dark-blue Chevy SUV had fled the crime scene. The witness had a license-plate number. Dale drove to the Mann residence. A police car and ambulance were already on the scene. The victim was being strapped to a gurney. Owen Mann, the guy he'd seen wearing a bathrobe in Dover Cemetery not two weeks back, was standing in front of his house, still in a bathrobe, now covered in blood.

Dale approached an officer on the scene and asked the name of the victim.

"Luna. Luna Grey," the officer said, checking his notes.

That was the name of the woman who'd found Irene Boucher, Dale thought. He didn't know what the hell was happening. A paramedic closed the doors to the van. Lights swirled. Dale phoned Detective Burns.

GREGORY WELLS SAW the police cruiser in his rearview mirror before the sirens blared and the lights flashed. He calmly clicked his right turn signal and pulled over, cutting the engine and keeping his hands visible at all times. He followed instructions as best he could, exiting the vehicle, clasping his hands behind his head. Some of the maneuvers were hard to accomplish with his hands intertwined. He lost his balance, lowering to his knees. The police told him to lie facedown on the ground. That seemed unsanitary. He tried to hover his face above the asphalt, but it hurt his neck. He told the cops that the gun was in the glove compartment. He was apprehended just fifteen minutes after the shooting.

NOAH WATCHED MARGOT answer the call. At first she seemed annoyed. Then confused, stunned, and finally angry.

"Fuck," she said, dropping her phone to her side.

"What happened?" Noah said.

"Oh my god."

"Margot," Goldman said, trying to get her attention.

"Shit," she said. "I didn't see it."

She was so stuck in her head, she couldn't even see her partner.

"Margot, what the hell happened?"

"We had it wrong from the start," Margot said.

OWEN STOOD IN the hospital bathroom, washing Luna's blood off his hands. He caught his reflection in the mirror and saw more blood, red streaks on his face and T-shirt. His pallor was vaguely green. The combo had a sick yuletide feel about it.

Owen had been in the waiting room for more than an hour when

322 / LISA LUTZ

those cops showed up. Burns and Goldman. They had the same inscrutable expressions. Did they teach that at the police academy? They were walking toward him. *What now?* he thought. It wasn't déjà vu this time around; it was Sisyphean. He really wasn't sure whether he could go through this again. The endless questions, the taped interviews, the murky status of not knowing if he'd be arrested or cleared or remain in limbo for an indeterminate amount of time.

Detective Burns asked Owen if he'd mind stepping outside. Owen told her that he wasn't going to the station. He was staying with Luna. Goldman explained that they just wanted to talk in a less crowded area. Owen followed the detectives outside.

The trio huddled together in the loading zone, under an awning. The air smelled of cigarettes, gasoline, bleach. Owen didn't want to look either cop in the eye. He was too worn out to deal with their suspicion, their judgment. He'd had enough.

"What?" Owen said.

"We got him," Noah said.

"Who?" Owen said.

Owen never saw the gunman; he didn't hear the car peel away. He just saw Luna on the ground, bleeding out.

"Your neighbor saw the shooter, wrote down his license plate. We got him right after that," Burns said.

"His name is Gregory Wells," Noah said.

"I don't understand. Am I supposed to know that name?" Owen asked.

"His sister was Lila Wells," Noah said.

Burns couldn't tell if Owen registered the name or not.

"Do you know who that is?" Burns asked.

"Yes," Owen said. "She was John Brown's second victim."

WHEN LUNA WOKE up, she didn't know where she was. There were bright lights. A cloying antiseptic smell. So much beeping. *What an evil alarm clock,* Luna thought. A nurse leaned over her and smiled. The nurse asked a lot of stupid questions.

"What year is it?"

"It's 2019."

"Who is president?"

"No."

"I'll accept that answer. What's your name?"

"Luna Grey."

"Do you know where you are?"

"Hospital."

Luna assumed she was at Chambliss Medical Center, where Sam worked. She asked for water. The nurse disappeared and said that she'd check to see if it was okay. When the nurse was gone, Luna remembered that she had another question. Sam entered her room. Then the nurse.

"What happened?" Luna asked.

"You were shot," Sam said.

"With a gun?" Luna asked, incredulous.

Many pharmaceuticals were roaming through her bloodstream.

"Yes, a gun," Sam said. "Those detectives are here. They want to talk to you."

"Who shot me?" Luna asked.

She thought of Owen. She remembered being outside his house. She didn't think it was him. It couldn't have been him. Could it?

"They're just outside," Sam said. "They'll explain."

"I'm really thirsty," Luna said.

Sam found a plastic pitcher and poured water into a sippy cup. "I'm going to let them in, okay?" Sam said.

Luna nodded, guzzled water.

"Slow down," Sam said, like she was drinking vodka.

The police came in. The same ones who'd asked so many questions. The woman detective—Luna forgot her name; must be the drugs or getting shot—told Luna the name of the shooter. She asked Luna if the name was familiar. It wasn't at first. Then she thought about it again, the last name. Wells.

"Wells?" Luna said.

"Yes," said the woman. "He was the brother of Lila Wells."

"Oh fuck," Luna said.

"Had he been in touch?" the young male detective asked.

"Not recently," Luna said. "A while ago, maybe."

"If that's all," Sam said, "she needs to rest."

The detectives shared a silent exchange. There was something else. Luna had an inchoate theory that her drug-addled brain couldn't fully grasp.

"The gun," Luna said. "Was it the same?"

The woman nodded; the man said, "Same man, same gun."

"I see," Luna said.

"What are you talking about?" Sam asked.

"When he shot Irene, he thought he was shooting me. Right?" Luna said, observing the female detective's expression to see if her theory was correct.

"Yes," said the woman. "He was waiting outside your house that day. He had an address scribbled on a piece of paper. He didn't know what you looked like. He just saw a woman leaving your home through the back door. He thought it was you. He followed her to the cemetery. There was no one around. He didn't realize his mistake until the story was in the news."

"Okay," Luna said, the tears falling freely.

The feeling was so familiar. Another death she'd have to carry around like dead weight.

November 2019

When Luna was released from the hospital, it was decided that she should return home with Sam. It made the most sense, all things considered.

It wasn't as uncomfortable as one might imagine. Caring for Luna would help Sam erase some of the guilt over his affair. Plus, she was heavily medicated and, even with a bullet wound, she wasn't that demanding. She camped out in the downstairs guest room, watching cable TV. One day, he found her crying. *The Sopranos* was on in the background. Sam asked if she needed another pain pill. No, she said. She was crying because Irene had the same tracksuit that Paulie Walnuts was wearing.

There were visits from Casey and Mason. Griff as well. Luna and he tried to avoid any meaningful talks while she was living under the same roof as her husband. And the past was also off-limits. They may not have spoken about the future, but it existed as an unspoken promise. They were on the brink of something, they both thought.

Owen called. Often. He tried her mobile at first. After ten unreturned messages, he tried the landline. He was surprised to find an ally in Sam.

"At least talk to the guy," Sam said to Luna, on more than one occasion.

Luna's memories of that day were thick and murky. She was

stuck in the moments before she stepped outside, before Gregory Wells took his aim. Luna couldn't get past the feeling that she didn't know Owen, that he might have been a murderer.

One evening while Luna was still in the hospital, dosed on painkillers, she woke from a fitful sleep. Sam had just come into her room to check on her.

"I need to tell you something," Luna said, beckoning him to her side.

"What?"

"Owen shot me," she whispered.

"No, Luna," Sam said, concerned that Luna might have suffered some neurological damage. "They got the guy. It was the same guy who shot Irene. Same gun."

The next morning, when Luna was more lucid, Sam reminded her of the conversation. She couldn't recall accusing Owen of being her shooter, but the feeling came back that there was a memory hidden in her brain. Scarlet, she thought. She remembered what Griff had told her. Owen knew what Scarlet was wearing the night she died, even though Owen claimed to have not seen her that day.

A few weeks into Luna's recovery, Sam had to leave town. He asked Mason and Casey if they'd stay with her for a night. Sam made the request, in part, to preempt any overnight Griff visits. Sam could deal with the divorce, mostly. But he really didn't want that guy and his shedding retriever taking over his house. There were limits.

Casey, Mason, and Luna had a quiet dinner, just the three old friends. Luna drank a glass of wine, which Sam had directly forbidden. Luna felt a tiny thrill of rebellion. The trio sat outside, around the firepit. It was chilly, but the wine made them warm. Casey asked about Griff, the frequency of his visits, whether they'd discussed the future. What would that future be?

"Why isn't Owen here?" Mason asked.

"Because I'm not ready," Luna said.

Mason refilled his wineglass. Casey gave him a look of warning.

"You and Owen were fine when he was a murder suspect, but

after his name is cleared you don't talk to him?" Mason said. "That doesn't make any sense."

"Things happened before I was shot," Luna replied. "He's not who I thought he was."

"No one is," Casey said.

"Before I was shot, I had started to think that maybe Owen wasn't innocent," Luna said.

"I don't understand," Mason said. "Innocent how? You know he didn't kill Irene. They have the gun; they have the shooter." Mason thought Luna needed another MRI.

"I know he didn't kill Irene," Luna said. "I'm not sure about Scarlet."

The couple exchanged a heavy glance. Their spousal language was impossible for Luna to comprehend.

"Luna," Mason said. "You're wrong. You've got to stop thinking that."

"Yeah, Luna, you really need to stop," Casey echoed.

"He knew what she was wearing. Scarlet. The day she died. He knew. How did he know?" Luna said.

"Maybe it was in the newspaper or the police told him," Mason said.

Casey drained her glass and opened another bottle of red. "You're angry about Griff and you're trying to find a reason to hate Owen. But you're wrong. And you need to stop this."

Luna didn't want to argue with her friends. She wasn't interested in convincing them of Owen's guilt when she wasn't entirely convinced herself.

"You're right," Luna said. "I'm just tired. I think I'll go to bed now."

Luna took her glass and retired to the downstairs guest room. Soon after, Casey and Mason headed upstairs to the master suite. Luna felt charged up and wide-awake. She watched television until she finally felt groggy. It was just past two A.M. when she nodded off. A knock. A creak. Then footsteps. She shot up in bed. Mason was standing over her.

"Shh," he said, finger to lips.

"Mason," Luna said. "What are you doing up?"

"I need to tell you something."

"Okay," Luna said.

Mason shut the door and sat on the edge of the bed. "I wanted to tell you sooner. Years ago, really. But Casey wouldn't let me," Mason said.

"Tell me what?" Luna asked.

"Owen didn't kill Scarlet. I know that—for a fact."

"How do you know?" Luna asked.

"Because I was there when Scarlet died," Mason said.

March 2004

A fter being ejected from Luna's dorm room, Owen, Mason, Casey, and Ted huddled outside and debated what to do with the rest of the night. Ted had heard about a party at Bing Hall and asked if anyone wanted to join him. Owen declined. He didn't want to risk running into Scarlet. And Mason was so stoned by then, any group activity seemed fraught with peril. Casey and Mason broke off and ambled around the quad. Casey kept looking up. There was supposed to be a full moon that night.

Mason stopped in his tracks and said, "I don't think I can do this anymore."

Casey turned to face Mason, steeling herself for the breakup conversation.

"Why not?" she said.

"I'm so thirsty. If I don't hydrate soon, I don't know what will happen."

Casey laughed, relieved. She took Mason back to her dorm room and gave him a tumbler of water, which he finished in one long, impressive gulp.

Casey went down the hall and refilled the tumbler at the bathroom sink. When she returned, Mason was out cold. She tried to wake him, but it was no use. Casey, still wide-awake, decided to check out the party at Bing. She scribbled a note for Mason and left.

Casey's room was at the end of the hall, conveniently located by the stairway, inconveniently next to the pay phone. Casey always wore earplugs to bed, since the phone ringing was as loud as any alarm clock. There was supposed to be a strict quiet time between ten P.M. and seven A.M., but no one paid attention on the weekend. The ringing phone eventually woke Mason. He tried to ignore it, but it kept ringing. He got up, propped the door open with a shoe, and answered the call.

"Avery Hall," Mason said.

"Is Amber or Bobbi there?" said a female voice.

"Hang on," Mason said.

He walked down the hall to Amber and Bobbi's room and knocked on the door. No one answered. He returned to the phone.

"They're not here," Mason said.

"Is this Mason?"

The voice was familiar, but Mason couldn't place it. He felt a tad paranoid that the girl on the line knew who he was.

"Who is this?"

"Scarlet."

"Oh hey," Mason said, less paranoid.

"Have you seen Owen?"

"Uh, yeah. We were hanging out in Luna's room earlier."

"When?"

"I don't know. I fell asleep. Where are you?" Mason asked.

"I'm waiting for Owen at Black Oak Bluff."

"Why? It's cold out, and you shouldn't be there at night."

"I'm so fucking over it," Scarlet said.

"Over what?"

"Doesn't matter. Everyone will know soon enough."

"What's going on? You sound weird."

There was a long pause. Mason thought the connection had dropped.

"You still there?" he asked.

"Luna is not who she says she is," said Scarlet.

Scarlet's tone worried Mason. He was afraid for Luna.

"Who is she, then?" Mason asked.

"Forget it."

"Come on, tell me."

"Remember that girl who lied on the stand and her brother got away with murder and then he—"

"I know the story," Mason said.

"That's Luna."

Mason's mouth was so dry he couldn't swallow. He thought he was the only one who knew. "You shouldn't spread ugly rumors. It says more about you than her."

"It's the truth, Mason. I went to the library, did some research. It all adds up. Luna's mom's name is Belinda. Belinda Brown is the name of John Brown's stepmother. Later she changed her name from Brown to Grey. How stupid. You can change your name and you don't pick something different or even cool."

"You should come back to the dorm," Mason said. "Why don't you meet me at the Mudhut. Let's talk about it."

"I gotta go," Scarlet said.

Mason didn't know Scarlet's number and he didn't have a mobile. He stopped off at his dorm room and got a flashlight. It had begun to drizzle when he stepped outside again. No one saw him as he crossed the quad and disappeared into the back woods.

Mason reached the base of Black Oak Bluff about fifteen minutes after he ended the call with Scarlet. A good ten of those minutes were the most frightening of his life. With only the narrow tunnel of his flashlight as his guide, Mason's hearing went on high alert. The rustle of leaves, a gust of wind, even the sound of his own footsteps terrified him. When the trail hit an incline, he knew he was getting close.

SCARLET HAD BEEN waiting for Owen at a high point on the Black Oak Bluff trail for over an hour. It was dark and scary and she wanted to leave, but she'd already made the precarious hike up the narrow trail. She was beginning to sober up. With sobriety came the realization that she was unlikely to change anything between Owen and Luna. And still, she waited, because she didn't want to walk the path alone again. It was an unseasonably warm night for early March, but it was still too cold to be just standing around in the woods. When it began to drizzle, Scarlet finally decided to turn back. She had to pee something fierce, though, and didn't think she'd make it down to the trailhead without bursting. There was a tree on the edge of the drop. She hiked up her dress, pulled down her tights, and leaned against it. As she was relieving herself, a light flashed over her.

"What the fuck," she said.

Startled, she scrambled to cover herself. Her foot lost purchase and she plunged down the twenty-foot drop.

MASON HEARD THE scream and the sickening crack of skull on stone. He stumbled down to the bottom of the trail, waving the flashlight around the base of the cliff. When he saw the angle of Scarlet's head, he knew she was gone. He tried to say her name, but he could barely speak. He thought he might vomit. Then, he thought he heard something in the woods. He tried to remember what bears did at night. Do they sleep or do they stalk their prey? He didn't know. He was pretty sure there had been bear sightings nearby. He didn't want to be attacked by a bear. He was hearing things. Some things were real, others were marijuana-induced embellishments. He followed the trail back to the main footpath that looped around campus.

He purged at the side of the footpath. Guts unburdened, Mason got his bearings, remembered the pay phone outside Bancroft Library. He jogged the path for twenty yards. He felt sick again. He picked up the phone. There was no dial tone. He rummaged through his pockets for coins. After depositing a quarter, he saw the OUT OF ORDER sign. He shouted a few expletives and fought back tears. He ran back to Bing Hall and used the back entrance to avoid any revelers. He climbed the stairs to the second floor. Some guy who didn't live on that floor was on the pay phone.

Mason climbed the stairs to the third floor. He picked up the pay phone. Then a girl whose name he didn't know asked him why he wasn't using the phone on his floor. Mason put the phone back on the cradle and walked away without a word. He returned to his room on the second floor and sat on the edge of his bed. He took off his muddy shoes and stuffed them in the back of his closet.

Mason tried to remember where there were other pay phones on campus. His plan to call 911 and leave an anonymous message kept being thwarted. Maybe that was a sign. He'd already played out what would happen if he phoned the police and gave them his name.

The cops would bring him in for an interview. He'd be nervous and act suspicious, because that's how he acted when he was nervous. They'd ask about Scarlet's fall. Did he cause the fall? Maybe he did. What if they gave him a lie-detector test? If they asked him if he killed Scarlet Hayes, he couldn't say no. He wouldn't pass the test. What if the police pinned it on him? They'd probably charge him with manslaughter. Mason smoked more weed to calm down. A mistake, no doubt. The particular strain of weed that he'd gotten from his dealer in Kingston made him extra paranoid. He had given Scarlet a few buds just last week. What if she had it on her or they found it in her room?

He'd be sweating under the lights of a police interrogation. Feeling guilty and therefore looking guilty. Accusations. Charges. A trial. He wasn't thinking clearly. He knew that. He needed sleep; then he'd be able to figure out what to do. He had a few Valium that he'd stolen from his mother's medicine cabinet. He took two pills. He figured with all the pot he smoked, he had a high tolerance. That was not the case.

Mason slept for ten hours. When he finally woke, Scarlet had been missing all night. He heard Amber and Bobbi stalking the halls, asking if anyone had seen her. They knocked on his door. He answered.

"Have you seen Scarlet?" Amber asked.

Mason shook his head.

"Let us know if you see her," Bobbi said.

"Okay," Mason said.

They were staring at him, their eyes boring into his soul. He wanted to close the door, but he didn't want to act odd or suspicious.

"Mason, can I be honest with you?" Amber said.

Mason braced himself for an accusation. "Uh, okay."

"You need to smoke less weed," Amber said.

Mason was so relieved he almost laughed.

"She's right," said Bobbi.

"I'll take that under advisement," Mason said.

November 2019

Mason thought he'd feel unburdened when he finally told Luna the thing they'd been keeping from her for years. Instead, he experienced an oppressive exhaustion.

"You watched Scarlet fall to her death and didn't tell anyone?" Luna asked.

"Not the police," said Mason. "I told Casey the next day. She went into town and made a call from a pay phone so they'd find Scarlet's body."

"Are you sure she was dead?"

"Yes. I swear, if I thought there was any chance she was alive, I would have . . . done something."

"Didn't you feel guilty?" Luna asked.

"Of course I did," Mason said. "I would have gone to the police. Casey talked me out of it. She thought I'd do something stupid like confess. Maybe I would have. I couldn't help but think that if I hadn't gone to the bluff, if Scarlet hadn't seen me, I wouldn't have startled her and she wouldn't have died. I'm sorry I never told you."

"Casey has known this whole time?" Luna said.

Mason nodded. "She called 911 from town and told them there was a body."

Luna had heard about the 911 call. The consensus at Markham was that she'd made it.

"You should tell Owen."

Mason picked at a hangnail. After a long pause, he said, "Owen knows. I told him years ago."

"When?"

"Remember when I went to visit him in London? We were at pubs every night. I was either drunk or hungover. Casey wasn't there to stop me. The guilt had been eating away at me. I'm sure I told him what she was wearing. I guess it stuck with him and he slipped up. I kept talking because I was afraid of how angry he'd be. But when I finally stopped, he wasn't upset. He was, but not that much. He was really cool about it. I think that's when we actually became friends."

"You all kept this from me. Why?"

"You know how Casey is with secrets. Steel trap. But, also, she said you wouldn't be able to keep quiet. You'd have to come clean. After I told Owen, we thought about it again, whether to tell you. Owen agreed with Casey. He said it was better if you didn't know."

"Why are you telling me now?" Luna asked.

"Because you keep thinking Owen did something, and he didn't."

Luna finally understood that her current stance on Owen had to change, but she wasn't yet ready to release all her pent-up anger. "The thing with Owen and me isn't just about Scarlet," Luna said. "He completely sabotaged my relationship with Griff."

"Sure," Mason said. "That was bad. But his own brother thought he was a murderer. You can't destroy a friendship because of one small mistake."

"It wasn't a small mistake," Luna said. "It changed everything."

"He lied to the cop for you. That has to count for something."

"What are you talking about?"

"After Scarlet was found and they brought him in. The detective saw Scarlet's texts. He wanted to know what your secret was. Owen refused to tell."

"He didn't know. Not then."

"Yes, he did. Griff told him after that weird Scarlet visit over Christmas. Owen knew what it would do to you if it really got out at school. Anytime after that, he could have changed the story, he could have told the truth and been spared a lot of shit. If anyone knew who you were, you would have been the suspect, not him. Maybe he told one lie a long time ago that was bad and fucked things up. But he also told another lie that probably made your life a whole lot easier. It's time to stop being angry."

Mason heard a creak on the stairs. "We cool?"

Luna nodded. Mason slipped out of the bedroom.

"What are you doing?" Casey whispered from the doorway.

"Checking on Luna."

Casey turned to Luna. "You okay?"

"I'm fine," Luna said.

"Come to bed, Mason."

It was quiet for the rest of the night. But Luna still couldn't sleep. She had to rethink her whole life yet again. She'd spent decades itemizing her sins, tracking her conscience like a loan shark. Guilt was a form of debt, and she was always in the red. Luna wasn't clear on whether that was the right or wrong way to live. She didn't have a strong opinion on what Owen, Mason, or Casey had done. When it came down to it, Luna's debt would always be greater than theirs.

In the morning, Luna was woken by the sound of whispers and rustling. She got out of bed and found Casey and Mason dressed and packed, with their suitcases waiting by the front door.

"Morning," Luna said.

"We were trying to be quiet," Casey said.

Mason gave Luna a tentative kiss on the cheek. Casey gave Luna her usual bear hug, which isn't advised with someone who's recently been shot.

"Ouch," Luna said.

"Sorry," said Casey. "What are you doing today?"

"I'm going to see Griff."

"Is he coming here?"

"No. We're meeting in Hyde Park."

"You're allowed to drive?" Mason asked.

"I was cleared a few days ago."

"Be careful," Mason said.

Luna thought he was talking about more than her driving. "I will," she said.

Mason carried luggage to the car. Casey turned back at the foyer and leveled her gaze at Luna.

"There's a full moon tonight. Don't forget to look up. You never know when it might be your last," Casey said.

Casey was telling Luna to live in the moment, to enjoy the easy gifts that life offered. But Luna couldn't help but feel a faint threat in the subtext.

November 2019

———

eo Whitman had no idea who had killed Irene. He'd hoped it was Owen. If convicted, Owen would lose his claim on Irene's estate and Leo might have a better chance at contesting the will. After hiring Amy Johnson as his assistant, Leo managed to convince her that Owen was the most likely suspect. Leo suggested Amy record her conversations with Owen.

"If you got him to confess, you'd be a hero," Leo had said.

Amy tried, that one time. Owen didn't confess. And he never spoke to her again. Amy wasn't sure what the old guy's angle was. She worked for him for two weeks and quit when her first paycheck bounced.

No one had called Leo Whitman to tell him that Luna was shot, Irene's killer was apprehended, or that the case was closed and the police would stop knocking on his door, suggesting he was capable of murder. He had to read about the gunman in the paper. For Leo, the story boiled down to one clear fact: Irene was dead because of Luna. As he'd said, where there's Luna, there's Owen. He blamed both of them. At least Luna paid a price. She was shot. Leo got drunk one night and called Owen. Leo had a few things to get off his chest. Before he could say a word, Owen interrupted.

"Irene told me about you. A long time ago. I remember now. You fucked her when she was a teenager. Then you married her mother. Don't *ever* call me again."

The police came to Leo's house a few weeks later. That awful middle-aged woman and that boy.

"What can I do for you, Detectives?" Leo said.

"It's what we can do for you," said Noah.

"I just want to give you a quick refresher on the law," said Burns. "Blackmail is illegal."

"What is your point?"

"We know you were blackmailing Irene. The DA is currently deciding whether to press charges."

"I'm afraid I don't know what you're talking about," Leo said. His hand tremor increased, like the signal on a metal detector.

"You found out that Irene was having an affair with Sam Burroughs," Noah said.

"And?" said Whitman.

"You used that information to extort money from her," Burns said.

"No. I simply asked for what was rightfully mine," Leo said.

"If that's your defense, you should discuss it with your attorney. It's not our business," Noah said.

Before the detectives departed, Burns said, "In case you were curious, the statute of limitations for felony blackmail is five years."

In the car, heading back to the station, Goldman said, "Feel better?"

"I do," said Burns.

Irene

On October 7, 2019, at seven twenty-three A.M., Irene left the house without a word to her husband. This was not how she wanted it. Irene liked niceties, customs, simple rituals. She thought couples should kiss on the lips before they parted, even if the return was imminent. But Owen had set a precedent for something very different.

The first time Owen disappeared on Irene was six months into their marriage. Irene had last seen him in the kitchen. She went upstairs to take a shower and when she returned, he was *gone*. A mug of lukewarm coffee sat on the island; the sliding glass door to their back porch was slightly ajar; even the shoes she thought he was wearing lay marooned down the hallway. His car sat cold to the touch in the driveway. It seemed to Irene that Owen had simply vanished, taken by a supernatural entity. Owen had said nothing about an appointment or heading to the studio. When Irene called his number, it went straight to voicemail.

Whenever Irene needed Owen's behavior explained, she'd go to Luna.

"Owen likes to disappear," Luna said. "It can take some getting used to. If he's not getting in touch, don't assume he's dead. That's the best advice I can give."

It took a full year for Irene to accept the fact that there was no curing Owen of this condition. Irene retaliated by disappearing herself, finding a small thrill in not having to tell someone where she was going or when she was coming back. When Irene and Sam started their affair, it was a seamless arrangement. She didn't have to account for time or arrange alibis. It required no extra effort whatsoever. It was too easy, Irene thought. Then Leo found out by chance. He was driving by the Sleep Chalet and spotted her car. He parked and waited, because there was no good reason for her to be at a motel. He tried to take a photo of Irene and Sam leaving together, but he was terrible with his camera phone. Leo had the nerve to spend Irene's money to hire an investigator to take proper, incriminating photos.

That night she planned to tell Owen she wanted a divorce. If she wasn't married, Leo would think he had no leverage. The truth was, Leo didn't even understand the leverage he had. Irene would have done just about anything to keep the affair from Luna. She wasn't even sure Owen would mind. She only knew that the first person he'd tell was Luna.

Irene wanted one more normal day before everything changed. She put on a Fila tracksuit, along with a giant gold chain that Luna got her for her last birthday. Luna was always ridiculously amused when Irene wore that combo. Irene jogged over to Luna's place, circled the house, and knocked on the back door. Irene wondered if it would be the last time.

November 2019

Luna was on her way to meet Griff when she made a detour onto Owen's street and parked in front of his house. While Luna wasn't certain she wanted to dive back into their friendship, she did feel lousy about her accusation and thought she ought to get her apology out of the way. She climbed out of the car and strode along the walkway in front of his house. She searched the sidewalk for the place she was shot, expecting to see a bloodstain. Instead, she found a layer of light-gray paint on cement. That must have been Maya, she thought.

"I was pissed off when she painted over it," Owen said.

Luna looked up. Owen was standing on his porch in his bathrobe.

"I thought you'd want to see it first," he said.

"You were right," Luna said.

"It's my sidewalk, right?"

"My blood," Luna said.

Owen started to laugh, then stopped himself. He was feeling a slurry of conflicting emotions. Anger and guilt were primary, but happiness was also in there. The last time he saw her, she was in a hospital bed.

"They caught the guy because of her," Luna said. "I'm inclined to forgive her other missteps."

"Me too," Owen said, taking a sip of his drink.

It was his second drink of the day. Luna's arrival made him want another. He was trying to decide how he felt. He understood that he owed Luna an apology, but he also believed that one was due to him. He didn't know if Luna was there to ask more questions or to make peace. She was eyeing the drink in his hand. He knew she was drawn to the sound of ice clinking.

"Don't judge me," Owen said.

Luna wasn't sure if he was talking about the bathrobe at two in the afternoon or the drink. Luna didn't have an opinion on either. Frankly, both sounded appealing.

Owen invited Luna inside by turning around and walking back into his house. Luna followed him into the kitchen. Half a pot of coffee was cold and stale on the counter. Luna took a mug from the shelf and poured a cup. She heated it in the microwave. The matter-of-fact way Luna made herself at home made Owen nostalgic for the days when he wouldn't have noticed.

"Mason and Casey were over last night," Luna said.

"I know. He texted me this morning."

"How did you keep that from me all these years?"

Owen shrugged. The microwave beeped. Luna retrieved her coffee.

"It wasn't my secret," he said. "Why are you here?"

"I came to apologize."

"Really?"

"Yep."

Luna had wanted to ease into it, wait for the right moment, but Owen seemed impatient.

"I'm so sorry about Irene," Luna said. "That sounds so . . . How do you apologize for being the reason someone died?"

"It's not your fault. She's dead because of the guy who shot her," Owen said.

"If I'm out of the picture, she's alive," Luna said.

Owen shrugged. That wasn't the apology he wanted.

"I'm also sorry about the things I said before. I was angry and it clouded my judgment," Luna said.

"My turn," Owen said. "What I did to you and Griff, it's unforgivable. There's no good explanation. I didn't want to lose you to him."

Both apologies were earnestly offered and accepted, but the timing was off. One was long overdue and the other still a fresh wound. Luna sipped her coffee. It was sour and stale.

"Well, I'll get out of your hair," Luna said, placing the mug in the sink, debating whether she should wash it and leave or just leave. She was going to just leave.

"So, is this like goodbye or something?" Owen asked. "You know, the more permanent kind?"

"I don't know," she said.

She'd believed up until the night before that the door to their friendship was closed. She hadn't had enough time to rethink that opinion. Watching Luna walk toward the door, Owen couldn't help but remember the last time. He could still hear the sound of the gunshot. He didn't want her to go.

"Well, you could leave," Owen said. "Or . . ."

"Or what?" Luna said, after a long pause.

The *or* held much more possibility than *goodbye*.

"You could stay for a drink. I never got to tell you about Irene, Leo, and the extortion scheme. What do you say?"

She would have said yes to a far less interesting invitation.

"You had me at extortion scheme," Luna said.

Owen whipped up a quick batch of greyhounds and poured two glasses.

He opened a cabinet drawer and showed Luna the photo Irene had taken of him fourteen years past. He told her the story behind the photo, the memory it jogged. He showed Luna a picture of Irene from her mother's wedding in London, said how Irene had told him about Leo years before he'd met the man. They sat on the deck and drank. It was like the old days, Luna thought. Aside from the constant ache in her shoulder.

Luna gazed, riveted, at the photo.

"Would you have known right away that this was Irene?" Owen asked.

"No. I mean, I see it now. I don't think I would have. Why didn't she tell you you'd met before?"

"I think she didn't want me to make the connection to Leo. Irene—who I thought was named Phoebe—told me all about him. She didn't say his name. But it was the night before her mother's wedding, and she was really messed up about it. If she'd reminded me of our first meeting when we met in New York, I would have remembered the other stuff. I never could understand what was going on with her and Leo. Irene's hatred was so intense and so un-like her."

Luna, eyes unfocused, was reframing her own set of memories. She was seeing Irene on her wedding day, her reflection in the mir-ror. The expression of complete panic when Irene thought Luna was going to leave her alone with Leo.

"I never told you this. Remember how I had two seizures at your wedding?"

"I assure you, no one has forgotten about that," Owen said.

"I only had one. I faked the first one, and then the real one was just bad luck."

"Wait, what? Why would you fake a seizure?"

"You sent me for booze or something and I went in to check on Irene. Leo was there. He had his hand on her shoulder. At first I thought they were having a moment, but then I got a really weird feeling. Leo was clearly trying to get rid of me. But when I saw Irene's reflection, I knew she was upset. It looked like she didn't want him to touch her. I didn't want to leave her alone. So what was I gonna do?" Luna said.

Owen busted out laughing. "Naturally, you faked a seizure. That makes sense."

"It all worked out. Leo had to leave to get help. Irene was so relieved, grateful."

"She never told me," Owen said.

"After I had the second seizure, she came into the room and gave me notes."

"What'd she say?" Owen asked.

"She said, 'That was a little over the top, no? Remember: Less is more.'"

Owen could picture Irene saying that. The memory warmed him briefly, but then he was reminded of her absence and a cold spell rolled in.

Luna raised her glass. "To Irene," she said.

"To Irene," he said.

Both of them looked away as they fought back tears.

"So, you and Sam are still getting a divorce?" Owen asked.

"Yes," Luna said.

Her glass was empty. Owen retrieved the pitcher from the kitchen.

"You have time for another?" Owen asked.

Luna glanced at her watch. She didn't. Not really.

"Do you have someplace you're supposed to be?"

"I told Griff I'd meet him. He's still upstate," Luna said. "I shouldn't have any more, since I have to drive."

"You could take a taxi or Uber."

"You're right," Luna said. "I could do that."

She wasn't making any moves to leave. Owen filled her highball glass and sat back down on the lounge chair.

"So, are you and Griff . . . ?" Owen asked.

"I don't know," Luna said. "It's been a long time."

Time wasn't the problem. Griff had planted the idea of Owen's guilt. Luna's loyalty to Owen made that hard to forgive. Whatever feelings remained were frozen in time. She had to wonder what would be left once they defrosted.

"I'm happy for you, if that's what you want," Owen said.

"I don't know what I want."

Luna checked the time again.

"When are you supposed to meet him?" Owen asked.

"Two-thirty," Luna said.

"It's three o'clock," Owen said.

"I know," Luna said, thumbing a text.

Not going to make it today.

After she sent the text, Luna asked, "Why didn't you just tell Griff how you knew what Scarlet was wearing?"

"I promised Mason."

"You didn't have to say Mason's name. You could have said enough to squelch Griff's suspicion."

"He's my brother. I shouldn't have had to," Owen said.

Luna could hear the crack in his voice. The wound was still fresh after so many years.

Her phone buzzed. She ignored it. Owen poured another drink.

"Luna, please don't sabotage on my account."

"I'm not," she said. "It's probably for his own good. People seem to die around me."

"Us," Owen said. "They die around us."

There was comfort in sharing the accidental guilt. Intellectually, they might be blameless, but that didn't matter. Statistically speaking, being in their orbit was more dangerous than that of most others.

"We've had some bad luck," Owen said.

"People we knew had some worse luck," Luna said.

"Yeah," Owen said.

"What do we do if it happens again?" Luna asked.

The first-person plural comforted Owen. Forgiveness can happen swiftly when you have no framework for living without the other person.

"If what happens?" Owen asked.

"If someone dies and one or both of us is suspected of murder," said Luna. "What do we do?"

"It won't happen again," Owen said.

"I hope not," Luna said. "But if it does, we'll need to take responsibility."

"Okay," Owen said. "If it happens again, we're through."

"Agreed," Luna said.

Both of them knew they were lying.

Acknowledgments

I'm writing this at the beginning of 2021, but you won't read this until 2022. I'll refrain from tempting fate with any bold fortune-telling. I think it's safe to say this: I hope 2021 treated you better than 2020. Congratulations! You made it.

To Stephanie Kip Rostan, my agent, thanks for everything. I don't know what I'd do without you. And thank you to everyone else who makes Levine Greenberg Rostan Literary Agency so wonderful: Melissa Rowland, Michael Nardullo, Miek (no, I did not misspell that) Coccia, Cristela Henriquez, and the rest of the team that I haven't seen in years. I miss you guys.

Kara Cesare, thank you so much for helping me wrangle this book. Your notes were sharp and collaborative, and your patience and faith in *The Accomplice* kept me going while I was plagued by distractions. Jesse Shuman, you are a delight. Many more thank-yous to all the wonderful Ballantine people: Kara Welsh, Jennifer Hershey, Kim Hovey, Karen Fink, Debbie Aroff, Colleen Nuccio, and Scott Biel.

Loren Noveck, my production editor, you get your own paragraph. In general, I owe quite a debt to copyeditors. However, the debt with this book might be bigger than usual. And another big thanks to Kathy Lord.

Austen Denusek: You've already impressed me.

Itzel Hayward: Thanks so much for the legal advice and help working out that plot hiccup.

David Hayward and Ellen Clair Lamb, who read endless drafts and clean up my literary messes. As always, your help is invaluable. I never thank you guys enough.

Anastasia Fuller, your encouragement after reading a partial draft meant everything. While I'm on the subject of my family, I'll mention a few more: Uncle Jeff & Aunt Eve, Jay, Dan, Lori, Mia, Ian, Kate, and Nancy.

Other thanks: Megan Abbott, for always keeping tethered to the outside world. Sarah Weinman, for her occasional wellness checks. And I'd like to apologize for my year-long Zoom boycott (Alison Gaylin).

Lastly, I'd like to thank all my West Coast friends. I love you all and I've missed you terribly. If you're ever charged with murder, I'll know you didn't do it. And if you did, we'll figure it out.

— The —
Accomplice

LISA LUTZ

A BOOK CLUB GUIDE

Dear book club people,

I keep mulling over an idea for a parlor game that's loosely connected to *The Accomplice,* the book that you've apparently chosen to read. (Or maybe you've just chosen to read this letter. Either way, thank you. Really. Now, back to my parlor game.)

Once you have secured the use of a parlor, you will need some supplies: stickers (round, I think) in three different colors. Assign to each color one of the following designations: murderer, accomplice, innocent bystander. For example: red sticker—murderer, orange—accomplice, blue—innocent bystander. Make sure you have enough of each sticker, in case there's a glut of murderers or not-murderers at your get-together.

As you and your guests mingle, drink, and eat canapés (yep, that's how I picture you), each person places a sticker on the back of every other guest, based on their assessment of that person's relative capability of committing murder. Don't overthink your decisions. Instead, go with your gut. This is no place to settle old business or legitimately accuse anyone of a felonious act.

After everyone has stickered everyone else in the room, each stickee tries to guess how many red, orange, and blue stickers they have on their back. The winner is the one who is closest to the correct guess.

Like the book, the game is less about discovering the truth than about exploring the gray, unknowable areas of even the closest relationships. In most cases, we have no idea what our friends would do or have done in a given situation. Unless you've actually committed a murder or abetted one, you don't know what *you'd* do. And that brings me back to the book.

What interested me most as I wrote *The Accomplice* were those moments when a person you know surprises you, forces you to rethink your idea of them. This experience can be destabilizing, in both good and bad ways. Because what's happening is not that the person you think you know has changed. Instead, something has changed for you—or even *in* you. And you've been wrong all this time.

My book is ultimately about the depths of a friendship and the limits of trust. And other stuff too. But I've already gone on way too long. If you want to dig deeper, check out the discussion questions.

I hope you enjoyed the book and my as-yet-untitled parlor game.

Warmest wishes,
Lisa Lutz

Questions and Topics for Discussion

1. *The Accomplice* is told by interweaving past and present story lines. How did switching between timelines affect your reading experience? What clues from the past informed the present, or vice versa? Did reading about the characters at different ages change your perceptions of them?

2. How do the themes of deception and integrity play out in the novel? Are all of the characters honest with themselves? Which secrets, in the novel and in life, are justified?

3. Memory plays a significant role in this book. In what ways does memory inform identity? Do you think that things you don't remember can affect who you become? What events in your life have been important in shaping who you are?

4. How does the past affect the present? What do the characters in the present learn from the past? How does this affect their relationships and help them heal?

5. Do you think Owen and Luna are equal partners in their relationship? In what ways are they unequal, and how are these inequalities balanced?

6. The "unreliable narrator" device is certainly at play in the novel, making it a challenge to know who's telling the truth, and when. Were you able to spot a lie from one of the characters at any point? If so, what was it, and how did you know?

7. Each of the characters in *The Accomplice* is guilty in some way, whether that is directly related to Irene's death or not. How

does guilt color each character's actions? Is anyone relieved of their guilt by the end of the novel?

8. Even though they are best friends, Owen and Luna keep certain secrets from each other. Discuss some of the secrets each keeps and why. Are they only trying to protect each other, or do they have selfish motives at heart? How does this affect their friendship in the long run?

9. Why do you think that so many people are drawn to Owen? How does he manipulate each of the characters in turn and why?

10. From the outset, Owen and Luna's relationship includes half-truths and mistrust. Do you think they ultimately overcome that enough to have a healthy relationship in the future?

Lisa Lutz's Guide to the Hudson Valley

For art

Dia Beacon—Beacon, New York

Storm King Art Center—New Windsor, New York

For books

Inquiring Minds—New Paltz and Saugerties, New York

Oblong Books—Millerton and Rhinebeck, New York

Rough Draft Bar & Books—Kingston, New York

For nature

Overlook Mountain Trail—Woodstock, New York

Walkway Over the Hudson State Historic Park—Poughkeepsie,
    New York

For food and drinks

Brooklyn Cider House—New Paltz, New York (April through
    October only)

Del's Roadside—Rhinebeck, New York

What Kind of Friend Are You? Quiz

You find the dead body of someone in your friend group—what's the first thing you do?

A. Call your best friend.
B. Call the police.
C. Run away.

You find out your best friend's secret while snooping through their stuff. What do you do?

A. Tell no one. It's their secret to keep and you respect that.
B. Tell your best friend you found out. You're a little hurt they didn't confide in you.
C. Secrets are for sharing! Tell everyone.

You're staying at your best friend's house for the holidays when a fight breaks out at the dinner table. Whose side are you taking?

A. Your best friend's side, obviously. You'll tell them how it really is later, no matter what.
B. Their family's. You're a guest and it's an awkward situation to be put in—your friend will forgive you.
C. Stay out of it. It's none of your business.

Your best friend asks you to lie for them and doesn't say why. What do you do?

A. Cover for them, no questions asked.
B. You'll do it, as long as they give you context . . . and it won't land you in any trouble.
C. No way. You're not getting wrapped up in something you know nothing about.

All A's

You're a ride-or-die best friend.

You're there for your BFF, no matter what, and are along for their adventure, no matter how extreme. You don't judge (okay, *sometimes*, but you won't sugarcoat it when you do). They are the most important person in this world to you and they know it.

All B's

You're a fair-weather friend.

You're close but not *that* close. You're a good friend when it is easy to be one, but let's be real: when the going gets tough, they become persona non grata.

All C's

"Die?" *Chokes back a cough* Everyone for themselves—you're the ready-to-bail friend!

PHOTO: MORGAN DOX

LISA LUTZ is the *New York Times* bestselling, Alex Award–winning author of the Spellman Files series and *The Swallows*, as well as the novels *How to Start a Fire* and *The Passenger*. She has also written for film and TV, including *The Deuce* for HBO and *Dare Me* on USA. She lives in New York's Hudson Valley.

lisalutz.com
Facebook.com/lisalutz.author
Twitter: @lisalutz
Instagram: @lisa.lutz

ABOUT THE TYPE

This book was set in Sabon, a typeface designed by the well-known German typographer Jan Tschichold (1902–74). Sabon's design is based upon the original letterforms of sixteenth-century French type designer Claude Garamond and was created specifically to be used for three sources: foundry type for hand composition, Linotype, and Monotype. Tschichold named his typeface for the famous Frankfurt typefounder Jacques Sabon (c. 1520–80).

RANDOM HOUSE BOOK CLUB

Because Stories Are Better Shared

Discover
Exciting new books that spark conversation every week.

Connect
With authors on tour—or in your living room. (Request an Author Chat for your book club!)

Discuss
Stories that move you with fellow book lovers on Facebook, on Goodreads, or at in-person meet-ups.

Enhance
Your reading experience with discussion prompts, digital book club kits, and more, available on our website.

Join our online book club community!

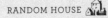 randomhousebookclub.com

Random House Book Club ™

Because Stories Are Better Shared